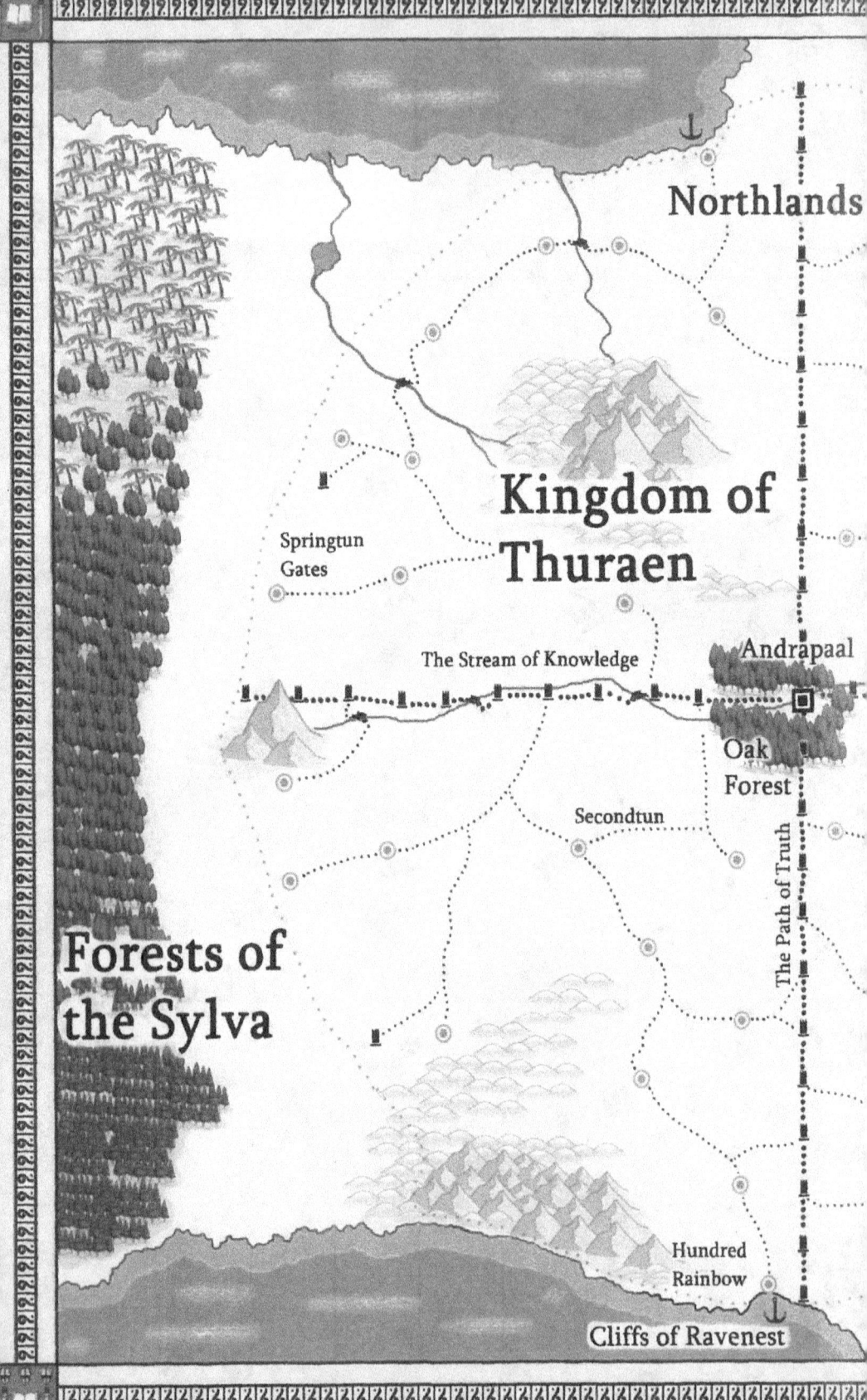

Lands of
the Vorsurk

The Path of Truth

Eaglehaven

The Blood River

Sylva   Thuraen   Vorsurk

The Picturesque Picaresque

Book Two of The Prophecies of Andrapaal

TIM LAW

DARK MYTH

www.darkmythpublications.com

This work of fiction. All of the characters, organizations, and the events portrayed in this novel are either products of the author's imagination or are used fictitiously.

The Picturesque Picaresque: Book Two of The Prophecies of Andrapaal

Dark Myth Publications
145 S Glenoaks Blvd.
Unit #3149, Burbank, CA 91502

www.darkmythpublications.com/

ISBN: 979-8-9925038-0-7

Our books may be purchased in bulk for promotional, educational, or business use. Please contact Myth Mart Sales Department at 1-818-940-4563, or by email at BulkBookOrders@jayzomondarkmyth.com.

First Edition: December 2025

Printed in the United States of America

10 9 8 7 6 5 4 3 2 1

Table of Contents

This story is dedicated to my wife's friend Petra. Your 'take no-nonsense' attitude is inspiring.

A special thank you goes out once more to Steph and Dave from Dark Myth Publications. Maybe one day, my *dream big* and my *real job* will both be writing stories, and when that happens it will be all YOUR fault.

Thank you to my son and my two daughters who are always happy for their dad to read them a story, especially when it is one of mine.

And finally, to my gorgeous wife Heidi who is my muse, my angel, and my greatest love. Your travel memories of the people you met along the way has helped to make this story what it is, for better or for worse.

Thank you my friends and family, near and far. I could do none of this without your support and encouragement.

XO

Tim

INTRODUCTION

This sequel was the story which *The Eleventh Tome* should have been. Paechra Lightheart was the initial inspiration for my first attempt at writing a novel (all those years ago) based on my ideas, my world, my imagination. My wife Heidi told me stories about her fierce friend Petra, but having never had the chance to meet this wonderful woman in person, I only had a vague idea of who she was. Couple this with the characteristics of every amazing person who had encouraged me, supported me, and loved me growing up, and you get the driving force of *The Picturesque Picaresque*. A little bit of this and a whole lot of that, and you end up with someone who is curious, fierce, vulnerable, naive, friendly, passionate, the perfect protagonist. To think the idea for book two in *The Prophecies of Andrapaal* came from a lot of reader feedback, me regularly being told, "My favorite character in *The Eleventh Tome* is that girl… Petra… You should write about her more…"

So, month after month, I let Paechra take the reins, month after month I was amazed by her passion for humanity and for doing what she considered to be right. I truly loved those times I got to spend with the sylvan and all her friends and family, the sisterhood. Through my excitement for this story and this character, I found I was chatting more with friends and family, and other ideas came to me through these conversations. Paechra grew from who I thought she was and would become into a true hero for the modern age. Paechra is all of us, or at least there is a little bit of all of us in her. And it is only from the way that people shared themselves with me that this story could grow into what it has become.

I want to take a moment here to thank a good friend whom I missed (twice) from mentioning in my dedication. Ben Spezzano, thank you, the time you spent on creating for yourself a visual map of my world, which then you gifted to me without charge or want of anything in return. It only seems right to share the source with the world of this map that has helped many a reader to find their way (and on occasion has helped to get me back on track). Thank you, my friend, for your support, your encouragement, and your skills as a cartographer. I don't know how I will ever repay you. Just know that you have my gratitude.

Thank you to my beautiful wife Heidi also. You may not know it, darling, but you drive me toward writing better stories, and for that I love you. And of course, to my kids, all three of you who inspire me with your strength and achievements. Don't be too surprised if you recognize yourselves in the pages of book three (when I finally get around to writing it).

Finally, I just wanted to thank YOU, the reader, for taking a chance on a fresh new face. There are so many incredible stories out there for the choosing. I'm so thrilled you've chosen mine.

Tim

The Picturesque Picaresque

Book Two of The Prophecies of Andrapaal

Prelude

The die rolls through the hall of Haven.

The thunder rolls.

The storm sings.

A city sleeps.

Nothing is eternal, but the goddess Herself

The prophecy of Andrapaal, twelfth stanza, translated by the sages of the Kingdom of Thuraen 514th year

HAVEN, THE HALL of the tri-gods existed beyond the lands of the mortal races. It lay out beyond the length of any mere mortal's ability to see. Its flooring was a simplistic pattern of squares, alternating black than white for an eternity. A fog, colored an insignificant grey, swirled about the hall as if alive. In the center of such an expansive space stood a table, unadorned, sandy in color, created from what looked like birch, stained with blood. The table was smooth to the touch, and of a sturdy construction. The four legs resembled the four elements, earth, fire, wind, and water. The earth leg resembled a craggy cliff face, the fire leg had what looked like lava running down it, the wind leg seemed to have fluffy clouds clinging to it and the water leg reflected a choppy sea.

Around this table mingled the fallen heroes and villains from all the worlds, those who had been prime pieces in the game of life. Some who did not believe in Haven discovered upon their death that they stood within the Divine Hall, much to their surprise. Some who believed with their whole hearts Haven was real never earned such an afterlife. Those deemed worthy lounged upon the squares black as pitch and white as ivory watching on as two of the three divine beings rolled the die of fate, battling each other in a game of tactics where all the worlds were the game board and the final prize. Each hero and villain urged on their chosen God while feasting, drinking, and celebrating their lives past.

In what was claimed to be the true world, the world of humankind, of the humans, vorsurk and others who dwelled there, not many knew of Haven and those that did believe in it, did so purely on faith alone.

In the true home of the fae such as the sylva, gnomes, demons and dwarves, messages from the Gods were common everyday occurrences. Representatives of these races usually had knowledge that such a place was real. Even so, few representatives of these races found their way to Haven, in life or in death.

The great table was the main focus of the hall. The right end of this table rested upon one of the white squares that made up the hall's marble floor. At this end of the table sat a gallant warrior dressed in perfectly fitting plate armor of platinum, a snow-white hood covering his clean-shaven facial features. Upon this figure's hooded head there comfortably sat a crown of white gold encrusted with the shavings of nine jewels; five diamonds, three emeralds, and one sapphire. This figure was young, handsome, strong, and felt both righteous and pious in the decisions that he made. This figure was Palidine, representative of all things good. Around him floated *Ithulii*, the brightly glowing Spirit of Peace, helpfully pointing to the table and sighing softly. At the feet of Palidine seated upon the white square was another spirit, *Adora*, the Spirit of Love; shaped as two soul-mates sharing an embrace. *Adora* ignored what was happening around it. Love remained lost in itself.

At the left end of this table impossibly far from, and yet impossibly near to this figure of piousness and good graces there sat another, upon a black square, the utter opposite of all things good. Cloaked in a robe that sucked color into oblivion, this figure looking as though an eternal age had distorted it, this figure had the distinct look of a mind twisted from eons of hatred. The figure at the end of the table had bone where skin should have been, shriveled orbs where eyes once had existed. Its tattered robe covered what remained of a humanoid figure. This resident of the black square leaned forward from his grand, ebony chair and smiled a fang filled smile. This figure was Sinestri, twin brother of Palidine.

"It so seems you have lost a great piece, my brother," the figure stated simply with a dry chuckle.

The words floated quietly and quickly across the vast distance that separated the pair. "And in such a loss the game is mine…"

"Hmmmph," replied Palidine without movement,

3

wondering where he had gone wrong, and yet still optimistic the game could still fall in his favor.

Around the one who was cloaked in tattered darkness, laughter erupted, a nasty, bullying bark. There was a flash, just like a ruby gleams when it catches the sun's light. It took flight from behind *Sinestri* and floated, still laughing cruelly, to land beside *Ithulii*.

"*Uncarne!* Spirit of Lust! Stay by my side!" boomed the one who sat upon the dark wooded throne. The laughter abruptly ceased and the ruby like gleam rushed back across the table to hide within its master's robes.

The figure encased in platinum, stroked the Spirit of Peace like a caring parent settling a young child, all the while whispering soft, soothing words. After a while Palidine spoke with an element of humor and great confidence contained within the statement made.

"You may claim to own Andrapaal for now, but I am brimming with a certainty that it will be returned to me. Not so much destroyed, I see a city that is merely sleeping... Your great city upon the waves, however, will become mine. It shall NOT be returned."

The black robed figure turned shriveled orbs away from the freshly erected barbaric fortress. The fang filled smile turned quickly into a clenched teeth frown. There was the booming sound as a single die of one thousand faces bounced across the game board that was so many worlds, all at once.

"Six!" hissed the skeletal figure, more of a curse than a statement.

"Indeed, it does seem already that fate has decided to change sides," the other replied mildly.

"Do not be so absolute in your thinking that such a fickle

thing as fate will remain befriended to you eternally," the dark-robed figure whispered harshly.

"I do believe that it be my roll," stated the one who sat upon the pure white square.

Again, the die bounced across the playing surface.

"Curse your luck!" screamed the figure who resided upon the black square as the die showed the highest possible score.

The gallant warrior merely smiled.

"You cheat, curse you!!" accused the skeletal one, a bone fist slamming down upon the world in a demonstration of obvious anger.

"Alas, unlike you, cheating is something that I just cannot do," laughed Palidine. "Now take up the die and let us continue our game." The pious one enjoying the way his nemesis' face contorted. For it seemed indeed possible that the fates were already turning back the way of all things good.

#

Raven Stormsong stared at the flames as he pumped the bellows in the old forge. It was hot work, thirsty work, and the kind of work that allowed him plenty of thinking time. He had come a long way since the attack upon his home of Andrapaal. Sacrifices had been made, and at the time they seemed like the necessary thing to do. Now? Well, Raven no longer knew with certainty what he would have done if faced with the same scenario. He had made his choice, and now he only had the words of dwarves, namely the McHallowhill clan, to guide him.

"Ye are the blackbird o' prophecy," Mick McHallowhill said

almost daily.

This was normally followed by a gruff, "So, learn how t'fly…"

The creatures carved from the mountains themselves had a funny way about them. They reminded Raven of the giant of a man, Gregory the Blacksmith. Gregory would have made a fine dwarf. He was gone now though, collateral in the fall of the fine city of Andrapaal. Raven knew that for the sake of his friend, he had to find a way back. The lost were lost, never to return, but those who remained still needed him. All Raven understood for certain was that his arms ached each night, as if he had flown for miles. Yet, he still seemed stuck in that strange world between worlds.

"Y' can go, lad," Mick told him. "Just as soon as ye learn where tis ye be goin' n how…"

So, Raven continued to pump the bellows, listening to the sound of hammers on steel, watching sword, axe, and shield being crafted by masters.

When Raven asked why, what was the purpose for so many tools of war, the McHallowhill dwarves smiled grimly.

"Forgive us, lad, if we'd rather have faith in something heavy we can wield ourselves," Mick would say as a form of explanation.

Raven never understood this, but dared not ask more. Each time he heard it though, or anything else Mick told him, he felt like it was partially his fault. He was still there with them, like a bird that had wings, waiting for someone else to show them what wings were for. Rest came every evening with dreams of his friend Paechra Lightheart. Her wings were widespread, and she was in full flight, but was she speeding toward her destiny or was the breeze of destiny pushing her away?

"I vow to be there for you, Paechra," Raven mumbled in his restless slumber. "I shall be by your side when you need me the most."

Another empty promise perhaps, but Raven used it as his mantra that drove him on.

Chapter One

Finding Her Freedom

There will be a great roar. It will be the voice of the lioness come from the western lands.

From the Eleventh Stanza of the Prophecy, translated by the sages of the Kingdom of Thuraen 514th year

PAECHRA WAS LIKE so many other members of her race, the forest-dwelling, and nature-loving fae-kin. She was of an average height, at just over five feet tall. She was of a weight that fit her frame, with toned and sun-kissed skin as was common for her kind. Paechra's childhood was that of the average sylvan who called Greenwood Vale home. With a father who was a scholarly linguist and a mother who was a Druid; a keeper of the forests that Paechra's people called home, the child Paechra had no inherited benefits, nor additional responsibilities to sculpt her, just the life of a free-spirited kinder. She was blessed with a childhood full of open skies, exploration, adventure, and the free time to make it so. Years of lessons in love for so many languages was a gift to Paechra from her father. Knowledge of the Mother Spirit and how to care for the flora and fauna of her home were playful lessons taught to Paechra by her mother and the other Druids. An only child, it was tough for Paechra, many a moment was there when she longed for a brother or sister with which to while away the days. When the time came though, her deep love for the earth outweighed her difficulties with other languages. Naturally, then she followed in the bare-footed dancing steps of her spiritual mother. Soon after Paechra had clearly made her choice it was fated that her father had needs to move away. After so many years of a carefree childhood, it was only natural for Paechra to wish for this life to go on forever. Then one day, as was traditional for her kind, everything in Paechra's life suddenly and abruptly changed.

The gray storm clouds poured their fury down upon the rich green grove, pitter-pattering a rhythmic splatter upon a crystal clear blue pond. A small group of Druids, the guardians and keepers of the forest had gathered here, away from the rest of their community. Seven of the small group took shelter from the frightful weather beneath the thick canopy of interloped oaken branches. One from this party rebuked the offered shelter, the storm that raged within allowing her to ignore the harsh weather for the moment.

"How dare he?" Paechra fumed. Her deep eyes of oaken-leaf green flashed wildly with anger as she spoke; giving her friends no reason to expect that she was anything other than furious.

"Sister, Sister Paechra. Please try to calm yourself." Sienna murmured as she slowly approached the irate Paechra.

Sienna's old frame made moving quickly impossible as if she had been a bear waking from hibernation or one of the giant oaks that these eight sylvan-kind had been selected to care for. Great drops of rain pelted the older forest dweller and soaked her quickly. Sienna continued her journey accepting the rain more as a caress of a friend than a hindrance. The other sisters of the grove respected Sienna's age, Paechra releasing her anger instantly so that she could rush to her friend's aid. Kneeling before Sienna, taking wrinkled hands in her own delicate ones of youth, and looking up into Sienna's paling blue eyes, Paechra sighed.

"I am sorry Sister. I feel too young to be betrothed, and what is more, the man I have been paired with is a pompous fool," Paechra added to that sigh, making it known to the sisters just what it was that angered her so.

The six other Druidic women all gasped in unison to hear a prince spoken of with so little respect. Sienna though, laughed an almost silent laugh.

"Young one, it is our way," the ancient sylvan began. Gently she released her gnarled, earth loved hands from the supple ones of Paechra's and dragged her long silver hair over a pointed ear.

"Daughter, walk with me awhile," Sienna suggested, shuffling away from the six gossiping sisters and taking Paechra with her. The grip of the elder sylvan was so surprisingly strong that Paechra found she had no choice.

"Indeed, it does seem an odd match," Sienna stated with sagely wisdom. By then the two sylvan, one ancient and one the replication of youth had walked far enough away from the others that they could not be overheard.

"Sienna, Derek is like a limp, wilted flower!" Paechra stated, exasperated.

"Paechra, daughter, perhaps not so much wilted," Sienna replied with deep lines of thought wrinkling her face even more than age had. "He is still of the royal house, though I will say that his sole resemblance to a rose be the prickles along its stem."

Paechra kept a slow pace with her old friend and listened respectfully. Her anger fumed within her exactly like the storm that continued to rage around them, but her respect for Sienna allowed her to listen.

"More like a colorful pansy. A bit faded, seemingly no plan for life. He seems like something that has bloomed simply to be seen. Certainly not rich in color and aroma like a rose. Neither does he have the sting of its thorns. Certainly, no rose indeed," Sienna added with great thought.

"Maybe I want a rose!!" cried the exasperated Paechra.

"Perhaps it is not any rose that you seek child. We are gifted with what we are given, Paechra. What we do beyond the gifting is what many consider the greatest test of life," Sienna answered with a laugh evident in her tone as she spoke.

Paechra laughed too, unable to refute the truth that rang in what her friend and teacher had said. The prince was the rose of his house, the rose of the forested principality. What girl did not want her prince though?

"Sienna, the bards will sing of your wise words forever," Paechra laughed.

"Perhaps they will not sing of them forever, my young friend," Sienna replied, her tone quite serious, her ancient eyes though reflected a childish mischievousness. "The occasional tune would be a nice surprise though," the elder Druid added with a smile.

11

Calmed again, Paechra turned upon her heels and guided her friend Sienna back toward her sisters, back toward her friends.

"Thank you, Sister Sienna," Paechra whispered as she led the other sylvan back the way they had come. Knowing that the wind and rain had easily drowned out her words, Paechra thought it strange that her friend was smiling.

The rain fell heavily and in what seemed to be one constant sheet, making the cobbled street chatter and laugh like young children not yet educated in the lessons of life learnt by their elders, the importance of silences and their place in a world often filled with chaos. Cursing the noise that continually broke his concentration, Ulan, Rose of the royal family of Greenwood Vale parried another clumsy blow headed for his unprotected chest. The wielder of the blade was none other than his younger brother.

"The crown is mine!" Derek screamed over the sound of the insistent storm.

I would only wish to be one of those simple droplets, Ulan thought longingly to himself. *My only responsibility would be to fall from the sky and be one with the earth,* Ulan continued to consider, before again he had to bring his blade up to swiftly block.

"Mine! Mine I say!!" Derek hollered with toddler like whining and consistent regularity.

Just as regularly as the storm's rainfall, Derek's poorly trained dagger blows struck out wildly towards the back stepping Ulan.

"Brother! Please stop this nonsense!" Ulan begged. A simple statement, yet it seemed to be the only way to get a message through to Derek at that very moment.

"Half-brother," Derek hissed. His correction of Ulan's urge for peace was like that of a physical slap in the face to the suggestion.

A brother considered to only partially be a member of the ruling family, the unending rain that just seemed to refuse to cease, a crown that had been thrust upon him; all of these things jostled in Ulan's mind, wanting to be the first issue to be addressed. Ulan's thoughts wavered briefly from the skirmish. Just long enough for Derek to score a hit.

The knife cut and cut deeply into Ulan's defensive left as so many compounding thoughts filled the mind of the sudden High Prince of the Greenwood sylvan. A river of crimson poured from that slice, as the knife blade slid free the pain of the wound caused the young High Prince's dammed-up temper to finally burst.

"I do not want it!!" Ulan exploded as the flat of his blade whipped around reflexively, crashing into his half-brother's cheek. Ulan felt remorse instantly as he saw rather than felt the shattering of the bones that he had struck so forcefully.

The rain continued to fall from the sky, not at all phased by this rare show of rage from the young ruler. The blanket of water from the sky disguised the argument of blades between Ulan and Derek.

"My liege, be you hurt?!" called one guard.

"My lord, are you alright?!" urgently asked another.

Those same two guardians, drawn by the noise, a noise that was almost impossible to hear over the roar of thunder from the foreboding sky, rushed into the courtyard and tended to Ulan's injured arm. They left the collapsed and cowering Derek to vomit a crimson mess that mixed insignificantly with the pool of water that flooded over the sandaled feet of the other three who shared the cobbled courtyard. Water erupted in small splashes as the two guardians led Ulan away.

"Enough!" Ulan stated, with an undertone of authority that was sufficient for the two that lent him unneeded support to let go of their assistance, allowing Ulan to rush back to the fallen Derek who gasped for air. Ulan saw that the waters from the storm flowed into his panting mouth with each gasping breath.

"Rise, brother!" Ulan urged.

Derek made a weak blow towards the one who had struck him such a vicious blow. An explosion of pain erupted in Derek's skull as Ulan lifted him under the armpits and clumsily tried to help him rise.

"Come to my aid!" Ulan ordered of the two guardians. They immediately responded.

Thus, together the two kindred left the storm and the flooding courtyard. The only sound that remained was the roar of the rain and the chattering laughter of its oblivious children.

As soon as the furious storm began, it seemed to slow and then was finally blown away by the wind. With the fading of the rain much of Paechra's fury vanished also. With a clearer head she went in search of her mother, Sienna's words of wisdom comforting her as she went.

It was thus that Paechra was deep in thought when she stumbled across Heidi the Dove-Spirit. Since the very day that Paechra chose her lifelong path, it was Heidi who became her best friend joining her in the same journey, from a novice to a fully-fledged Druid.

"You are dedicated to the earth! You are a Druid, keeper of The Mother Spirit and all her children," Heidi panted in

disbelief as she heard the news of Paechra's betrothal. "Those who call themselves our rulers obviously have little understanding of what that role actually demands."

Paechra loved her friend. As all best friends did, Heidi knew exactly what to say to make the nerves vanish and the laughter rush forth. Today though she was a listening ear and a sympathetic voice, features of only the truest of friends. Together Paechra and Heidi spoke of the strange and sudden match between Paechra and Derek as they continued their search, but even together they could find no sign of Sarah Lightheart. That was because Paechra's mother had business where Paechra and Heidi dared not to look. She had business at the palace.

Of all the structures of the forested sylvan community, the palace was the most permanent. Made of hard strong stone, where most of the other buildings were formed from that which the forest alone supplied, the palace was the home of the elders, the decision makers, and others of that sylvan race whose protection and position was most important. During darker times, the palace served as a barrier against enemies, but now that times seemed peaceful the main role of this stone fort was to keep the worst of the cold and the heat from the youngest and the oldest of the citizens. It was by tradition that those classed of having the blood of the original forest spirits from whom the sylvan had spawned; those then considered of royal blood resided within the palace too.

When any of royal blood required medical attention of any level they asked only for the best. Sarah came as quickly as she could to the palace, but she could not disengage from her feelings towards Ulan and his choice for her daughter. As

15

Paechra's mother pulled tightly upon the bandage that bound the deep knife wound, her thoughts were motherly, but certainly not towards the royal.

"How could you?" she asked through gritted teeth. "Join my daughter to€¦ him?"

Ulan looked up pleadingly, yet he dared not speak a wrong word to his healer and at that very moment every word seemed wrong.

"Have I vanished?" Ulan's brother tried to say. The healing salves that Sarah had applied to his face were dulling the pain but had no effect on making his speech any clearer. The words came out as a jumble of slurred and sloshed sounds, something that Sarah and Ulan both found easy to ignore.

"It is a girl's decision finally who it is she shall love, but our ways are there to guide this decision," Sarah continued. Both Ulan and Derek listened as though their very life depended upon the Druid's words.

"Do you understand? This boy is not what I nor Paechra's father would have happily chose for her. Neither, I believe, would Paechra choose him for herself."

"Boy!" interrupted Derek. Even with his jaw giving the word an unusual pronunciation, both Sarah and Ulan clearly understood what he had said.

"Yes, you act as a mere boy!" Sarah stated as a plain fact. "Your current actions cannot be considered those of a man."

"How is it that you dare…?" growled Derek, his words unclear but his threat clearly evident.

"If it were not for your childishness, would we be both sitting here getting wounds tended?" Ulan asked kindly. His patience with his half-brother was well known. With great effort the sylvan ruler attempted to diffuse the tension before it worsened.

The fires of frustration still burned in Derek's eyes of gray, but at Ulan's words the young prince turned his head away. As Sarah and Ulan talked quietly together, dark thoughts ebbed into Derek's mind.

"Ulan took away my prize. Father should have given me the role of highest prince. And now the menial prize that Ulan has given me will be whisked away, simply because she doesn't like it," sulked Derek.

I shan't let this treasure be taken from me, Derek vowed silently.

Without a sound, the young prince slipped away.

For what purpose and how that was to affect Paechra and the others only time would tell.

#

Prince Derek was missing. Brother of High Prince Ulan he had vanished from the palace after the injury to his face had been tended by Sarah, one of the many Druids who tended the forest, healed the sick and injured and cared for the sylvan community. Once alert to the fact that his half-brother was missing the High Prince called for the assistance of the eldest Druid, Mother Sienna.

"My prince..." Sienna began, but with his hand held up for silence, the prince of the sylvan ones of Greenwood Vale stopped the older Druid short. His deep discussion with Sarah and then the disappearance of his brother had left the Royal Rose exhausted.

"I understand your love for your sister Druid. Her own mother lectured me on my poor choice and the unfortunate path that I have unknowingly forged for her daughter," Ulan complained, "I was hoping that you Sienna would at least see some wisdom in my choice, or better yet enlighten me upon the path that I should set for Paechra."

Sienna chuckled to herself, her ancient eyes twinkling like those of an infant's.

"My prince," she began again. "It has indeed come to my attention that the suggested joining of your half-brother to the young Druid Paechra has caused some minds to contemplate your wisdom."

"Suggested? Do you patronize me Sienna? You knew my father well and I had hoped that you would use your words to aid me also. I never expected from you such a slap to my face, verbal that it be. I believe Paechra is strong enough... It is for Derek's sake..." Ulan gasped.

Sienna laughed again.

"Ulan, my prince, you are the ruler of our sylvan people but think truly of the race that you rule. Do you believe that even your father in the last of his years considered that his decisions were thought final and correct by each and every one of the free spirited, nature caring creatures of the sylvan life that he called subjects? We are the people who question, who live freely and think freely. I do not patronize you with my words, instead I embrace the sylvan ideal, just as Sarah does, just as Paechra does, just as you should also."

"Of course, when it is put so elegantly, I feel as though the role of High Prince is more an honor and less a burden," Ulan said with a smile.

"Come my friend, that I may call you such... It is time to share in the midday meal. Perhaps as we feast upon the gifts that the Mother Spirit has supplied we can attempt to bring Paechra and Derek together," Sienna suggested, offering High

Prince Ulan her hand. Taking the Druid's hand in his own, the prince led Sienna at a slow but steady pace. His thoughts were suddenly happier, so much more confident that his choice had been the right one.

At the communal gathering Paechra finally found her mother. With the two princes tended to, there was no need for Sarah to remain at the palace. Before Sarah could even give greeting, she saw the trouble in her daughter's eyes.

"Mother I wish to run. I cannot help but feel detest towards what Ulan has chosen for me. Not only do I detest his brother, but it is as Sienna suggests. I cannot feel love for any other than The Rose. It is Ulan who has my heart, he, and the earth. If I cannot have one love I shall dedicate myself wholly to the other," Paechra pleaded.

"I have spoken with Ulan and told him of my thoughts. My thoughts are your thoughts, daughter. But they are not the thoughts of our High Prince. I can see nothing we can do but follow his will. Derek does need you. Your level head and your determination… I feel that your father and I should be proud of you and saddened by your destiny. The spirits have been kind, but they certainly could have been kinder," Sarah replied with a verbal sigh.

Both women continued to eat in silence. All around them the others of the community chatted and laughed through the midday meal. Sarah and Paechra though, were deep in thought. They only broke their somber silence at Sienna's arrival. Even then , the additional arrival of Ulan did nothing to improve Paechra's mood.

"Have you seen Derek?" Ulan asked, innocently.

What do I care of Derek, when in truth I love you? Paechra thought to herself.

19

She offered Ulan a dark look, to disguise her true feelings. Ulan turned his eyes away, not willing to witness what he thought was Paechra's look of anger. Instead, he held the gaze of Sienna and Sarah, pleading with them for any information that they may have heard.

The eldest Druid, Mother Sienna, met the prince's gaze with such sadness in her eyes.

"I was certain that he would be here," she answered.

"I've not seen your brother since tending to his wounds," Sarah explained. "I would like to see him though. In my mind his treatment is only half complete."

When Ulan's look of worry deepened, Sarah broke into a soft smile.

"All that I mean by that is he has offered no thanks."

"I believe, Sarah, that when Derek and Paechra are together, Derek will change. I must believe that" Ulan replied, his eyes still filled with worry.

"Jealousy is a feeling that naturally occurs in siblings," Sienna began. "I fear that in Derek though, it has become less a feeling and more an illness."

Paechra remained silent until she heard Sienna's words.

"I'll not be wed to damaged stock! It is a poor match indeed if the role of either partner is to fix their betrothed!" Paechra stated, much louder than she had intended. Silence followed, as almost everyone present stopped mid-mouthful, focus drawn away from their meal. As her feelings of helplessness overwhelmed her, Paechra rushed away from the table and into the forest. Silent tears glistened in her eyes and streamed down her cheeks as she ran.

"Paechra!" Sarah and Ulan called together.

"Leave her," Sienna murmured. "It be more important now, our need to find Derek."

"Be it not just as important to make certain Paechra is safe?" suggested the sylvan High Prince.

"Paechra is strong," replied Sienna, firmly. "Our Daughter of the Forest just needs some time to be alone."

Sienna, Sarah, and Ulan dismissed themselves abruptly from the communal meal. As they too vanished into the woods, the other sylvan returned to the shared task of feasting.

"Heidi I must leave. My mother understands and so too does Sienna, everyone seems to understand. It is only I though who can do a thing about it." Paechra panted.

She had already gathered up some of her possessions, everything she thought necessary to travel far and fast.

"But where will you go?" Heidi pleaded as she handed the torch and tinder that Paechra motioned toward. Paechra's friend had snuck away from the meal soon after Ulan, Sarah and Sienna had left. Even in that short time Paechra had gathered together much of what she needed for a long journey.

"My father..." Paechra replied with utter excitement igniting her eyes. "I plan to find him and explain my ill-fate lot."

"How will you aim to venture beyond our borders then? What scheme have you thought through? Hasn't your father left our lands in his search for more examples of foreign speech?" Heidi asked in earnest.

"Here..." Paechra offered in response, passing a piece of folded parchment to her dear friend. Heidi scanned the paper for a moment and then passed it back with a quizzical look plastering her face.

21

"Oh, I forgot. Your struggle to comprehend languages other than our own is worse than mine." Paechra laughed.

"I can make out a few of the words…" Heidi agreed.

"It is a letter. I wrote an explanation of who I am; daughter, sylvan, betrothed. With this letter and what I know of the strength and the great power of The Mother Spirit I hope to be able to travel safe."

"You believe yourself to be safe?!" a voice growled from the doorway of the wooden hut, the hut that Paechra shared with Sarah as her home, the same wooden hut where Heidi and Paechra now sat, otherwise alone.

"Get Sarah," Paechra mouthed silently to her friend.

"How do you expect me to do that?" Heidi mouthed back. The only exit from the hut was blocked.

"Show yourself, Derek," Paechra stated plainly, trying to dismiss the fear that gripped her.

"How can you possibly think you are safe?!" Derek growled again. The early afternoon sun reflected off his drawn dagger as he stepped into view. "You are certainly not safe from me."

"Leave now Derek, before anyone gets hurt," Paechra warned, her fear turning into anger.

Derek's stance, the look in his eyes, everything about him said bully.

"You warn me about getting hurt, my betrothed," Derek sniggered. "And yet, I am the one holding the knife."

"Why are you doing this?" Heidi pleaded, almost in a whisper.

"Why?" Derek growled, turning on her harshly. His eyes narrowed into slits like his dagger blade. "I have lived in Ulan's shadow for always. Never was I father's favorite, and now my elder brother treats me as a burden…" Derek hissed.

"If you stopped acting like a child, you would find more people would treat you with the respect you seek," Paechra interrupted. Heidi flashed her friend a look of fear, but Paechra was inspired.

"People respect arms, a quick blade," replied Derek, keeping his eyes trained on Heidi.

"People fear such things! If you seek respect you must prove that you deserve it. Your actions have always been self-centered. Derek, how can you expect me to respect that, how can you expect such feelings from any of us?"

Heidi recalled hearing such a speech from Sienna; the same words of wisdom seemed to flow easily from Paechra's lips. Both of the Druids watched Derek fight an inner battle.

"How?" the younger prince argued aloud. "How can I change, and why should it be me who has too?"

"Derek, it is you who must take the first steps because it is you who must choose to change. The moment you accept responsibility for your own actions…" Paechra explained gently. For a moment all the anger left Paechra, the frustration at having her planned life of forest keeper whisked away, her disappointment at Ulan's inability to see her feelings, the panic at seeing her long life stretch out before her as nursemaid to the troubled Derek, all this vanished. The feeling that she was left with was a hope that Derek indeed could be saved, that in fact he could save himself.

"You are just like all the others, both of you," Derek accused. Without warning his eyes locked with Heidi's once more and he lunged, leading with his dagger.

Maybe that is simply because everyone around you has tried to help, Paechra thought to herself. She kept the thought within

23

her though; Derek was already beyond the point of listening anymore.

"Derek! You are the one holding the blade, and yet again I warn you about getting hurt," Paechra said instead.

Heidi jumped further back into the simple hut, avoiding another clumsy blow from Derek. The prince, frustrated and getting angrier by the second turned his eyes away from Heidi and focused upon Paechra as he made his next lunge. Heidi took that moment to slip passed and rush for the doorway.

"What witchery is this?" Derek hissed as his eyes locked onto Paechra noticing for the first time that a strange faint light had enveloped her.

"The Mother Spirit gives her blessing, you are indeed favored in Her eyes," Heidi sighed in awe at the sight.

"Run Heidi, find the High Prince, Mother Sienna and the others," Paechra urged, her dear friend needing no more encouragement to do just that. With one final forlorn glance at leaving her friend Heidi fled, calling out for Ulan as loudly as she could.

"For the third time I urge you, Prince Derek, to lay down your weapon and look beyond your own selfish center," Paechra pleaded.

With a savage, animal like cry, Derek thrust his dagger. Somehow Paechra struck first, confidence in her own ability and the justness of her cause enabling her to land a true blow.

So, it has come to this, Paechra thought, gravely. All around her the battle raged on, but she was beyond it all, above it all. It was Derek's personal struggle, but he refused to have it with himself. Instead, he tried to target everyone around him with his anger. Paechra saw what she had to do. In the next moment Derek found himself encased in the strange light, trapped by the strange magic. Paechra refused to continue to fight a battle that would not end, a battle that was not hers and that she refused to inherit. Paechra gathered up her things and left without a word. Derek screamed after her, but to the prince, Paechra had no more words to give. The light was her parting gift, but Derek had to work beyond his fear of it. Paechra hoped beyond hope that he would.

Ulan and Sienna watched the tiny figure of Paechra disappear, the young sylvan following the path of the afternoon sun. They stood hidden from her sight, and for a few moments they watched in silence.

"Tell me Sienna. What must we do?" Ulan begged of the elder Druid. The day had been one of the worst that Ulan could remember. He felt a deep feeling of responsibility and despair.

"Ulan my liege, we must let her go," Sienna stated, simply, always seeming to know the right thing to say.

"She is so young… How can we just let her leave?"

"Paechra's life is her freedom. She has earned it; we can do nothing but let her go. She will return to us wiser and stronger. I only hope that when Paechra walks among us again we are ready. For now, we must focus upon your brother. He is a troubled soul."

When the High Prince and the Elder Druid checked on Derek they found that he too had disappeared.

Hours later, Paechra continued to journey alone, but happy. The Mother Spirit had blessed her with everything Paechra needed to reach her father safely. Paechra had friends that she could rely upon, and they in turn upon her. The young sylvan had courage, intelligence, the gift of wisdom and above all, a precious self-belief and confidence. This was Paechra's magic.

25

This was the source of her freedom.

Chapter Two

Answering Destiny's Call

In their time of freedom, they should not forget what it was that came before.

From the Eleventh Stanza of the Prophecy, translated by the sages of the Kingdom of Thuraen 514th year

DRUID PAECHRA, A sylva from the land of the forest spirits left her home with a light heart. She walked through the forest of dreams with her head held highly. The great fir trees were friends, gigantic guardians that the young-one felt would protect her. Paechra's betrothed, Low Prince Derek was wounded, his pride certainly but there had been a physical element that the sylva thought she had gifted as well. Paechra hoped she had given Derek much to consider, and she planned to give him sufficient time to dwell upon the lessons taught. He had allowed his anger and jealousy to rule him and guide him and Paechra would not settle for a beloved she needed change so much. Derek's brother must have seen something in Paechra but there would be time for her to ponder upon this. For now, though there was the thrill of adventure ahead.

The sylva had not traveled far from home before but she was striding in her father's footsteps, Therdous had taken his love of language and other races beyond the forest and Paechra felt now was the time in her life she needed to be with such a man. Having no experience traveling beyond the forest realm did not mean Paechra had no knowledge of such a path. In fact, she knew of many pathways that one could choose to travel in a way of moving through the world between worlds. There was the way of the mountain, this way of peace and self-discovery Paechra associated with her father and perhaps the High Prince, certainly her mentor Mother Sienna. Too long it would be for Paechra though. The way of fire and darkness Paechra knew her betrothed would follow, should he choose to hunt for her, the fool that he was. Not through choice would fire be his route, but Low Prince Derek would choose naught with a clear head. Paechra had seen in his aura that Derek was a boy of no-thought, only do; do from anger, do from pain, do from jealousness and fury, and hurt and then the circle began again. The way of sea Paechra feared the most. That way could be chosen but it was chosen at great risk. Some who chose the way of sea left early but remained forever changed, some never left and some never found the courage to set sail and trust in the journey. Paechra thought with excitement that her travel would be via the way of air. The most challenging and the most exhilarating, Paechra's heart had filled with joy and longing the first time she had heard her elder sister Druids speak of such a

way.

"The thrill of touching the clouds while the wind plays with your hair," one had said, Rachella, daughter of Mother Sienna and beloved of The Lady of Possibility.

"For me it was the feel of the creature's skin and mine so close to be almost connected, to feel its spirit even before we took to the skies," another had added, both Druids sharing a look, a mutual knowledge of a life's achievement that they could share.

It was the same thrill that Paechra planned to experience, a story to share when she next saw Therdous Father.

The land rose slightly, and a small smile creeped across the sylva's features. She was warm from how far she had walked that day already but the pending thrill of traveling through the air spurred her onwards. The strange sun remained a constant light in the place between worlds. One step then another, Paechra continued her journey, farther and higher up the path. Soon the forest of firs thinned, and the path became rocky. A mile ahead the land became hilly, hinting at the mountainous terrain to follow after. At the base of the hills Paechra could easily see a hollowed out cavern, a small fire burning in the cave's entrance.

"Good day!" called the sylva, hopeful of a reply.

It had seemed almost an eternity since she had left a dark, verbal battle with the Low Prince. The Druid was in great need of conversation, a voice full of warmth. Not the sounds of angry jealousy she played back over and over to spur on her walking. At the sound of Paechra's call an ancient figure dressed in animal furs similar to the Druid hobbled forth from the darkness of the cave.

"Ho, Paechra!" the ancient one called back.

Paechra thought at first this figure was Mother Druid Sienna but as the figure spoke she discovered it was certainly not the case. The voice was male.

"Greetings old one," Paechra stated as she hurried toward the cave. "How do you know of me?"

Closer to the hermit of the cavern and able to stare into the man's eyes Paechra discovered a strange reptilian nature to those eyes, golden in color and showing a youthfulness where the body obviously stated age.

"Child, what you wish to ask is why do I know of you so well where you know naught of me."

Unsure of how to react to this Paechra merely nodded.

"I see the wisdom of elders has drawn you to silence, child," laughed the hermit.

The old one turned and wandered back into the cavern, stumbling as he moved by the fire's flames. Paechra was swift in closing the gap, there to catch the old one under one arm to halt his tumble.

"The Mother Druid Sienna did say that you were a kind one," said the hermit. "Glad I am to discover that this is indeed the case."

"Know you Mother Sienna?" asked Paechra.

"Indeed child, she has come this way though not for many years, more than a hundred or more," lamented the elder.

"Do you have many visitors come this way?" Paechra asked as she helped the hermit rise again to his feet.

"Not as many of late," sighed the hermit. "Perhaps there was a male of your race, one or two years ago."

"My father, Therdous?" asked the Druid, surprised. "I was

certain he would have chosen to walk the path of the mountain."

"Yes, I do believe Therdous was his name…" considered the hermit. "He wished to test my knowledge of languages, but many have come before him and many will come after."

"That sounds like Father Therdous," laughed Paechra. "Always testing, hoping you are concentrating and wishing that the knowledge would just stay put."

"Have you come to test me too, child?" then asked the hermit, his eyes flashed for a moment as if there were a terrific fury awaiting release.

"Many of my sister Druids have spoken of the wise old dragon," began Paechra, honest and straight to the point. "I am hopeful that you may know where this creature can be found."

The hermit pondered a moment, gnarled fingers drawn to a wispy white beard that adorned his chin.

"The dragon appears only to those who offer a gift."

Paechra pondered for a moment, she had left home with little but what she thought to grab. Thus far her journey had supplied her with everything she needed.

"My father would have gifted the ancient beast a word," she thought. "Mother Sienna perhaps the gift of respect."

"I know the gift that I wish to bestow upon the wondrous dragon," the Druid announced but with caution. "For what it is worth I offer to you the gift of my friendship."

The eyes of the hermit grew wide as if surprised but then filled with warmth.

"Paechra Lightheart, daughter of Therdous Lightheart, I knew of your arrival, and I knew you would not disappoint," announced the hermit.

Before her very eyes Paechra watched the old man transform. His body grew larger and more elongated as silver scales appearing across the old man's wrinkled skin. The beard became like leathery vines, the eyes larger but still holding that warmth and humor.

"I know child when you guessed the truth and discovered my identity," the great beast gushed. "I accept your gift and as a friend I offer you the ride you seek."

"I thank you my friend," replied a gracious Paechra.

As she spoke she felt in her mind the name Fythrania.

"I honor you, Fythrania, Dragon Friend," stated the Druid with a bow.

"As I honor you, Paechra, Sylva Friend," the dragon replied.

Dragon flight was a strange feeling, wondrous and terrifying. Paechra climbed between the giant's shoulders, just in front of his wing joints, just as Fythrania asked her to do. As she sat and patiently waited she found the beast connect with her, mind to mind.

'I will keep you safe child,' the mind of the dragon promised, the eons echoing, betraying the true ancientness of the creature and the old man it pretended to be. Then suddenly the flight began.

As promised Fythrania did protect the sylva, flying while grounded and yet mentally Paechra experienced all the thrills of bursting through the clouds and seeing the true world from such a vantage. It was as if she was dreaming but experiencing this physical thrill at the same time.

"Is this how flight always feels?" Paechra cried, her voice barely a whisper as she battled the wind whistling past her.

'Speak with your mind child and I will hear you,' the dragon replied, an echo amongst the madness that was Paechra's thoughts.

'Is this how...?'

'Flight always feels?' laughed Fythrania. 'I did hear your question as you thought before you spoke.'

'Of course,' replied the young Druid, embarrassed but happy.

'To answer your question, Paechra Sylva Friend it is not how flight feels for the birds and other creatures that fly and glide using the air for travel... For those who fly by dragon though it is the safest way to experience the speed and height.'

'Show me truth then, what it is to fly for real,' Paechra asked.

Again, there was a moment of pause as the dragon, like the hermit considered the request.

'As you wish,' he stated.

Immediately Paechra fell. Tumbling through the open sky she screamed, panic overfilling her mind where previously there was calm, excitement, happiness. Just as quickly Fythrania returned, his solid promise of protection like a shield.

'Wish you to experience that again, young one?' the dragon asked.

'No, please, never again," Paechra replied. 'I have learned to simply trust you and your wisodom, Fythrania.'

'Paechra, Sylva Friend, I sense that our friendship will be a strong one,' stated the dragon.

Paechra thought she detected some humor in the creature's tone.

'Wise and wondrous Fythrania, I sense the same,' she

replied with a smile of her own.

The dragon landed in a forest clearing far from Paechra's homeland. The sylva slid from the creature's shoulders and looked back to see a number of trees uprooted as if Fythrania had crashed into them. Thanks to the mental connection the pair shared Paechra had felt none of that impact. As she inspected her friend she found slight cuts and abrasions where the great oaks caused harm.

'Please, allow me to help,' asked Paechra, her aura flaring as she touched each wound.

They were only shallow, so they closed up swiftly.

'I thank you friend, I shall watch your journey with interest,' said the dragon. 'Now though our paths go separate ways.'

With a gracious bow Paechra turned away from the dragon and entered deeper into the wall of trees. She felt rather than saw Fythrania take flight again, headed back to the cave and identity of the hermit.

Alone again the sylva wandered east. Her heart seemed to say that was the path her father had trodden. The voices of the trees and animals were her company, and the Druid quietly chatted with them all as she went. Now the sun was a ball that moved and Paechra could feel the passing of time. As the morning became afternoon she felt the mood of the forest change. As if like a curse there came the sound of steel clashing upon steel reverberated throughout the once quiet forest, sending its native inhabitants either scurrying away or taking to the air with just as much noise as the combat that startled them. Paechra felt the flight instinct evident in each and every beast that raced by her. Driven toward the danger the sylva caught the bridal of a milky white horse that tried to race past. Encasing the beast in her aura the Druid spoke calming words as she connected with the majestic mare.

'Master… Danger… Flee…' the horse chanted at a galloping pace. 'Master… Danger… FLEE…'

'I am friend… Come, show me the way,' urged Paechra. 'We can save him together.'

Paechra leapt into the saddle and tried to work out the unnatural set up as the horse lead her back to its master. The two burst into the clearing to witness a lucky hammer blow from one of a half dozen vorsurk warriors. A lone human trying to fend off all of the dog-like monsters was struck sharply upon the helmet. The human swooned, Paechra seeing and feeling the effects of the blow in the man's outline. The bright red outline of adrenaline faded quickly to a sickening purple. As the hammer fell again, the human's new state of dizziness cost him his shoulder. Paechra saw the human continued fighting valiantly on, but she could tell his strength was fading fast. Urging the horse to fight through its fear the Druid used a mixture of calming thoughts and urgency to drive it onward with earnestness.

The horde of creatures that had caught the human by surprise now looked up in shock themselves. The human, dazed and in agonizing pain from the blow to his head and shoulder Paechra was certain would be broken, watched with his mouth opened wide, as the Druid a vision, blonde haired and dressed in mixture of furs, skins and cloth of various earthen colors leapt from the galloping steed and entered into the fray. With an ease Paechra molded her aura of sky blue light into what could only be described as the image of a great angry grizzly bear. All of Paechra's built up frustration was released in a flurry as Vorsurk flesh was ripped effortlessly and soundlessly from Vorsurk bones, almost like the five hundred pound monsters of muscle were really dried Autumn leaves blown from the branches by a cruel, cool wind. As the last limb fell quietly to the forest floor and the fallen Vorsurk all twitched their last, the girl turned on the spot to face the human and gave him a beaming smile 'The Look of Paechra'. The Druid was surprised such a skirmish had not even caused her a moment of breathlessness, with a moment's pause to allow the savage she-bear to slip from her aura Paechra felt fury-free and ready to meet her first human.

"You seemed like you needed some help," Daughter of the Forest Paechra began with a shrug and no sign of a shortage of breath. "My name is Paechra. Paechra Lightheart," the girl added, her beaming smile seeming to make the greeting a proclamation, not the plain statement that it was. She thrust out her hand but then retracted it apologetically, wiping the Vorsurk muck from her fingers upon the lush forest greenery before extending it again. The human took it and winched as excruciating pain shot up his agonized right arm. Paechra let the warrior's arm drop immediately

"You're hurt!" she cried.

The human let the obvious statement pass, answering affirmatively with just a single nod. Even this action of little effort caused him severe pain. Letting his sword drop, the warrior clutched his shattered shoulder and willed the pain to ease to a dull throb, without any success.

"Here let me…" the girl kindly offered as she gave the dark haired warrior another knowing smile. The human warrior released feeling of uncertainty then, unusually unnerved. As Paechra placed her hands upon the horribly damaged shoulder, the blue light flared up around her again. The human, shied away as if he expected to see the bear and face the same fate as the Vorsurk before him. Tempted as it was to bring out the ferocity once more Paechra decided to heal instead of hurt. The human warrior was both surprised and relieved to see the image of a dove instead envelope the girl. Beyond this was the feeling of warmth as Paechra helped his pain vanish away. A moment later, with a clearer head, the human looked again, with greater scrutiny, at the sylva before him and discovered that the blue haze had vanished.

"Paechra?" the human asked. "You found my horse?"

"No, human," Paechra replied. "Your horse found me."

"Raven, please," requested the warrior as he tested his shoulder. "My name is Raven."

"Raven it would bring me great joy if I could call you my friend," Paechra gushed.

"As you wish," replied Raven.

His yellowish aura betrayed his uncertainty.

"Come, friend Raven," laughed Paechra. "Lead me to my father."

"Strange lady, I travel to Andrapaal," replied Raven. "We can enquire there about your father."

"Few of my kind have ventured lately among your people," stated Paechra. "Should my father be at this Andrapaal I am sure he will be easily found."

"Well, you seem on good terms with my faithful steed," said Raven, indicating the saddle.

"It shall be no Fythrania, perhaps I shall ride with you," stated Paechra.

"As you wish," the human said with a sigh, the second time already since meeting Paechra.

Climbing back up into the saddle Raven lowered an arm. With great strength he helped Paechra onto the horse's rump. Testing his bearings Raven then turned the steed eastwards.

"Onwards to Andrapaal then," he said with a humorless grin.

"Indeed," agreed Paechra. "Onwards to Andrapaal."

*

The Druid Paechra thought often of that time when she made her own choice and left her homeland. It was strange to think that this fateful day had occurred already some two or so years in the past. Betrothed to limp flower Low Prince Derek, favorite of Mother Druid Sienna, discovering her powers and how to best use them for the benefit of sylvan-kind and their forest home, Paechra made her choice to leave her betrothed, her sisters of the wood, family, and friends behind. It seemed like the right personal choice deciding to seek out her father, the linguist Therdous, and since leaving the safety of her forested homeland much had happened to the sylva.

Of those happenings Paechra considered the most fortuitous being that of her meeting with the Truth Seeker Johannas Stormsong, a human that she considered friend, one whom she even wondered whether there could be other feelings, but she knew there currently was little time to consider such though as Paechra witnessed the loss firstly of her father, then Johannas and finally the invasion of Thuraen by the shared enemy the vorsurk. Under the cover of chaos as the city Andrapaal transformed the sylva was luckily able to guide what few citizens she could safely away from the fallen city. The use of magical means was risky in the land of humanity, a place where magic of any kind was forbidden. Traveling with Paechra, fighting over the role of leadership were Anton and Michael, Johannas' master, and his father. Between the two neither could clearly take charge, nor would one or the other step aside to allow a leader to be chosen. Instead, the pair fought like toddlers, arguing over when the other had made a mistake and the gravity of such an error. Thomas the Butcher, one of the Council of Eleven, though Paechra could never understand why, was always buffer between the pair of older men trying to side with one and then the other as the arguments between Anton and Michael seemed to provide a winner until it were finally evident that neither was right.

Paechra wished for those early days again when she had just left home and started her personal quest. Had she had known that Lady Fate would guide her faithful servant to this point in time Paechra believed she would have thought twice about even beginning that journey.

For such an innocent desire had led to Paechra's discovery of the monster Morthos. Thinking of Johannas caused Paechra to smile but memories of that trickster Morthos quickly caused that smile to vanish. The path that Johannas had undertaken was gifted to him by Morthos in a similar way that Paechra had chosen the path of the humans, such thinking led to a deeper sadness and an understanding for Paechra of her responsibility. Too many mixed memories, too much distraction, in truth though Paechra needed to focus upon the now, the world toward which she was going and the path she had chosen for all. Paechra's own path was again that of guide and support, the spirits had advised that the sylva's place was with Queen Catherine of the Kingdom of Thuraen and the infant growing in her womb. Paechra missed Johannas and the friendship that was growing between them. She hoped that the path of Druid and Truth Keeper would cross once more. Until then though there was the ship.

"What is this place you lead us towards, witch?" demanded Anton, the time of prophecy had seemingly affected the Head of the Truth Keepers as badly as the city of Andrapaal itself.

"Must you insult our guide?" Michael sighed, his elderly eyes showing more disappointment than anger.

"To guide you must let me lead, I have merely set your course and then followed the sound of your bickering," replied Paechra, her anger evident.

"I thought the sylva kind and benevolent," chimed in Thomas.

Queen Catherine remained silent.

Paechra looked on the fleeing monarch and not for the first time did she see a waning figure.

"Queen Catherine of Thuraen you must have food, you must have wine," urged Truth Keeper Anton. He too had noticed the poor state of the queen.

"Food, water and rest is what is needed," stated Paechra with a frown. "No wine."

"The queen's color is poorly, and wine will do wonders for such a condition," barked back Anton.

"Are you a sage, Anton?" called Michael, louder than the bark. "Do you wear yellow or red robes beneath your armor?"

"No," growled the Head of the Truth Keepers, his eyes like daggers.

"We must reach the docks before the ship sails," muttered Paechra.

She took Queen Catherine about the shoulders and guided her in a kindly way to continue the journey.

"What is this talk of docklands?" whined Thomas the Butcher.

He looked to Michael first and then Anton, waiting for a supportive comment from either. Paechra could see in his aura that the butcher was in truth hoping both the older men would

back up his fear.

"Leave well alone," muttered Michael wearily.

"Boy, the witch has set our path," added Anton. "It is our own fault we have walked it."

"Walking this far I fear what awaits us is not near as terrifying as what we have left behind," the queen whispered, something only Paechra overheard.

For the humans it seemed a strange journey, walking steadily along a path through a dense forest of firs. A distinct lack of other people, animals and towns had left the men disorientated. Living in a kingdom where each city, town or village was only a day's travel away even by foot, it was difficult to comprehend wandering this forest and then having to set camp. The nature of the light caused Anton trouble as well, the lack of sun's rise and set. The strange world between worlds that Paechra walked with confidence was foreign to the humans.

"How far, witch?" demanded Anton.

"We camp here and rest," ordered Paechra. "I'll not push Queen Catherine and the child another mile today."

"Thomas, pitch the tents," instructed Anton.

"I will find firewood and begin a meal," offered Michael.

Paechra yearned to demonstrate her power, the magic of nature. Within moments she knew it was possible to have a sturdy, safe camp with blazing fire and fruits suffice for a hungry army to feast upon. Such was the way of the humans though that a display of such power would be feared. So instead, she stood and waited, quietly singing to the queen and the unborn child. A soft glow of blue light enveloped Paechra, but the men were too busy to notice, and the queen was sunken so deeply into her own thoughts that the outside world was a

41

mystery.

"Thyn kint fyss g hoolalee," crooned Paechra, almost whispering in the queen's ear.

Queen Catherine sighed, remained squat, and hunched over.

"Fyss g haalalae fyn o lathereryn," the sylva continued.

With some level of satisfaction Paechra noted a soft rose color return to what she could see of the queen's complexion. Soon after which there came from the monarch the sounds of slumber. Much needed rest for both mother and child.

Paechra then chose to take a rare moment for herself. Slipping into a state of reverie she was immediately flooded with the thoughts and feelings she had spent so many days keeping at bay. Images of Morthos and Vladimir combined with Johannas while the spirits Aiera and Thur servants of light and air flew in and out and around trying to guide but creating more chaos. As the city grew up around Paechra she knew she was still dreaming.

"You are not true, you cannot harm me here," stated the Druid, strength in her voice which surprised her.

The face that stepped out from behind one of the great grey stone walls was that which resembled the creature part man and part wolf, a vorsurk. Cloaked in the robes of a runecaster the creature brought forth from within its garments an ancient book.

"Your certainty amuses me forested one," the doglike magician growled. There was humor in its eyes but a vacancy in its tone.

"This is my dream and again I state that I see you for what you are," said Paechra calmly, just as her mother and The Mother Druid Sienna had taught her. "You are but a vision of my dreaming and I bid you move on."

"You must be wary, forested one," again growled the vorsurk. "Truth on the road of dreaming can be twisted and retold; one's dream can become another's path."

"Then let me awaken that your pathway would end here," boldly suggested the Druid.

This only caused a hollow laugh to emanate from the wolf's jaws.

"Child, do not threaten what you do not properly comprehend."

"You call me child and yet my knowledge of your kind leads me to estimate our years are similar, if not the same."

The vorsurk's laughter ended.

"I call you child to merely highlight that your knowledge is obviously infantile," growled the magician.

"With my awakening we shall discover whose word speaks truly," called back Paechra, but for the first time in that short time she felt her confidence waiver.

The vorsurk flipped open his ancient book and gracefully stepped back behind the great stone wall. Paechra heard an eerie chanting fading as the magician began to move away.

"Wake up! Paechra wake up!" the Druid urged of herself.

The sylva did not see but sensed the vorsurk as it appeared behind her.

"Shall I take your soul with my knife, girl?" growled the dog in Paechra's almond shaped ear.

A bright blue light suddenly surrounded the sylva, her inner aura brought forth. The vorsurk hissed as the hand that wielded the soul-stealer was caught in the light. With satisfaction Paechra noted the knife was dropped and a mark of harm appeared upon the clawed hand that had once held it. The sylva stood firmly upon the fallen blade and beneath her boot it shattered.

"You may have proven yourself true, magician," announced Paechra. "But you will not harm me here."

"Perhaps I shall take one of your charges then," suggested the magician.

"Be on your way my enemy," stated Paechra coolly. "Reflect upon the fact that it has been too long between battles, you forget our powers."

"I am Gwyn-Thul-Tur, and I shall tell me brothers of you," promised the vorsurk. "I know you Paechra Lightheart and promise we all shall know your name."

As the vorsurk stepped away and closed the book it held so reverently Paechra felt her dream state fade. Seeing the creature step behind the wall once more the Druid began to relax. The city walls vanished, returning to the forest floor and revealing once again the woods that Paechra realized had never gone. As her weary eyes flickered open her enemy left her with a parting gift.

"I shall not take one charge from you, girl," a whisper on the wind promised with a growl. "You'll need them all to pay passage for your journey ahead.

"Gwyn-Thul-Tur I shall remember you and vow we shall meet again," announced the Druid, unsure yet whether she wished such a vow to come true.

"What do you grumble about in our queen's ear, witch?" growled Anton and Paechra was immediately reminded of her dream battle.

"Queen Catherine must awaken," demanded Paechra,

urgency obvious in her tone. "I thought us safe here, but I was wrong."

Anton made to retort, upset he had been ignored but this time Michael and Thomas sided together and cut the Head of the Truth Seekers off in his tracks before the grizzled warrior could say more.

"I shall dismantle the tents then," sighed Thomas.

"Catherine, my queen, you must wake," urged Michael, taking the monarch by her shoulders and gently shaking her.

"Fredrickson? Fredrickson, my love, is it you?" asked Queen Catherine, hopeful, dreamily.

"No, my queen, it is only I," replied Michael, sharing in his queen's sadness.

"No, you are not a king," agreed Catherine. She rose and wiped the sleep from her eyes while Michael stood ashamed.

Paechra looked around, warily while the men packed up the camp.

"What did you see, lass?" Michael asked, shaking off his strange conversation with Queen Catherine.

The Druid paused for a moment, considering what to say. Seeing Michael standing before her and seeing something of his son Johannas in the father's features Paechra decided to reveal the truth.

"Dark magic, our shared enemy, they hunt us even in our dreams," the sylva explained.

"Even in sleep, this far from home," replied Michael, disbelief obvious across his features. "Is anywhere safe?"

Paechra loved the man as she loved his son. Other humans would not have believed her as Michael had. The sylva was so grateful for the immediacy, with trust she continued to speak freely.

"There is one place these creatures dare not venture," began Paechra. "It is where I lead you, but I did not realize until now just how important our next stop will be."

"The dockland we shall go then."

Paechra nodded grimly. She had hidden from Michael as she had hidden from the others the true nature of that place, the docklands. The Druid understood that revealing such a truth would turn all, including Michael against her and what she thought was necessary. The sylvan people of the past had helped these humans, and it was many of those same forest dwellers who would need to help again. Leading so many humans through the forest of dreams Paechra had decided it was to be impossible to return the same way she had come. These humans, fragile as they were, would need to find an inner bravery. Paechra understood their weariness from what they had witnessed and the fact that they were not used to traveling so far. This would indeed test them as it would test her. The Picturesque Picaresque was the ship that the Druid sought. Passage on such a vessel would be costly. Paechra hoped that all would survive.

As Paechra's magic subtly guided the humans deeper along the path of the forest of dreams she caused the firs to grow thinner in number, smaller, sparser. It was not the Druid's doing as the fog rolled in.

"What is this...?" began Thomas, echoing Anton's usual cry.

A silent look from Michael caused the younger man to swallow the word witchery before it began.

"Where do you lead us?" growled Anton, not willing to give up a chance for a fight so easily.

"We follow Paechra to safety," assured Michael.

For the first time the sylva felt the pangs of guilt.

"We travel to the Docklands to seek passage to my people," Paechra stated quickly. "They have helped humankind before, and I believe they will assist us again."

"So, you think yourself human now do you, girl?" Anton barked.

Paechra shivered as she was reminded of her meeting for the vorsurk magician. The tone was the same, the words spoken by the Head Truth Keeper almost identical. With a deep breath the Druid attempted to slow her heart before she responded.

"Anton, I represent the people of the forest realm," Paechra began, slow and calm. "I do not consider my race altered from the brief time I have spent in Thuraen."

"Right, well, good then," replied Anton.

"I hear the ocean," suddenly announced Queen Catherine.

A light wind had carried sound and scent of the waters to the party, the queen the first to notice.

'There is still hope,' thought Paechra then.

The sylva had been worried for the kingdom's monarch, the queen's condition possibly too fragile for what trials lay ahead.

"Double time then!" ordered Anton, urging Thomas to quicken the pace.

It was only a mile left to travel Paechra knew. With some relief she allowed the leader of Thuraen's knights to do what he had been doing for most of his adult life. The Druid passed the care and guidance of Queen Catherine on to Michael. Hanging back a few strides behind the rest the sylva returned to the state of reverie.

"We have naught that we can part with," Paechra reminded herself of. "So it must be that I negotiate work in exchange for passage."

"Daughter, you may offer translation as a skill," suggested Paechra's father.

Paechra stopped and turned to hug the man as she discovered his presence.

"But what of the others, what might they do?" the Druid asked, ending the embrace as quickly as it began.

"The men can be put to work," Therdous stated simply.

"What of Queen Catherine and the child, father?"

"Daughter you must have faith that even the Ghoul will respect the blood of royalty."

As her father faded away Paechra nodded, decision made.

'The humankind enjoy playing dice," she muttered. "Let us dice then with their souls."

Stepping out from her moment of rejuvenation Paechra felt the land beneath her feet change from soft, lush grass to the hard cobbled stone of the Docklands.

"Wait," she made to say but discovered that the humans had already stopped in their tracks.

Through the fog three great ocean vessels could be seen. They creaked from age as they struggled with their moorings, eager to be free and sailing. The first ship was covered with lizardmen. They slithered across the decks and up and down masting's. The second was crewed by humanoid creatures crossed with a menagerie of animalia.

Across the deck of the third ship shuffled the groaning undead. Upon the rear of that ship was painted in a dark scrawl like blood the name Picturesque Picaresque. Toward this ship Paechra strode.

"Remain here, silently," demanded the sylva. "I go to negotiate our passage."

Dumbfounded, for once all of the humans did as asked.

Chapter Three

Riding the Wave

The wave of life does rise and fall. The wise do not resist.

**From the Ninth Stanza of the Prophecy, translated by the
sages of the Kingdom of Thuraen 408th year**

PAECHRA FELT LIKE a prisoner between cells as she lay in her
allocated hammock and let the sea rock and sway her. The great
ship, The Picturesque Picaresque groaned and creaked as it
powered its way through the ocean waves. The sylvan's almond
ears could distinctly hear the wind and rain as it affronted the
vessel, to the Druid it sounded like a war.

"Is it over yet?" moaned Queen Catherine, she searched
frantically for the bucket which was located under her own
hammock and released what bread and water she had eaten to

break her morning fast.

Without answering Paechra made her way the three steps across the cabin and placed a hand upon the queen's burning forehead. A pale blue light enveloped the delicate fingers of the forest dweller that was so far from home. The royal from Thuraen sighed as the fever momentarily left her and she closed her eyes. In turn Paechra placed her still faintly glowing hand upon Catherine's belly and sent vibes of peace toward the child that grew within.

"We still have much distance to travel," the sylvan sighed.

The journey from the Docklands had been rough from the beginning.

*

Paechra thought back, not more than three days past, when with a bravery that was partly hers and partly that of Johannas her friend she stepped aboard this ship and called for its Captain.

"Welcome, forested one," announced the Ghoul that approached, bowing low. "Is it passage home that you seek?"

Paechra had tried hard to ignore the foul stench of the undead creatures that shuffled about the top deck, it was almost impossible to remain stone-like as the most senior aboard the Picturesque Picaresque appeared and then spoke. The grey skin of the creature drooped on the left side, a rat poked forth out from one sleeve of a tattered black coat, as the creature smiled Paechra could see the jaws were filled with jagged teeth designed for ripping and tearing flesh. Paechra's knowledge of these creatures led her to believe that flesh was preferably warm, heart still beating, victim screaming.

51

"Indeed, Captain..?"

"Overtian, oh forested one," replied the Ghoul.

"Such a name means sea explorer in your language, true?" suggested Paechra, not completely confident with her translation.

"Sea traveler, oh forested one," replied Captain Overtian, genuinely surprised. "Your linguistic abilities could be useful to us on this voyage."

"I wish not for payment but am willing to offer my knowledge and abilities as a linguist while we travel together," explained Paechra.

"In exchange for..?" enquired the ship's captain as an off colored drool ran from his top lip's gum down his chin to then drip upon the head of the rat.

With a squeak the creature turned tail and disappeared, Paechra following its passage down the sleeve and amongst the body of the shirt the monster wore. The sylvan suppressed a shiver as she considered whether the vermin nested somewhere within the Ghoul's clothing or within his actual body.

"I wish only for a dual cabin, I travel with royalty," announced Paechra as she indicated the other members of her party.

With milky white eyes, ancient and knowing the captain turned away from Paechra and examined the humans.

"You travel with this?" asked Captain Overtian, for the second time genuinely surprised.

"It is my business what company I keep," replied Paechra.

"Indeed, oh forested one," replied the captain, returning his gaze to the sylvan and offering a respectful bow. "Do they know where and to whom you lead them?"

All of this occurred so far from the waiting humans that they could not overhear, something that Paechra was grateful for.

There was a period where neither spoke. The silence told the Ghoul all he wanted to know.

"I see," continued the Ghoul with a grin that enabled Paechra to count each and every pointed tooth. "Perhaps it would be a better fate for them all that they should join my crew now."

"No!" Paechra replied with a fury unexpected.

"No?" questioned the captain, the grin becoming a frown.

"No," stated Paechra again but this time her voice was level, a confidence and control returned. "I have not led these few from a fallen city to doom them to a fate worse than death."

"A fate worse than death, Druid?" asked the Ghoul. "You hurt me and my kind with such words."

The captain's face contorted into that of a whipped dog.

"How would you describe the existence of yourself, your crew and the others like you?" enquired the sylvan, her face unchanged.

"Perhaps a fate similar to death, no better, no worse..." replied the captain, his smile returning.

"I would not know," said Paechra. "Nor would I wish for myself or those I choose to travel with to know of such a fate."

"Then it is agreed, oh forested one," announced the captain thrusting forward a clawed hand that missed half a thumb.

Paechra reluctantly took the offered hand and shook it once.

"There shall be a cabin set aside for you, the human queen and..." began the captain, pausing for a moment to sniff the breeze. "Joining you both of course shall be the unborn prince."

"Agreed," stated Paechra. "The men who travel with us shall assist your crew thereby retaining their flesh and their souls."

"As you are no doubt aware any failure to pay through work will forfeit said agreement and result in myself enjoying quite a meal," laughed the captain as his forked tongue ran across his dried and flaking lips.

"I shall make sure that all members of my party are aware of the finer details of our agreement," Paechra promised.

*

That was the hardest conversation that the sylvan had to have.

"Is there no other way to get to where you are trying to take us?" asked Michael, Johannas' father.

"To what fate have you doomed us, witch?" Anton demanded, butting in before Paechra was able to answer Andrapaal's blacksmith.

"Yes Paechra, what would you have us do?" whined Thomas. "We should have made a deal with the animals."

"And who is to say," growled Anton. "Where this stranger wishes to lead us is where we want to go?"

"The sylvan-kind saved us in the past," suggested Michael. "It is written so it must be true."

Anton spat upon the cobbles as he heard what Michael said.

"I believe what I can see and strike with my sword," stated the Head Truth Keeper. "The written word is for the sages, to keep, to read and to govern us by."

Paechra sighed. She could see Anton was going to be typically difficult.

"Thomas, those other ships do not travel to the lands of my people," the Druid tried to explain. "Where they go I do not know, and I cannot say what welcome we would get when those ships dock at port."

"Perhaps that is a risk we are all willing to take," announced Anton. "Aren't I right lad?!"

Thomas gasped as he was thumped on the back. Anton's surprising attack of comradery had caught the butcher off guard.

"Maybe," mumbled Thomas with a cough.

"That is, you, out voted again, Anton," suggested Michael.

Paechra leveled her eyes at the Head Truth Keeper then.

"Follow me, I shall settle us in," she announced. "We have lost enough travel time already."

"So, you say, witch," replied Anton before he broke off from the group and marched toward the gangplank.

"Thank you," the sylvan whispered to Michael before she took Queen Catherine by the elbow and wrist and guided her toward the ship.

Michael nodded and then thumped Thomas on the arm.

"Come along butcher's boy, adventure awaits us."

Paechra knew that Michael and Anton both worked the oars, deep in the belly of the ship. Their strength had quickly been identified by Captain Overtain's more senior crew members. The sylvan wondered if on those nights when the wind had died down she could faintly hear the boom of the drum as the First Mate set a grueling pace. It was that or the heavy footfalls of the larger, half-giant crew rushing about top deck to bring in some sails and furl out others to keep the ship cruising with the aid of what wind there was. The Druid hoped it was the crew, else the noise she would hear from Michael and Anton both would be relentless. Paechra knew she might never be able to call the Head of the Truth Keepers a friend, but she hoped that what respect she had somehow gained from Johannas' father Michael Stormsong was not to be whittled away from this sea voyage. Paechra had wanted to explain that she could not possibly have led Queen Catherine and her unborn child over the mountains and none of the humans would have believed in the existence of the dragon. That would have literally been a dead end there. Paechra convinced herself for the hundredth time that the sea and this boat were the only way she could have returned home.

There came a knock at the cabin door, followed by the meek voice of Thomas.

"Paechra, your midday meal has arrived."

The Druid cursed under her breath, in the semi-darkness Queen Catherine stirred at the sound of the butcher's voice. With care the sylvan unhooked the cabin door's latch and allowed the butcher a view of her facial features.

"I am sorry, oh forested one," stated the butcher with his head lowered.

Paechra noted one of the Ghouls stood waiting a step behind Thomas. The creature had no weapons that the Druid could see but the creature's claws, those teeth and an eternal hunger were enough to cause Thomas to ooze fear.

"Come, bring the meal that I may share it with my companion," announced Paechra, hurrying Thomas into the cabin.

The sylvan swiftly shut and latched the door before the accompanying Ghoul could follow after. Paechra pitied Thomas, not strong enough to man the oars he had been relegated to the kitchen. Thomas had been allocated the task of distributing the bread and water to those who worked the ship who were not Ghouls. From day one he had been looked over and sniffed at by the undead and he had witnessed a number of dwarves and fellow humans attempt to leap overboard only for them to be quickly caught by Ghoul crew members and bustled off towards the kitchen.

"Paechra I have been asked by so many if I carry with me a knife," moaned Thomas as the door closed behind and the Ghoul began a rhythmic thump upon it.

"I bet they send you around the ship with naught but a wooden jug and a cloth sack of bread," replied the Druid with a sigh.

Paechra wondered if she had doomed Thomas to the worst time aboard the Picturesque Picaresque. His eyes were widened more than they had been that morning.

"A knife to cut the bread they claim," continued the butcher, ignoring Paechra's attempt at sympathy. "But I know for sure that they would use it on their wrists."

"How could you be so certain?" asked Paechra, but she was sure she already knew the answer.

"Because I would use it myself," hissed Thomas, madly. "I would do anything to get away from this accursed ship and its monstrous crew."

"Calm yourself, butcher," demanded Paechra, though she looked upon Thomas with kindly eyes.

"Of course, Queen Catherine," considered the young butcher.

He turned his attention to the monarch and noted her eyes were open wide.

"Fredrickson, my love," cried the eerie voice of the queen

from her hammock.

"Feed her," instructed Paechra and without question Thomas obeyed.

As Paechra had shown him the day before and as he had done for the evening meal, Thomas broke from the small loaf bite sized pieces. He then poured a small amount of water into a bowl and began dipping the bread and placing it at Catherine's lips.

Queen Catherine accepted the food, chewed it, and then swallowed as if she did not know what was happening. Thomas held back a tear as he watched the process he was a part of.

"She retains her color," murmured Paechra. "We just need the body to fight the fever itself."

"You all fight for me," the voice of Queen Catherine stated suddenly, for once clear. "Who fights for you all?"

"My queen!" announced Thomas, joyful for that briefest of moments.

"You are not my husband!" Catherine stated, staring with suddenly fearful eyes at Thomas and the bowl into which he was dunking the pieces of bread. "You are certainly no king."

"Perhaps I am the king of fools," thought Thomas.

He placed his hand upon Queen Catherine's forehead.

"Paechra, she is hot again," the butcher announced.

There came another round of thumps and scratches upon the cabin door, the Ghoul on the other side demanding entry.

"You need to go," ordered Paechra. "I will finish here."

"Must I?" whined Thomas, his eyes pleading with the sylvan to let him stay.

"Please pass on to the men down below that I am hopeful our time upon this ship will be for only a few days more."

"As you wish, witch," replied Thomas.

The cabin door opened and then closed, and the butcher was gone.

Out of sight Thomas' voice could be heard protesting as the monstrosity manhandled him away from the safety of the cabin.

Dutifully Paechra latched the door before picking up bowl and bread and continuing to feed the small, wet morsels to the hungry queen. As she dipped she sang, and tendrils of blue danced about her fingers.

"Rest now, Queen Catherine," urged the Druid. "Rest and remember happier times."

*

Paechra stared down the length of the dining table. So many candles, their lights flickering. The sylvan thought perhaps their existence were purely for her benefit, a way of keeping the stench of undeath at bay. The combination of rose, forest fruits, sea breeze and so many more fragrances, impossible to single out. The affect was distractive yet still thoughts of death assaulted Paechra's mind.

"Try the chicken," suggested the captain of the Picturesque Picaresque, a rotting hand indicated the fine bird that was the table's centerpiece.

"You will not join me?" asked the Druid though she already knew the reply.

"Nay oh forested one, the food I eat usually still lives and

59

squirms and screams... I am sure you have heard my feasting at least once already..."

Paechra had twice thus far during the sea voyage. Twice her dreams had been disrupted and her sleep then stolen as she prayed to whatever spirits listened that the poor soul being devoured was not Thomas, Michael or even Anton. Queen Catherine had been the worst to console then. There was something about those initial screams that had even cut through the royal's fevered delirium. Sleep vanished like the stars as day dawns and Paechra had been in the worst of moods on those mornings that followed after.

Her thoughts returning to the meal before her, Paechra reached for the golden goblet filled with wine. A sip turned into a gulp. The ship's captain gave an open lipped smile that revealed his razor sharp front teeth. It was frightening how the ghoulish curse turned humans into creatures that were more animalistic, almost like they had never lived a previous life, never been anything other than the monster they had morphed into. As the goblet was returned to the overflowing table the ship pitched portside. The goblet toppled as Paechra reached out to steady her sliding plate and what dishes she could reach.

"Why not distribute this fine food amongst the others on board?" asked the sylvan.

"If the rowers rowed faster than me and me crew would miss out on a chance to feast upon the weak," replied Captain Overtain with a smile. "No, we need them afraid and tired, so they make mistakes."

Paechra shuddered at that logic, knowing the verbal agreement, knowing the ultimate price for breaking contract. Her fear continued to grow deeper as from out of the shadows came another figure. A sigh of relief followed as the Druid discovered it was one of the living, not the undead.

"Thomas?" she asked, taken slightly aback.

"No ma'am," came a squeaky reply, the human only a teen, Paechra guessed he would be fourteen years at the most. "My name is Aaron, Aaron Hollantain."

"I promise to remember your name, Aaron," said Paechra solemnly as the boy righted her goblet.

"I thank you, ma'am," replied the boy with a courteous nod of honest relief. "I fear I shall remain aboard this ship for so long it gladdens my heart that someone will remember me."

From behind her Paechra felt, heard, and could immediately smell one of the deathless approach with a pitcher of wine.

"Water please," she asked, placing a hand over the mouth of the drinking vessel.

The creature wordlessly turned to the captain who nodded. With a gnashing of teeth the ghoul then withdrew, dragging the boy Aaron along with it, back toward the galley.

"Please don't hurt him," stated Paechra, her voice level, trying not to beg.

"For your refusal?" asked Captain Overtain of the Picturesque Picaresque, a dark laugh following after. "Oh, forested one, it will not be for your refusal that he shall be punished."

There was something about the captain's tone that alerted the sylvan to the fact that the boy was not safe.

"Aaron is but a child, how can you hold him accountable for his own fears and mistakes?" demanded Paechra Lightheart.

"This child, as you call him, has agreed to the same conditions of passage as you, oh Forested One," stated the captain, face blank, unreadable.

Paechra made to respond but the captain barreled onward, his face becoming a carnivorous smirk.

"Besides, it is the youngest flesh that is the tastiest, that boy shall be fought over by my crew."

"Poor soul," Paechra murmured sorrowfully. "It is a damned eternity deserved by none."

"Fear not for the child, oh forested one," assured the ghoul, still smiling. "That tasty boy shall be torn into many pieces before he is devoured."

"And what? That is a better fate?" growled Paechra, a faint glow of blue glimmering at the tips of her fingers.

The ghoul's smile faded, fast.

"I assure you when one such as he dies it is not a path to that of an eternity of slavery..." the captain stammered. "It is the ones who are bitten and then brought back of whom the Picturesque continues to punish."

"So, she is a sneaky mistress?" asked Paechra, all the while wondering to herself 'How could I have been so foolish to not hear the word thief in the very name of the vessel?'

Guilt caused the tendrils of magic to fade just as quickly as they had appeared. Overtain hid his relief at such a sight.

"Aye, oh forested one," agreed the captain, his voice unusually quiet. "She be a rogue who fools with her great size and her greater promises... Many have had stolen their lives... Those who stay on to set the sails or swab her decks have had their very souls taken in the night."

As a pair of rats appeared from the neck of the captain's fine shirt Paechra pushed her plate away from her.

"I have a queen to attend, she and the ocean disagree," the

sylvan announced. "I have had my fill of your table and your company."

"What of the water you requested?" came then the voice of Aaron.

The teen presented the ceramic jug, pure white with a slight crack running from the lip to the base.

"You are safe," announced Paechra, surprised and delighted.

As Aaron leaned past the sylvan to pour accurately, Paechra was able to see the boy's shoulder bled from a bite.

"You promised!" the Druid growled, again the evidence of arcane fury enveloped Paechra's fingers then hands.

Those hands reached out to touch the gaping wound, but a guttural sound came from the captain's throat which caused the sylvan to pause.

"You should consider your strike for the villain, not the victim," urged the captain then.

"I mean only to undo the injury and hope to return at least some of the humanity," explained the Druid.

"Your touch will burn and torture, a poor fate made worse," the captain replied with an explanation of his own.

"Please, do it," muttered Aaron. "I already feel the change upon me, my life ebbing away."

"I cannot," mourned Paechra. "I have done you enough harm already."

The boy dropped the jug as he reached for the knife.

Paechra heard the porcelain shatter around her feet and then caught herself as the ship pitched again. With great effort she stopped a gasp from escaping as Aaron fell across her lap. Far lighter did her feel compared to how hefty Paechra assumed a human teen boy to be. Hands still glowing blue accidentally fell upon Aaron's face and shoulder and the creature he was already becoming squealed like that of a frightened rabbit.

"I am so sorry!" cried Paechra as Aaron struggled to roll away from her and under the table.

The rats scurried over to the sylvan's plate and nibbled briefly at the chicken uneaten. As Aaron vanished from sight Paechra watched one rodent vanish after the teen. There was a moment or two of near silence before the tiny beast then scampered away with an eye in its mouth.

"Do not look at me, mistress," begged Aaron as he crawled away from the table toward the captain and the dark shadows.

"I'll take that, thank ye lad," stated Captain Overtain, leaning down as the teen crawled by. "Not a great deal of good will it do ye, you're one of us now."

Paechra noticed that the captain pulled the knife away from Aaron with ease.

"Only good for the living these," the captain then said.

There was a sound like a butterfly flapping its wings as the blade went through the captain's shirt and into the ghoul's flesh. Overtain stabbed himself a number of times, his sharp teeth evident as he smiled, unhurt.

Paechra watched on in silent shock.

"No point stabbing a heart that don't beat," the captain explained. "A true pain when we lose a limb, but nothing we cannot somehow move on from."

The captain laughed, a dry chortle this time mixed with the weariness of eternal damnation.

"So, if we are finished with yer eating perhaps you'd be willing to do some translations for me?"

"But, what of Queen Catherine?" asked Paechra, the sylvan hopeful of getting away from the smell and sight of undeath.

"Your friend Thomas is taking great care of our royal passenger," assured the ghoul. "Certain am I that he would like it not if you returned too soon."

Paechra thought of poor Thomas and wondered just how often he too drew close to Aaron's fate. Day after day the butcher of Andrappal mixed with the fretful living and the cursed undead. Day after day he begged Paechra for release.

Returning her focus to that of Captain Overtain the sylvan gave in, her only foreseeable option.

"As you wish then," she stated with an audible sigh. "Where do you wish to begin?"

*

Paechra knocked lightly upon the cabin door.

"Thomas, please open…" the Druid requested. "It is me, Paechra, returned at last."

"What if I tell you, no?" whined Thomas. "Queen Catherine and I are quite comfortable together."

"You know what fate awaits you if you remain in and keep me out," stated Paechra.

Immediately she regretted her words.

"Should I be more fearful of you, witch?" spat back the butcher of Andrapaal, one of the chosen Eleven.

"Thomas, I am your friend," Paechra then said, attempting to reassure.

"For how much longer do you tie us to this pontoon of

death?" hissed Thomas, the cabin door opening a crack.

"The pace of the rowers, the strength of the wind, should we hold this speed and have no greater storms assault us I believe I shall be back on home soil by late tomorrow morning," announced Paechra after a moment of thought.

The cabin door closed again as Thomas saw Paechra was not alone.

"Thomas, you must come out," demanded Paechra, a slight waver in her voice.

This time when the butcher opened the cabin door he opened it wide.

"I am not afraid of you and your blue glow witch," Thomas announced. "Nor am I afraid of the monster…"

Paechra sighed as the moonlight revealed that her companion that night was young Aaron. It were a cruel joke played by the captain. The newest edition of the Picturesque Picaresque's crew had been forced to remain at hand as Paechra was forced to attempt to translate so many passages, maps, and intercepted correspondences. Aaron wanted to merely vanish, to crawl into that rat hole or a shadowy hole of his own and to think why he had chosen such a dangerous voyage. Instead, the enchantment of the ship and the power of the one named captain made the teen nothing but a puppet, a slave, something to command for the rest of eternity. Considering herself greatly responsible for such a fate Paechra in turn had wished nothing more than to either take back her actions or remove herself from the poor boy's sight. The captain had enjoyed his time watching the two squirm in silent agony. It was well past midnight when the cruel jest had finally run its course, and the captain had released the pair with a dry smirk and the sinister words "We should do this all again sometime."

Paechra had decided there and then that the return trip to

Andrapaal with or without her kindred would certainly not be by ship. There were other ways to tackle such a distance.

"Thomas, why must you call me witch?" asked the Druid. "Please try to understand that I am who I am, and I want to be your friend."

"I have seen what fate awaits those who befriend you," replied Thomas, carefully.

The butcher watched the young one who stood silently beside Paechra.

"What do you know of this boy's fate?" asked Paechra, somewhat surprised. "Can you smell death upon him, or do you sense somehow my guilt?"

"I speak not of this boy who follows you, witch," replied the butcher, eyes wide. "Though now I wonder what you have brought to the door of my queen."

"Then of whom do you refer?" asked Paechra.

"Johannas Stormsong, the one whom you have proclaimed to be your friend," spat Thomas, eyes drifted away from the silent figure, finger raised in accusation.

"Raven is my friend!" cried Paechra. "It was not me who set him on his current unfortunate path, I did not drive him into the darkness."

"And yet you lead us now along a path that is filled with danger and for what end?" demanded Thomas.

"The sylvan peoples have helped to free humanity once before," argued Paechra, though she and Thomas both were uncertain if it were the butcher or herself she was trying to convince.

"True, witch," agreed Thomas. "Your kind did have a moment in your history and ours when your hearts shone brightly."

"And that is what I hope will occur again," stated Paechra.

"But after how many years of suffering? How many decades of slavery? The tomes do not lie," argued Thomas, with the blindness of the faithful he clung to the belief all humans of the Sagedom of Thuraen had been taught.

"Surely my people can be convinced to help again?" asked the Druid, this time it was obvious she questioned herself. "It is for that reason I bring you to me homeland."

"You have set us upon a path that gambles greatly upon the truth of that conviction," accused Thomas, adding, "I only hope that your dice roll high."

The argument was broken as Aaron stepped forward and grasped Thomas by the wrist. The pointing finger of the butcher was retracted.

"Hey!" cried Thomas and Paechra together.

It was only then that the moonlight revealed Aaron's injured shoulder.

"I know you, boy," stated Thomas in disbelief. "I saw you this morning, a frightened little child who asked me, no actually you begged me for some rope, for what reason I can only guess."

"Be silent, please Thomas," begged Paechra, the sylvan's voice suddenly a mere whisper.

"What have you done to this poor young soul, Paechra?" growled the butcher.

Paechra lowered her head, not willing to meet Thomas' cold gaze.

"While the sun was up this boy lived," growled the butcher. "Now he walks with death in his eyes, his heart, his clouded mind."

Aaron pulled causing Thomas to stumble forward.

Not wishing to talk anymore, Paechra stepped around the pair.

To the living she bade goodnight. Of the undeathly she begged forgiveness.

As Thomas was led away Paechra listened to his cries. Shouting accusations changed to a begging for release.

"You did this, witch!" the butcher called out as loudly as he dared.

"Please save us, Paechra!" Thomas then added a second or two later.

'I did do this,' thought Paechra to herself. 'It is my foolery that has set us on this merry path.'

To try and block out Thomas' fading pleas and accusations Paechra stepped into the darkness of the cabin that she shared with Queen Catherine and closed the door behind her.

The night had been a long one. To Paechra's dismay it was only to get longer.

"He is right," announced the voice of Queen Catherine in the darkness.

Paechra thought at first it was her own conscience speaking, guilt mixed with uncertainty and exhaustion.

"From what that butcher boy has told me you have given us all little choice," the queen continued.

"Catherine, are you well?" asked the Druid, as she placed her hand upon the forehead of the royal Paechra found it cool to touch.

"Between you both I feel I have been nursed back to something that resembles health," replied the queen of Thuraen. "I guess that is something I must be grateful for."

Paechra went to feed the queen another morsel of bread and water but found both bowls to be empty.

"I am doing this for you," announced the sylvan. "For you, Queen Catherine and your unborn child."

"I know," replied the queen, her voice tight, not willing to allow her built up emotions to spill forth.

"I am doing it for my friend Raven too, a Truth Keeper and someone whom I consider to be my friend," continued Paechra. "I lead you all on this perilous quest in hope that we can return to find there is still some of Thuraen left to save."

"And what if there is not?" asked the strengthening voice of the royal who lay thinking in the darkness. "What if all of the walls have crumbled and all of my people slain?"

"Then we must remember that you and your child are Thuraen," replied Paechra Lightheart confidently. "Wherever you are the kingdom is also."

"Thank you, friend Paechra," sighed Queen Catherine.

There was a silence then shared by the two women. A promise of sorts. In the moments that passed Paechra finally heard the soft sounds of Catherine's slumber. It was then that the sylvan felt the full force of the day that had been. Latching the door to the cabin shut Paechra was thankful to find her hammock and some rest.

#

"It is time for you to fly, blackbird," ordered the voice of

Palidine.

#

Raven awoke from restless slumber; his dreams vague memories of an ocean he'd only seen long ago in nightmares and the rocking of a great ship he had never sailed upon.

"What could this possibly mean?" he asked his dwarf friend.

"Ye are in the sights of the gods, lad," Mick muttered. "It be not a good place, so say us dwarf-kind…"

"I have spent so many years of my life just trying to blend in," Raven replied. "If the gods have a purpose for me, than let them know I am ready."

At that moment, two of Mick's kin escorted a figure into camp. He was tall, but not as tall as the human. He was strong, but his strength stank of anger.

"Seek… Paechra… Druid… Wife…" the figure growled. "She… Mine…"

"Paechra Lightheart is my friend," Raven replied. "She is not here, but I am, and I will defend her right to be nobody's property."

"Hu-man… Prepare… You smell… Her smell… I crush… All… Who take… What given… To me…" announced the sylvan.

"You must be Derek, Paechra has spoken of you, and not fondly," stated Raven.

The sylvan gave Raven's comment a look of genuine surprise, which quickly turned to contempt.

"Paechra... Disrespect... Leaving... Talking... She shall learn..." vowed Derek, Low Prince of Greenwood Vale.

"Not if it is I who teach you the lesson of respect first," suggested Raven as his hands became fists.

"Make them hands o' ye wings, not weapons," called out the voice of Mick.

"Listen you... Man... Creatures of stone... Know best... Slink into shadow... Else those hands... I cut free..."

Derek's words were an obvious threat, made even more obvious when he clicked his tongue. In a flash of light, a thin, long blade, deadly sharp, was in his right hand.

"There shall be no blood spilled here upon the soil of the McHallowhill clan," the dwarf announced.

"Think you... Matching... Sylvan cunning... With mountain might?" stated Derek, fury building.

"I know this land, I know the prayers that have been said upon it, sewn into it," stated the dwarf. "And, what's more, I know me clan, so know it not be a threat but a promise to ye both..."

"Spill blood and the land swallows us whole?" asked Raven. "You did not believe that an important enough fact to tell me when I first arrived?"

"The land knows its visitors, whom it can trust, lad, n who tis that needs a stern voice..." Mick hurriedly explained. "What's more, ye have no blade to draw blood with..."

"True," Raven agreed. "But my people have been settling differences with tooth, nail, stone, long before we found axe, sword, spear, and staff in our hands."

"Aye, true," Mick agreed. "But the land doth know the truth in all our hearts, and she did tell me yer heart be pure."

"But, not his heart," suggested Raven, clearly indicating the newly arrived sylvan prince.

"Aye, lad, the sylvan be of the earth just like we, but his heart be elsewhere," the dwarf agreed.

"No judge… But Goddess… No more… Secret thoughts… Where… Is… My… Wife..?" growled Derek, attempting to take a step toward Mick and Raven.

The two stout guards brought the flat of their battle-axe blades hard up against the sylvan, at his back and upon his chest.

"Nay, release him," ordered Mick. "The low prince has been warned, what he chooses to do next is not on us…"

"I will say what I know if it will keep the peace of this place," stated Raven.

"I am… Listen…" stated Derek as the axes fell away and he took another purposeful stride.

"Then know this, Low Prince," said Raven. "I am Paechra's friend… Perhaps that is why we seem connected…"

"Friend… Betrothed… There is difference…" the sylvan pointed out.

Connection… Nothing… Between these there is also a difference," Raven countered. "You hunt for Paechra, and you have arrived here."

"…" Derek opened his mouth to deliver a rebuttal, but nothing came out, the spiteful words refused to form.

"Let us both find Paechra, as I fear, my visions of her are telling me she will need all the help we can give," suggested Raven, reluctant, but wise enough to realize the truth of what he was saying.

"Embrace, that such a bond not be broken," commanded

Mick.

Derek nodded.

"Together…" he stated.

The sylvan and the human clasped forearms and promised to work together to find Paechra Lightheart.

"That what is done here, must ne'er be undone," announced the McHallowhill clansman, and then rest of the clan shouted a resounding "Huzzah!!"

"Huzzah indeed," agreed Raven as he metaphorically felt his wings unfold.

Chapter Four

Home

The spirits play with the lioness. The die rolls through the hall of Haven.

From the Twelfth Stanza of the Prophecy, translated by the sages of the Kingdom of Thuraen 514th year

PAECHRA STOOD ABOARD the deck of the Picturesque Picaresque and stared through the fog that surrounded the ship. She watched for any sign of sunlight and anything that would show her how close they were to land. There was something tingling in her senses, a feeling that home was so near. The creatures who crewed such a vessel shuffled around her, not daring to draw too close to the sylvan. Left in peace Paechra watched and waited.

"Witch, you have been asked for by Queen Catherine," announced Thomas the Butcher, with blundering thoughtlessness he broke the Druid's moment of tranquility.

With a sigh and a nod Paechra then left the deck and returned to the cabin she shared with Thuraen's queen.

"How long?!" Queen Catherine demanded to know the very moment she heard Paechra begin to open the cabin door.

The sylvan almost regretted leaving the fallen city of Andrapaal with the monarch, but in truth she was gladdened to see Catherine recovered from her feverish state.

"Good morning to you as well, your majesty," replied Paechra. "It is wonderful to see you up and about."

"I'll not step foot outside this cabin until we reach land," continued Queen Catherine, ignoring the sylvan. "A sea voyage, in my condition."

Paechra noticed that a bump was becoming evident where the queen's child was growing. In a few months there would be no denying that a new member of the royal family would arrive soon.

"I promise you, Queen Catherine, the sea voyage was necessary," Paechra began in explanation. "As dangerous as it is it would be considered far safer when compared with dragon flight."

"Dragon flight?" exclaimed Queen Catherine. "The royals of Thuraen do not fly."

"Regrettably…" muttered Paechra.

Catherine offered a cold stare and then asked again her question.

"How long?!"

"If all goes as I hope, your majesty, it shall be within a day."

"Humph," replied Queen Catherine, a noise Paechra knew to be a dismissal.

Gladly the sylvan left, the healthier queen of the humankind was far more difficult now that she was stronger in mind and body.

Paechra felt better upon the deck of the ship, the sky above and the smell of the sea evident all around her. The wind concerned the sylvan however, blowing the ship and all upon it away from their destination. As the ship's captain had stated though it was in the interest of the ghouls to slow the journey. The more chance there was of a mistake the greater the chance of a meal, a soul to snag and another victim for the Picturesque Picaresque to claim for eternity.

"Row! Row faster and harder!" Paechra quietly prayed, wishing that Anton, Michael, and the other poor slaves in the belly of the ship would heed her words and add an extra effort.

As the wind changed for a moment Paechra glimpsed forest in the distance and her heart leapt with joy. An idea dawned and Paechra began to make her way around the deck.

In a little nook where Paechra hoped nobody watched on the Druid began to sing.

"Tha-i o'lette, tha-i o'hnee... Anth-thlik rethull rethullii..."

As she sang, the Druid made a sign of the fishes with her hands. The faint blue glow of magic appeared at her fingertips and then flowed outwards to drift towards the surface of the choppy sea. As the soft singing continued the eerie blue glow broke the surface and made its way under the ship. School upon school of fishes large and small were drawn to the magic. School upon school of the scaled creatures bumped upon the vessel's hull, bit by bit, inch by inch, driving it forward against the push of the wind.

Within half an hour the ship was clear of the fog, happy with what she had achieved the Druid stepped out into the sunshine. Regardless of the horror of the monstrosities on board Paechra still managed a sigh of contentment. That was until the ghoul named Aaron came in search of her.

"Paechra!" he called mournfully. "Paechra you know not what you have done…"

Paechra greeted the ghoul with a mix of disgust and guilt, it was she felt somehow because of own words or actions that the teen had suffered the fate of becoming an accursed ghoul.

"Aaron please explain," requested Paechra, though she thought it possible she knew already what the creature was to tell her.

"You have driven us forward far faster than the captain and the ship desired," accused Aaron.

"What proof have you that such a thing occurred?" asked Paechra.

"Do you deny such an accusation?" then asked Aaron.

"If I was not seen then I see no reason to admit such guilt," replied the Druid.

"You have spent far too long with humankind," suggested Aaron.

Paechra made to retort that the boy was of that same kind, but it had only been the night before that Aaron did serve the ship as a young human teen. Once bitten by the ship's crew and not devoured the poor boy was human no more. Paechra noticed already the usually bright and frightened eyes of Aaron had become clouded and emotionless.

Two larger ghouls came up behind Paechra and grasped her about the shoulders. The Druid thought to summon the magic to strike and free herself, but she could also see that Aaron would have stepped in should she have tried to escape. Succumbing to her fate the Druid sighed and allowed herself to be half marched, half carried toward the captain's cabin.

"You have broken the rules, Druid," growled Captain Overtian. "To hasten the ship is against nature and I was of the understanding that you foresters loved nature."

"To keep the ship cloaked in an unnatural fog, slowing the journey, controlling the wind… Is that not also breaking rules?" suggested Paechra, willing herself to show no fear.

Captain Overtian smiled, sharp fangs revealed.

"It be not cheating if ya be the one making up the game," the captain suggested. "Me and this here ship has an understanding."

"So, what is the penalty you would have me serve?" then asked Paechra, wishing nothing more than to end the time she was spending with this ghoul.

"Since ye wish to be rid o' me and me crew it just so happens that the Picturesque Picaresque wishes to be rid o' ye as well," the captain announced with a grin.

"What does that mean?" queried Paechra.

"Our contract is cancelled, girlie," announced Overtian. "Now before ye start accusing me o' eating yer friends I must tell ya that we still hold true to the bargain struck."

A look of relief crossed the sylvan's features.

"My companions remain unharmed?"

"Even the child that grows within that queen."

"You knew of the child?"

Captain Overtian sniffed the air and then gnashed his teeth.

"Girlie, we monsters smell souls…"

The ship slowed and slipped back into the fog. The wind blew back against the sales, agony for the rowers as they tried in vain to propel the ship onwards. For Michael and Anton such torture was finally over. They rubbed at their aching shoulders as they stood with Paechra, Queen Catherine and Thomas the Butcher awaiting their disembarking.

Captain Overtian was there was well, along with Aaron and a few of the other ghouls who had taken an interest in Thomas.

"Be ye certain that ya wish to follow the forested one?" asked the captain.

"Most certainly," replied Michael, without hesitation.

The others were a mixture of muttered responses.

"Well then, shall we make ye jump?"

"Certainly not," replied Anton, immediately he stepped up to Queen Catherine and placed a protective arm around her shoulder. "You would not dare place the life of a royal of Thuraen in such jeopardy."

"I would and I can," replied Captain Overtian with a sharp toothed smile. "Lucky for you lot though we have little need for them lifeboats."

"You hear that Michael," laughed Anton humorlessly. "We get to row again."

"I would much prefer rowing our own boat that this accursed ship," said Michael.

Time and time again did Thomas offer to take over the oars from either Anton or Michael, but the older men refused him each time.

"Be quite, Butcher," grumbled Anton. "You are disrupting my rhythm."

"Please don't apologize again boy," begged Michael. "It is that which puts me off."

Paechra ignored the men, instead willing away the last of the fog that somehow seemed to blind her.

"And what is our plan once we reach the shore at last," stated Queen Catherine, obvious to everyone it was not a question.

"This is not my plan," began Paechra defensively.

"Of course," laughed the queen dryly. "If I recall correctly you were taking us to your people to beg for help."

"I knew that you were not human, Paechra," added Thomas. "But I did not think you were a sea creature."

There was a moment or two as the oars dipped in and out of the choppy ocean. Then Anton began to laugh, followed by Thomas and then even the queen began a gentle chuckle. A tear threatened to drop down Paechra's cheek. Not for the laughter, but for the lack of support from Michael Stormsong.

The laughter ceased immediately as the fog fell away and all aboard the rowboat discovered just how close to shore they were.

"Quickly men, row," ordered Queen Catherine.

Michael and Anton waved away Thomas' offer and began to stroke double time.

The boat was pushed up onto a pebbled beach, this time

Thomas was allowed to assist. Catherine took Paechra's offered hand as the sylvan jumped ashore.

Before them all was forest, but nothing like the humans had ever experienced. It was vibrantly alive, so lush, and green; utterly enriched with a ferocious spirit. Thomas and Anton looked at each other and then the queen. Michael only had eyes for Paechra, and her eyes were sparkling.

"It feels so good to come home," announced the Druid. "A true pity that home is still so far away though."

Without hesitation the Druid made her way confidently from the beach through the undergrowth and within moments she was gone.

"Paechra, wait!" called Michael.

At a brisk pace he too bravely ventured across the pebbled beach. There was a moment of uncertainty and then he thought he caught sight of Paechra, and he crashed through the undergrowth.

"Michael! Michael Stormsong!" cried Queen Catherine. "I am your queen, and I order you to wait!"

"I will fetch him back, your majesty," announced Thomas and with the energy of youth he raced at the blanket of greenery.

"Thomas you fool!" cried Anton after the boy. "Stay with us! Always remember there is safety in numbers!"

It was too late though. The butcher, one of the Eleven of Andrapaal was beyond the undergrowth and lost to all sight.

"Thomas, over here!" called Michael as he spotted the younger man.

Thomas raced towards the voice and then faster still when

he too saw Michael. It was incredible how easy to was to hide, it was almost like the forest was helping to keep figures hidden.

"Your queen as ordered that you return to the beach," demanded Thomas, the butcher sounding like a somewhat spoilt child.

"Even if I wanted to return to the beach which way would I go?" asked Michael.

Confused, Thomas looked about him. Everything had a similarity to it. Each tree was almost like each and every other tree. In fact, Michael and Thomas could not tell what type of tree they were, so different they were to the flora of Thuraen.

"Ironbark they are so named," explained Paechra as she appeared to step out from the very trunk of the tree Thomas was looking at.

"Ironbark?" asked Michael.

"With bejeweled axe-heads do we chop them down and use their bark for weapons and armor," Paechra continued.

"Using sticks against swords," laughed Thomas. "What witchery is that?"

"Our weapons are as strong and sharp as any fine crafted by your people," suggested the Druid.

Michael knew it not to be a boast but a plain truth. Thomas though was not as wise.

"I call witchcraft," the butcher cried. "Your people use spell craft upon the wood.

With all of his strength Thomas then attempted to break off a low hanging branch. For all his efforts all the young man was able to break was a sweat.

"If you are finished with your foolery, Thomas," began Michael as he stifled a smile. "Can you please tell us where the others are?"

"I was so enchanted by this strange place that I almost forgot them," cried Thomas in surprise.

"They are this way," announced Paechra confidently.

"Come on, boy," said Michael as he took Thomas by the arm and dragged him after Paechra.

"We have been calling for hours!" grumbled Anton.

The look that Paechra, Thomas and Michael saw on the face of Queen Catherine seemed to suggest that it was not only Anton who called out.

"My queen," stated Michael and Thomas together.

"In all truthfulness your cries did not penetrate the wall of wood," stated Paechra.

"Ironwoods it is," said Thomas.

"Actually, it is Ironbark," added Michael, correcting the younger.

"Come, we must enter the forest together, otherwise it is highly likely you will become lost," stated Paechra.

Again, the sylvan walked away from the group and again Anton and the queen made argument.

"Why should we follow you?" asked Anton.

In a huff the Druid turned to face the head of the Truth Keepers of Thuraen.

"In the city of Andrapaal you knew where you were, what you could and could not do and how you needed to live your life," stated Paechra.

"And you stole that certainty away from me," growled Anton.

"Your own stole that away when they smuggled the black tome into your city," spat back Paechra. "I just happened to be there to smuggle you out when everything went wrong."

Anton swallowed his next argument as he recalled their escape from the fallen capital.

"Well, I know where I am now, follow me and bet on the help of my people and our weapons made from trees or hope back in that boat and see if you can find your own way home and your own solution to a very big problem," the sylvan added.

"Lead the way and I will follow, Paechra," announced Michael as he took a stride toward the forest.

"I will follow you while there is no other option," added Thomas though he remained beside the queen and looked to her for confirmation.

Paechra smiled inwardly, glad that once again she had the confidence and support of Raven's father. The fickle nature of Thomas' support she was happy to take as it came. To lose Michael's faith though made Paechra think she was losing Raven's as well.

"Of course, Thomas, I would expect nothing less," stated Paechra and Catherine together.

As the Druid turned away from the group once more and towards her home she marched forward with a prayer in her heart.

'I do so hope this works,' she stated.

Half the battle was won though as this time all followed her and none remained behind.

In the thickest part of the forest darkness came quick. Paechra

85

had hoped that as a group they could have moved faster. Anton was very protective of the queen however and so their race against the remaining daylight was a futile one. As the group began to come across signs of sylvan life, signs that only Paechra could see, there came a renewed effort to move faster. All of this came to a very sudden halt, however. As Anton deviated from a path that Paechra asked them all to follow there came a snap and then a flourish of movement along the forest floor. Ropes, thick and strong, erupted from within the undergrowth and suddenly a net flew up into the trees. Caught within the highest treetops the party swayed in the wind.

"Now what do we do?" whined Thomas.

"This is all entirely your fault," began Anton, trying to catch Paechra's eye.

The sylvan however, was far more interested in the figures she noticed coming silently through the branches of the Ironbark trees.

"Who be it that approaches us?" called Paechra, sylvan words that sounded to the humans like a strange song.

Casting a quick spell the Druid enabled her words and the words of her people to fall upon the humans hearing and to be translated.

"She returns!" cried one voice and then the chant was taken up by that of the three others who stepped out from the cover of the forest's foliage.

"It is indeed you, Paechra of the Lightheart clan," stated one of the sylvan, all four males. Each was dressed in an odd garb of tree bark from head to toe. Each wielded a six foot spear, each weapon expertly carved from a sole branch.

"It is indeed Paechra Lightheart whom I be," replied the Druid. "I return home, and I have brought with me guests."

"Cut her down, cut down the princess," demanded one of the sylvan.

"Princess?" asked Anton.

Queen Catherine also heard the term though she chose to say nothing.

As the net was sliced free of the ropes and gently lowered the humans had a chance to look closely upon their captors. Short and lean, well-tanned, these figures were built for the wild.

"Your majesty," echoed all four of the sylvan figures. In unison they all knelt before Paechra, a surprise to the Druid as much as it was to her companions.

"Please explain this to us, Princess Paechra," demanded Queen Catherine.

"Honestly, I am as much at a loss as you all are," replied Paechra. "I too do not understand."

Paechra, Druidess, returned home at last looked into the eyes of her fellow sylvan. The soldiers, protectors of the forest of Greenwood Vale stared back.

"You call me princess," stated Paechra, not for the first time. "Why?"

Finally, one of the sylvan plucked up the courage to speak to the Druid.

"Sister Paechra do you not recall the announcement made by High Prince Derek and Mother Druid Sienna?" the soldier asked.

The humans, Thomas the Butcher, Anton the Head of the Truth Keepers, Michael the father of Johannas Stormsong and Queen Catherine all listened in with various levels of interest.

Thomas and Anton, who had the least amount of interest, spent most of their time examining the weapons and armor of the forest creatures. The two humans exchanged smirks, for the equipment seemed primitive, when compared with the steel blades and the ring mail undershirts that they wore at their hip and across their chest under their cotton shirts.

"Yes, the betrothal," replied Paechra to her kin. "So much has happened to me since leaving Greenwood Vale that I had clear forgotten the reason for my going in the first place."

"Princess Paechra," continued another of the sylvan males. "We had made the assumption that your fiancé had finally found you and brought you home."

"Low Prince Derek?" queried Paechra. "He is not here?"

"No princess, the Low Princess also left Greenwood Vale," explained one of the sylvan soldiers.

"Let me guess, Derek followed after me the same day that I left, correct," stated Paechra.

"Correct, Sister Paechra," replied the one that seemed most likely to be the decision maker for the six sylvan soldiers that were there. "We initially thought both you and your betrothed would have returned in a day or two."

"We were surprised that you were absent for many months and more surprised now that you have returned but we can see no sign of the low prince."

"So, Derek is still missing?" asked Paechra.

"You are to be a princess?" suddenly asked Queen Catherine.

Finally, the sylvan soldiers acknowledged that the humans were there. The soldiers seemed surprised that Paechra's companions could speak, even though each of the humans had exclaimed shock and surprise just as Paechra did when their guide had at first been addressed.

"Please show respect to our ones of royal blood," begged one of the soldiers, his hand hovered close to his weapon's hilt but at a sign from his superior he visibly relaxed.

Paechra and her human companions all noticed this. Anton quickly drew his own blade halfway from its hilt before Michael stepped across the forest floor to meet him face to face.

"Do not be a fool, Anton," whispered Michael into the Head Truth Keeper's ear.

"Who is the fool that you come across and lay a hand upon me?" asked Anton gruffly.

Slightly behind with what was going on, Thomas a moment later drew his own hand to his sword hilt but Paechra stopped him with a simple glance.

"Come, release this guests into the capable care of a princess of Greenwood Vale and I will lead them to my home," commanded the Druid.

"As you wish, Princess Paechra," announced the leader of the sylvan soldiers and with a single note from his lips he ordered the other five forest born to depart.

In the blink of an eye all six vanished silently into the undergrowth as if they had never been there.

"Amazing," murmured Thomas the Butcher.

"I have seen Truth Keepers on the boarder do it far better," said Anton with his arms crossed and an unimpressed look.

"Nonsense," scoffed Michael.

Before he had been given the role of carer of prisoners, Michael Stormsong had been a well-respected Truth Keeper.

"Are we going to stand around and argue until we are caught off-guard again?" asked Paechra. "Or will you all just happily follow me?"

"We have been following you blindly for some time now, witch," growled Anton. "So far we have followed that now you give us no choice."

Michael again made to step in and address Anton but before he could Paechra merely nodded.

"Good," she said. "It is decided then."

With that the Druid led confidently through the thick forest. Queen Catherine was the next to follow after, then Michael. Thomas stayed back, waiting to see what Anton would do.

"Come boy, we must not lag behind or the witch could just disappear, and we'd be lost forever," stated the Head of the Truth Keepers.

"Right you are," agreed Thomas, stating this to Anton's back.

Like a snake the five flowed through the trees and into the darkness.

It took five hours of trudging along to reach something that resembled a stone structure.

"Are we there yet?" moaned Thomas.

"We have been here for at least half an hour," Paechra laughed in reply. "Look up above you."

Amongst the treetops, as the humans paused to peer upwards they all discovered strange huts and other buildings made from lumber with vine bridges joining them together creating some sort of thoroughfare. Figures stared down at the humans curiously.

"Daughter, Paechra!" called one figure, similarly dressed as Paechra was.

"Mother!" Paechra called back joyously. "Shall you come down to meet my companions?"

"Of course I shall," stated Paechra's mother.

Queen Catherine looked on with interest while Thomas, Anton and Michael all seemed distraught as the older sylvan woman scampered down the trunk of the tree skipping from branch to branch without fear or failure. Soon she was at ground level, embracing her daughter with a kiss on both cheeks.

Paechra in turn greeted her mother with an identical ritual. After this she turned to address the four humans.

"Queen Catherine of Thuraen, Anton, Michael and Thomas, please meet my mother, Sarah Lightheart."

Thomas squawked like a parrot as his cheeks were suddenly brushed by Sarah's lips. Michael smiled and silently returned the greeting gesture. Anton tried to avoid the light kisses causing Paechra to rumble with disapproval. Sarah's kisses for Anton became air pecks. The Druid did not flinch when Anton offered no kisses in return. Queen Catherine looked on with distrust as Sarah Lightheart approached her. To the human queen's surprise, the older Druid bowed towards her with closed eyes.

"I can feel your blood is regal," announced Sarah which in turn caused Catherine to blush scarlet at her cheeks almost as if she had been kissed all along.

There was a moment when Sarah suddenly gasped.

"And you are with child," she whispered, so quietly that only the queen overheard.

Queen Catherine nodded mutely.

"Come!" called Sarah then, up into the canopy above. "We must treat these companions of my daughter Paechra just like

91

the guests they are."

There was a scurry of movement and a crowd of sylva made their way from the treetops, each one with as much agility as Sarah had shown. Each of the humans was offered a wooden goblet filled with a refreshing brew.

"What is this?" asked Michael in awe.

One of the sylva, the man who had given him the drink smiled broadly.

"It is a local drink, a mix of seasoned fruits and the crystal waters of our steam."

"It is utterly delicious," replied Michael.

"It is satisfactory," added Anton.

"It is way better than that!" cried Thomas.

Immediately the Butcher caught Anton's glare, and the far younger man suddenly withdrew.

Queen Catherine graciously sipped her goblet and sighed as it began to relieve her aches and pains.

"Magical," murmured the queen dreamily.

Suddenly Queen Catherine gasped as she felt her baby kick.

"You must rest, oh royal one," announced Sarah.

"Come, Mother, lead on to the Druid's Grove," suggested Paechra.

Sarah nodded.

"Come sisters, we must away," then said Sarah, taking Queen Catherine by the hand.

"I will not allow you to take my queen," growled Anton.

"Yeah, Queen Catherine stays with us," added Thomas the Butcher, suddenly springing out of his embarrassment.

"You are being a fool once more Anton," announced Michael although this time he did not approach the Head Truth Keeper. "And you Thomas, you are acting like the child that you are."

"Michael, you this time are the fool," countered Anton. "You are swanning around like these creatures are your friends."

"We don't know them," added Thomas. "We have only just met them."

"Be quiet, all of you!" commanded the queen. "You are not my keeper, none of you are."

There was a moment of silence in the forest and then Queen Catherine released a sigh.

"Now I am going with these women to a place of peace where I plan to find some much needed rest and some time away from all of you," the queen explained in such a way that she was certain there would be no arguments.

Thomas made to speak but a single stern look from Anton and Michael both caused him to only make a little squeak.

"As you so wish, Queen Catherine," replied Anton.

Michael bowed.

Arms linked with Paechra and Sarah the queen then turned and left with a trail of seven more Druids falling in behind them.

"What do we do now?" Thomas whispered as the Druids left.

Catherine did not remain behind to see if there was a response.

The Druid's Grove was a pristine place of peace. A crystal clear waterfall gushed musically down a limestone cliff face. As

Catherine arrived with Sarah and Paechra beside her she laughed in delight at the blanket of flowers that greeted her, a rainbow of colors with a perfume easily able to still the troubling thoughts of her mind.

"This is paradise," the queen suggested.

From a little away from the roar of the falls Catherine could see ten or more of the sylvan women bathing in the gentle current. Their clothing all sat in neat bundles resting upon the stream's edge. The women were all chatting and laughing, enjoying their swim.

"Sisters! Sisters! Be there room for more swimmers?" asked Paechra as she let go of Catherine's arm and began to undress.

"Sister Paechra," chorused the bathers. "It is so wonderful to have you returned to us."

"I have missed you all," cried back Paechra. "But it is you Heidi that I have missed the most."

"And I in turn have missed you dearly, my friend," called back one of the women, one who Catherine assumed was Heidi.

As Catherine looked around the grove she felt a true comradery. It was something that she missed when she married her husband, Prince Fredrickson who in turn became King of Thuraen. She wondered how long she might be able to stay amongst those women and that feeling.

"Sadly, nowhere near long enough," Queen Catherine considered, choosing not to share such thoughts aloud.

"Come, your Royalness, please come and share with us this ritual," urged Sarah.

Catherine noticed that this Druid as well was already partly undressed.

There was only one who was not swimming. Catherine saw that one lone figure lay comfortably with her back to a broad, ancient oak.

"Who might that be, resting there?" Catherine asked as she too began to struggle with her clothes.

"That is our Mother Druid Sienna," called Paechra before she slipped from the edge of the stream into the water.

"She is often at prayer," added Sarah.

"But that is not always the case," announced the figure.

Milky white eyes slowly opened, and Catherine realized that the figure was actually quite old.

"Come, daughters one and all," called the Mother Druid. "Who will gain my blessing and help me to rise?"

"I shall," called back Catherine and swiftly she made her way to the great tree.

"I felt your presence," announced Sienna as Catherine gentle took her hands. "The presence of two in fact of royal blood."

Catherine nodded and then remembered the milky eyes.

"Yes, I am with child."

"Then we must bathe you and rid you of the stink of the ghoul," suggested Sienna. "Why my daughter thought to travel that way is anyone's guess."

"Mother Sienna!" cried Paechra from the water.

At this outburst, the other Druids laughed.

"Child of adventure you always were, Paechra," Mother Druid Sienna then said with a laugh of her own. "To expect anything less would be to expect the unexpected."

Queen Catherine hurriedly finished undressing before she

then reached out to help Sienna.

"I am fine as I am, human girl," said Sienna. "Too old am I to waste my time peeling back skin after skin only to put it back on again."

True to her word Sienna then took Catherine's hand in both of hers and with confidence she stepped forward, gently gliding into the steam.

As Sienna led Catherine further into the water the queen felt all of her worries just melt away.

"What is this place, this paradise?" said Catherine with a sigh.

"It is the heart of the forest and our sacred home," replied the Mother Druid.

"Now queen it is time for us to place you beneath the water," stated Heidi.

"Fear not Catherine, open your eyes and witness the wonder," then added Paechra.

The two younger Druids were at Catherine's right and left. Gently they each placed a hand upon a shoulder and slowly pushed the human downwards. Catherine kept her eyes open as suggested. As her head dropped beneath the water's surface a whole new world was opened to her sight. Aquatic creatures, more colorful than the wild growing flowers flittered and floated like a smorgasbord of delight. Pretty rock formations, statues and altars littered every visible space. More Druids swam in and out of tunnels, seemingly able to hold their breath forever.

"Arise, Queen Catherine and child unknown," cried the Mother Druid, her voice heard muffled through the water.

As bidden Queen Catherine rose again she felt reborn. Her baby kicked as if it were broken free and swimming itself. The glorious feeling of butterflies caused Catherine to giggle and gasp.

With arms raised high and milky eyes shut tight Mother Druid Sienna began to pray.

"Spirit of this sacred grove please bless our guest and her precious gift."

"Of this we pray," the other Druids all echoed, almost one voice lending its support.

"Please relieve of them this burden that is held in the mind and the heart."

Again, the chorus of voices replied.

"Grant them peace and happiness while they gift us with joy in return."

"And please make certain that my loyal company find the same peace and happiness also," added the queen.

There was a gasp from the gathered Druids as it seemed like Queen Catherine had interrupted the prayer.

"Yes, such peace and happiness your companions can find here," stated Sienna. "We must all help them to find it."

As the prayer came to an end Catherine felt a weight lifted from her.

"Thank you, Mother Druid," the queen said graciously.

Then Queen Catherine rose from the waters to her full height and bending forward she lightly brushed Sienna's cheeks with her lips.

"Thank you for your welcome, I feel I shall be happy here," Queen Catherine announced. "Thank you Paechra, thank you for showing me what I never knew I needed."

With a beaming smile upon her lips Paechra came up to

embrace Catherine and then Sienna.

"You have done well my daughter of the Druid's Grove," announced Sienna. "That my eyes were not so blinded that I could look upon you once again."

"Mother Sienna, I thank thee for your kindest of praises," replied Paechra. "Let your heart tell your eyes what you see, and I pray that my image will live up to your imagination."

"You need not live up to my imagination," answered Sienna as she embraced Paechra in return. "You must only live up to your own hopes and dreams."

"I promise I shall," said Paechra with a smile.

As Queen Catherine watched on and listened closely to the joy around her she realized all it was that Paechra Lightheart had given up to seek out the human realm. Such a sacrifice, resulting in such a benefit for Catherine and hopefully a peace for the others that she traveled with. There was much to be grateful for.

Chapter Five

Another World

A song will be sung that remembers all which came before

From the Twelfth Stanza of the Prophecy, translated by the sages of the Kingdom of Thuraen 514th year

QUEEN CATHERINE REMAINED with the Druid sisters for most of that first day spent in the Princedom of Greenwood Vale. Catherine was shown special places, sacred places, places of peace located within Greenwood Vale. As the sun began to set upon that first day the queen realized that there was a strange feeling of peace both in her heart and her mind, something she had not felt since the fall of Thuraen and the circumstances that came before such a fateful day.

Paechra in turn shared such a feeling of peace. The time

spent away from her people had given her a chance to ponder upon her surprise betrothal to one of the princes of the vale. Paechra's search for her father in the city of Andrapaal had been a distraction though and still the young Lightheart had yet to settle upon a decision. Her friendship with Raven, a friendship which had the potential to be more was additionally confusing. As the sun set, Paechra, like her sisters brought her fingers to her eyes and then pointed skywards.

"Thank you glorious Sun for lighting our way," chorused the Druids. "Welcome Luna and Stella that you may cast your illumination upon our darknesses."

"How curious," murmured the queen.

"Queen Catherine," began Mother Sienna and Sister Paechra together.

There was a second or two of embarrassment before Mother Sienna spoke again.

"Sister Paechra, please take a moment to explain our prayer while we travel to the fortress."

"But I was hoping..." began Paechra, causing Queen Catherine and Mother Sienna both to laugh.

"Daughter do you believe it possible for your arrival to go unnoticed by our High Prince?" Sienna asked with a mix of humor and kindness in her tone.

"I know that very little happened in the city of Andrapaal without my husband and I knowing quite quickly of it," added Queen Catherine.

Mentioning her husband, King Fredrickson caused Catherine to sigh.

"Catherine please feel free to dwell upon your memories but know that your husband will always be with you," kindly stated Mother Sienna.

"It is our belief that the spirits of our loved ones are all connected, as we are connected also," added another Druid.

"We are all a part of Mother Spirit's web," explained Paechra. "The forest is central and our spirits the threads."

"And what of the sun, the moon and the stars?" asked Queen Catherine. "Are these all a part of the same web? Do you believe them to be your ancient ancestors perhaps?"

"You mock us," suggested Paechra. "You mock what you do not understand."

"Now Sister Lightheart you must give our guest a time to understand before you judge how she comprehends our beliefs," suggested Sienna.

Queen Catherine did not detect a berating tone in the elder Druid's voice, only kindness. For some reason, the queen could see Paechra's cheeks flush in the twilight.

"Yes, Mother Druid, as you have suggested," murmured Paechra.

"So then please explain this to me," asked Catherine, she locking eyes with Paechra's.

"Queen Catherine we believe and understand as you do that the celestial bodies are existing beyond our world," began Paechra. "We have been studying the worlds beyond our world for thousands of years."

"It is difficult for me to comprehend a history that far outstrips my own kind," replied Queen Catherine in awe. "The centuries that humankind have been recording our history, both mundane and wondrous is merely a single drop in the well compared with far more ancient cultures than ours."

The two sylvan Druids that flanked her nodded in agreement with the human queen.

101

"You are starting to understand and yet there is still so much that you do not know," laughed Mother Sienna.

The trio walked on in the twilight in silence for the next few minutes, the other sister Druids keeping step while maintaining a respectful distance. Once the Druids finally returned to the homesteads Mother Sienna turned and dismissed the Druids behind her with a nod.

Paechra too made to move off but with a click of her tongue Sienna caused her to halt.

"Have you forgotten already, Sister Paechra," Sienna laughed. "You have a date with a queen and a prince."

"Derek?" asked Paechra, her breath suddenly short.

"No, my daughter," assured Paechra's mother. "Low Prince Derek has not been seen by his people since he left to follow after you."

"I have not seen him, Mother," replied Paechra, feeling accused. "I have not seen nor felt the presence of my betrothed."

Queen Catherine was intrigued by this statement but remained silent, listening intently.

"Where have you been?" then asked Anton, barging in on the conversation.

"I tried to stop him, beg you forgive us," stammered Michael, a few strides behind.

"Anton, Truth Keeper," quietly and calmly began Mother Druid Sienna.

"I need not hear an excuse from you, blind lady," growled Anton disrespectfully. "I do not wish to remain here amongst these tree-folk."

There came a gasp from Catherine, Michael and Paechra but

Sienna remained silent, and stone faced.

There was such a minimal movement from the ancient sylvan that Queen Catherine and Paechra almost missed it. Sienna's hands flared the color of spun gold and then the elder Druid lightly touched Anton's chest.

"Ga!" cried out the Head Truth Keeper and then he was frozen, unable to move or speak.

"Much better," murmured Sienna.

There was a moment of stunned silence.

"Where we have been and for what purpose is of no business of his to ask," the Mother Druid continued.

The statue of Anton remained still.

"Should your queen decide to inform you then that is her business," the elder Druid continued.

"Please watch over Anton," requested Paechra to Michael. "We have a prince that we cannot keep waiting."

The Forest Fortress was the only permanent structure built in Greenwood Vale. It was large enough to house the entire population of sylvan who resided under the guidance of High Prince Ulan, Low Prince Derek, and Mother Druid Sienna. Usually, the large stone structure was home only to the two princes and those sylvan who kept the structure running like clockwork. This was as things should be during the time of peace, when the doglike vorsurk were a distant memory and thoughts of war were just as hazy. In the past, when humankind were the slaves of the vorsurk and the sylvan were constantly at battle then the sturdy forest fortress had been the only safe haven Greenwood Vale had. Now it was a place for meeting, a place for discussion, a place that Paechra wished she could have avoided.

"Please, daughter Druid," requested Sienna to Paechra. "Please announce our arrival."

"So, you have requested, Mother Druid, that I shall obey," replied Paechra courteously.

Queen Catherine watched on as Paechra took up a small hammer that hung from a chain on one of the double doors. With a twirling of her wrist Paechra beat out a series of knocks upon the door. Within moments it swung open, and a sylvan soldier welcomed the four inside.

Paechra saw the impressed look that passed across Queen Catherine's features, and she smiled.

"Our engineers are just as clever with earth and rock as they are with timber," Paechra suggested.

"So, it seems," murmured Queen Catherine.

"Daughter Paechra, you ooze pride for your people's skills and history," injected Mother Sienna. "Be wary though that your words are spoken in kindness and that they are not aimed to belittle."

"It is as you suggest," murmured Paechra. "I will not allow my pride to become an unkindness."

Before any more could be said all four women were approached by a regal looking figure.

High Prince Ulan entered the fortress foyer from where Paechra knew the fortress kitchen was located. Paechra, her mother and Mother Druid Sienna all gave a small bow to this figure. Queen Catherine made her own shallow bow very soon after that of the three sylvan.

"You disappoint me, Mother Druid Sienna," began High Prince Ulan.

"Why do you suggest such a thing?" asked the elder Druid,

obviously taken aback.

"You bring into my home a princess without her prince," explained Ulan. "Also, we are graced with the presence of a queen but without her king."

"That is true, High Prince Ulan," agreed the Mother Druid. "It is impossible though to present to you one who cannot physically be here."

"As you so wisely do suggest," agreed the prince.

Ulan then smiled.

"Queen Catherine of Thuraen, please allow me to welcome you to the Princedom of Greenwood Vale and to my home here," stated the prince, this time he bowed to the human queen, it was a bow that was deep and graceful.

As High Prince Ulan looked up from his bow he locked eyes with Queen Catherine again.

"What of the rest of your entourage?" he asked.

"Of whom do you refer?" asked Queen Catherine, somewhat confused for a moment.

"Queen Catherine I ask of the whereabouts of the three human males that travelled with you into my realm," explained the sylvan prince.

"If they were to be considered anybody's entourage they would be yours, would they not?" Queen Catherine then suggested, turning her eyes away from High Prince Ulan and instead finding Paechra's.

"I did what I thought was right," explained Paechra.

"Your choices were the best that you could have made under the circumstances," suggested Sienna. "At least the choice that you made to leave that city."

"It is just a pity that you were not able to bring more along with you," then said Paechra's mother.

Both mother and daughter thought then of the sylvan, Paechra's father who was left behind in Andrapaal.

"I ask again," began High Prince Ulan. "Why have you not thought to bring along Thomas, Anton and Michael?"

"We thought it best to introduce all of the humans slowly to you, High Prince Ulan," suggested Paechra. "No offence was intended."

"Nonsense! Nonsense! I have decided that I am ready to meet everyone," beamed the sylvan high prince. "I have had the soldiers escort the humans to the dining area."

"Oh, you have made such a regal decision, have you?" smiled Mother Druid Sienna.

"Please," oozed the high prince, waving everyone towards the doorway next to the kitchen.

Paechra knew what to expect but Queen Catherine did not. The room that the small group entered into was a great hall large enough to seat over a thousand civilians or soldiers. Four long tables all carved out of the finest polished wood showed their ancient age as did the timber chairs alongside. Michael and Thomas each sat upon one of the chairs with Anton standing nearby. Paechra noticed that the Head Truth Keeper was at that time flanked by two sylvan soldiers.

"Please, Mother Druid, release our guest?" asked Ulan.

"As you so desire, High Prince Ulan," replied Sienna.

With Paechra's help Sienna made her way deeper into the hall until she stood before the frozen figure of Anton.

"I release you," the Mother Druid announced.

In that instant Anton seemed to come back to life as if instantly thawed from an iced prison.

"This realm is overrun with witchery!" the Head Truth Keeper roared. "Forbidden magicks are thrown about like words are merely toys!"

His voice carried so far that it bounced off the walls of the near empty hall.

"Indeed!" laughed High Prince Ulan. "Call it Druid's craft or witchery it is something that has helped to keep my people safe for thousands upon thousands of years."

Anton looked about him in surprise. Paechra knew that Anton would have no recollection of how he had left the forest and arrived at the fortress. For a moment she almost felt sorry for the man, almost.

"Come, Anton, sit as my guest," beckoned the sylvan prince. "I am High Prince Ulan; I rule Greenwood Vale with the help of my brother. "Regrettably my younger brother Derek is currently away."

"Finally, someone in charge," stated Anton, refusing to sit.

As the Head Truth Keeper began to march his way towards the high prince the two sylvan soldiers made to draw their weapons. With the simplest gesture of raising one finger High Prince Ulan gave both of the soldiers the order to pause.

"Friend Anton, what is your grievance?" asked the high prince.

"This woman!" gruffly accused the human, pointing obviously at Paechra. "Has threatened my life, my comrade's lives and the life of my queen!!"

"As I understand it," stated the sylvan prince. "My kin has actually saved all of those lives by escorting you all away from a place of extreme danger."

"Yes, well, I supposed that what you say is also true," pondered Anton for a moment. "It does not change the fact though that there were threats made and made with accompanying evidence that had us all believe such threats would not stay threats for long."

Paechra made to speak but her mother gave the young sylvan a look that kept her silent.

Michael instead came to Paechra's defense.

"Nonsense, Anton!" Raven's father called from the table where he sat next to Thomas. "I struggle to recall even one time where Paechra spoke out in anger though there were numerous times in our journey where I wanted to bop you one."

"See!" Anton appealed to High Prince Ulan for sympathy. "All I ever hear is more threats!"

Ulan laughed, giving the humans a bright, beaming smile.

"If anything, you short lived humans are indeed entertaining," the sylvan prince chuckled. "Now if we are all hungry as I am, I believe that we should sit and eat."

One of the sylvan soldiers disappeared from the great room and turned towards the kitchen. Everyone noticed that the other soldier remained.

"Mother Druid, Sienna," then stated High Prince Ulan, turning his beaming smile directly upon the eldest figure standing in the hall. "Shall I have our chairs brought to the table or are you happy to sit with everyone else?"

"My prince you do as you please," replied the ancient one. "I shall sit with my daughters."

"As you so desire," stated Ulan curtly.

"It makes it far easier to follow the conversation," stated Sienna, quietly in Paechra's ear.

Paechra stifled a laugh and took Sienna's hand.

"Come Mother Druid and Mother," Paechra said. "I shall

assist you to your seats.

Along the table on one side there was Michael, Thomas and lastly Anton. Opposite them was Paechra's mother Sarah, Mother Druid Sienna and then Paechra on the end. Paechra tried hard to ignore Anton's seething gaze and stony silences. An intricately carved, high backed chair of a dark red wood was brought to the end of the table and High Prince Ulan sat. The two sylvan soldiers stood beside their high prince but in a relaxed state. Another chair, far less decorated was brought in and placed beside the throne where Ulan indicated that Queen Catherine should sit. The soldier at Ulan's left stood behind the human queen, still leaning upon the great chair of dark red wood.

"High Prince Ulan," began Michael as he admired the chair. "Is there any significance to the carved hunting scenes we can see reflected in the woodwork?"

"Indeed, Michael," replied High Prince Ulan, pleased. "Each prince's chair is uniquely designed by our master carver and her team upon the prince becoming of age."

"I can see lots of hunting scenes on yours, your Princeness," stammered Thomas.

"It speaks!" cried the high prince, again beaming. "Yes, Thomas, I do hunt when I can find the time."

"In fact, I believe that it was you who trapped the beast that we will be sampling this very moment," mentioned Sarah.

"I was merely one of our many sylvan hunters who know this forest and her creatures so well," replied High Prince Ulan.

At that very moment six kitchen hands dressed in finery entered and approached the table. They bore, hoisted upon their shoulders a great wooden board upon which steamed what at first looked to be a pig.

"Oh, High Prince Ulan," moaned Mother Druid Sienna. "Was it indeed necessary to slaughter another defenseless woodland dweller?"

As the wooden board was gently and reverently placed upon the table the humans could see that what they initially thought was pork actually had lightly colored scales and a mouth full of sharp, needle-like teeth.

"An orthnoxut," announced Ulan with a flourish. "It was trapped fresh this morning just prior to sunrise."

"You dragged us through a forest containing monsters like this?" growled Anton, again trying to catch Paechra's eye.

"Sadly, there is less and less orthnoxut alive each season to continue the population," muttered Sienna.

"Come, eat, enjoy," encouraged Ulan, either not hearing or choosing to ignore Mother Druid Sienna's comment.

Cautiously Michael made to peel away some of the creature's flesh, but he was stopped by a gentle hand. One of the kitchen hands removed a dagger from behind them and elegantly sliced off a piece of the creature's flank. It floated lightly to rest upon a provided wooden plate.

"Thank you," murmured Michael in awe of the process.

"Try it," urged Ulan.

Michael did, finding that the creature's flesh tasted divine.

"It is the finest meat I have ever had," Michael stated.

High Prince Ulan nodded, happily. He watched on as Thomas and Anton also tried the orthnoxut. A plate of steamed greens was presented to the Druids. The kitchen staff waited beside Queen Catherine's chair for her to decide which she preferred.

"I shall try both, thank you," the queen decided.

High Prince Ulan watched on as the others ate, happy to see them enjoy the meal.

"Firstly, we feast!" ordered the sylvan prince. "After we talk…"

The High Prince Ulan watched patiently while the Druids and the humans finished their meal. The enormity of The Great Hall where they all sat eating muffled any noise leaving a calming silence. When Ulan was satisfied that the meal was over he clapped his hands and the sylvan from the kitchen appeared to take the dishes away.

"Are we all satisfied?" the high prince asked.

There came a chorus of noises from the humans, especially Anton, who all seemed surprised by how satisfied they were after the sylvan fare.

"Mother Sienna, are you well and satisfied?" Ulan then asked of the elder Druid.

"Our High Prince Ulan refers to Sienna Alknown as Mother due to her role," whispered Paechra to the humans, her tone hushed. "He does not call her his mother; she did not birth him."

Thomas blushed at the mention of birthing. Anton grumbled under his breath. Michael just nodded to show that he had heard and understood.

"Paechra!" cried Sarah Lightheart, Paechra's mother. "If you must speak of such things your tone must be minimal."

"As you so say, Mother," replied Paechra.

"Daughter, Sarah I understand that you speak as a mother," added Sienna. "Please see your daughter's words as guidance for our guests."

111

"Your words are wisdom as always, Mother Sienna," stated Sarah with a bow. "Sister Druid Paechra it was indeed of pure purpose which guided your speech, I retract my advisement and request that you carry on."

Paechra sat in silence. She nodded thanks to the Mother Druid and then thanks to her mother.

"That which I had to say I have said," Paechra replied. "With graciousness I now request that our high prince continue."

"As you so wish," laughed High Prince Ulan. "If it is to the satisfaction of you all I ask that you please follow me."

High Prince Ulan then rose from his chair and the sylvan guards that escorted him both stood beside their high prince, ready.

Paechra took the hand of Mother Sienna and Queen Catherine, the trio were the next to leave as Ulan and his guards made their way out of the great dining hall.

"See here!" announced High Prince Ulan as he paused in his walk along the fortress passageways.

As a group they had stopped at the entrance to a great stone room full of magnificent statues. Some of the works of art had been carved from still living trees while others were built from stone similar to that which made up the fortress walls, roof, and flooring. Many were statues of figurines; fighting sequences between sylvan and vorsurk, a scene of love between two forest dwellers, or a regal figure hunting a dazzling creature of the woodlands. Other works of art were placed in and around the statues, a painting of a younger Sienna which looked so lifelike, a bust adorned with a necklace of precious jewels, spears and blades carved from wood that honed mean looking edges and dangerously sharpened points.

"This is beautiful," murmured Catherine as she stopped briefly to stare.

"If you should like such things," grumbled Anton.

Paechra noticed the look that the Head Truth Keeper gave to the weaponry, he was interested and impressed. Thomas had eyes for the jewelry. Michael Stormsong admired it all.

"Come, we have much more to see," announced the high prince.

"He is showing off, isn't he," Sienna mumbled to Paechra and Catherine.

"Well, I for one am certainly impressed," announced Queen Catherine of Thuraen.

"Next he will be showing us the orchards," Paechra grumbled.

"And please take your time to admire," stated Ulan next.

Again, the group paused and as Paechra predicted the high prince had paused at the entrance to an internal garden.

"Please we must stop," begged Michael.

Before he had been given his role at the human kingdom capital as jailer, before Anton had been promoted to the role of Head Truth Keeper, Head Truth Keeper Michael Stormsong had kept the most beautiful garden in the whole of Andrapaal, perhaps the whole kingdom of Thuraen.

"As you wish," said High Prince Ulan with a smile.

"How?" Michael wondered as he reverently made his way under the ivy arch.

"Why?" grumbled Anton, the Head Truth Keeper deciding not to enter, instead remaining in the passage with his back to the wall.

"Is that a peach tree?" asked Thomas. "Those fruits are enormous."

The butcher followed after Michael and then pushed past the figure in front. Striding purposefully Thomas was before the tree he sought within mere moments. In less time than that he had plucked three ripe fruits the size of wine skins.

""Apples too?" Thomas cried in disbelief.

The butcher's hands were already covered in honey like nectar as he left the peaches, two whole and one partly eaten and ventured deeper into the orchard.

"How can you eat after the meal we have just had?" asked Sienna in disbelief.

"Oh, Mother Druid," laughed Paechra. "Once you have lived with these creatures, even for only a short time, you discover what it is that they are indeed capable of."

"Do you speak ill of us, do you degrade my kind," grumbled Anton, standing behind the two sylvan.

"Oh, Anton," sighed Paechra as she turned to face the human. "It seems that you must discover a fight in each and every moment."

"Indeed, human," agreed Sienna though she chose not to turn and face Anton. "Each and every moment you have spent here with us you have sought to find and expand the argument, the disappointment, where is your understanding of beauty?"

"Beauty is seen in a ready soldier," replied Anton without pause. "Beauty is found in the opened belly of an enemy, a fallen vorsurk who will never rise again…"

Paechra inwardly shivered at that statement.

"Come Mother Sienna, come Queen Catherine," Paechra announced. "We have some exploring to do."

114

Leaving Anton to brood the three then made their way arm in arm through the doorway and under the ivy arch. Paechra noticed Catherine's eyes light up as she took in each fruit tree, each blade of grass, every flower and other plant.

"This is a true marvel of nature," sighed the human queen. "It would be impossible for my people to reproduce nature so accurately in an indoor setting."

"Indeed Catherine," replied Paechra. "It is a balance of understanding what is possible and ignoring the improbable."

"Something that you humans seem to struggle to combine," suggested Mother Druid Sienna.

"You are right," sighed the queen again. "Instead of regretting that which shall not be I will instead enjoy what miraculously is."

"Perhaps there is hope for you then," said Sienna, a faint smile appearing upon her ancient features.

"Not for me," suggested Catherine. "Though I thank you for suggesting such."

"Not for you?" asked Paechra, surprised.

"No, my generation is stuck in its ways and thinking," explained Queen Catherine. "My hope is for the next generation."

The human queen brought her hands around her unborn child as she spoke those words.

Michael and Thomas meanwhile made their way throughout the marvel that was the indoor orchard. They sampled what foods they thought they recognized, often discovering that an item's flavor and even its nature was different than that of Thuraen.

115

"Hear this, Michael," called Thomas as he crunched upon a pea pod.

The crack was like a sword blade being sharpened by a whetstone.

"How is the flavor?" Michael asked.

The elder felt like a boy again and thinking of such it made his heart rise and fall equally.

"The taste is like that of a fresh stream trout, strange for something so green and crunchy," laughed Thomas. "I must say the rainbow of sweet and sweeter from that giant peach is still my favorite."

"Indeed," stated Michael.

The elder Stormsong's thoughts were far away wondering what fate had befallen his son Johannas.

"I wish you were here and seeing this, boy," Michael muttered under his breath.

"But I am!" announced Thomas with a playful laugh.

For the butcher, this world within a world was so utterly different to the strange ship where he had almost lost his soul. This place was freedom, this place was joy.

"I wish we could stay here forever," Thomas announced as he bit into a rosy, red apple.

"Be very careful what you wish for," warned Michael.

"Nonsense," said Thomas. "These people have welcomed us; they are our friends."

"Paechra, yes," agreed Michael. "I trust her, the other Druids too of what I have seen of them."

"There you go," laughed Thomas. "I was right."

"This high prince though," pondered Michael. "I am still not sure what to think of him."

"You worry too much," suggested Thomas with a grin.

"Because you worry too little," suggested Michael in return.

"I worry about getting my belly full and keeping my head attached to my shoulders and you know in the whole time we have left home it is here that I suddenly feel the safest."

"I know what you mean," said Michael. "Still there is something…"

Paechra smiled as she overheard Thomas speaking. Her smile wavered slightly as she heard Michael's replies. The young Druid considered how long she had been away from her home and her people, truly not long when the life span of the sylvan race was considered. She agreed though that there was indeed something about High Prince Ulan that did not sit right with her.

Sarah Lightheart interrupted her daughter's ponderings.

"Come, it is time for us to move on," urged the elder Lightheart. "High Prince Ulan still has much he wishes for you to see."

"Me?" asked Paechra, curious and a little confused.

"So it seems," answered Sienna.

Druid Sarah had already moved on, calling to the humans that it was time to leave.

"I still have so much more to explore!" Thomas complained, loudly.

"Come, Thomas," urged Michael. "Perhaps they will next show us the kitchens."

There was a complete change of mood as the group ducked

under the ivy arch and entered the passageway again.

'What has happened?' Paechra thought.

Immediately Paechra noticed that the two guards who flanked High Prince Ulan both had their hands hovering close to the hilt of their weapons. Anton was giving Ulan a seething glare and the high prince was deliberately ignoring the human.

"Come!" ordered High Prince Ulan as Thomas ducked under the arch.

"I hope to visit you again soon," Paechra heard Thomas whisper longingly.

"What is happening, daughter Paechra?" asked Mother Druid Sienna and Paechra realized that she still gripped the elder Druid's hand.

Letting go of both Sienna's hand and Catherine's hand, Paechra tried to interpret the situation.

"I believe our high prince has done or said something that has greatly annoyed Head Truth Keeper Anton," she began.

"From the little time that I have spent with the man, that would not be difficult," muttered Queen Catherine.

"I agree," added Sienna sagely. "It is impossible to tell what has happened while we have been in the orchard but both Anton and Ulan show signs of distrust and frustration in their auras."

"I see it too," said Sarah as she snuck up behind the trio.

Paechra shifted her sight and cast her inner eye over both men. She gasped in surprise as the dark purple shadows enveloped both the human and the sylvan. It looked to Paechra as if blood were about to be spilled.

"No," she whispered. "We cannot allow this."

"What worries you so, ladies?" asked Michael.

He was a few strides ahead of his queen, close enough to Anton and yet the elder Stormsong seemed oblivious.

"It is Anton," began Paechra at a murmur.

"When is it ever not Anton?" asked Michael with a laugh.

"You speak of me, witch!" growled the Head Truth Keeper, turning midstride.

Anton's fists were clenched tightly and his eyes narrowed.

"Now see here…" began Michael as he strode forward and made to place a hand upon Anton's shoulder.

Aggressively Anton knocked the hand away while it was inches from its target.

"Hey!" cried Michael in surprise, annoyed.

Paechra saw Michael's calm aura of clear-sky blue turn suddenly orange. Anton's aura had turned from dark purple to a smoking charcoal color. Ulan, well his aura seemed to laugh, a dangerous red flaring with the blue and yellow hews of a crackling fire.

"Further evidence that little has changed of your race over the years," announced Ulan. "We show you advanced beauty and you wish to fight about it."

"My prince," called Sienna down the passage. "You give our guests little opportunity."

As always Paechra saw the Mother Druid bathed in the white aura of wisdom.

"How so?" asked High Prince Ulan.

"You have truly only met one human, for but a brief moment," suggested Sienna. "You cannot make judgement so swiftly, not if you truly are a sylvan prince."

"Mother Druid Sienna, you know me and you know who I

am," replied Ulan. "You were there at the time of my birth, and you know of my parents and my parents' parents."

"Indeed," agreed Sienna.

"I am High Prince Ulan of the Greenwood Vale."

"Then my prince, please act as High Prince Ulan of the Greenwood Vale," order the Mother Druid.

Paechra did not need her inner eye to see the demeanor of the high prince immediately change. A deep, dark blue aura overtook the fiery one. Turning away from those behind him the high prince sighed.

"Come," he muttered, leading on.

The two sylvan guards gave Anton one last look before they returned their hands to their sides and marched after the high prince.

"This is not over," growled Anton under his breath as he followed.

The rest of the group quickened their pace, not wanting to be left behind.

"Hold my hand and I will guide you," advised Paechra, touching Sienna's hand with her own.

Ulan had veered off the path of the corridor and taken a doorway that led to a stairwell. The spiral stair made its way upwards.

"Can you please aid Queen Catherine?" Paechra then asked of Thomas or Michael who were at the rear of the group.

"Thomas?" Michael suggested.

"It would be my honor," stated the butcher.

"Thank you," Queen Catherine stated plainly. "That will not

be necessary though."

"It would bring me great pleasure to escort you up these stairs, Queen Catherine," announced Thomas as he took the queen's hand.

"How can I then refuse?" replied the queen with a gracious smile.

As the group stepped out at the top of the turret they all took in the view of Greenwood Vale.

"Magnificent," gasped Catherine.

"What an incredible view," murmured Michael.

"Home," whispered Paechra.

"You ask me to risk all of this," stated Ulan.

The high prince waved at the land then above to the sky and below to the fortress beneath them all.

"Who does?" asked Michael and Thomas together.

"We do," spat Anton. "Or at least she does," he added, indicating Paechra.

Paechra looked from Anton to Ulan and then to the other members of the group.

"Daughter," murmured Paechra's mother. "Do you wish to explain?"

"Please, Sarah, allow me," interjected Ulan. "I speak of the past as I speak of the present."

"Helpful," blurted Thomas, still holding hands with Queen Catherine.

"Hush, Thomas," the queen demanded.

Immediately the butcher let go and went silent.

"I have come to realize that you Paechra have not returned

to us as a sign that you have finally agreed to become my brother's wife," Ulan continued, ignoring the two humans.

Paechra made to reply but Sienna placed a hand upon the younger sylvan's back and caused her to pause.

"High Prince Ulan, it is indeed Paechra's decision where it is she lets her heart lead her... We have made a suggestion, merely that..." called Sienna loudly and clearly.

"As you so say, Mother Druid Sienna," sighed High Prince Ulan. "I do wish that this were all simple to piece together."

"Nothing is simple except the comprehension that nothing about life is ever simple," suggested Sarah.

"Witch's babble, nothing more," complained Anton.

"Regardless of the simplicity or complexity of life there is something that I comprehend clearly now," announced Ulan. "Paechra you return home with a request."

"I do, High Prince Ulan," stated Paechra.

Making her way to stand before the high prince Paechra stared straight in the royal's eyes. Purposefully she then lowered her head respectfully.

"I do not wish you to kneel," said the high prince. "No Druid however young should kneel before any being."

"Of that I am grateful, my prince," replied Paechra. "I do come before you asking that you pledge your support to the human cause."

There then came a gasp of surprise from Sarah and Sienna as well as the two sylvan guards.

"We can fight our own war," grumbled Anton.

The other humans all stood in silence.

"Oh High Prince Ulan of Greenwood Vale," then said

Michael as he stepped up to stand shoulder to shoulder with Paechra.

"You, human, should kneel," Ulan demanded.

Michael Stormsong immediately sank to his knees and bowed his head.

"The vorsurk, our shared enemy have returned to the kingdom of Thuraen," explained Paechra.

"It is with thanks to this Druid that I, my queen and others stand before you," continued Michael.

"I believe that our only hope of driving out these forces of evil once again from the human lands is to strike with the mighty force of the sylvan people," stated Paechra. "This time I wish to stand beside my kindred, I wish to play my part in this war."

High Prince Ulan surveyed all those before him. After a moment he spoke one word.

"No."

Chapter Six

Sylvan Politics

It shall be a song to herald that which still must come to be.

From the Twelfth Stanza of the Prophecy, translated by the sages of the Kingdom of Thuraen 514th year

THE HIGH PRINCE Ulan watched all those who were present on the fortress rooftop with him. His focus was specifically on Paechra Lightheart, for it was the young Druid that the high prince expected to speak first. It had been Paechra who had come home to Greenwood Vale bringing the humans with her. It was Paechra, the youngest Druid who was asking much of the sylvan people, her people; a race that had known peace and prosperity for so many years. Paechra was asking them to go to war.

Instead, it was Alknown Mother Druid Sienna who spoke.

"High Prince Ulan, I hear in your words a passion for your people," began the elderly sylvan. "I hear your desire to keep us all safe, to keep safe our way of life and our sheltered grove."

Ulan beamed at these words. This was exactly what he hoped to hear, affirmation and support from Alknown Mother Druid Sienna. Paechra could see in the royal face that there was a fierce confidence that the Mother Druid would side with his decision.

"High Prince Ulan, you are a fool," Sienna continued, her tone changing from that of a caring grandmother, becoming instead the voice of an accusing matriarch.

"But" began High Prince Ulan, only to be cut off by the elderly Druid.

"You cannot see the bigger picture, you do not have the experience," Sienna continued, obviously frustrated. "You have not lived through the times before and therefore do not understand the importance of the present arrangement."

"I know our history," announced Ulan, defensively.

"You have read the scrolls that record our history," argued Sienna. "Words can only say so much, they do not give you the memories of what has happened before."

"I feel quite ill," murmured Queen Catherine as she clutched her midsection. "Please, is there somewhere quieter where I may sit?"

Immediately Paechra and Sienna turned to the human queen, High Prince Ulan for the moment was forgotten.

"We have walked so far without a moment to rest," considered Paechra. "We have not stopped since the meal."

125

"We must take you to a place where you can be more relaxed," announced Sienna. "Sarah, will you please take the queen to somewhere quieter and more private?"

"Of course, Mother," agreed Sarah Lightheart with a bow.

"No, I must remain here as a representative of the city of Andrapaal and as Queen of Thuraen," injected Queen Catherine. "I fear that in this moment there balances the fate of humanity, and I will not turn my back upon a difficult conversation."

"Please, my queen," said Anton with a curt bow. "Allow me as Head Truth Keeper to represent the kingdom in this matter."

"Are you a jester, Anton?" laughed Catherine. "Should I imagine you wearing colored cloth with bells attached?"

"My queen, you should know that I do not speak humorously," replied Anton, a look of confusion obvious across his features. "And my clothing is that of a keeper of the truth, I have worn such from the day I first received my blade and swore the oath."

"I can sense your mood is a poor one, Anton," replied Queen Catherine. "It has been skeptical since our arrival."

"Better to be wary when in the land of witchery," suggested Anton.

"We are guests in paradise," suggested Catherine. "It is your own disillusionment that seems to blind you to this fact."

"Nay, my queen," growled Anton. "It is you who are illusioned, enchanted by these creatures and their magic to the point where you can no longer see the truth."

There was a moment of shocked silence before Michael spoke.

"You call Catherine your queen and yet show her no

respect," said Michael Stormsong. "To speak as such to me or Paechra or any of the others is rude but to do so to our queen…"

"I know that you are all blinded and cannot see," accused Anton, pointing to Queen Catherine, then Michael, then Thomas, and finally to Paechra. "And it is you witch, who is the blindest of them all."

With that Anton stormed from the roof and disappeared from sight.

One of the sylvan soldiers made to go after the head of the Truth Keepers but High Prince Ulan caused him to pause with a single princely gesture.

"Let him go, it gladdens me to no longer need to hear his words or see his features." High Prince Ulan announced. "In fact, all of you can go, now, be gone from my sight."

"We will take you to a place of rest," suggested Thomas and Michael as they each stepped up to stand beside Queen Catherine.

"Thank you," said the human queen as she allowed herself to be led away.

"I will show you where to go," offered Sarah Lightheart.

"I will come with you," added Sarah's daughter, Paechra.

"No, Paechra, you will remain here with me," commanded Sienna. "We have much yet to discuss with High Prince Ulan."

"I have demanded my own space," replied Ulan. "Can one not seek silence in one's own home?"

"Not when one is in a position of leadership," replied Sienna, wisely. "A truly great leader makes time for the difficult as much as the enjoyable and I believe you have it in you to be such a leader."

As the others retreated Alknown Mother Druid Sienna gave High Prince Ulan another matriarchal glare.

"Leave us," Sienna said to the guards.

Ulan nodded to the two and they made to move away.

"Remain at the bottom of the stairwell," Ulan commanded. "We are not to be interrupted."

"As you command," replied the sylvan before they marched away.

Paechra strained her ears to hear the tromp, tromp marching as the pair of sylvan soldiers left the roof top. The rhythmic sound of marching strides grew quieter and quieter until it could be heard no more.

"Now, what is the meaning of this?" Ulan demanded to know.

"My prince I wished not to embarrass you in front of our guests," began Sienna.

"Alas embarrassed I am," announced High Prince Ulan.

"Then grow up and listen," stated Alknown Mother Druid Sienna.

Milky white eyes turned to face Ulan and although both Ulan and Paechra knew the extent of Sienna's blindness there was no denying that in that very moment the elder sylvan was staring straight through the high prince's very soul.

"As you request," murmured Ulan, meekly, all bravado sucked from his persona under Sienna's extreme glare.

"Better," Sienna huffed. "Now you must understand that in our past the battles with our mortal enemy almost wiped out the sylvan population."

"I am not afraid," stated Ulan proudly.

"You should be," Sienna Alknown replied. "Your father and mother had peace and prosperity, but they were wise enough to fear the wolf that howls in the night."

"Peace and prosperity is not weakness," argued the high prince.

"And bravado is not wisdom," Sienna argued in reply.

"I wished only for the support of my people," stated Paechra meekly. "I thought that we could be there for humankind again, as we were all those centuries ago."

Ulan and Sienna both turned to face the younger Druid.

"You also do not know the true history of that time," replied Sienna.

The old Druid's voice was steady, no hint of age and yet she spoke with the conviction of ancient memory.

"My father has spoken to me of that time, I have read the pages of history, I know what you know," announced the high prince.

Alknown Mother Druid Sienna shook her head.

"No, my prince, you know nothing," the elder Druid stated. "Words are only words; they do not paint a true picture of the horror and fear of that time."

"Then tell us of that time and make us understand," demanded High Prince Ulan.

"I can do better than tell you," suggested Sienna, mysteriously. "I am the only one who can show you."

Paechra noticed a white light shadowing the older Druid, the outline resembling that of a wise old owl. Sienna cautiously reached out her gnarled hands seeking Ulan's face. Bravely the prince took those reaching hands and placed them upon his temples. Paechra saw the mix of uncertainty and determination in Ulan's eyes before Sienna found those eyes with her searching digits and gently placed her thumbs over the eyelids, sliding them closed.

"Share with me your memories, show me the truth that words cannot reveal," requested High Prince Ulan.

In silence Paechra watched as the prince stiffened as his mind was flooded with Sienna's visions. Gradually he fell to his knees with a moan. Paechra, feeling sympathy was immediately enveloped in a healing blue light. Straight away she embraced the two and felt some of the pain ease from both Sienna and Ulan.

"So much blood, so much suffering," murmured Ulan.

Paechra felt his silently falling tears wet her cheeks.

The memories continued to flow between Sienna and Ulan; the fear and pain of battle, the plan to involve humankind, freeing the land of the vorsurk and finally the feeling of peace and freedom. All of these memories experienced by a child and then interpreted through eons of wisdom and experience. The prince began to shake as Sienna finally removed her hands.

"Help me up, daughter," begged Sienna of Paechra and without question the younger Druid obeyed.

"I thank you, Alknown Mother Druid Sienna," whispered the sylvan high prince. "Thank you for sharing with me your knowledge."

"Now you know why we can't say no," said Sienna. "Surely now you understand why it is that we can only say yes, committing the might of the sylvan people to such a worthy and necessary cause, just as we did in the past to save humankind from this fate."

"No, Sienna," muttered the prince. "Now I see for certain that my choice is the correct one, I cannot be the one to commit our people to such a cause, I am not as brave as my ancestors."

"Come, Paechra, there is nothing more that we can say here," stated Sienna sadly, offering Paechra her hands so that she could be led away.

"Foolish, foolish, foolish princes..." muttered Sienna as she and Paechra made their way down the flight of steps.

"Please slow down, Mother," begged Paechra. "I am supposed to be the eyes for both of us."

"Child I know each and every one of these steps, should I choose to I could dance up and down them with the help of spells," answered Sienna.

The elder Druid's face twisted into a look of anger and frustration. As Paechra gave a look of shock in reply Sienna's face softened.

"I am sorry, my daughter," cooed Sienna. "It is not you that I am angry with."

Paechra sighed, relieved.

"You were innocent in your request, you were too quick to jump to the conclusion that what happened in the past is the right solution for the present," continued Sienna, pausing on the steps to take Paechra's hands in her own.

"Was I wrong?" asked Paechra. "Should I have not brought the humans here?"

"Paechra Lightheart you have journeyed far and already experienced much in your few years, your heart is that of the dragon and your mind is that of the unicorn," Sienna suggested.

"Courage and purity," Paechra stated with a smile.

"Courage and purity with no wisdom," answered Sienna

with a tone of forgiveness. "In the same position I would have done the same as you, but I would have been seeking a private audience with our foolish high prince."

The two sylvan guards waiting at the bottom of the steps looked over their shoulders in surprise at hearing such words.

Paechra gave them a wide eyed glance, but Sienna merely pushed her way past them.

"High Prince Ulan has need of rest," Alknown Mother Druid Sienna suggested. "Please escort him to the royal chambers and do not allow him to refuse."

"Of course, Mother Druid," replied the two respectfully.

As Paechra led Sienna onwards she heard the rhythmic march of the pair making their way up the flight of stairs. She wondered what they would find when they reached the top.

"What is that noise?" grumbled Sienna.

Paechra paused for a moment and tried to focus. Up ahead there was a sound of shouting, it seemed likely that an argument had broken out between the humans.

"Quickly, Mother," urged Paechra.

"You go on ahead," suggested Sienna. "I will be fine young one, I shall follow the ruckus."

Unsure for a moment Paechra caught the distinct sound of blades clashing.

"What stupidity will I be walking into?" she muttered to herself before rushing forward.

The noise led Paechra along the fortress passageways until she arrived at the Great Hall once more. There she found two sylvan soldiers sharing blows with Anton while Thomas danced around them like a flightless Arkarokk waving his empty hands about.

"Stop! Stop!" the butcher was shouting.

It was obvious to Paechra that nobody was listening.

"This is how a Truth Keeper teaches his lessons!" growled Anton as his sword arched around in a backhanded blow aiming to hamstring one of the sylvan warriors.

As a pair the sylvan blocked the blow with crossed spear poles before one stabbed at Anton's chest causing the Head Truth Keeper to quickly duck under the thrust.

"Enough of this foolery!" cried Paechra as she stepped into the Great Hall.

The two sylvan looked up for only a second to see who it was that had spoken. This was just enough time for Anton to nick the shoulder of one of the sylvan causing a ribbon of red to spray across a table.

A foreboding purple shadow appeared around Paechra as she saw Sylvan blood spilled.

"I said that is ENOUGH!" the Druid boomed.

Dropped weapons clattered to the stone floor.

"I tried, Paechra," Thomas cried out in fear.

"Yes, so I could see," replied the Druid.

The purple shadow still without a distinct outline faded as Paechra's anger vanished as quickly as it had flared.

"You there, help him to a healer," commanded Paechra, ordering the uninjured sylvan soldier to support his fellow.

"The foolishness of men is common, regardless of the race," announced Sienna as she appeared in the doorway.

"So, it seems, Mother," agreed Paechra.

"I believe that the wisest course of action is some time

apart," suggested Sienna. "Perhaps Anton you would like to take a walk with me."

"You are the worst of the hags here!" growled Anton as he made to pick back up his dropped blade.

"Well then, perhaps you would prefer to take a walk outside yourself," said Sienna, her milky white eyes flashing green.

Paechra noticed a similar green pass as a shadow over Anton's face.

The Head Truth Keeper forgot his blade then and nodded.

"Fresh air will do me good," he said.

"Would it trouble you if an old woman happened to be walking the same way?" asked Sienna with a soft smile.

"I guess not," considered Anton.

To the surprise of everyone but Paechra the Mother Druid and the Head Truth Keeper left the Great Hall then, headed in the direction of the forest. As the pair left the fortress Paechra noted Thomas the Butcher collected Anton's blade. The young human held the weapon reverently and seemed confused about what to do with it next.

"I think it best that we all have some time away from one another," Paechra then suggested, to which there was no argument, just murmurs of concurrency.

An hour later Paechra found herself in the company of Queen Catherine. Michael Stormsong was with her, keeping the queen company.

"It is wonderful to see you at rest," Paechra announced. "May I spend some time with you both in silence, I have many thoughts that I need to set straight."

Queen Catherine was relaxed upon a bed of lush grass; a

gentle stream ran alongside where she lay. Michael sat upon a thick fallen branch supplied but a great oak nearby.

"Please do join us," begged Michael. "I would love to speak with you on the subject of my son, if you are willing."

Queen Catherine yawned a dainty little yawn and smiled.

"Yes, please Paechra," said the human queen. "Your presence would be a fine addition to our small but satisfactory party."

Grateful Paechra found a place on the other side of Catherine, sitting upon the grass and facing Michael.

"So, what did you want to know?" the Druid asked.

"Well for one thing I was hoping that you could tell me where he is?" asked Michael, hopeful but uncertain.

Paechra pondered upon the question wondering just how to explain the fate that had befallen Michael's son and what she should reveal regarding her involvement. Before she could begin her reply the party of three was interrupted by Paechra's friend and sister through Druid commonality, Heidi the Dove Spirit.

"Here I find you, Paechra my friend," puffed Heidi.

She looked as though she had been searching for Paechra for some time.

"Indeed, friend Heidi, here I am," replied Paechra. "Come sit and rest with us."

"As tempting as that offer is, alas, I cannot rest, and neither can you," Heidi said with a sigh. "The Mother Druid has summoned us for a meeting in the Sacred Grove."

"Alas indeed," sighed Paechra, turning to address Michael and the human queen she continued. "Please enjoy the peace and the song of the bubbling stream."

"That will not be possible," Heidi added. "Queen Catherine and Michael Stormsong have both been summoned also."

"A man invited to the Sacred Grove?" asked Paechra. "This has never happened before."

"Come quickly," urged Heidi. "Anton and Thomas are already there."

The sylvan Druid Paechra Lightheart, the human of Andrapaal Michael Stormsong, and Catherine, the queen of the human kingdom of Thuraen followed after sylvan Druid Heidi, Paechra's friend. Paechra knew the way to the Sacred Druid Grove in Greenwood Vale well, yet she hung back and allowed her friend to lead the way. Paechra believed it more important that she help Michael to aid Queen Catherine who had her growing baby to worry about. It was almost as if the child growing within the human queen knew where they were headed as it kicked with eagerness, slowing Catherine as she tried to keep up with Heidi's pace.

"Friend Heidi, please slow down!" called Paechra.

Heidi turned to look behind her and visually sighed.

"Mother Druid Sienna asked that I find you quickly and bring you to the Sacred Grove," Heidi said, obviously troubled.

Leaving Queen Catherine in Michael's care, Paechra made up the distance between her and her friend. Placing a reassuring arm around Heidi's shoulder Paechra gave her a squeeze.

"I shall personally tell Sienna that you've fulfilled your duty as per her request," said Paechra. "You did find us quickly and you will take us to the grove."

"I am not sure that Mother Druid Sienna will see things that way..." Heidi said, unsure.

"I think that our wise Mother will appreciate your consideration for the poor, pregnant human," Paechra suggested. "They are not as physically robust as we are."

Heidi considered this before she slowly nodded.

"You are right, as always, Paechra," sighed Heidi before she gave the younger Lightheart a weak smile.

By then Michael and Queen Catherine had caught up with the two sylvan.

"Thank you, Paechra," puffed Catherine. "This child saps me and I do not seem to have the same energy as my younger self did."

Paechra nodded, offering her arm to the human queen.

"I am sorry for my haste," said Heidi. "Paechra has suggested that we travel at a slower pace the rest of the way."

"I am sure that Queen Catherine will appreciate this," suggested Michael. "I for one am not as young as I used to be."

Paechra noticed a pink hue appear around Catherine, an aura that suggested annoyance.

"You go at your own pace then, Michael," Queen Catherine commanded. "I shall happily be escorted by Heidi and Paechra and we shall arrive when it is that we do."

Unsure of what he had said wrong, Michael Stormsong could only stand and watch as Catherine released her grip upon his supporting arm and instead hooked arms with the Druids.

Seeing Michael like this reminded Paechra of her friend Johannas causing her to wonder where Johannas had gone, hoping that he was ok.

'I am sure that we will see each other soon,' Paechra thought to herself.

"Come, Paechra and Catherine," urged Heidi, causing Paechra to return to the moment, all thoughts of Johannas postponed.

Paechra took one of Queen Catherine's offered arms while Heidi took the other.

"Let us lend the queen strength," suggested Heidi. "That we may hasten our pace."

"Would that please you, Queen Catherine?" Paechra asked of the human.

With satisfaction, Paechra saw the hue that enveloped the queen turn from pink to white and then disappear.

"Queen Catherine, you wish only to be asked," murmured Paechra. "To be consulted rather than be directed and spoken for."

"Indeed, Paechra," replied Catherine. "As queen far too often, my decisions were made for me by King Fredrickson or by one of the sages."

Paechra and Heidi both nodded, urging the human queen to go on.

"Leaving the city of Andrapaal and Thuraen I was in no fit state to make decisions for myself, so with trust and gratefulness I went where it was that you led us, Paechra," Queen Catherine added as the trio continued to walk.

"Since your arrival in Greenwood Vale I have noticed a change in you, Catherine," suggested Paechra. "You are becoming your own entity."

"Indeed," agreed Catherine. "Although I miss my home and the life I once had, although my heart is still heavy with sadness, this place has acted like some sort of healing sanctuary."

"This is how we feel also," suggested Heidi. "We feel like the grove, our home, heals us of our fears and sorrows."

"We would do anything to protect it," added Paechra.

"Would you think it possible that I could remain here?" asked Queen Catherine, hopeful but unsure.

"Why, of course," announced Paechra, confidently.

Heidi gave her friend a look of utter surprise. She was not so sure that a human would be accepted by the community. This was unheard of and certainly not something that Heidi thought would be possible.

'Are you so certain?' Paechra heard the voice of Heidi echo in her mind.

Hush, Heidi-friend, replied Paechra, both Druids using a special bond, the bond of the sisterhood to communicate without sound. *I shall convince High Prince Ulan to allow the human queen and her unborn child to stay.*

Just as you convinced High Prince Ulan to send our people to war, mused Heidi.

To this Paechra said nothing.

As both Druids bathed themselves in a blue, healing light Queen Catherine found herself strengthened.

"Come, let us hurry," the human queen announced as she quickened her pace.

"Queen Catherine!" called Michael who was still a few strides behind. "Please wait and I will walk beside you."

Paechra noted that the human queen purposefully did not respond to Michael's call.

Soon the distance between Michael and the trio in front of him began to grow. It continued to grow until it was a lengthy gap just as Heidi, Paechra, and Queen Catherine reached the edge of Greenwood Vale's Sacred Grove. All three stopped and gasped in surprise. It was here that Michael found them, he rested, bent double with his hands on his knees.

"No, I must admit I am certainly not as young as my Truth Keeper days," gasped Michael. "I thank you for waiting," he then added with a grin.

When the two sylvan Druids and the human queen did not answer Michael looked up and finally witnessed what it was that had stopped Heidi, Paechra, and Queen Catherine. In the center of the grove, not far from the water's edge, a figure stood bathed in moonlight. All four could clearly see Mother Druid Sienna Alknown, painted in the bright colors of pink, yellow and sky-blue. The paint was streaked through Sienna's hair, across her face, down her body, and over her arms and legs. There seemed to be no part of her skin that was not marked. The moonlight seemed to focus upon Sienna's upstanding form, the markings glowing brightly with some regal, arcane power.

"Ah, at last," called the Mother Druid, her voice loud and confident, almost youthful. "You have arrived, now we may begin."

Paechra made to move towards where Sienna stood and addressed the gathering.

"Nay, daughter Paechra," called Sienna's surprisingly strong voice. "For once it is not you that we are waiting upon."

It was then that Paechra and Heidi both noticed that Thomas and Anton stood beside Sienna, off to the side and out of the curtain of illumination gifted by the moon.

"I believe you are being summoned," whispered Heidi to Queen Catherine.

"Michael it seems that your presence is needed also," suggested Paechra, turning to look behind her, catching Michael's eye.

"Queen Catherine, if you would please allow me…" began Michael, again offering his arm for support.

"If I must," announced Catherine, reluctantly. "I am still displeased about your comment earlier though, Michael."

"My queen, please, I wished no disrespect," mumbled Michael apologetically.

"And yet, disrespect you did achieve," Paechra overheard Queen Catherine reply as the duo slowly made their way towards the waiting Mother Druid.

"Poor Michael," Paechra suggested as she watched the pair disappear amongst the gathered.

In the evening's light, it was difficult to tell who was present, but Paechra sensed it was not only her sister Druids and the humans. Switching her sight to that which could detect auras Paechra smiled as she discovered staff from the fortress, tinkers, carers, and pickers, even some of the forest guardians.

Paechra heard a gasp come from her friend Heidi and so she returned to normal vision.

"What is it?" Paechra asked but Heidi did not need to answer.

There standing beside Heidi was High Prince Ulan.

"I am surprised that so many have come to the sacred grove this evening," the high prince muttered. "I am still trying to determine if it is a betrayal against me and my brother's rulership or if it is just the curiosity of an ancient people."

"High Prince Ulan," Paechra said in greetings. "I would suggest it is less disrespect for you and my betrothed and more a show of respect for our Mother Druid."

'Jhathrani,' Paechra then thought to herself as she witnessed her friend Heidi blend into the gathering, leaving Paechra on her own to deal with the prince.

Heidi had been just like the winged little forest hens, slinking into the shadows of the forest when the Ffnenk came stalking. Heidi had been smart.

"High Prince Ulan," Paechra began.

She was cut short though as the prince raised his hand.

"Hush, young Lightheart," urged the high prince. "We have come to listen, have we not?"

"Indeed, we have," agreed Paechra before she thankfully returned her attention to Sienna.

"... followed our daughter, Paechra Lightheart, sister Druid of this sacred grove..." continued the Mother Druid with all eyes upon her. "They trusted that Paechra had in her mind and heart the best interest for the safety of the human kingdom of Thuraen..."

At the mention of her name Paechra completely tuned in on what Sienna was saying and so she noticed the figure of Anton in his usually agitated state push into the moonlight, Sienna stood her ground though forcing Anton to share the space, this made Paechra smile.

"Not all of us followed so blindly," announced the Head Truth Keeper.

"Anton," hissed Thomas, so loudly that even Paechra at the back of the crowd could hear him. "You cannot say such things."

"Quiet lad," growled Anton towards where Thomas

remained in the darkness. "I can say what I like."

"Agreed," stated Sienna, her voice still strong, confident. "Yet follow you did and here you are."

The matter-of-fact delivery of Mother Druid Sienna's words made Anton pause for a moment to think them over. Sienna took that opportunity to address the crowd once more.

"What Paechra did not realize though is that there is a deeper, darker reasoning for why the sylvan of the past drove the vorsurk into the desert lands…" announced Sienna. "Our reason for giving the lands to the human people, for gifting them with language and for helping them to flourish was not through kindness, but instead was purely for preservation… We wished only to protect ourselves and our own way of life."

'No,' Paechra thought to herself. 'Surely that is not true.'

As she opened her mind's eye Paechra felt and saw many of her kith and kin were feeling the same. Far ahead of her Paechra could see the aura that surrounded Mother Druid Sienna Alknown. It was the aura of truth.

"I was there as a child, a child that listened, that learned, and remembered," continued Sienna.

The Mother Druid's voice grew louder as the gathered crowd of sylvan began to mutter and murmur. Paechra could see that Queen Catherine was surrounded by confusion, as was Thomas the Butcher. Michael had worry forming as a solid mass while Anton's anger was growing darker in color.

"We, the sylvan of Greenwood Vale and that of other settlements throughout our lands, we did tell ancestors of these humans in our midst that our actions, our sacrifices, our gift to them of so-called freedom was a blessing," added Sienna, somehow her voice becoming even louder and stronger. "In fact, it was a curse!"

At this, the gathering erupted in a cacophony of wild noise. Paechra could just make out Anton mouthing the words 'I knew it' while Queen Catherine and the other humans seemed overwhelmed by exactly the same feeling Paechra herself felt, disbelief.

"For more than five hundred years," continued Sienna, the magic she sucked from the moon's beams fueling her elderly voice so that it somehow managed to be clearly heard amongst the chaos. "The human kingdom has acted as a shield for us, a way that we could protect ourselves from our jealous enemy…"

Paechra and Heidi both saw that Anton had drawn his weapon, a forbidden act in the sacred grove. Sienna was oblivious, so caught up in her spell to notice. Certain that the worst was about to occur both Paechra and Heidi were surprised to witness Michael come up from behind Anton and tackle him backward into the darkness. Thomas came up beside Queen Catherine as she suddenly fell. The young butcher held his queen and her unborn child up for a moment before guiding her to a sitting position. All the while, Mother Druid Sienna continued to cry out to the crowd.

"I say enough! I say it is now time that we do what should have been done all those centuries ago," announced Sienna. "It is time that we truly commit to saving the humans and treated them as equals."

'Equals?' thought Paechra, and at this, she smiled.

"It is high time that we march from our safe haven and reveal ourselves to the humans, the vorsurk, and all of the other races," urged Sienna.

"Yes!" cried some members of the crowd in reply.

"It is time that there was a show of strength from the sylvan kind, a true demonstration of our love and gratitude for the human people," added Sienna.

Again, the crowd responded, again there was a cry of support.

"Our high prince says no, we cannot go, we must send these humans away," continued Sienna. "But I say we are free spirits, and those who wish to, shall have their own minds decide."

The gathering calmed for a moment, Paechra could see that those present seemed to hang on Sienna's every word.

"I say that we go to war with or without the blessing of High Prince Ulan and his missing brother," announced Mother Druid Sienna Alknown. "I say that we owe this to the human kingdom, for five hundred years of betrayal and trickery."

At this Sienna paused, the moonlight faulted, flickered, and then vanished. It did not matter though. The paint upon Sienna's body still pulsed brightly with power, a chaotic rainbow of raw energy. When the Mother Druid spoke again and broke the moment of silence her words were but a whisper. It mattered little though, for all there who were present in the sacred grove strained to hear. No one wished to miss a single utterance.

"Those who agree need but to follow…" was all that Sienna had left to say.

At this, the gathered crowd erupted. Some argued, others shouted with joy. Paechra turned to gauge the high prince's reaction, but as silently as Ulan had arrived at the gathering he had also vanished. Paechra wondered just when it was that he had left and how much he had overheard.

'Enough,' she thought to herself. 'What Ulan does not know already he shall discover sooner rather than later…'

Regardless of what High Prince Ulan thought though of the words of the Mother Druid, such words had been spoken, and the seed had been planted within the hearts of the sylvan people. Paechra could sense that there was a change in the winds, a choice that needed to be made. Sienna had opened the eyes and minds of Greenwood Vale showing all that it was their choice and not one that they needed to have made for them.

"Well, that was completely unexpected," said Heidi as she once more stood at Paechra's side.

Paechra nodded to her friend and smiled.

"What do you believe will happen next?" Heidi asked, trying to hide her obvious feelings of worry and concern. "Friend Paechra, are you not afraid?"

"I do not know, Heidi, I do not know how to feel," laughed Paechra. "What I do know though is that the sylvan of Greenwood Vale will choose for themselves, and I sense that they will make that choice quickly."

Paechra watched as the crowd dispersed, many different conversations were beginning to form, proof that Sienna's seed had in fact been planted and in some places was already sprouting.

"Come, Heidi my sister," Paechra said, motioning towards where Sienna had spoken. "I feel that our presence is required in the aftermath of the storm."

"As you say, friend Paechra," agreed Heidi, making her way through the last of the gathering.

When the two Druids reached the Mother Druid and the humans they discovered disaster.

"I don't know what to do," groaned Thomas.

The butcher had one arm around the shoulders of Queen Catherine, supporting her as she winced in pain. His other arm was patting Sienna on the back as she breathed in short, shallow breaths.

"Quickly, Thomas and Heidi," urged Paechra. "Help me to get them back on their feet."

"But..." began Thomas.

"We need to get them to the water," Paechra urged.

Michael came over to help, Paechra noticed that Anton had vanished somewhere.

Between the four of them, quickly, Queen Catherine and Sienna were stumbling towards the water.

"Now let us go," ordered Paechra.

As she entered the water with Sienna and felt Heidi and Catherine follow after there was one thing on Paechra's mind.

'I hope that we are not too late...'

Chapter Seven

Forces Gathering

It will be the voice of the lioness come from the western lands.

From the Eleventh Stanza of the Prophecy, translated by the sages of the Kingdom of Thuraen 514th year

PAECHRA STARED IN awe over her shoulder, and not for the first time. The view of the column of her kindred was inspiring. It gave Paechra great hope for the people of Thuraen, but it also rekindled in the young Druid a strong belief in her people. The sylvan race could come to the aid of any who were in genuine need, as the humans were from a vorsurk invasion.

It had been three days since Mother Druid Sienna Alknown had addressed the gathered crowd in the Sacred Grove of Greenwood Vale and a great deal had transpired since that night.

#

High Prince Ulan had vanished into the fortress, ordering that no one be allowed entry. Paechra had worried that the sylvan prince would make an announcement that no sylvan of Greenwood Vale would have permission to leave with the blessing of the royal house. Thankfully such an announcement never came. Ulan was leaving it to the people to decide their own fate, just as Sienna had encouraged everyone who had come to the grove to do. In response, nearly a thousand sylvan had chosen to leave their home, uncertain of whether they would ever return.

Sienna had shown signs of stress the morning following her speech, yet she had refused to remain behind at the grove, regardless of how much the other Druids insisted.

"Nonsense," the Mother Druid had huffed. "I have tossed this leaf into the wind; I shall not turn my back upon it as it floats in the breeze."

"I afear that this breeze may become a hailstorm, or worse, a hurricane," suggested Paechra's mother, Sarah Lightheart.

"What you fear may well come true," replied Sienna. "Still, what may become real is no reason to give up on something when there is an equal possibility it may only remain a possibility."

Paechra had been witness to that discussion and she had seen her mother eager to reply, but Sienna Alknown had waved Sarah Lightheart away from her as another coughing fit erupted from the Mother Druid's aged frame.

"If you wish to be useful," suggested Sienna. "A broth

would make an old woman grateful."

"I shall boil…" Paechra had offered, hoping to ease the tension between these two whom she respected.

"Nay, daughter," stated her mother. "It will be my honor to prepare this."

Paechra thought that she would be given another task to undertake, leaving the Mother Druid to rest, but Sienna had other ideas.

"Good, peace at last, no more nagging from your mother," Sienna had sighed. "Finally, I have you alone to speak with, Paechra Lightheart."

"I am here to listen, Mother Druid," Paechra remembered announcing in reply.

"I do so hope you are eager for more than just listening," grumbled the Mother Druid. "I have a far greater role in mind for you."

"I am ready," Paechra had replied, and at that moment she hoped that the words she spoke were indeed true.

Looking back over her shoulder again, the younger Lightheart still wondered.

'Why me, Sienna?' thought Paechra to herself. 'There are so many others more experienced, more worthy.'

While it had been just the two of them Sienna had informed Paechra that she wished for the younger Druid to take up the mantel of leadership.

"Young Lightheart, I have planted the seed, and I wish to witness the growth of that which I have planted but I have not the energy to water and weed and tend to each leaf, each root, each blossom that shall turn into fruit."

"What do you mean, Mother Druid?" Paechra remembered

asking, her confusion causing Sienna to laugh.

As the laugh turned into another hacking fit of coughing Paechra had helped Sienna to stand.

"Paechra, I will be unable to stand at the front of the line and lead those who choose to join us," stated Sienna, slowly. "That is a task I am gifting to you."

Without thought Paechra had agreed wholeheartedly.

"I shall not let you down," she had said.

When Sarah Lightheart had returned to Sienna and Paechra she had given her daughter a strange look. In silence she had offered the healing broth to the Mother Druid.

"Focus upon me," Sienna had grumbled then.

Broth had dribbled down her chin and over the front of her robes.

"Apologies, Mother Druid," Sarah had said, aghast at what she had done, tearing her untrusting eyes away from her daughter to focus upon the disaster.

Paechra had taken that opportunity to dismiss herself then and to go off in search of her friend Heidi. Sienna had given Paechra a sagely nod before again scolding Sarah. Paechra had left the pair with Sienna's cries of angst and discomfort ringing in her ears.

Heidi had not been difficult to find. She was with Queen Catherine and Michael Stormsong. Straight after Sienna's speech there had been the moment of chaos and panic. The moment when Thomas the Butcher, one of the chosen Eleven of Andrapaal, the capital city of Thuraen had tried to support both his queen and the Mother Druid. It was the moment when Paechra could see the aura surrounding both human and Druid was flickering and fading. In that moment Paechra had seen the pool in the sacred grove was glowing brightly with healing light. With assistance from Thomas and Michael Paechra and her friend Heidi had been able to get Queen Catherine and Mother Druid Sienna into the water. Thankfully, it was just at the very moment when the arcane powers had pulsed. Paechra did not know if it were their abrupt arrival that had caused this reaction or if it were some perfected or lucky timing. Either way those waters had done the trick.

Sienna had broken the surface and swum back to the shore. Likewise, Catherine had come up for air and had laughed joyously as her baby kicked. It had been a wondrous moment, Paechra and Heidi both feeling the euphoria from the waters as well. Paechra had felt electrified and prepared to tackle the whole vorsurk army on her own. The moment was brief and as all four had stepped away from the pool such a feeling of unnatural strength had slipped away.

"There is a true wonder in this place," Queen Catherine had announced.

"My Queen," Michael had cried, rushing over to support Catherine.

Courteously the queen had taken Michael's offered hand.

"Allow me to support you, oh ancient one," Thomas had then said, copying Michael and offering support to Sienna.

Paechra had been surprised but pleased to see such behavior reflected by Thomas. She had left the two men to care for the queen and Mother Druid, wanting instead to find Anton whom she did not trust. With Heidi's help the two Druids searched the remainder of the night for the gnarled Head Truth Keeper but always found themselves to be one or two steps behind him.

"Yes we have seen that wounded Hgaphannup," some of the sylvan had said with worried looks.

Paechra and Heidi both knew the danger of an injured Hgaphannup and Heidi had suggested they cease their search early. Paechra, thinking that she knew Anton's character was determined to push on. Finally, they found the whereabouts of Anton, his trail of disgruntlement leading to the entrance of the fortress. By then though High Prince Ulan had made his announcement and the way into the fortress had been barred.

When Paechra had found Heidi most recently she had asked her friend again if there had been any sighting of the Head Truth Keeper.

"Still none," Heidi had sighed. "We watch and we listen but there is still no sighting or any word."

"I have offered to approach the fortress," said Michael. "But even I am turned away, unable to enter."

After the euphoric feeling of the waters of the pool had left Catherine she had felt quite tired, Paechra had dismissed the queen's offer to also enquire about Anton and Ulan, asking that Catherine instead focus upon herself and the child.

"All will reveal itself soon enough," Paechra had suggested, and she had indeed been proven right.

On the second morning following Sienna's speech word spread that those who wished to help the humans were to gather again at the Sacred Grove with the expectation that all who chose to gather would then leave with the humans the following sunrise. Paechra had expected perhaps a throng of fifty at most. As Greenwood Vale's residents had proven her wrong Paechra's eyes and smile had both grown bigger and bigger until they could grow no more.

"This is incredible," Paechra had said to Heidi and her friend had agreed.

"To see so many gathered at Sienna's call," Heidi had

whispered in awe. "Such respect for our Mother Druid, and all of our sisters."

"And such defiance shown towards our princes," Paechra had laughed.

"Well, perhaps defiance is too strong a word," Heidi had suggested, cautiously.

"What else should we call it?" asked Paechra then.

"Perhaps we could call it democracy?" Heidi had said with a great deal of uncertainty.

"Democracy spoken loudly and proudly," Paechra had suggested.

As the numbers passed nine-hundred Anton had reappeared, not willing to explain his disappearance and certainly not willing to reveal whether or not he had spoken with Prince Ulan.

"My time is my own," he had announced.

After which the Head Truth Keeper had sought out Thomas the Butcher for a private chat.

Paechra had been tempted then to use her arcane powers to eavesdrop upon the pair but there was still too much to organize, and she was starting to discover what exactly leadership entailed.

Sienna's insistence that she come along as witness was the first difficulty that had been brought to Paechra's attention.

"We shall acquire a beast upon which the Mother Druid shall ride," Paechra had suggested to the older Druids.

Some had thought such an idea had merit but others, especially Paechra's own mother, had highlighted potential issues.

"Sienna dozes often," Sarah had said. "Should the beast

rock her to sleep she would tumble."

It was finally agreed that a carriage would be built to transport Sienna, a respectable vehicle for one of such age and status. Paechra made the decision that Queen Catherine would join Sienna Alknown, but the human queen refused the offer.

"I am ever so grateful for your offer and thoughtfulness," Queen Catherine had announced in reply when she heard of Paechra's suggestion. "I have made the difficult decision however to remain here in Greenwood Vale."

When Paechra and others pressed the human queen for more, Catherine frowned and narrowed her eyes in disappointment, unfamiliar with her decisions being questioned. Regardless, Catherine did choose to elaborate.

"Since my fortunate arrival in this special place I and my child have felt like we have come home at last, my husband's passing has left upon me a darkness that I associate with Andrapaal, and the feeling of peace I have gained from this forested world will be of great benefit to myself, my child, and our soul healing."

Since there could be no arguing against such a premise, Paechra turned her focus toward other things. The human queen was left to find her own lodgings and it was rumored that she had been allowed to take shelter with Ulan.

"I shall join you," Michael had said when he heard of the queen's decision.

"This cannot be," Catherine had announced in reply. "I must be allowed to recuperate alone and in peace."

After this Paechra had noticed Michael seemed at a loose end so she had given him and Thomas the task of gathering enough food for the journey.

"How long will this journey take?" Thomas had asked,

adding with a pleading look. "And please tell us we will not be getting on any ships."

"That I can promise you, no ships," Paechra had said. "Go ask some of the sylvan for help, we will need food for at least ten days."

Paechra had relied on her sister Druids to organize those who came willing, to march to war. Each member would need weapons and shelter as well as the food Thomas and Michael were tasked with gathering. The Druids were only happy to help organize tents and blankets for the gathering. Of the ways of weaponry and warfare the sisters knew little. Paechra turned to Anton, reluctantly.

"You have taught young men to take up swords and to run into battle in the name of freedom," Paechra had said to the Head Truth Keeper. "For the sake of your race I ask that you set aside your anger and distrust of us, of me, and you find it in your heart or at the very least your mind the same abilities to become my army's captain."

"I will do nothing for you, witch," Anton had growled. "To aid my own kind though I can see that it is necessary for me to share some of my knowledge and experience."

"That is the best that I can ask for, you may begin at your leisure," Paechra had chosen to state in reply.

Thankfully, Anton had realized just how little time he had, quickly the Head Truth Keeper with the permission of High Prince Ulan had acquired a number of spears from the fortress armory. As the numbers gathered had continued to swell it was determined early on that those weapons the fortress could spare would not be enough. Alan had ordered for wooden spears to be made, and the sylvan wood smiths obliged. There was a competition to see who could produce the most perfect wooden spear, then sword, then shield and breastplate. Paechra sense that Anton and the other humans were impressed with the sylvan ability to work wood in a similar way to a human smithy that worked metal, never once did Anton voice his opinion. Paechra could detect the changes in the Head Truth Keeper's aura though. He seemed both surprised and proud, yet his response did not match that which his aura had revealed.

"I will promise to do nothing for you, witch, promise to be able to do little with you and your forest dwellers and those sharp sticks," Anton had stated, loudly and cruelly. "I will teach the basics, that is all, make sure this ragtag bunch are not overrun the first time we come across the one-thousand or more wolf pack."

"If that is the best you can do then that is all we can ask of you," Paechra recalled saying in reply.

The interaction with Anton had left her confused, she became even more confused when Anton demonstrated what he considered minimal training. The sylvan who had been given spears, men, and women both, had been awoken before the dawn and forced through drill after military-style drill. Having never seen the Truth Keepers fight as a group, Paechra made sure she was awake in time to witness, and she found herself to be most impressed by what she saw.

#

All of this and the comradery that seemed to be blossoming within the sylvan and amongst the humans too all added up to equal a feeling of pride for Paechra. That was why she felt both taller and stronger as she set the pace at the front of the column, leading it through sylvan homelands, gathering more eager kindred to the cause.

157

"Isn't it wonderful," said Paechra's friend Heidi as she joined Paechra at the very front of the pack.

Paechra smiled at her friend and took another look over her shoulder.

A river of color, greens, browns, blues, and whites snaked out behind her. Many wore the wooden breastplate and held high spears, ready for anything, though still they chatted and joked amongst themselves.

"We are indeed already a formidable force," Paechra replied to her friend. "What we have in numbers we lack in experience though."

"Agreed," grumbled Anton as he suddenly appeared by Paechra's side. "You forest dwellers have no sense of fear, no idea of the dangers ahead."

"There is nothing that can possibly stand before the greatness of our people..." began Heidi with confidence and conviction.

"Hush, Heidi," urged Paechra.

Heidi stopped in surprise.

"You sense I am right, don't you, witch," smirked Anton. "Any chance you could dream up one of those wolfmen, or perhaps a pack?"

"You speak of folly and foolery, human," Heidi said with a frown.

"No, Heidi, what Anton suggests may have merit," said Paechra, deep in thought, genuinely considering Anton's suggestion.

"Will ye need to discuss this with the other women?" Anton asked, though both Heidi and Paechra both sensed that there was a challenge in Anton's tone.

"I shall ask the Mother Druid for her advice," replied Paechra. "I walk at the front of this army, but the call was Sienna's that these people have answered, I do so ask as a sign of respect."

"And if the old one says nay?" asked Anton.

"I shall make my decision based upon that which Sienna Alknown advises," replied Paechra.

Heidi swung her head from Paechra to Anton and back, eyes growing wider.

"What you suggest is reckless, dangerous even," Heidi whispered.

"Indeed, friend Heidi," Paechra said, agreeing with her friend. "But this could be the introduction to danger that our people needs."

"Or it could be the thing that drives all of our kindred away," murmured Heidi.

"If that turns out to be true then it is better that we know it now," growled Anton.

"Agreed," stated Paechra with a nod.

"I shall wait to hear from you then," said Anton.

"You cannot expect the unexpected," said Paechra. "Only expect to be surprised."

"Oh gosh," murmured Heidi. "Here we go…"

#

It was much later when Paechra Lightheart, sister Druid of Greenwood Vale found some time to sit, feeding a small campfire the occasional log to keep it burning brightly. She did

159

this more out of habit than necessity, the night was warm and still. She watched the yellow and orange flames dance, looking for signs from the spirits that the world was fuming and agitated just as she was, but such signs could not be found. For the moment, at so late an hour, those around Paechra were at peace, slumbering soundly and deeply. The crackle of the happy blaze gave the Druid the chance to reflect back upon the journey she and so many of her sylvan kin had undertaken.

A full day had passed by since her conversation with the human, Head Truth Keeper Anton of Andrapaal, capital city of the human kingdom of Thuraen. Paechra's friend, and sister Druid Heidi had been present also when the discussion was had. It was a conversation in regards to how best to test capabilities of the army of just over a thousand sylvan people that had chosen to gather and leave Greenwood Vale. Paechra had been in awe to see just how many chose to leave after Mother Druid Sienna Alknown had made a passionate speech in the Greenwood Vale Sacred Grove. So many of Paechra's kind now followed towards certain battle.

Both Heidi and Anton had suggested doubt at the battle worthiness of those simple forest folk who had never picked up a weapon. This doubt had been of no surprise to Paechra to hear it from Anton, but to hear Heidi agree with the Head Truth Keeper had caused Paechra to second guess her plan, this had led to Paechra's frustration, a feeling she just could not seem to shake. Since initially discovering the presence of the vorsurk in Thuraen, and in Andrapaal, the heart of the human kingdom, Paechra had thought of nothing else but asking the sylvan people to come to the aid of humanity, just as they had over five thousand years before. It had been challenging to bring a small representation of Thuraen to Greenwood Vale, but Paechra had managed to accomplish this feat. It had then been a greater challenge to convince High Prince Ulan to willingly send sylvan to the aid of the invaded kingdom, a challenge that Paechra still could not believe she had failed. Out of such a failure though had come something beyond the young Druid's hopes, with the support of Mother Druid Sienna Alknown, Paechra's army had gathered and grown. The people had made their own decision, sylvan heart coming to the fore at the cry for support of what had to be a worthy cause. What could possibly go wrong? And yet Anton and Heidi had both agreed that Paechra's army was not yet capable of facing vorsurk forces.

"We are fierce," Paechra told herself. "We are ready."

Paechra was alone, sitting by the fire. There were a number of tents and other makeshift shelters spread out like a moving village, each shelter holding three or four humans or sylvan, the gathering making a pilgrimage from Greenwood Vale to Thuraen, and eventually to Andrapaal at the heart of the human kingdom where Paechra suspected they would find hordes of the wolf-like warriors and sorcerers battling with humans for control of the city.

Centuries ago, the vorsurk had enslaved the whole of humanity and many of the other races as well. History recorded that the sylvan race had driven the vorsurk back from the lush lands that bordered the mystical forest groves like Greenwood Vale and hounded the wolf pack to the sandy deserts in the far east.

Thanks to a tome of dark magic, smuggled into Andrapaal, the vorsurk had been allowed to return. Paechra was determined not to let them stay long enough to get settled again.

"Sylvan of history were able to drive back these beasts, I myself have fought some on occasion," Paechra muttered to herself. "How dare Anton suggest that we are not ready... How dare Heidi, my faithful friend Heidi... She has suggested that we will flee..."

Paechra shook her head, the flames catching her blonde locks and making them shine.

"I know that we will prove them wrong," vowed the young Lightheart. "I have faith in my people and in the humans who we travel with, we are indeed ready, and I will find a way to prove it."

Staring deep into the flames of the campfire Paechra felt herself begin to doze. In her mind Paechra knew that she had a way to seek out the wolfish enemy, they were always seeking a way to join minds with and then overcome the sylvan, especially Druids who had a magical connection with the world. The vorsurk sorcerers were always hunting for an opening, seeking prey to devour, mind, body, and soul. Traveling with the small group of humans Paechra had almost been caught out, her personal mission finished before it had truly had a chance to begin. Paechra had been able to drive back the sorcerer though, she had proven herself strong enough. Considering Anton and Heidi's words, Paechra now wondered if her strength would be enough for all. There was a tingling in Paechra's mind as she felt that same sorcerer who had battled her before trying the same again. So far from Greenwood Vale and the sacred grove there, the protective spirits that watched over the sylvan and hid them away from enemies no longer had that capability, the sylvan had travelled too far for that. The wolves were hunting and they rarely hunted alone.

"No, this is not the time or the place," the Druid said to herself, she tried to fight the feeling and disengage. "I need rest, we shall try this during the daylight of the morrow."

As she sat, to distract herself and break free of the vorsurk's probing, Paechra thought back to Sienna's speech and counted in her mind just how many had answered that call. As the group had made their way through other sylvan forests their number had swelled and continued to grow, the stone tossed into the pond did indeed ripple far and fast.

"We are almost double our initial number," Paechra whispered to the fire, and she smiled, thinking of the size of the army helping her to grow more confident again. "I wonder just how many more will come in support of our cause, to fight for the freedom of humankind."

Paechra considered the lateness of the hour, and the long day of travel planned and decided that she would have to eventually at least try to sleep.

Retiring for the evening she joined her friend Heidi in the shelter that they shared with another sister Druid. The smell of the smoke from the extinguished campfire still tickled Paechra's nose as she climbed beneath her simple blanket. The shimmering starlight in the dark sky above comforted Paechra and soon she drifted into slumber.

"I see you," hissed a voice.

Paechra, eyes closed tried to discover whether the voice was in her mind or not. Realizing that the sound was spoken, close by, and not a mental message she opened her eyes slowly and discovered that she was again crouching before the campfire. The flames that she was sure she had extinguished only moments before burned brightly. This time though the flames glowed green, purple, and blue, not the normal orange and yellow. Also, strangely there was no heat from the fire although it burned strongly. What radiated instead from the flickering tongues was a bitter cold that sank deep into Paechra's very soul.

"I told you to leave me be," stated Paechra bravely.

"Your wish and what is reality can be two very separate things, little lamb," replied the voice.

Paechra tried to rise from the flames but found she was being held in place by some unseen force.

"Show yourself, that I may truly know my enemy," demanded Paechra.

"You know of me, little one, we have met before."

Paechra cast her mind back to the time only days ago, perhaps not more than a week passed when she tried guiding the small group of humans towards the ghoul ship, The Picturesque Picaresque. It had been a short battle of wills then and Paechra believed this encounter would prove to be the same.

"You know that I have beaten you before," stated the Druid. "Why have you foolishly chosen to engage with me again?"

"I the fool?" sniggered the wolfish voice. "That first engagement perhaps but not this time…"

"What is different this time?" asked Paechra, uncertainty creeping into her voice.

"This time I am not alone," howled the vorsurk.

"Well neither am I," announced Paechra.

With brute mental strength she forced herself to avert her eyes from the strange fire's flames. As her head rose, Paechra found the pressures upon her weaken and she was able to stand up.

"Look about you, little lamb," stated the hooded figure that stood only five yards away from Paechra. "You are surrounded and here in this realm you ARE alone."

Quickly Paechra flicked her eyes around the darkness and

saw that behind the vorsurk sorcerer there were well over a hundred wolf-like foot-soldiers. Some bore spears, swords, but all were equipped with the deadly claws that vorsurk were born with.

"One hundred and twenty creatures of death," stated the sorcerer. "Each one of them merely awaits my command to stride through the vale and into your sleeping campsite."

"If that is the case," thought Paechra quickly. "All I must do is this…"

The words of power came forth from the Druid's lips immediately, a spell conjuring an arcane spider-like web which wrapped around the sorcerer's maw.

Eyes narrowed, more annoyed than angry and the wolf-like vorsurk simply ran a sharp claw through the bonds. They sliced through easily and fell away.

"Who is the fool now, little one?" growled the wolf.

Paechra wrapped herself in the guise of a she-bear, but in this place her magic felt wrong. Instead of a pure blue the shadow that surrounded her was purple, black, grey, and swirling not solid. The spell felt as though it was eating away at her, so she let it go. Instead of fading away, the spirit form remained. The spectral she-bear growled deeply and then rose up before Paechra, meaning to strike.

"Jhathrat feeloo tha ghurtnun…" stated Paechra in a soothing tone.

The bear was not happy to hear such words though, normally a calming spell. Instead, it gave another deep, throaty growl before raking Paechra with its fore-claws. Paechra gasped in pain as the claws dragged down her front. Hurriedly Paechra stepped back and watched the bear cautiously.

"Your spells do not work as you wish here, my lamb, not as

mine do," announced the vorsurk. "Now let us see how well your so called army handles mine…"

"My magic has failed me, but I still have my hands and my feet," cried Paechra.

As the sorcerer began to flick through his tome of dark magicks Paechra rushed towards him and threw a punch. The bawled fist smacked into the creature's maw, behind it all of Paechra's frustrations and fears.

"What is the meaning of this?" cried the sorcerer. "One of you seize the girl!"

As one, a hundred and twenty foot soldiers rushed forward to obey their master. The scene was one of undisciplined chaos. Vorsurk collided with one another and tumbled sideways, armor screeched, and spears knocked, one soldier fell wounded followed by two more. Paechra kicked the sorcerer before sidestepping to the left as the bear charged at her. The sorcerer grunted as he was knocked over instead.

"Gotcha!" growled one of the wolfish soldiers as Paechra felt his claws upon her shoulders. Struggling Paechra found another soldier grappled her around the waist, as the third tackled her around the knees and knocked her down to the ground the Druid knew she was caught.

"You three, hold her still…" ordered the sorcerer.

All Paechra could do was watch and hope as the curtain between the real world and the realm of magic was for a moment cast aside.

"Kill them all," ordered the sorcerer.

"Arise! We are under attack!" screamed Paechra.

The vorsurk ran through the camp with torches lit and

weapons drawn. Tents smoldered and then came alight. Sylvan rushed out and were struck down by the soldiers. The smell of fire and blood caused the creatures to howl with lust. Paechra struggled to break free from the trio that held her down. She could see herself kneeling beside the extinguished campfire staring at the dead coals.

"Paechra! Paechra!" called a voice over the sounds of battle.

"I am here!" Paechra cried, in frustration she saw that her figure in the real world remained silent and still.

In the haze of battle Paechra saw a figure approach her and wrench her to her feet. The she-bear spirit struck out at the three vorsurk that held her firm, and they scattered, releasing her. As Paechra felt her soul join again with her body the arcane figure of the angered bear appeared around her. This time the magic was true, a beautiful blue that Paechra trusted.

"To me!" cried the Druid and she saw with relief a number of her sisters with their own outlines ready to strike out as a pack.

The vorsurk foot soldiers made a good fight of it but the determination of the sylvan was too much for so few numbers. Eighty swiftly became forty and then ten. Finally, all that remained was the sorcerer.

"Remain and be destroyed," vowed Sienna who had joined the fight as the tide had turned.

"As you say, old one," replied the vorsurk before stepping back through the curtain which then vanished from sight.

"Bury the dead and bring back those who have run away," ordered the Mother Druid.

"Come, daughter, we have been given our task," suggested Paechra's mother, beckoning towards Paechra.

The younger Lightheart was looking around at what have

previously been the village, home away from home. Not one structure remained untouched. Of the sylvan who had answered the call of Sienna Alknown not even half remained. Paechra heard the groans of suffering coming from her people, perhaps fifty or so. Beside them quietly wept those whose kin had closed their eyes for the last time, struck down in the battle, never to rise again.

"I did this," thought the young Druid, whispering the words.

"Paechra my friend you must not say such things," replied Heidi, close enough to have overheard her friend.

"I thought that we were ready, we are so not though," Paechra continued, a sadness tinting her voice.

"You were not to know that the vorsurk would attack us this day, none of us could have known that" said Heidi as she gave Paechra's shoulder a reassuring squeeze.

Paechra shrugged off the gesture and turned to face Heidi.

"I did know, Heidi," she said, almost shouting. "At least I felt the sorcerer trying to make the connection and I chose to tell no one."

"Why then, Paechra?" asked Heidi, shocked to hear this admission. "Why ignore such warnings?"

"I thought I was strong enough," whispered Paechra in disbelief. "I thought that you and Anton were wrong."

"And now look at what such foolish thoughts have achieved," stated Sienna as she hobbled towards the pair.

"You are injured!" gasped Heidi, rushing to the ancient sylvan's aid.

Paechra saw the deep claw marks that oozed bloody crimson from Sienna's left thigh. Her guilt multiplied tenfold.

"It is but a scratch, child," stated Sienna, waving Heidi away. "It shall be naught but a scar in a day or two."

Again, Paechra forced herself to look around, calculating the level of destruction.

"I am not fit to lead," she suggested and hung her head.

"Nonsense," spat Sienna. "When you were captured and forced to watch on as we were attacked you risked everything to shout a warning."

"Yes, that is true," agreed Heidi. "Your cry woke us from our slumber."

"Daughter, your actions have saved many," said Paechra's mother with a weak smile. "Your initial cry and then the way you called us all together; they are indeed the actions of a leader."

"But those who have perished could still be alive, those injured could still be whole," the daughter replied. "And that also is because of me, my stubbornness, my determination to do things my way, myself."

Many of those who had run at the first sounds of battle had started to return. They seemed shocked at the state of the army, trying their best to help extinguish the structures that still smoldered.

"Paechra this skirmish was my first experience of battle," said Thomas, the butcher joining the conversation. "You hear stories from Truth Keepers about war and battle, but nothing prepares you for the real thing, not until you experience it yourself."

"I thank you then Thomas, for keeping your head and coming to my aid," stated Paechra graciously.

"No, Paechra it was not me," admitted Thomas.

"Not you?" Paechra replied in surprise.

"I thought about it, but I do not hold the courage such an action would require," Thomas stated sadly, not willing to meet Paechra's grateful gaze.

"Then who?" asked the young Lightheart, confused. "Who chose to help me in my moment of need?"

"Me," said a voice from the edge of the gathering. "It was me who saw that you needed aid…"

Paechra's eyes grew wide in disbelief and her confusion deepened.

"Why, why did you do such a thing for me?" she asked, unsure if she wanted to know the answer.

#

"Where are you taking me?" Raven asked Derek.

The pair had woken from slumber, just as the strange orb which illuminated the world between worlds appeared, brightening the darkness.

"Home," stated the sylvan.

"Surely not my home, to travel there would mean our capture," cried Raven. "You are not that foolish."

"You fool… Ask now… What way… After so much days…" replied Derek.

"You follow my visions, and none of them seem like home to me," said Raven. "Explain yourself…"

"You say… House in tree… Everywhere green… This my vale… Take you… Home…" explained Derek.

"Well, is there a faster way?" asked Raven, eager to know. "I sense that Paechra may be in some sort of trouble."

"Only Druids… Walk such paths…" stated Derek. "Path of dreams…"

"I can feel myself being dragged into such a path…" said Raven.

His right arm had vanished from sight, but he could still feel its presence.

"This not same…" stated Derek, suddenly grasping hold of Raven's left arm, that he not be left behind.

Metaphorically, Raven felt his great wings threatened.

Chapter Eight

A Leader and Her Doubts

The rains will not fall forever.

What came before shall come again.

From the Eleventh Stanza of the Prophecy, translated by the sages of the Kingdom of Thuraen 514th year

PAECHRA LIGHTHEART, SISTER Druid of Greenwood Vale crouched beside the place where a small campfire had once been brightly burning. She looked up into the faces of Thomas, Anton, and her sylvan kindred.

"Who?" asked the young Lightheart, confused. "Who chose to help me in my moment of need?"

Only moments before the campsite had been overrun by

vorsurk foot soldiers who had crossed over through the realm of magic and into the real world with help from one of their sorcerers. The vorsurk sorcerer had been following Paechra's mind, trying to find a way to connect with the young Druid and to abuse that connection. Paechra had been foolish enough to think she could keep the wolf-like creature out of her head, but she had been proven very, very wrong. Some of her kindred had been injured in the attack, some had died. This weighed very heavily on young Lightheart's conscience.

"You ask again who it was that came to your aide," said a voice from the edge of the gathering. "Again, I tell you it was me; I saw that you needed aid and so I aided you."

Paechra's eyes that had grown wide in disbelief suddenly narrowed.

"I asked you why did you do such a thing for me?" Paechra said again, but then she followed up with another question. "How did you do such a thing?"

From the shadow stepped Ulan.

"The day that you spoke with me as we looked over Greenwood Vale I told you I did not support your request to go to war," said the high prince. "I worried for our people, a people that are not battle hardened, experienced in fighting against the vorsurk."

Paechra looked around the campsite as Ulan indicated the fallen.

"I heard you, but I did not believe," replied Paechra, moving to stand before the sylvan prince.

Paechra took up Ulan's hand and then knelt before him, looking up into his saddened features.

"Please, arise, Paechra," requested Ulan. "It is I who should be apologizing."

Paechra slowly rose back to her feet and was joined by her mother and her friend.

"What do you mean, High Prince Ulan?" asked Heidi, confused.

"I thought that I was speaking for the people," began Ulan. "I thought that I knew their mind, that they would be afraid and shy away from war."

High Prince Ulan took a moment to again look around the campsite and he sighed.

"So many have flocked to the call, not only in response to Mother Druid Sienna's words, not only to your passionate plea, Paechra," the high prince continued. "They have responded because it is the right thing to do."

"You now think it is right to die for the humans?" asked Paechra.

"To die is always a shameful waste," stated Ulan. "I have always thought this, and such thoughts have not been altered."

"Then what is right? What has changed?" asked Paechra's mother.

"It is right to fix the mess that we have made and have allowed to remain for so many centuries," Ulan tried to explain.

A crowd had gathered as many caught wind that High Prince Ulan had appeared in camp. The crowd parted as one of the more senior Druids escorted Sienna so that the Mother Druid could look the high prince eye to eye.

"You speak of the pact made with the humans," said the ancient one, sagely.

"Indeed, I do," agreed the high prince.

"Why have you come all this way to tell us though," queried Sienna. "It would be sufficient to send word that you have changed your mind."

"I spoke with the human queen Catherine on the evening before you all left Greenwood Vale," explained Ulan. "She told me of her decision to remain with the sylvan people and how it was the right choice for herself and her unborn child."

"Greenwood Vale is safety, it is where you should be too," suggested Paechra. "It is where I believe Mother Druid Sienna should also be."

"Daughter Paechra Lightheart," laughed Sienna. "Your heart and mind are linked in such a way that there is never any wonder what you are thinking."

"Indeed, Sienna, you speak the truth," said the elder Lightheart. "My daughter has always spoken freely regardless of the what, why and to whom."

"And I speak now seeing just how close we have stepped toward danger and disaster," interrupted Paechra. "That is why it is so important we return you home."

"I thank you for your concern, Paechra," replied Ulan. "I am sure such sentiment is shared by many here."

"I shall be staying," argued Sienna. "My words have brought many from the safety of home and I will not be the old woman who hides in the shadows while others do what is right."

"If I may be allowed to continue..." stated High Prince Ulan.

"Of course..." murmured many from the group that had gathered.

"Paechra's words had initially caused me concern," continued the sylvan prince. "My conversation with Queen Catherine had me reconsidering, if the humans are already finding our mutual enemy in the heart of their kingdom how long will it be before we find them once more howling in our own heart, in our sacred grove, taking us as slaves again, the past will not stay the past forever."

"So, you have thought to join our crazy crusade," stated Sienna.

"I have," agreed Ulan. "I left under the light of the full moon the very night after you began your initial march."

"You have been with us the whole time?" asked Paechra, surprised.

"Indeed, young Lightheart," laughed the prince. "I have watched, I have listened, and I have been most impressed with how quickly sylvan from beyond Greenwood Vale have answered your call."

"Only for us to fall when we needed to stand strong," murmured Paechra, disheartened.

"But we did stand strong, Paechra," suggested her friend Heidi. "We fought back against trained soldiers who had ambushed us, and we have managed to defeat many and drive away the rest."

"Well yes, but what of our own losses?" questioned Paechra.

"It is indeed sad those who we have already lost to the fight and so early on," agreed the prince and Mother Druid Sienna.

"And that is where you and I must better work together," grumbled the voice of Anton. "Your people have shown me what they are capable of but none of you are Truth Keeper material."

"We must learn to fight the sylvan way," suggested Heidi.

"Such a decision is one that our prince should make," stated Paechra.

"Nonsense," replied Ulan. "I have not made my presence

known to all so that I may make this cause mine and mine alone."

"The cause is still ours, Paechra," added Sienna. "Mine, yes, but yours also, and the cause of sylvan and human alike."

"All that we ask is that you share with us your thoughts, young Lightheart," requested High Prince Ulan. "Whether you believe we would want to hear you voice them or would not, we need you to share them all."

"Well then," began Paechra after a pause. "We will need to somehow make sure that the vorsurk do not find a way to ambush us again."

"Your sisters and I shall work on that," promised the Mother Druid.

Many of the Druids present nodded.

"And we must make sure that you are protected, High Prince Ulan," Paechra continued.

"I will need no such..." Ulan immediately protested.

"I am responsible for having both you and your brother leave Greenwood Vale, no word has been heard regarding Derek's fate so I will hear no argument regarding your protection."

"The sylvan of Greenwood Vale are in the care of Queen Catherine, one who radiates care and compassion," stated the high prince.

"I fear not for Greenwood Vale, especially if our journey is successful," stated Sienna, speaking just before Paechra could respond with the same. "Paechra is correct though in understanding the importance of both our roles as figureheads."

"Should either of you not survive the sylvan people will

continue existing but we will not be the same," added Paechra. "You are both representatives of a way of living, a way of peace, something worth fighting for and protecting."

"I understand," sighed High Prince Ulan. "But I refuse to be locked away in a covered wagon to only be paraded when morale is low."

"Fear not our prince," said Sienna with a wrinkled smile. "We shall find sufficiently royal tasks for you to occupy your time."

"Such as...?"

"Such as making your way through this camp and introducing yourself to all who have flocked to this cause," ordered Paechra Lightheart. "There is a rumor that has started to spread regarding your appearance, perhaps we should reveal that such a rumor is in fact true."

"I shall accompany you," added Mother Druid Sienna. "I can lend some strength to the fact you really are who you say and not some vorsurk imposter..."

"I shall gather the sisters and contemplate our problem with this vorsurk sorcerer," suggested Heidi.

As Paechra's friend hurried away she gave Paechra a reassuring hug.

"Thomas and I shall check over the damage done to the structures, the sooner we can move on the better," suggested Anton.

"As you suggest, Anton," murmured Thomas, seemingly thankful for having such a simple task to occupy him.

One by one Paechra found the group that had gathered began to move on. Finally, she was alone, almost.

"Mother," Paechra sighed. "How have I failed so?"

"You are your father's daughter, always believing that you are enough, that you need to be the one to fix, even if there is no problem or the problem is not yours, not yours alone," answered the elder Lightheart.

Paechra knew she would not receive sympathy, but even so it was difficult to hear her father mentioned.

"Somehow I have this connection that I cannot seem to be able to break," Paechra explained. "I am afraid that this sorcerer will again try to surprise us, to strike when we least suspect it."

"Remember my daughter that the vorsurk treat the number eleven as such a holy and important numeral," suggested Paechra's mother. "Never will the vorsurk strike without the required number of soldiers."

"So, we have bought ourselves at least a little time while the wolves regather," replied the younger Lightheart, unimpressed. "Perhaps we have a day, two or three at the most."

"You are wrong, daughter," suggested Sarah Lightheart. "It will take time for this sorcerer to convince his kind to strike again."

"So, we are safe for now?" asked Paechra, unconvinced.

"The vorsurk are often trying to compete with each other… We are therefore far from safe."

"You mean I am far from safe," suggested the daughter.

"Once again you are trying to take on all of the responsibility," replied Sarah Lightheart, patiently. "This sorcerer will still try to exploit your connection as will others of his kind."

"Then what can I do?" Paechra asked, demanding to know

the solution.

"Come, join us, sister," stated the voice of Heidi.

"As you wish," sighed Paechra, begrudgingly.

Sarah, Heidi, and Paechra left the extinguished campfire and joined the gathering of Druids.

"What is the feeling that comes over you?" asked one sister.

"Is there a moment when you sense this sorcerer is trying to connect with you?" asked another sister Druid.

Paechra made to respond but a third sister questioned her again before she could say two words.

"Is it always the same sorcerer?"

The large group of Druids had gathered on the outskirts of the camp, hoping for some quiet to help them focus. There were at least twenty present, but Mother Druid Sienna Alknown was absent, still with High Prince Ulan.

"Yes," said Paechra before she could be asked yet another question. "Yes there is a moment when I am at my tiredest that the sorcerer seems to be able to force the mental connection between us to open."

"Do you feel tired now?" asked Heidi, eyes wide with worry.

"Fear not, my friend," reassured Paechra. "There is no possibility of this sorcerer wanting to connect again, his forces are scattered and what is more I am awake and ready."

Heidi sighed, smiled and her body relaxed. Paechra noticed then that her friend had a cut under her chin which still dribbled blood.

"Heidi you are injured," Paechra gasped, reaching out to

lightly touch the wound. "Please let me heal you."

Heidi stepped back and she held up her hands defensively.

"Please Paechra, allow one of our other sisters to do it," Heidi begged.

"Of course, my spell failed me initially in the battle," said Paechra as she dropped her hands to her sides. "When I needed it most though, my magic proved true."

"Please forgive my mistrust," murmured Heidi, dismissing herself from the group.

"This creates yet another problem," stated Sarah Lightheart. "We hope that our own magic will be enough to counter the darkness of the vorsurk sorcerers but what if we are forced to fight in the place between worlds?"

"We use such a place to travel so often but it seems we truly do not understand it," added one of the other Druids.

"We will need to meditate on this," suggested Paechra's mother.

Paechra dismissed herself from the group as her sisters turned inward.

"If any have further need of me I will be looking over the camp," she said before she left, receiving nods from some of her sister Druids.

It did not take long for Paechra to spy Thomas and Anton clearing away the shell of a burnt out tent.

"This is the tenth structure that we have found that is no longer viable," grumbled Anton. "What were you thinking, Paechra?"

"What, not witch this time?" replied the younger Lightheart.

"Just answer the question," snapped the Head Truth Keeper.

"So many questions," sighed Paechra. "You deserve an answer to yours though."

Anton and Thomas put down what they were carrying and waited for Paechra to say more.

"I should have listened to you Anton, you and Heidi both," said Paechra. "I wanted to believe though that my people are the warriors of the past just waiting to wake up."

"Tonight, has proven that the warrior spirit is there," suggested Thomas.

"What do you know of the warrior spirit, butcher?" asked Anton, cruelly.

"I know what I saw, but you are right Anton," Thomas replied, bravely, looking Anton in the face and not averting his eyes. "I have been lucky as one of Andrapaal's chosen not to have had to face the might of our enemies, at least not until now."

"And now you think yourself a warrior?" grunted Anton.

"Is it not enough to be right?" asked Paechra of Anton.

"No, I need everyone to know I am right," replied Anton. "Whether the warrior spirit of the past is still with the sylvan people of the present time is not the point."

"Then what is the point?" asked Thomas and Paechra together.

"The point is can we make warriors out of what we have before we need them," suggested Anton. "Before we reach Andrapaal..."

"And...?" asked Paechra.

"I have witnessed farmers, woodsmen, butchers," began Anton. "Regrettably I am yet to see a single soldier."

"You are wrong," mumbled Thomas, but he did not dare say it too loudly.

"You should have listened to me," Anton said, ignoring Thomas. "You should have listened to the advice of your friend."

"What can I do now to fix things?" asked Paechra.

"Leave us to the physical, this magic stuff I don't understand," Anton admitted.

"Yes, focus on yourself and what is in your head," urged Thomas. "Find a way to fix that, for the sake of both of our races."

The sylvan conducted a ceremony thanking the forest for the materials needed to construct more tents. Soon the gathering of human and sylvan could continue their journey. As what remained of the gathering moved from sylvan settlement to sylvan settlement Paechra was surprised to discover that more of her kindred continued to swell the ranks. The Druid sisterhood focused as one upon investigating the connection that the vorsurk sorcerer had established. Frustratingly this connection continued to remain a mystery. Paechra also focused her energies upon exploring the connection. As her mother suggested the vorsurk sorcerer did not attempt to make a connection over the days that followed. Any attempt that Paechra made to establish a connection was replied with by silence.

"Licking his wounds," suggested Sienna.

"Perhaps," considered Paechra. "Or they could be waiting for the time we are no longer ready."

"Our numbers are growing, daughter," suggested Mother Druid Sienna. "And we are ever vigilant."

On the sixth night Paechra felt the tingle again in her mind.

"Be ready," she murmured.

"We are," assured her mother.

"You have been busy, young one," hissed the voice of the vorsurk sorcerer.

Paechra opened her eyes to discover she was once more in the place between worlds.

"You cannot control me," said Paechra.

"And yet it is I who determine the time and the place for our... meetings..." stated the sorcerer with a sneer.

Looking around her Paechra noticed that although the sorcerer was confident, he was alone.

"You have chosen this time to meet, to talk," agreed Paechra. "You have re-opened the gate..."

"But" said the voice of Sarah Lightheart. "You have forgotten to close it behind you."

From the shadows the sorcerer discovered first one, then two, then four, then ten of Paechra's sister Druids appeared around him, surrounding him. As one the Druids all focused their power upon the single vorsurk. Soon he was nothing but robes, a threat no longer.

#

True to his word, sylvan High Prince Ulan remained in the shadows, not taking up the leadership role of the gathered forces that flocked to Paechra's call for war. True to her own word Paechra made sure that the prince remained busy mixing with the people, listening to them and encouraging them. Sienna Alknown and Ulan watched on as Paechra grew in confidence in her leadership role, the young Lightheart finding it far more challenging when compared with leading the small group of humans. Paechra's mother Sarah Lightheart was always a step behind her daughter, ready to talk down the doubters. Paechra was disappointed to discover that the most vocal of these was still her close friend Heidi.

"I need your support," Paechra stated with earnest one evening when she found herself alone with Heidi.

"I can sense your need, my friend," Heidi agreed. "But I cannot blindly throw my support behind an idea that risks so many and so much."

"I cannot understand Heidi why it is you sounded so supportive before but now you share doubt of our cause, and my plan," said Paechra. "You have not seen the humans in their own environment, I get that they are strangers to you and why you might ask should we risk our precious, safe, culture and life for strangers…"

"You are wrong to think that way, my friend," argued back Heidi. "You paint me as a shallow creature; you paint our people as pretentious."

"Not our people, no," stated Paechra. "You have witnessed just as I have the numbers who gather under our banner knowing fully well where we travel and why."

"Yes, I am one of the first to heed such a call, or have you forgotten such a fact," said Heidi to her friend.

"But you state truly now that you believe it impossible to support such a calling," said Sarah, joining the pair of friends.

"Mother, are you spying upon me for Sienna?" Paechra suggested, frowning.

185

"Daughter Paechra, young dove," replied the elder Lightheart. "I only tell the Mother Druid of your successes."

"Fear not, Paechra," echoed Heidi. "There are more than enough other sisters who report to Sienna your failings."

There was a silence, brief, that existed between the three Druids, filled by the crackle of a hungry campfire.

"What then can I do to convince you to believe and follow again?" asked Paechra of her friend.

"Change the plan," Heidi responded without needing a moment to think.

"Is this all you ask of me?" laughed Paechra, humor absent from her eyes, the laugh a hollow sound of disappointment. "If that is so we may as well turn around and go home."

"No, my friend, I am not asking you to abandon your plan," stated Heidi, placing her hand upon Paechra's shoulder just as she had done thousands of times before then.

"Hear out what it is that Heidi has to say, please Paechra," urged Sarah to which her daughter sighed in reply.

"Speak then, Heidi, tell us of your thoughts," requested Paechra, her tone telling her friend that she was still not eager to listen.

"Well," began Heidi, taking a deep breath. "You have shown great bravery by firstly traveling alone to the human kingdom and then by bringing humans back home with you to Greenwood Vale."

"Yes, yes, Paechra's bravery is unquestionable," said Sarah Lightheart. "It is not her bravery that is under scrutiny."

"Please allow my friend to speak, mother," injected Paechra.

"Your cause was greatly assisted by Sienna Alknown, her speech at the Sacred Grove was indeed inspirational and having the Mother Druid travelling with us indeed helps to quash much talk of doubt," continued Heidi, ignoring the mother and daughter.

"The discovery of High Prince Ulan amongst our numbers has also assisted in strengthening my claims that I am leading us to something worthwhile," argued Paechra.

Heidi nodded.

"Yes, that is true," the friend agreed. "But having Ulan here also reminds us of his initial doubt, his refusal to back you immediately."

"In actual fact the prince was heard apologizing to my daughter for such doubt," argued Sarah. "He has realized that my daughter's voice is the voice of the people."

"Why then are the people asking a human to teach them to fight?" Heidi asked.

Again, there was a moment of quiet.

"So, this is the source of your doubt?" asked Paechra. "Anton, the Truth Keeper?"

"Friend, I was able to find a way that we could protect you from vorsurk sorcery," stated Heidi. "When you doubted yourself I was one of the first to tell you that it could be done."

"Anton is your fear, your thoughts of failure revolve around him?" asked Paechra again, seemingly ignoring Heidi for that moment.

"Yes, a human soldier and his militant fighting style, is that so difficult to understand?"

"Who else do we have that knows of combat?" asked Paechra. "As much as I struggle with his mannerisms and his bluntness he is the only one who has recently fought our shared enemy."

"Wrong Paechra," stated Heidi. "We have all recently fought the vorsurk."

"We cannot count the experience from the other night..." began Sarah Lightheart.

"And why not?" asked Heidi, cutting the elder Lightheart off. "Sylvan have not fought with the wolves for centuries, not since the human people were given the gift of the written word."

"A gift given by us," stated Sarah.

"For a grave price," argued Heidi.

"Think you the price grave for us or for them?" asked Paechra's mother.

"I believe Mother Druid Sienna when she said that the price paid by the humans, a price that they are still paying has been far more than we should have asked."

"Which is why I have asked the sylvan people to join our cause," suggested Paechra. "We go to save the humans from eons of slavery, but equally we go to right such wrongs as that which we caused in the past."

"Then we must fight as sylvan and not as humans," argued Heidi.

"For a people who have not needed to fight for so long I ask you, Heidi my friend," said Paechra "What does it mean to fight like a sylvan?"

"And so, we go around and around again," groaned Sarah.

"How often do we find ourselves upon an open field?" asked Heidi, ignoring the elder Lightheart's comment.

"Never, or hardly ever," Paechra agreed.

"How often do we need to fight with blades of steel?" questioned Heidi.

"That is a human weapon," Paechra agreed.

"So that then is what is not to fight like sylvan-kind," stated Heidi.

Sarah watched her daughter Paechra's face changing from thoughtfulness to frustration.

"Anton is used to drilling the young boys of human aristocrat families, teach them how to fight upon the open fields of the empty desert," murmured the younger Lightheart.

"We need to learn to fight with the trees, amongst the trees, for the people," stated Paechra.

"Wrong again, my daughter," stated Sarah.

"Wrong?" asked Paechra and Heidi, together.

"You both forget where it is that we are headed," suggested Sarah.

"You have been there, Paechra, please tell us what the human city is like," begged Heidi.

"Stone... Like little mountains, some piled upon each other... Unlike forest there is no life, only the lives of those who call such stone home..." Paechra began.

"Strange it would be to live in such a way as that," stated Paechra's mother, Sarah. "I could think of nothing worse."

"Please excuse me," begged Paechra then. "I must find Anton and speak with him a moment."

"I shall accompany you," suggested Heidi.

"While I shall seek out Mother Druid Sienna Alknown," said Sarah with a smile. "Perhaps she is not so all-knowing after all."

"And hopefully High Prince Ulan is with her so you can inform them both," said Heidi.

"We can only hope," said Paechra before the three parted ways.

Anton was just where Paechra and Heidi thought that they would find him. Where the great gathering of sylvan had camped there was only one place that had flat ground and very few trees. If they had been unsure of the Head Truth Keeper's whereabouts as they drew nearer to the place known as The Clearing he could easily be heard.

"No! No! Again! Faster!"

"Come, sister, we must hurry," urged Heidi.

"Agreed, my friend," said Paechra in reply. "That we may at the very least relieve our kindred of the endless shouting."

"Anton! Anton! May we please speak with you?!" called Paechra.

The human was waving a sword around above his head as two groups of sylvan ran towards each other and then past each other. Swords occasionally clashed but not often.

"Thomas, please do what you can," the Head Truth Keeper begged as he handed his sword over to the young butcher.

As Anton strode towards the pair of sylvan Druids they noticed he was shaking his head and muttering.

"I didn't think I would ever say it, but I miss the presence of Michael Stormsong," the human said.

"Perhaps we have something even better to offer you," suggested Heidi.

"What could possibly be better than someone else with military experience, and knowledge of tactical warfare?" grumbled Anton.

"This," announced Paechra cryptically.

Turning towards the treeless space Paechra spoke to the earth in a sing-song voice that began low but then grew higher in pitch and steadier. The earth rumbled and shook before it began to rise. Paechra sculpted the land, forcing it to mimic her memory of how the streets of Andrapaal had changed. Tears pricked her almond-shaped eyes as she tried not to think of her father and instead created hollowed out buildings and cobbled streets.

"This is…" rumbled Anton as the sylvan he was trying to turn into soldiers dropped their practice blades and turned to watch.

"Amazing?" Heidi suggested.

"Yes, actually, it is utterly amazing," stated Anton. "This will have to be the first and probably only time when I will ever admit that magic is useful."

"You are welcome, I guess," stated Heidi as Paechra continued to create the new practice field.

"Can you make the wolf-men appear as well?" asked Thomas. "Not real ones of course…"

"I will see what I can do," replied Paechra through gritted teeth.

World shaping was more difficult than she had initially thought it would be.

"Here, let me help," offered Heidi.

The images of oak trees began to spring up amongst the dirt buildings followed by half-sized vorsurk, some in robes and some brandishing crude dirt weapons.

"How are you still doing this?" panted Heidi, shaking after only a few moments of helping Paechra.

"What is the meaning of this!" the voice of Sienna could be

clearly heard by all present.

Paechra released her connection to the earth as did Heidi, a blue haze of magic that shimmered around the pair faded to nothing. The earth that had been sculpted up to that point shifted, settled, and then remained standing.

"Well met, Mother Druid," called Paechra and Heidi as one.

Sienna Alknown was enveloped by a clearly seen purple halo. Paechra and Heidi both knew that was not a good sign. Anton did not, however.

"Greetings, old one," stated the Head Truth Keeper. "Is it not marvelous?"

"Yes, it is not marvelous," replied Sienna crossly. "Is this your idea, Anton?"

"Well, no, it was something two of your Druid girls were creating," the human replied. "It is to help me train your people; I am discovering that it is so difficult when we cannot visualize the battlefield."

Sienna ignored the babbling Anton, instead turning her narrowed eyes upon Paechra and Heidi.

"Did you not hear the screaming?" murmured the ancient sylvan.

"I promise you, Sienna, there have been no injuries upon my training field," continued Anton.

"Yes, oh great one, zero injuries, zero deaths…" added Thomas the Butcher. "Unless you included that unfortunate incident a day or so ago…"

"Hush lad, hush," murmured Anton as he waved Thomas behind him.

"Yes, please hush," growled Mother Druid Sienna.

"You heard her lad, hush," agreed Anton.

"Both of you please, silence," demanded the ancient one.

"What screaming, Mother?" Paechra asked, slowly, cautiously.

The angry purple faded from Sienna's form.

"I thought we were under attack again," the old sylvan explained. "The land was screaming out to me, to all of your sisters."

"We swear, Mother," said Heidi with her head drooped. "We could not hear anything."

"Shall we return The Clearing to its original state?" asked Paechra, embarrassed.

"No, please, leave the land as it now is," begged Sienna. "We have tortured the land enough for one lifetime."

"We are sorry, Mother Druid Sienna," stated Heidi and Paechra. "We know what we need to do."

"Then do it," commanded Sienna. "I shall remain here so you can use my tent in private."

"But..." mumbled Anton.

"Hush, Anton," said Sienna, Heidi and Paechra.

The two friends approached Sienna's tent with scrubbed skin, dressed in clean clothing. Heidi carried a burning stick of incense and Paechra brandished a wooden blade.

Inside, the tent was modestly furnished; a sleeping mat for Sienna, a daybed for High Prince Ulan, and a place where the Druid who was caring for Sienna could rest. There was a low table with plate and goblet and in one corner of the tent an altar, upon which sat a stone bust resembling the shape of a woman. As Paechra and Heidi adjusted to the darkness of the tent's inside they each pointed towards the altar and nodded in silence.

"We come to the altar of Pit-Ta-Raha," the two sylvan murmured reverently, just as Mother Druid Sienna Alknown had told them to do.

Heidi placed the burning stick in the right hand of the statue of the goddess that took up most of the altar. At the feet of the statue was an ivory bowl. The two friends looked at each other before again facing the statue.

"We have wronged You, Pit-Ta-Raha and we have wronged the earth," stated Heidi reverently.

"We ask of You, great goddess, Your endless forgiveness, though in truth it is a greater gift than we deserve," murmured Paechra as she stepped closer to the statue and alter.

"I guess, now we make the offering?" whispered Heidi.

"I've never had to do this before, have you?" Paechra whispered back.

"I have seen it done, only once," replied Heidi. "But never have I needed to make my own offering."

"Pit-Ta-Raha, please guide my hand," begged Paechra. "That my offering may please You and right my wrong."

There was a presence then that the two Druids felt enter the tent. Paechra ran the point of the wooden dagger across the tip of her pinky and index fingers. Blood dropped with a plop into the bowl. When six droplets from each finger had fallen Paechra withdrew her hand and placed her fingers into her mouth, sucking to try and stop the bleeding.

"Your turn," she mumbled to Heidi as she stepped away from the altar, statue, and bowl.

Heidi took the weapon, surprised to see that the blade was clean. She showed Paechra who shrugged, her eyes wide in surprise.

"Goddess, we have wronged You and harmed the earth we care for and love so dearly," prayed Heidi. "Please accept my offering in payment of such crimes, that You may find in Your wisdom the ability to forgive me."

Again, the wooden blade was used to prick the index and pinky, this time on Heidi's hand. The droplets plopped into the bowl to mix with Paechra's offering.

"Now what?" asked Paechra.

"Now we extinguish the taper in the bowl, I think…" said Heidi uncertainty evident in her tone.

"Like this?" asked Paechra of her friend as she reverently took up the stick of incense and placed the burning end into the pool of blood.

With a hiss the stick immediately went out, Heidi and Paechra then watched on in awe. The blood became a cloud of crimson mist. As it left the bowl it hovered around the face of the statue before the image inhaled it.

The feeling of a holy presence left the tent just as suddenly as it had arrived.

"That was really weird, Paechra," whispered Heidi. "Don't you think it was weird?"

Paechra indicated the statue and then pointed to her ears.

Considering the possibility that the deity could possibly still be listening, Heidi panicked.

"I mean no disrespect!" she stammered.

There was no reaction from the statue or the altar.

"I think we've been forgiven," suggested Paechra.

"I hope so," murmured Heidi. "I truly hope so."

When Paechra and Heidi returned to The Clearing they found Anton distraught as much of the earth had returned to the way it had originally been. All that remained was a full-sized grey rock carved in the image of Pit-Ta-Raha. Painted around the rock's neck and breasts was what resembled a crimson chain from which hung a beautiful ruby.

"Did you do this, Mother Druid Sienna?" asked Heidi and Paechra.

"No, young ones," the ancient sylvan replied. "This was an answer sent for the two of you; it was your offering, your sacrifice that has made this come to be."

"I believe we have been forgiven," said Paechra with a smile as she gave her friend Heidi a quick hug.

Heidi squeezed Paechra back in return.

"Yes," agreed Sienna. "The goddess smiles upon us again."

"Tell me exactly what is going on!" demanded Anton.

The sylvan he was trying to train in the art of combat all knelt reverently upon the earth of The Clearing, faced towards the stone statue with eyes closed.

"Hush, Anton," stated the three Druids as one. "Please, just hush."

Chapter Nine

Beautiful and Dangerous

They who be yellow as the sun play, youthful abandonment.

Red as blood is blood forgotten.

Only those of ancient blue recall, remember, rewrite.

**From the Eleventh Stanza of the Prophecy, translated by the
sages of the Kingdom of Thuraen 514th year**

THE SYLVAN AND human gathering remained at the site
where the statue of Pit-Ta-Raha had appeared. No further
training of combat drills took place upon this section of land
previously known as The Clearing, everything but worship was
deemed forbidden.

"This is ridiculous," Paechra and Heidi overheard Anton

mutter to Thomas.

The young butcher from Andrapaal nodded but did not dare to utter a word of agreement. Thomas, like Anton, was a long way from home and he knew it. Unlike Anton, Thomas tried not to rock the boat; memories of the last boat he had been on, The Picturesque Picaresque, and the horrors he had experienced were still fresh in his thoughts.

"We are so close to Thuraen, to home, to facing the enemy, our common enemy," grumbled Anton, Head of the Truth Keepers, and in his mind, key militant strategist. "And yet we remain stationary, stalled, we are unable to budge because of some stone."

"We would not expect you to understand," said Paechra as she left from her morning of worship. "You cannot possibly understand that our people's connection to the land and the spirit of the land runs deep, and long, and true."

"Humph," muttered Anton, though he could not deny that since leaving Andrapaal and Thuraen he had seen in the presence of Paechra and other sylvan things he did not think were possible.

The most recent example of this of course was the existence of the statue in The Clearing. It was undeniable. Anton knew that he could touch it, though he dared not do so while the sylvan were close by. He could see it, and he knew that only days before the same area of forest was clear, flat, no stone statue had been anywhere close by and there was no way that a statue of that size could have been brought in and then dug into the ground so deep, not without everyone knowing about it. Paechra could see in the human's eyes that he did not want to believe in the existence of gods and spirits, but it was very difficult for Anton to continue to deny that his truth, the truth he was so vigilant in protecting was perhaps not the whole truth.

Thomas on the other hand had seen things, things that Paechra regretted she had shown him. Seeing such things had made Thomas far more open-minded though.

"We must be patient, Anton," Thomas continued to say while the elder human had paced like a caged wolf. "We will move on, we will continue to train, to learn to fight."

"When though, Thomas, when will this happen?" Anton always rumbled in frustrated reply.

It was seven days, a timing that was important to Pit-Ta-Raha, after which Sienna had called for a meeting in the sacred place. Standing beside the statue which towered over her, the elderly sylvan had placed a loving hand over the place where Pit-Ta-Raha's heart would have been.

"Oh, great one," the Mother Druid had cried out. "We leave this place in peace; we pray that we may return this way one and all to again thank You for Your protection, Your love…"

"And Your forgiveness and mercy," Paechra mumbled under her breath.

"And Your gracious understanding," Sienna finished.

"Come, one and all," announced Paechra. "We continue our journey, onwards to Thuraen to grant the humans true freedom."

"Finally," grumbled Anton.

It was not as swift an exodus as Anton had hoped for. Each and every sylvan needed to pause beside the statue of Pit-Ta-Raha to bid their own farewell to the goddess, some choosing to have a conversation, and not a short one at that. High Prince Ulan was the last to stop beside the statue, spending five minutes with his head resting against the holy stone, seeming to Anton like he was saying nothing.

"What could you have possibly needed to do, your highness?" Anton had asked when the army finally got moving.

"Listening, Anton," Ulan had replied. "It is funny what you can learn from listening."

"Just listening?" Anton had spluttered in disbelief.

"One day you should try it," High Prince Ulan had then suggested. "All of the great leaders do."

Over the following days the gathering sylvan known unofficially as Paechra's Army continued to grow. Paechra used her memories of Thuraen, especially that of Andrapaal to show her sister Druids how to build a city environment. The other Druids at first struggled to visualize the solid stone houses, buildings, streets, and open squares. Human cities and towns were so unlike the forest dwellings of Paechra and her kin. All, with the exception of Paechra Lightheart only had the stone fortress as reference.

"No, too large," Paechra continued to say as her sisters tried to create the vision of houses, shops, halls, a fortress, and everything else that made Andrapaal and Thuraen unique.

"Smaller, rounder, more square..." Paechra said again and again and again until the visions became closer to what she recalled.

After that it was Thomas and Anton who helped to add in the extra details that Paechra, being not human, still managed to forget. Paechra was discovering the limitations of her powers, often it was the younger Lightheart that the other

Druids requested help from when their own spell power did not seem enough. The sister Druids would have previously asked Sienna for aid, Paechra truly enjoyed her new role, although it did at times test her health and sanity both.

"You must rest, for your sake and the sake of us all," stressed Heidi, Paechra's closest friend.

"Yes, my daughter," Sarah Lightheart agreed. "Paechra, you have become the focus of this force, through the attention of the vorsurk, your words and deeds, and the mantle of leadership that has been thrust upon your shoulders."

"Worry not, Mother Sarah and friend Heidi both," reassured Paechra. "I am at no risk with the two of you and Sienna Alknown all keeping a hawkish watch over my every move and Anton and Ulan both examining and dissecting everything that I say. I cannot speak or walk a single step without having a barrage of questions fired upon me like a flight of arrows."

"At least they be not poisoned tips," suggested Heidi.

"Perhaps not poisoned," agreed Paechra. "But some do seem to have been soaked in pitch and set aflame."

"The questions from Anton seem more like they are catapulted boulders," laughed Heidi.

Sarah and Paechra Lightheart failed to see the humor.

"Like great rocks that crumble to mere pebbles as soon as they strike a reasonable response," Heidi added as an attempted explanation.

"Ah, yes," Sarah agreed. "Comments and queries that be simple in their unravelling, yet complex in their delivery."

"Exactly," smiled Heidi.

"I could do with far less interruptions from both Head Truth Keeper Anton and High Prince Ulan, less interruptions and more assistance."

"Assistance, how?" asked the sylvan high prince. "I overheard my name and thought I was needed," he added. "Is that correct?"

"You are needed to leave me in peace," grumbled Paechra. "It is nearing the moment that we travelled faster, the peak of our journey's parabola and distractions and waylaying will not assist us at this time."

"How shall we travel, Paechra?" asked Heidi.

"This is something that I will need to discuss in depth with the Mother Druid," replied Paechra. "I have some ideas but none of them are as of yet perfect."

"Before that Anton is also in need of you," said Ulan. "He asked me to seek you out, something about combat training and new scenarios."

"When will this day ever end?" cried Paechra.

"How is this day different to any other?" asked Heidi with an audible sigh.

"This is what we continually warn you about, daughter," said Sarah.

In reply Paechra merely groaned.

As the days went on and Paechra shared with them all her time spent looking for her father, the emotional connection helped her to paint a clearer picture which in turn led to a more accurate training environment for the sylvan fighters. Anton was amazed with how much Paechra, and her sisters were able to make Andrapaal come to life, and Sienna was pleased with how Paechra carefully created the environment as an image only, purely created from magic.

"Your daughter's power is growing swiftly," Paechra overheard Sienna telling her mother, Sarah. "Her control over such power is quite impressive."

"Thank you, Mother Druid Sienna," Paechra said, graciously accepting the compliment.

"Daughter, your power exceeds even mine at the same age," continued Sienna. "Of that I am certain."

"What does that mean?" Sarah Lightheart asked, proud of her daughter but worried also.

"I believe that I am being asked to stay wary," suggested Paechra, answering her mother's question before Sienna had the opportunity. "A Druid's power is a gift, not a plaything."

"Your daughter understands," said Sienna, smiling, her wise eyes proud.

"Such power is a weapon that we must harness," suggested Anton, a silent Thomas beside him.

"Are you eves dropping?" accused Sarah.

"How else am I supposed to know what is going on?" asked Anton, neither confirming nor denying the accusation.

"You need not know of everything that happens," suggested Sienna. "None of us can truly know of everything that happens."

"Even with your magic and your goddesses and spirits and such?" said Anton. "Don't they whisper in your ear at night and tell you predictions of the future?"

Sienna, Paechra, and Sarah all stood for a moment in shocked silence, eyes wide. Then Sienna began to laugh, a dry chuckle that almost caught in her throat. The elder Druid began to cough and splutter, Sarah and Paechra coming to her aid until she could slowly breathe again.

"Is that what you believe?" asked Sienna Alknown. "I have heard you call us witches but did not think for a moment you actually believed in such nonsense."

"Sadly, we are taught to fear what we do not understand," said Thomas, finally breaking his silence.

"Yes such is sad, and also true," agreed Paechra. "And what we have shown you, what I especially have shown you, would not help to dispel such a belief."

"We are not the same, there are many differences between human and sylvan," suggested Sarah, Paechra's mother. "But in this instance we have the same wish, the same desire."

Thomas nodded, slowly, in agreement. "We are trying to work together on a common goal."

"We must stop trying and just do," said Anton. "I must set aside my distrust, but I will only be able to do so if you share with me your thoughts, no matter how odd I may think them."

"Well then Anton, you will be pleased to know I have taken now to announce that we should be changing the training scenarios to explore the under-city of Andrapaal," announced Paechra. "This is something I have been considering for a few days, but an idea that I have not even shared with my friend Heidi."

Anton stood gob smacked, so surprised was he to hear of such a suggestion.

"The undercity of Andrapaal?" he asked. "Why would we need to train there?"

"Because that is where I found my father and that is the last thing that I remember seeing before we escaped the city and your homeland," explained Paechra.

"Yes," agreed Thomas, groaning at the memory. "There is something that I recall about the city beneath awakening and rising up."

"Impossible," said Anton, dismissively. "There would be no city beneath, the sages would have spoken about it... It would have featured in some law somewhere, somebody's history, I would have known..."

"You cannot know everyone's story, Anton," stated Sienna sagely. "Not even a million, million tomes could capture every piece of information."

"I am the protector of truth, and my truth is my belief," replied Anton. "I still choose to believe what I have been taught to believe."

Paechra made to reply but felt an ancient hand upon her shoulder.

"Belief is a strong form of motivation," murmured Mother Druid Sienna. "Allow the humans to have their belief. Right or wrong it helps them and us to share a cause."

Paechra nodded, understanding her elder's wisdom.

Paechra spent a bit more time in Sienna's tent speaking in depth with the Mother Druid. They discussed Paechra's idea of travelling faster, Sienna agreeing that the time was right.

"There is little more that we can do to prepare the sylvan who have flocked to our cause," said Sienna. "There are fewer settlements between here and the border of the two worlds."

"We cannot travel by dragon, or dream," said Paechra, not denying what it was that Sienna stated.

"Far too many of us for even a hoard of flying lizards," agreed Sienna. "And I do not know how well I would cope with a dragon flight, though I would suggest both Thomas and Anton would not cope at all."

Paechra smiled at that and then added a log to the small fire that burned in the fire pit that had been added to Sienna's sleeping tent. As the journey had drawn closer to the place where human and sylvan realms joined it was becoming evident that the season was changing.

"Your human companions have experienced a voyage by sea, yes?" suggested Sienna.

"They have, though I would strongly suggested they would prefer to avoid such again," said Paechra thoughtfully. "Thomas still wakes from nightmares and Anton…"

"Yes," agreed Sienna. "Though he tries to sound strong, Anton has an aura that is somewhat scarred."

"Is there any other way?" Paechra asked, hopefully that the Alknown would know.

The Mother Druid shook her head.

"I fear I would not survive a forced march like that which Anton continually threatens."

"I do not believe any, but Anton would arrive at Andrapaal's gates if such a grueling march was our chosen option," suggested Paechra. "Perhaps the captain of the Picturesque Picaresque would grant us all passage if it were you who summoned it."

"We can only hope, daughter," sighed Sienna. "Those poor souls respected our kind a millennia ago, but it has been too many years that I have chosen to ignore them and focus only upon Greenwood Vale."

"Try, Mother Druid Sienna," begged Paechra. "I shall break the news to the humans."

"No, no, No, NO, NO!!!" stammered Thomas. "You will not be

getting me back on that ship."

The butcher gave Paechra and Anton wild eyes, pleading, and obviously frightened.

"Try spending the voyage below deck, lad," muttered Anton. "I'll not be wanting to do that again. Not in this lifetime or the next."

"I hope that the presence of Mother Druid Sienna and my sister Druids will help convince the captain of the ship that we will not need rowers, nor will any of us need to interact with the captain or the crew," explained Paechra. Her own experiences, still recent memories did not sit comfortably with the young Druid. She would have preferred a different means of travel but alas the ship and her crew seemed the only option.

"In that case, sign my name and welcome me aboard," suggested Anton, this statement causing both Thomas and Paechra to stare at the Head Truth Keeper in surprise.

"Really?" asked a shocked Thomas.

"Truly?" asked a somewhat relieved Paechra.

"Sarcastically," replied Anton.

"We are not going by THAT ship," stated Thomas, firmly.

"Then I guess we will just need to strap you to the tail of a dragon then," sighed Paechra. "I shall inform Sienna we will need to summon one."

"A dra... dra... dragon?" stammered Thomas, his eyes growing even larger.

"Don't fall for it lad," warned Anton, too quiet for the fearful Thomas to hear.

"I have travelled by giant lizard many a time," lied Paechra. "The view is amazing."

"I would far rather walk," stated Thomas.

"To walk, to march, even to run would have us arrive far too late," suggested Paechra. "I sense something in the change of season, something that tells me we are ready to fight, and we must fight now."

Paechra saw that the call to battle stirred in Anton's aura, there was a silver strand that suddenly ran up the spine of his courage.

"Come, Thomas, I guess it is once again time for us to show these forest dwellers what it is to be human," growled the Head Truth Keeper.

Paechra considered the pair of auras and understood even in that pair of examples there was plenty revealed about the human people. She kept her thoughts to herself though and listened for Thomas' response.

"If I must then I must," the butcher sighed.

"Good lad," said Anton as he gave Thomas a thump on the back.

It took two days of travel by foot for Paechra's Army to catch a whiff of the smell of the sea. Thomas was already green about the face when the dock finally came into sight. Paechra noticed that Anton had also paled. She was proud of the pair of humans when neither uttered a word of complaint.

"Are you going aboard, witch?" was all that Anton said.

"I am not the one who has summoned the ship this time," said Paechra. "We must wait and see what Mother Druid Sienna Alknown can negotiate on our behalf."

All three looked on as the ancient Druid hobbled her way slowly up the gangplank with the assistance of Sarah Lightheart. Paechra was not certain but thought she saw the familiar Captain Overtian smile that sharp fanged smile as he pointed one claw towards Paechra, Thomas, and Anton. Sienna slowly shook her head at which the ghoul turned away. Sarah waved them all aboard. Thus did the journey endure.

#

Paechra noticed that the march up the gangplank from the misty dock to the great ship, the Picturesque Picaresque was a difficult climb for not only her but the two humans that chose to travel with her also. They did not have the same physical frailties as the ancient Sienna, and a small number of other older Druids who had undertaken the journey that had begun in the sacred grove of Greenwood Vale, destined to end, Paechra hoped, in the heart of Andrapaal, Capital City of the human kingdom of Thuraen. What Paechra, Anton, and Thomas all shared though was a memory of their previous travels aboard the ghoul ship. Paechra noted that it gladdened Anton to discover that he was not sent below the deck of the Picturesque Picaresque, instead he had been given run of the ship as Thomas had been on the previous voyage. Likewise, Thomas had not been sent below to row, for the young butcher though it was not as great a relief. Paechra Lightheart joined the two humans on deck, pretending that she wanted to keep an eye upon them. In reality though the sylvan only wished to avoid contact with the ship's captain, Overtain.

"Why so many complaints boy," laughed Anton, Paechra noticing that silver still persisted in the old warrior's aura, silver with a touch of pink. The silver was evidence of bravery while the pink was that of a pleasant mood, a mood Paechra had never seen Anton wear before.

Thomas on the other hand was all grey and a deep dark blue where his aura was concerned. Around his face the

209

butcher from Andrapaal was green, and those bits not sickly were ghost-white. Grey was concerning for Paechra, an aura reflecting a physical illness or injury. The deep dark blue was not so concerning, pure fear in its most natural form. Paechra was certain if she chose to examine her own aura she would see the same color there too.

"It was not like this," moaned the younger of the humans. "The deck was swarming with monstrosities; each way I turned I was faced with a reminder of death and decay."

"You should have seen what awaited Michael and me below then, lad," chuckled Anton. "The dead filled every seat but for a handful."

Thomas gulped loudly as he tried to stop himself from being sick.

"I know that they are hidden away somewhere, perhaps at night they will come out to haunt my dreams," suggested Thomas as he looked left and right, expecting an undead sailor to appear, reaching out to grab him. "Why did we have to travel by boat again?"

"I have ways to help you deal with your nausea," offered Paechra, she was also looking for distractions from her own memories.

"The boy will be fine," stated Anton with a smile. It seemed he was happy watching Thomas suffer.

"Why are you not with Sienna, the old one?" asked Thomas, before he gulped again, his eyes growing wide with panic.

"Just let it out, boy," urged Anton. "We will all feel a hundred percent better if you do."

"I for one do not wish to witness such a spectacle," said Paechra. "And to answer your question there are enough of my sisters chanting at present to keep the sails full."

It had quickly become known that the Druids Sienna and Sarah had negotiated with the ship's captain, Captain Overtain, that they would supply the wind that would propel the great ship. Overtain had dismissed his crew of rowers and shipmates, deeming them unnecessary. The poor lost souls wandered aimlessly past the waiting sylvan and vanished into the mist, groaning, moaning, and complaining. Paechra tried to look away as the young boy she had doomed shuffled by her, but he caught her eye, and the look they shared made Paechra shudder. As luck would have it many more of the ghoul crew came up behind that fresh corpse and shuffled him along. As she made her way cautiously up the gangplank Paechra still expected to see young Aaron behind every hidey-hole, around every blind corner. The ship seemed empty though, empty of all ghouls but one.

As Thomas made the noise of sickness Paechra overheard Anton's chuckling.

"Sister Paechra," called one of the other Druids. "Your mother has requested your presence."

"Get it all out, lad," Paechra heard Anton say.

"Much thanks, Isobella-Ann," murmured Paechra, truly grateful for the summons.

Should Thomas have need to become sick again, as his aura seemed to suggest, Paechra wanted to be far away from the two men, as far away as possible.

The wind blew strong and straight, not faulting as Paechra made her way, surefooted across the deck of the rising and falling ship. Unlike the voyage that the sylvan took with the human queen and her handful of citizens, a terribly rough sea voyage made even more uncomfortably with the presence of the stench and vision of death, this journey seemed likely to be

211

far more pleasant. The sky was a pretty blue, not a cloud in the sky, the ship travelled far faster with the magical wind propelling it. Paechra thought of her own use of magic, how she had chosen to use the life beneath the waves to propel the vessel out of a foggy storm. Such use of power had gained her a personal meeting with the ship's captain. This time around though Captain Overtain seemed not to care that Sienna, and the other Druids were blatantly manipulating the natural order. It seemed, as in nature, that it was one rule for some but a completely different set of rules for the rest.

"It seems unfair," Paechra mumbled to herself. "But why should I try to figure out the thoughts and intentions of a ghoul, undead and cursed to prey upon the living and yet imprisoned, destined to spend eternity tied to single place."

Paechra considered what Captain Overtain may have been like before he came upon the Picturesque Picaresque. The ghoul would have to have been a person, a human or other race that had somehow made his way through the world between worlds before suffering the fate that befell him. But this was far too difficult a notion to examine, there were far too many unknowns and so many questions that the young Lightheart would have needed to ask, and that would require Paechra spending time with the ghoul. Paechra considered the blatant fact that not all ghouls needed to stay aboard, but it seemed even in death the captain must go wherever it be that the ship wishes to take them. Otherwise, Paechra considered the other possibility, the possibility that the captain had remained on board the ship for his own reasons, reasons that involved her.

With this disturbing thought in the forefront of her mind, Paechra continued to make her way across the deck to where she believed that Sarah Lightheart would be waiting.

"Sister, Paechra, please wait!" Isobella-Ann's voice cried, Paechra only just able to hear it over the wind that filled the sails and caused them to balloon outwards, almost tearing them due to their agedness.

"What is it that you need from me, sister Druid?" asked Paechra. "I fear that I have kept my mother and the other Druids waiting already long enough."

"I can see from your aura that something plagues your thoughts, thought that is not why I have stopped you, Paechra," said Isobella-Ann, coming up to stand beside Paechra under one of the great sails when she saw that the younger Lightheart had heeded her call.

"Yes, I have travelled by dragon, by horseback, and dream," explained Paechra. "Traveling by sea, this sea, upon this very boat, with this same captain, it is not a new experience to me as it is to all of you others."

"I understand," said Isobella-Ann.

"How can you though?" asked Paechra. "How is it that you can say you understand?"

"We are sisters, we are Druids of the Greenwood Vale," suggested Isobella-Ann.

"This is not my first time beyond our home," said Paechra.

Isobella-Ann saw as Paechra felt her aura change as memories poured into the younger Lightheart's mind.

"Sisters talk," said Isobella-Ann plainly, as if that explained everything.

"Let me guess," sighed Paechra. "My friend Heidi has shared with some of you what she knows of my adventures in the human realm."

"I wish not to betray any of our sisterhood," began the other Druid. "But, yes, Heidi has spoken of the citizens of Andrapaal, a blacksmith, a seamstress, one who is a bird…"

"The black bird, Raven?" half asked, half laughed Paechra. "No, not a bird, but a man, and a strange man at that."

"It sounds as though all from this kingdom of Thuraen are strange," suggested Isobella-Ann. "Who in their right mind would take the life of one such as us?"

"Who in their right mind would give up their life for one such as us?" asked Paechra in return.

The young Druids both sighed, Isobella-Ann was contemplating the complexities of humankind, while Paechra was trying to recall her friend Raven's facial features and found her memory to be a blur of vagueness and uncertainty.

"So, what is it that you actually wish to know?" asked Paechra.

"What is so important to you, sister, that we risk so many precious lives?" asked Isobella-Ann.

Paechra stared out across the empty ocean, tracking the sun as it ebbed towards late afternoon.

"One man, only one human claimed the hours of my father's life," Paechra began. "I am certain that there are other humans like that one man… Not all of one race can be kind, thoughtful, caring, selfless…"

"Agreed," murmured Isobella-Ann.

"That one man who captured my father and forced him to use his knowledge and understanding, that one man who chose to steal my father from me," continued Paechra. "My father gave to me the parting words that I not paint all humans with the experience of one who is selfish and cruel, I will honor that request."

"You still have not told me why the two of us are standing upon this deck, why we go to a foreign world where peace does not reign, where enemies may be friends, and the creatures

214

who are our shared enemies attack us from our thoughts and dreams," said Isobella-Ann, an edge creeping into her tone. "I ask you why as a sister Druid and you dance around the question like you are your father's daughter."

"I am a linguist, but I am a Druid first," replied Paechra, her arms open wide. "You know me, Isobella-Ann, you know my parents and my upbringing, and that you have discovered such an upbringing has gifted me with the best and the worst of both worlds... Of that you cannot point to my heart and my mind and call foul."

Isobella-Ann made to argue back, she raised her finger and opened her mouth, but then she remained silent. Her accusation was caught in her throat and as such was unspoken.

"There, see, you cannot say the words, but I can see your frustration written upon your face and simmering at the very surface of your bubbling aura," stated Paechra. "Sadly, I cannot give the answer to you that you need to hear, sister."

"Then what can you give me, Paechra Lightheart?" Isobella-Ann demanded to know.

"A surface like the calm ocean, sister," suggested Paechra. "Ask yourself why if you doubt this cause do you still follow when none have told you that you must stay."

"Sienna Alknown, our Mother Druid, she has spoken and all must follow," stated Isobella-Ann, her arms crossed over her chest.

"No! You are wrong, sister," said Paechra, her finger jutting forward to poke Isobella-Ann in the arm. "Sienna's message was that all had a choice, and that nobody had to obey."

"Then, I guess I have chosen to follow the path like a gHjunkith, one wandering blindly after the one before until all are caught in the carnivore's den," sighed Isobella-Ann as she rubbed the place where she had been poked.

"Galumph, galumph, galoo..." laughed Paechra, giving Isobella-Ann a smile and a huge hug. "Let us both be gHjunkith together then... Better that than a feathered Urt."

"Agreed," said Isobella-Ann, a smile creeping across her face. "A bunch of gHjunkith can bite and kick all but the largest of carnivore."

"The Urt merely sing as their feathers are plucked one by one," said Paechra. "Caw... Caw... Why?"

"Why? Why? Why indeed?" laughed Isobella-Ann. "I do so sound like the helpless Urt."

"Helpless, but for its small, sharp, pecker," said Paechra with a nod.

"Watch where you place your prodder, or you may find my pecker draws blood," warned the other Druid.

"Then, may I ask that you fly free, young Urt?" begged Paechra. "I must away myself, Mother has called, and I have kept her waiting for far too long."

"I thought that all had a choice?" smirked Isobella-Ann.

"Such were the words of the Mother Druid," agreed Paechra. "But such rules do not often apply when you are dealing with your own mother."

"Especially true when your mother is Sarah Lightheart," Isobella-Ann laughed. "Perhaps you are the Urt who must fly."

"Something that we can both agree upon," said Paechra. "Sister Isobella-Ann I do hope at the end of this all that you discover what has been sacrificed and what sacrifices are yet to come are worth it for sylvan and human alike."

Isobella-Ann nodded and then turned, walking away from Paechra.

The younger Lightheart spent a few moments more looking out over the ocean before she noticed that the wind in the sails had died down slightly. Not sure of what that meant, Paechra hurried on towards the bow of the Picturesque Piceresque.

When Paechra arrived, she discovered looks of confusion, shared amongst her sisters.

"What is the meaning of this?" asked Paechra. "The ship must sail, the wind must blow, if those sheets of canvas slack there are no rowers but us sisters."

"I fear that what you believe is canvas may in fact be cured skins, human, sylvan, ghoul, who truly knows," murmured Heidi.

Paechra gave her friend a look which quietened Heidi immediately, but Paechra knew that her friend was possibly correct. She made a mental note that she would need to offer apologies to Heidi later that same day. For now, though it was important to get the strong wind blowing again.

"Sisters, we should be chanting, we need to be speaking to the wind," urged Paechra. "What is the reason for this pause?"

"Sister Lightheart," cried a couple of the Druids. "You need to see this…"

The group of Druids parted to show on the bow-deck what looked to be a large, sky-blue colored cocoon.

"What matter of creature is this, sisters?" Paechra demanded to know. "Is this some ghoulish trick that the captain has pulled?"

Heidi and a few other Druids sucked in deep breaths of shock.

"Paechra, my daughter, unfortunately I must inform you

that you have just suggested Mother Druid Sienna Alknown is some sort of insect larvae."

"The Mother Druid?" gasped Paechra. "That is Sienna Alknown."

"I am afraid so," said Sarah Lightheart as she gave a look of disapproval to her daughter.

"How?" said Paechra, both embarrassed and confused. "Why? How did it happen?"

"We hoped that Sienna may have said something to you daughter," said Sarah. "We were all chanting the prayer, the wind was blowing strong and steady, as you are well aware."

Paechra nodded but said nothing, not trusting her voice at that moment.

"As we continued to sing the song to the wind we all witnessed Alknowing Sienna was yawning, not adding her voice to the song."

"The Mother Druid is Alknown," muttered Sarah though she did not say this too loudly.

"One by one, we all slowed in our prayer as we watched Sienna transform," continued Heidi.

"The yawning became longer and more often and then this strange substance began to rise up from the deck to encase our Mother Druid," stated some of Paechra's sisters.

"It coated her feet and then rose up to her knees..." continued others.

"We tried to continue speaking to the wind," suggested Sarah Lightheart. "But eventually such a sight, such a strange transformation proved too great a distraction."

Paechra nodded, she understood, such a sight would have stolen her focus also.

"And the wind; is no one guiding the ship?" Paechra asked.

"Daughter Paechra, the wind blows where e'er it will," replied her mother, the older Lightheart.

"You summoned me, mother?" said the daughter.

"Yes, Paechra," replied Sarah. "I sent Isobella-Ann to find you as soon as Sienna started to transform, she was supposed to return with you, to hurry you to assist."

"She did not," said Paechra. "In fact, she waylaid me and then walked away… There was no mention of urgency."

"I see," murmured Sarah.

"I must seek an audience with Captain Overtain," announced Paechra. "We must know if this has happened before, is it a curse from the ship, an effect of our spell, some trick that the ghouls have played upon us?"

"Halt, daughter, this is not your sole responsibility," announced Sarah Lightheart. "I shall join you when we face this ghoul."

"Mother I have faced Overtain before," stated Paechra. "I'll do this."

"Have you forgotten, Paechra, I have been the last one to speak with this ghoul, if any of us are to speak with him about this it should be me."

Paechra sighed as she realized that there would be no winning an argument with her mother.

"Come, then, we go together," she said.

Chapter Ten

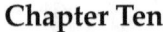

Dangers upon the Sea

In the realm of Dreams, who can truly believe they are master?

**From the Fifth Stanza of the Prophecy, translated by the sages
of the Kingdom of Thuraen 306th year**

ABOARD THE GHOUL-ship, The Picturesque Picaresque, the
sisters of the Sacred Grove of Greenwood Vale stood idle. The
wind that they had conjured had died down to a mere whisker
of a breeze, the ship slowing to a snail's pace. Paechra thought
not of this, focused instead on the mystery of the strange
cocoon that had formed about the Mother Druid, Sienna.

"Have you never seen anything like this happen before?"
the younger Lightheart asked of her mother, Sarah.

"No, never daughter, Paechra," admitted Sarah Lightheart. "This is the first I have witnessed such a strange phenomenon, I worry what will emerge when the cocoon breaks open."

"None of you others have heard of such?" asked Paechra then, especially focused on catching the eye of the elder Druids.

In turn each one shook their head, indicating that over the centuries they had lived such a strange sight had never been witnessed, nor recounted.

"This must be the work of the ship then," decided Paechra. "Some form of revenge orchestrated by Captain Overtain, since he could not claim me for his crew, so he has instead found a way to claim someone close to my heart for his ship."

"I am yet to be convinced that this is not some other such thing," suggested Sarah, suddenly doubtful.

"Mother, do you question my logic?" replied Paechra, almond eyes narrowed. "Or is it your own courage that is in question?"

"Daughter, Paechra, I have taught you far better than that," stated Sarah as the pair marched across the deck of the Picturesque Picaresque, the name given to the ghoul-ship.

Paechra stopped and looked deeply into her mother's eyes.

"Daughter you speak of logic where there seems little to no evidence that such exists," Sarah stated, calmly, not fazed by the look Paechra was giving her.

"Mother, you speak of lessons you have taught me, where both of us know much of my learning came from my father, not you Sienna, and of course my own exploration," retorted the daughter.

Paechra expected her mother to bite back with her own retort, but instead Sarah Lightheart began to laugh. It was a laugh that was less full of mirth, more a dry chortle, an

221

admission of failure, or the closest thing Sarah would offer of such an admission.

"What you accuse me of I cannot deny," the elder Lightheart finally said.

To this Paechra nodded, but remained silent, listening.

"But as a child you were always in your father's shadow, something that Mother Druid Sienna asked me to encourage," Sarah continued. "I went against my instincts, not that I would have every considered myself as motherly anyway... We did have moments shared though when it could be confirmed we were mother and daughter, and sister Druids..."

Again, the elder Lightheart smiled, and laughed. This time it was an honest sound, Sarah recalling fond memories.

"I guess you saw the beautiful relationship that had grown between me and my father..." said Paechra.

"You soaked up what he taught you, lessons of the world, tales of places beyond the forest, realms I had never considered, never thought about, not until you left us dear daughter," Sarah explained.

Now it was Paechra's turn to reflect, to reminisce.

"I thought of you, mother, of you and of Greenwood Vale," Sarah's daughter said. "The world of humans was a strange one, is a strange one, made stranger still when I befriended Raven."

"And yet, you did not think of turning your back upon this strangeness and returning to the familiar?" asked Sarah. "Not even a message to ease my worries?"

"No," replied Paechra. "What was before my very eyes took all of my focus and thought to understand, mother."

Paechra and Sarah both wavered as the great ship lurched.

"Much as now, my daughter?" suggested Paechra's mother.

"You believe me not, but your mind will change when we arrive in the land of the humankind," replied Paechra. "You will see, as I did, I just know it."

"Before we can arrive, we must go again," said Sarah Lightheart, giving her daughter a look of urgency.

"Agreed, mother," Paechra replied. "The cabin of Captain Overtain is just up ahead."

"Why though does the wind remain so flat?" asked the elder Lightheart. "The sails have become so lifeless."

"Mother Sienna was leading the song…" Paechra explained. "When the curse encased her it seems the song was forgot."

"Nonsense, daughter," snorted Sarah. "You and I and all of the other sisters of the Druid's belief, we all know the song to sing."

"Then let the two of us sing it now," laughed Paechra, suddenly the solution seeming so foolishly obvious.

"You begin, I shall follow your tone and harmonize," urged Sarah.

Paechra took in a deep breath of pure sea air, but when she tried to find the words that the wind wanted to hear, her mind was empty, blank.

"Daughter, will you not sing?" asked Sarah of the younger Lightheart. "Know you not the words?"

"Nay mother," said Paechra, a whisper. "I know not the spell, not in sylvan, nor human tongue, nor the natural tones of the song."

"There is more to this mystery," Sarah suggested. "We must find the captain and find him now."

"Come, this way," Paechra said, she beckoned to her mother,

and without another word shared Sarah Lightheart followed.

Paechra searched frantically for the familiar cabin door. She passed by the place where she had previously resided, sharing a cabin with the human queen Catherine, her unborn child, and the butcher Thomas. This cabin had forced Paechra to answer some difficult questions, and Paechra considered where it was that all would reside during this voyage. That had all been arranged this time by Sienna and Sarah, and Sienna was unavailable to ask, while Paechra found her mother was less than open with those details. When she and her mother faced Captain Overtain, Paechra vowed to pry from the ghoul what information she sought.

There seemed to be a clear sky of blue in front and behind the ship, to the port and starboard also. Paechra began to realize that the mist she associated with travel aboard The Picturesque Picaresque was now all in her mind.

"Mother, Sarah, I understand now why the song has left us all," exclaimed the younger Lightheart.

"Why then, Paechra," asked Sarah. "What is the solution to this mystery?"

"Look inwards," said the daughter. "Bring forth the magic, engage with the spirits."

Paechra watched as her mother attempted to cast even the simplest of spells.

"I... I... I can't," murmured Sarah.

"In the past I have heard speak of the mist that shrouds this nightmare ship, I myself have experienced such when I did travel with the humans," said Paechra, resting a calming hand upon her mother's shoulder.

"I too have heard of such a mist, every mention of The Picaresque never fails to include the mist," grumbled Sarah Lightheart.

"But now the sky is clear, it is as if we have outrun this mist," Paechra continued.

"I had assumed that our spell had caused the ship to outpace the mist, to break free of the blanket, revealing all secrets as the sun beamed down upon us," said Sarah. "You believe, daughter, that such is not the case?"

"I thought at first mother, that our combined power was far greater than captain and ship," explained Paechra. "As did you, and in fact all of us believe, I thought we had broken the spell and removed the threat that ghoul and ship presented."

"Daughter, Paechra, we are dead in the water, what you need say please say it now," urged Sarah.

"I believe that the mist has entered our minds," Paechra finally told her mother. "The minds of us all."

Sarah shook her head in disbelief.

"No, such magics cannot be possible…" stated Sarah. "And yet… It would explain so much…"

"Feel what the ship is telling us mother," suggested Paechra. "Not with your mind, not with your memory, just physically feel…"

"We are traveling backwards!" cried Sarah in alarm.

It was true. The breeze that was magically propelling the great ship towards Andrapaal as the Druids sang had died down to nothingness. Now the wind had begun blowing the opposite way, the strange sails had billowed out against the mast and The Picturesque Picaresque had begun moving at a slow pace in reverse.

As if the magics that had frozen her to the deck, just like the Mother Druid, had suddenly become undone, Sarah broke into a run.

"Hurry daughter, to the cabin."

"Mother slow, wait!" Paechra called, urgently. "You and I know not what to expect once we enter that cabin."

"We can wait no longer, child," called back Sarah.

The distance between mother and daughter seemed to grow exponentially. Finally, though Paechra was able to motivate her limbs to push against the fog that had invaded her thoughts. Step by step she made her way further up the deck of the ship. The distance between the two main masts seemed to take forever to cross.

"No, mother," moaned Paechra as she witnessed Sarah Lightheart reach the cabin of Captain Overtain and seemingly without a moment of thought throw open the doorway and step inside.

As if chains were suddenly broken, with the door to the captain's cabin closed again, Paechra felt herself released. Enveloping herself in blue and chanting the familiar words of a protection spell the younger Lightheart bounded along the ship's deck, wolf-like, upon all fours.

"Release her!" demanded Paechra, snarling. "Release my mother, it is me you want."

As usual, the cabin of Captain Overtain was dark, a true contrast to the glorious sunshine that poured warmly across the deck of The Picturesque Picaresque. As Paechra's almond eyes adjusted to the change in light, she gasped. The captain, more deathly, diseased, and afflicted by the ghoul curse, sat again at the head of the table, but this time there was a figure nestled, comfortably within his lap.

"Isobella-Ann?" said Paechra in surprise.

"Indeed, Isobella-Ann," growled Sarah.

Paechra's mother was surrounded by a purplish glow, the shape of a falcon, a very angry falcon.

"Yes, Isobella-Ann," laughed the other Druid. "I am surprised that the Lightheart Druids did not suspect me as being a traitor."

The Druid turned her head to reveal marks upon her neck resembling the disease that covered Captain Overtain.

Paechra took one look at those marks and her narrowed eyes opened, sympathy quickly replacing fury.

"How? When did this happen?" Paechra asked.

"We care not to know such trivial details," growled the elder Lightheart. "Regardless of when and how, what remains and that we have been betrayed."

"Come, come, Sister Sarah," Isobella-Ann continued, her voice like tiny bells, melodic, slightly maniacal. "Let me explain…"

The shadow of the falcon flapped purple wings and exposed claws that wished to tear at Isobella-Ann's throat, to wipe away that confident smile.

"Mother, please let her speak," requested Paechra.

Sarah looked at her daughter in such a way that Paechra thought mayhap her mother had forgot she was even there. Silence was created between the two of the Lightheart name, a silence that Isobella-Ann was more than happy to fill.

"You are not the only one who dreams, Paechra Lightheart," Isobella-Ann began. "Though your dreams are of our enemies, the wolves who cast long shadows with arcana so dark that it

227

shrivels their tiny hearts."

"Such dreams have jeopardized our mission," stated Paechra, carefully choosing her words. "But we have been able to refocus, and we have found a way to harness such dreaming in the end to our benefit."

"Of whom do you dream?" Sarah asked of Isobella-Ann, though she asked in such a way that she suggested the answer was already known, known, and despised.

Isobella-Ann ignored Sarah's tone.

"Thank you for your asking, sister Sarah," Isobella-Ann replied with her smirk remaining. "I was dreaming of a darker power, a darker promise, a darker love."

"My love," said Captain Overtain, milky white eyes softened as he tilted his head and with a claw-like hand cupped Isobella-Ann's cheek, drawing her towards him so their lips could embrace.

"So, you have sold out all of Greenwood Vale, that you may share in this monstrosity and his sickness?" asked Sarah in disbelief.

Paechra could understand though, seeing Isobella-Ann and Captain Overtain together brought on thoughts of Raven, the Truth Keeper Johannas Stormsong, Michael's son. For a single moment Paechra wondered what fate had befallen her friend. That moment passed by swiftly though as her mother, Sarah, rushed forward.

"You should be punished for your foolery," announced the elder Lightheart as the purple light that surrounded her glowed brightly.

As luck would have it the long table that Paechra was familiar with blocked her mother's path. As Sarah came within a yard of striking, Isobella-Ann revealed just how far the transition of the ghoul disease had already progressed. A face that was partially melted, sliding from muscle and skull uncovered razor-sharp, elongated teeth that hungered to pierce through delicate, sylvan skin.

"I wish to eat, to feast!" announced Isobella-Ann, her lips that were only moments before caught up in the embrace of lust were then mere inches away from Sarah's wrist as they snapped shut.

"Calm, my love, we will both enjoy the banquet that stands before us," sedated the captain.

Paechra pulled back her mother as quickly as she could, before Sarah or Isobella-Ann could jump upon the table and bridge the tiny gap between them.

"You ooze of confidence, captain," stated Paechra. "And yet I see that there are only two of you, and we are numbered the same."

"Ah, young Paechra, sweet flesh and clever mind," smiled Captain Overtain, revealing his own fangs, a tongue flicking out and running along cracked lips. "Once again you miss the point, the big picture, that which is hidden in plain sight."

"Reveal your trickery, Overtain," growled Sarah, the purple light growing stronger, brighter.

"Paechra, do you wish to see how the trick is done?" asked the captain, ignoring the elder Lightheart's comments.

"Or would you rather remain as you always seem to enjoy being?" laughed Isobella-Ann. "In the darkness, unknowing, unsure, lost?"

"I am not lost," stated Paechra, though her voice lacked its usual confidence. "I know exactly where I am."

"You think you are aboard a ship, my ship," said the ghoul, smiling wickedly. "But where is my ship?"

"Upon the sea of dreams," Paechra stated, just realizing their potentially fatal mistake.

The captain's cabin became darkness all around the edges, door, walls, ceiling, and floor, all vanished, replaced with nothingness. All that remained were the table, the chair, and the four figures. Then four became eight, twelve, twenty... From the darkness came the growl and howl of the vorsurk.

"You are not the only one who can dream, Paechra Lightheart," laughed Captain Overtain, believing he had finally won. "And aboard this ship, I am master of the dreaming."

In panic Paechra dug deeply inside and a brilliant light of pure white burst forth from out of her very core. The younger Lightheart heard her mother cry out her name, at the same time Isobella-Ann screeched in pain.

"You will not defeat me twice upon my own ship," vowed Overtain. "Never have I been beaten once, I promise you, I shall claim my revenge, my prize, your soul shall be mine."

Paechra sensed rather than saw the effects that her light had had upon the vorsurk, half of them stumbling back into the darkness to get away as their ghoulish hides bubbled and boiled. The remaining pushed forward to reach her, to distract her, to break the spell she had cast in an instant. Paechra's mother bit, scratched, and clawed at the wolves that strove to bring down her daughter. And then where no door had been before, suddenly the cabin portal burst open.

"To my shoulder, boy!" cried the voice of Anton, heard by Paechra clear as a thundering gong.

"Here?" squeaked the voice of Thomas, obviously wanting to be anywhere else but there at that moment.

"I said, my left, boy, my left..." berated Anton. "Now strike!!"

Paechra saw Thomas' aura waver from a sickly yellow to a pail blue. It was then and only then that she also noticed the black, shadowy aura that surrounded the ghoul captain, a similar shadow faintly enveloping Isobella-Ann and the vorsurk she could see.

As Thomas thrust clumsily with a ship's spear and Anton struck one of the vorsurk with a broad-bladed blow, Paechra focused upon her hands. Two claws of bright-white flew forward and grabbed hold of the black shadow that surrounded Overtain.

"You dare!" the captain cried in disbelief.

He slumped in his chair as all of the ghoul's physical presence vanished, bolstering his arcane, his pitch-black soul.

Paechra found her spiritual hands that had attempted to rip the soul apart, suddenly faced a great struggle. Overtain pulled, Paechra pulled back. The two powers engaged in a tugging match that the Druid was not certain she could win. If the battle had taken place in the sacred grove it would have already been a victory for Paechra, aboard the ship in the realm of dreams, Overtain had the advantage. As the physical battle continued to play out around them Paechra and Overtain only focused upon each other. The dark aura syphoned off more and more of Paechra's dazzling purity, the young Lightheart having need to draw more and more inwardly. All the while the darkness from outside seemed to squeeze Paechra tight, the fog in her mind threatened to become everything and then nothing. In a last-ditch effort, the daughter felt her mother's presence; together they struck.

#

Paechra, surrounded by darkness, found herself in a great spiritual struggle against the ghoul Overtain. As the captain of the Ship the Picturesque Picaresque pulled, Paechra pulled back. The two auras were engaged in a tugging match that the Druid was not a hundred percent sure she could win. Paechra could only just sense the physical skirmish that was happening close by in the captain's cabin, her focus solely upon herself and the ghoul, unable to allocate even a slither of her focus to anything but the battle in the ethereal. Overtain's dark aura syphoned off more and more of Paechra's dazzling purity, the young Lightheart having need to draw more and more inwardly. All the while the darkness from outside seemed to squeeze Paechra tight, the fog in her mind threatened to become everything and then nothing. In a last-ditch effort, the daughter felt her mother's presence, joining her in the battle of spirits.

"I will not lose you, daughter," announced Sarah Lightheart. "I did have you away from my side for so long already, I'll not accept that such absence will be eternal."

"Is the battle beyond already won?" the daughter asked, surprised, but hopeful.

"Nay, it still continues," said Sarah. "Though it seems, our captain does not know well the beliefs of the vorsurk."

"I believe enough in my own power, upon my own ship," growled the ghoul. "I have turned one of yours against you, it will be child's play to claim those that remain against me."

"You'll not have us as your ship's crew," replied Paechra as her aura clutched the spectral hand of her mother.

Sarah Lightheart gasped, and her aura shimmered as Paechra drew deeply upon her mother's soul, the younger Lightheart then yanked with all of her mental might, tearing the ghoul's dark shadow right out of his body.

The aura smiled, wickedly, suddenly growing to double its size now that it was free of the physical restraints of a body.

Paechra released her ethereal grip on her mother and then allowed her mind to return to the physical realm. In doing so she let go of the dark, growing shade, and it snapped instantly back into the ghoul-shaped cage that held it captive.

Choas ruled the cabin, still dark, but not nearly as purely dark as the ethereal realm. Anton stood shakily, fending off a slice from Isobella-Ann whose purple aura resembled a fierce jungle cat. Back to back with Anton was Thomas who somehow was keeping two vorsurk on the back foot, a flurry of random strikes with a pair of dancing daggers, each blade equally confusing and deadly. Paechra counted seventeen of the vorsurk, too many for the cabin space and way more than the eleven, or factor of eleven that the religion of the wolf-like creatures demanded for a battle. Normally there would be present one sorcerer, accompanied by ten, one hundred and twenty, or sometimes one thousand, three hundred and thirty of the grunt soldiers. It seemed to Paechra that Overtain had opened up the portal of dreaming and drove in as many soldiers as he thought would fit. Paechra imagined the furious sorcerer, located somewhere, suddenly short so much fodder, without meaning, Overtain had probably saved some humans or sylvan, possibly both.

"We're not done yet," growled the captain, suddenly returned to his physical form, sword drawn, tip held under Paechra's chin.

"Oh, I feel we are," stated Paechra, she could both sense and see that her mother still remained in the spiritual tug-of-war.

Satisfied, Paechra watched the light vanish from Captain

Overtain's eyes as his soul was again dragged out of his physical form. The sword tip scrapped across Paechra's throat lightly, drawing a single droplet of blood. Paechra cloaked herself in the blue image of a hawk before she ran a claw down Isobella-Ann's exposed back.

"Ahhhh!" cried the Druid that had been bitten by Overtain the ghoul. "You shall pay for such."

"Catch me," demanded Paechra. "If you indeed dare to try."

With a single kick the young Lightheart burst forth from the darkness of the cabin and into a world of mist. With the cry of a hunter, she took to the sky. A moment later Paechra felt that she was pursued as Isobella-Ann made her own transformation. The pair put on quite an aeronautical show, though there were none, but maybe Sienna Alknown, who had the opportunity to watch, though none truly understood what had happened to the wise, aged Druid.

Paechra in hawk-form took a quick glance over her left wing and cursed. She had chosen the spirit of a fast flyer, just as previously she had chosen a fierce combatant in the bear, but Isoballa-Ann had chosen to take on the form of the Akknoo-Ruu, a sylvan forest bird whose speed far our striped any animal known to humans. Perhaps too long had Paechra been in the realm of those other than her own, she was forgetting much, relying on knowledge that seemed to be no longer there, or at the very best a distant second in consideration. The very instant that Paechra thought of the creatures known to the sylvan people she immediately changed her form into the littlest bug known to her kind. The Thy-Lth-Rewoln was similar in size to a flea, but far greater at distant flights. In her new form, the youngest Lightheart vanished in the strange mist, part ocean, part ship's creation, and with satisfaction heard the cry of frustration come from Isobella-Ann. Hovering in the thick mist, Paechra made a great gamble, waiting with tiny mouth open, hoping that Isobella-Ann would continue the same flight path. With a cry of triumph, the Akknoo-Ruu appeared quite suddenly, at the very moment that Paechra transformed herself into the largest sea creature known to the sylvan people, a Mth-Hja-Ioiputh…

As Isobella-Ann flew into the wide, opened maw it snapped shut on the great, leathery beast and, broadtail first, Paechra and her captive plummeted back towards the Picturesque Picaresque. There came a great crash as Paechra's gigantic form took out one of the ship's masts, before a meaty slap announced she had returned to the deck. There was an awkward feeling inside Paechra's great gut as Isobella-Ann made a transformation of her own. In a pool of orange sickness, the ghoul-bitten Druid reappeared in the shape of a Juu, known to those humans who had witnessed such a creature by the name of Puff-Spines, due to its ability to grow in size during times of danger and sprout large, spear-like quills that could be fired towards enemies and threats.

"Curse you," growled Paechra, pulling a quill from her thigh and watching her veins turn black as they absorbed the poison.

Isobella-Ann also returned to her natural form.

"Give up, sister," she demanded of Paechra. "You have lost, and you will die."

"Not yet, will I die," Paechra replied. "Today is not my day."

Muttering under her breath a spell, Paechra then enveloped herself in the brilliant white light of her inner being.

"The Juu poison will work through your body, quicker than even you can react," Isobella-Ann then boasted. "Face it, Paechra Lightheart, you have lost, and I have won."

235

At that moment Paechra activated her spell. She focused the dazzling white light upon her thigh where the poison resided and, painfully, dragged it out from her body.

"Impossible!" hissed Isobella-Ann, a mixture of frustration and awe. "None have ever managed to remove the poison before now, let alone so quickly."

Paechra risked a moment to glance up at her enemy and give her a gritted-teeth grin. She dared not retort though; focus was paramount at that very moment. The poison seemed to have a life of its own as it struggled to seep back into Paechra's form, even trying to bond with her aura. Eventually the whole black and purple mess was drawn out, writhing in the sea air.

"What now, dear Paechra," said the voice of Sarah Lightheart.

Paechra's mother had stepped out from the cabin of Captain Overtain, covered in scratches, and deeper wounds. Paechra's friend Heidi appeared beside the elder Lightheart, helping her to stand.

"See, Isobella-Ann," muttered Paechra, under deep strain. "The captain is vanquished, you are alone."

Sarah began to speak, but Heidi placed a gentle hand upon her shoulder and Paechra's mother stopped before she had even begun.

"If such is indeed the case, then return the poison from whence it first did come," begged Isobella-Ann.

"I will not," announced Paechra. "Not until you reveal what curse you and Captain Overtain have placed upon Mother Druid Sienna Alknown."

"A curse? I know nothing of such a thing," replied Isobella-Ann.

"But you must," stated Sarah and Paechra, together.

"Isobella-Ann was present when the Mother Druid began to change," stated Heidi.

"But so too were you," Isobella-Ann bit back. "All sisters, except for Paechra Lightheart, the precious one... All others were there when the change began."

"Are you suggesting that my daughter played a part in why and how the Mother Druid was captured and cocooned?" Sarah demanded to know.

"We were all casting the wind spell," argued Isobella-Ann in her defense. "None of us noticeably altered the words, none of us could have known such a strange change would occur."

"None of us thought it possible that one we call sister could possibly betray us, such as we have witnessed you do, Isobella-Ann," suggested Sarah Lightheart.

"Wait!" cried Paechra. "If what our sister says is true then there is only one explanation for the change that our Mother Druid has undergone."

"And that is..?" Sarah, Isobella-Ann, and Heidi all begged to know.

"For some reason, perhaps, Sienna Alknown has undertaken this cocoonment on purpose, herself," Paechra suggested.

"Strange, but possible," considered Sarah. "I've not heard of it happening before, though."

"Perhaps, our Mother Druid is the first to discover it," Heidi suggested.

"I believe sister Isobella-Ann when she claims no knowledge of how the transformation did come about," said Paechra. "I sense no ill magicks emanating from the ship, and I do not believe that our captain has any great knowledge of the dark powers of captivity."

"I sense it too," announced Sarah Lightheart. "Captain Overtain is more a captive than a captor."

"As now am I," added Isobella-Ann, her tone reverberating melancholy and regret. "Is there any chance perhaps sister Paechra that your brilliant light may have an effect on ghoul bites?"

Paechra awoke in that moment to the fact she still had in her possession that cloud of Juu poison.

"It seems a very sisterly thing to do," stated Paechra then. "To act rashly and consider afterward the consequences."

"Be ye human, sylvan, or other race," suggested Heidi. "Such a show of thoughtlessness seems natural for all."

"The monster is free!!" suddenly announced the panicked voice of Thomas the Butcher of Andrapaal, bursting from the captain's cabin.

"The monster?" mouthed Paechra, catching her mother's eyes.

Anton was at Thomas' heals.

"Move lad! Make haste! Make way!" demanded the Head Truth Keeper, both he and Thomas wishing they were back home again, far from the ship and the mysterious sea.

Billowing out from the cabin came Captain Overtain, or whatever it was that the captain of the Picturesque Picaresque had become. Over the course of the skirmish that had occurred in the dark, cramped space of the cabin and in the ethereal realm, the world between worlds, it seemed to Paechra that the ghoul had melded and molded with some of the souls of the vorsurk soldiers that he had brought to his side via the dreaming. The younger Lightheart could count at the very least five heads, including two half-heads that sprouted from the underside of the beast. It was difficult to determine where physical ended, and aura began. The creature roared, gurgled, and then made a noise like laughter.

"You lied!" cried Isobella-Ann. "The ghoul does live, if such can be called living…"

"Wish you to side with such a beast?" asked Heidi, genuinely surprised.

"I am bit," said Isobella-Ann, mater-of-factly. "I fear I have not a great deal of choice."

Again, the purple aura encased the Druid and once more the Juu landed with a slap upon the deck of the ship. Paechra quickly forced the struggling cloud of poison towards Overtain.

"Paechra, just let go and leave!" urged Sarah her mother. "We must all take cover, transform and fly…"

"What of the humans?" questioned Paechra. "I'll not leave them, nor will I leave the Mother Druid."

"Curse you and your kindness," replied Sarah, but she smiled, proud of her daughter's pure goodness.

"I shall counter our sister, fear not," announced Heidi, and in a matter of moments she had cast a glowing sphere of protection atop the fish, just as it reached full expansion, just as the spears shot out one by one.

Each spear was stopped, except for one which flew across the starboard side of the ship and vanished into the sea. Isobella-Ann transformed once more, this time into the form of a hulking forest beast. Sarah took on a similar form and the pair rose up upon hindquarters and, with meaty claws, sought an opening to slash. Heidi took a differing approach and took on the form of a tiny Thy-Lth-Rewoln, flying about the two combatants, seeking a place to land and bite. Paechra forced the cloud of poison to strike one of Overtain's faces, a wolf-like maw that howled and snarled as the darkness vanished up nostrils and into other orifices.

"And… You call… ME… evil…" gasped and gargled the voice of Overtain.

"I cannot go on!" cried Thomas. "I am sorry Paechra, I am sorry Johannas… Anton…"

With that said, the butcher then tossed his weapons and ran, fleeing from the ghoul, the skirmish, and the battle. Paechra heard Anton curse.

"Looks like it's up to us, witch," the Head Truth Keeper laughed.

Paechra watched on as Anton then danced in and swung at the beast Overtain had become. The human's blade struck true and two of the heads howled in pain. Paechra witnessed the poison seeping across their eyes, black blood mixed with aura drifting out to be caught by the wind.

"The wind!" cried Paechra.

The other Druids had once more begun the chant, and the ship was again on the move.

"Anton, stop!" Paechra then commanded.

The human swung again, and his sword sliced another wound.

"We cannot stop!" growled Anton. "Not until this monster is slain!"

"No, you are wrong, but equally right!" Paechra argued. "Even with the aid of the wind, we cannot reach the shore without the captain."

"You speak in riddles again, witch," growled Anton, raising his blade to strike again.

"We need someone to steer the ship!" explained Paechra, her urgency causing Anton to pause.

"Kill me..." gargled Overtain's voice. "You... will... sail... FOR... EVER..."

"What do we do then?" Anton demanded to know.

It was dawning on the human that this was not a battle he wanted to win, but equally, none of them could pay the price of losing.

"Protect me," commanded Paechra, then trusting that Anton would do as she asked, she closed her eyes and allowed her aura to guide her.

Darkness, all around her Paechra sense nothing but darkness. Her brilliant light could not penetrate the dark and it felt as though the very essence of evil was surrounding her. Paechra pulsed and the presence retracted, burnt by goodness. In this way the younger Lightheart navigated the dark, hoping beyond hope that she could find what she sought. After a moment she saw it, another glowing presence, a beacon in the dark. It was far, but it gladdened Paechra's heart to see that it was there.

"Mother?" Paechra's spirit called. "Sienna?"

"Daughter, you have found me!" a much younger version of Sienna called back.

And then they were together, side by side, and Paechra sensed that she had physically made her way to where Sienna Alknown still stood, cocooned upon the deck of the Picturesque Picaresque.

"Why did you choose to leave us, Mother?" Paechra asked. "Why did you leave us in our time of need?"

"It is because I foresaw this time that I chose to leave you all," Sienna replied. "I was given a vision, and I was told by our ancestors of a way to preserve my powers..."

"But you are all powerful!" stated Paechra.

"What I am, or what I was at least, I was old, and frail, and tired," explained Sienna. "What I am now is strong, strong enough to help you, strong enough to right this ship and return its captain to the helm."

"Let us work together then," said Paechra. "Let us banish the darkness and find a way to continue on to Andrapaal."

"Take my hands," requested Sienna.

When Paechra did as she was bid she felt youthfulness as well as wisdom, the best of all states.

"And now?" asked Paechra.

"Patience, daughter, listen, learn," urged Sienna.

Paechra thought that the Mother Druid was scolding her, but then she opened her mind and began to hear the chant, to feel the rhythm that was trying so hard to break up the dark.

"I feel it, I hear it, I know it," stated Paechra in awe.

"That is because it is you, daughter," Sienna explained. "You, me, us, life… The goodness will drive away the dark… There will be balance… Good and evil existing together…"

"I understand," whispered the younger Lightheart.

Together Sienna and Paechra began to chant, with each syllable entuned a tendril of light flew out from the embracing pair and wrapped around the dark. The world then became lighter. Bit by bit it changed.

#

Raven groaned as the pain in his arm throbbed. Whatever challenges Paechra faced, Raven thought his and Derek's predicament was a hundred times worse. His link to the lasting effects of shared dreaming that he thought would transport him and Derek to Paechra's side had instead landed the pair in the midst of a small force of vorsurk. Monstrous, wolf-like humanoids who had an equal hatred for sylvan and human alike. In fact, any race not vorsurk were either food, slaves, or both in the eyes and minds of such creatures. The force had been somewhat defeated, dilapidated enough that Derek's blade could slay two more, but the brutes still outweighed the pair by size and numbers. Swiftly Raven and Derek found themselves bound together, by hand and foot, and then chained by the other arm to the top bar of the cage they were brutally herded into.

"At least we are alive," Raven said.

Derek laughed at this, a dark, manic sound without hope.

"You not… Remember vorsurk…" the sylvan stated dryly. "Of course… You do not…"

"My people know them more than you do," Raven argued. "For it was your race who stuck us as a barrier between hunter and hunted…"

There was a grunt from the beast who limped along beside the cage, not understanding what was being said between the pair, but not happy the pair were talking.

"You know… Warriors harass your boarder… But forget… Cruelty of vorsurk camps… Your ancestors enslaved…" continued the sylvan low prince, ignoring the barbaric beast.

Raven watched the sylvan's face screw up in pain as he was stabbed between the cage bars, a spear shaft jabbing him in the ribs. This was followed by another grunt from the vorsurk.

Raven tried to stretch to comfort the sylvan, but any effort was waved away.

"Rest... Sleep... Energy needed... Later time..." Derek said.

Raven nodded and tried to find what sleep he could. The rocking of the wagon eventually sent him into the realm of nightmares; thoughts of past experiences he had had with the vorsurk, and visions of what was yet to come.

Chapter Eleven

What Little We Know

The wisdom of the Lioness is trust

The words of the serpent merely the summer's breeze

From the seventh stanza of the Prophecy, translated by the sages of the Kingdom of Thuraen 514th year

PAECHRA STOOD IN the world between worlds, hand in hand with Mother Druid Sienna Alknown. The world in which the pair existed upon the deck of the great ship, The Picturesque Picaresque, was real, but so too was the spirit realm where the pair stood together as one, singing away the darkness. With each note harmoniously sounded, a tendril of light flew out from the embracing pair and wrapped around the dark. The world then became lighter. Bit by bit it changed.

Bit by bit the dark became grey, the good and the evil becoming balanced once more, neither any more powerful than the other. The world of chaos becoming just a little saner.

Paechra sensed her mother, Sarah Lightheart, and friend Heidi, battling the changing Druid Isobella-Ann who had been bitten by Overtain and was sadly becoming a ghoul like he was. In her heart, the younger Druid felt for her sister, Isobella-Ann, and wished there was something that Druid magic could do to help. Alas, the bite from a ghoul was something beyond even Sienna's understanding, it seemed that Isobella-Ann's fate was sealed.

Beside Sarah and Heidi, fought Anton. Brave, foolish, human, Anton, he was, Paechra hoped taking on the monstrosity that was the ship's captain, not wanting to destroy the ghoul, but equally not wanting him to claim more victims with his bite. For all had come to realize that the Picturesque Picaresque needed a captain, if Overtain was slain in battle then Paechra and her army would be doomed to sail forever.

"Paechra, daughter, heed my words," said the voice of Sienna.

"I hear you, Mother Druid, I am your Daughter of the Forest and I am listening," replied Paechra.

"The darkness has turned to the grey mist of old," stated the voice of Sienna. "I feel the ship has heard the song of the wind, it has picked up speed, and soon we will be clear of immediate danger."

Paechra paused for a moment and found that she too could hear her sister Druids chanting, equally she could feel the soul of the great sea juggernaut cruising through the mystical waters.

"What have you need me do, Sienna Alknown?" asked Paechra.

"Leave me, child, return to those who need you most," suggested Sienna.

"And you? What of you, Mother?" asked the younger of the Lightheart family.

"Fear not for me child, I will be safe within my cocoon," said Sienna with a smile. "I think you, Paechra Lightheart, for your concern."

Paechra nodded, and then, with a mere thought, she stepped away from the realm of spirits and souls and again found herself upon the bow of the Picturesque Picaresque, the mummified figure of Mother Druid Sienna seemingly a mystery, a statue, still beside her. Midship the world was not still, however. While the breeze filled the sails causing them to bellow and flap, the Druids, twenty in total, sang and chanted, helping the wind to rise, and whip, and play with the grand ship. Further along Paechra found the battle still continued, Anton desperately pressing the monstrous ghoul, Captain Overtain, pushing the giant slug towards the ship's wheel that simply span freely, like a child twirling, without rhyme or reason. Each blow landed by Anton, Head Truth Keeper of Andrapaal, seemed to sever free a vorsurk which in turn was slashed and cut down by the capable human. Wolfish limbs, jaws, ears, all littered the deck, a pile of trophies that were a reward to Anton for his efforts. As she came swiftly closer, Paechra could see though that the warrior of old was tiring. Overtain struck with open maw and two claws simultaneously. Anton had no hope to deflect all three of the trio of attacks. The maw was met with sword blade, but the two claws both struck home.

"Thomas I need you!" called a clearly angered Anton.

"Good!" laughed Captain Overtain. "I feed on your aura! Your frustration gives me strength!"

247

"I am here to aid you!" called Paechra.

"Have you no other fight but mine? grumbled the Head Truth Keeper, but Paechra could sense that Anton was actually relieved to have someone assist him.

Paechra adopted the form of a great sea serpent, wrapping herself around the chaotic form of Overtain and squeezing tight. The captain's claws tried to dig into the snake's skin but time and time again they just slid off.

"I give in! I give in!" cried the ghoul.

He slid free of the mass and landed gracefully upon the deck of the ship. The vorsurk that made up the bulk of the monstrosity also drifted apart as the enchantment came to an end. Paechra quickly calculated that six of the wolf-like creatures remained. Surprisingly two of the six were dressed in robes instead of armor.

"Sorcerers," hissed the Druid.

"Leave the warriors to me, witch," announced Anton.

Without waiting for Paechra to reply, the human leapt at two of the vorsurk with a tired and clumsy swing of his sword. It was easily knocked aside as too was Anton. He rolled to rest against the door to the Captain's Cabin and was still.

"Anton!" cried Thomas, the butcher, appearing from the shadows caused by the sun upon the great mast.

Paechra considered for a brief moment that the chant of her sisters must be working successfully if the great ship had pulled so far clear of the mist that the sun was able to be seen.

Thomas took up Anton's blade in two shaking hands and swung it wildly. One of the vorsurk was cut across the face and the other three stepped backward to create some distance between them and the human.

"You keep away from my friend!" Thomas cried, giving each of the wolfish warriors a wide-eyed glare.

As if drawn to the scene from commotion or will alone, a swarm of sylvan arrived, grappling and grasping the warriors. Paechra took her eye off the sorcerers for only a second, but that was all of the time that the pair needed to disappear.

"We are not finished with you yet, Druid..." one whispered harshly in Paechra's ear, a faint, but clear warning.

"Well, I am not finished with you, either," Paechra replied, but she knew that the threat had already gone.

"What do we do now?" Thomas asked, sword still held out awkwardly, looking for a target.

"If you can, heave that vorsurk over the side, and then tend to Anton," Paechra ordered.

Thomas nodded and then gently put down the blade.

"Mistress Paechra," asked the sylvan. "What is it that shall be done with the remaining vorsurk?"

Paechra paused for a moment, pondering before she chose to reply.

"We certainly cannot bring them with us?" said the Druid. "It would be far too risky to transport them the remainder of the way to Andrapaal, only to have them then escape and join the others of their kind that I suspect will be there."

"May I make a suggestion?" enquired Captain Overtain.

"Of course you can, captain," said Paechra in reply.

Although the young Druid thought that she perhaps already knew what the ghoul was going to suggest, she wanted to give Overtain the opportunity to voice his idea out loud.

"Why not leave these creatures in my capable care?" asked the ghoul. "I solemnly do vow that they will remain upon this ship, my ship, the Picturesque Picaresque, never to be released from duty."

"I did so wonder from where you were planning on recruiting a replacement crew, since we did force you to offload your last cast of monstrosities," pondered Paechra.

The gathered sylvan did look on in wonder, knowing the difficulty of the decision that faced the younger Lightheart. Paechra's friend Heidi and her mother Sarah were especially keen to discover how the Druid would respond.

"As much as I would not like to wish such a fate even upon our very worst of enemies, alas I believe it is the only option that is available to us," muttered Paechra. "Already one of our own has been gifted such a wicked life."

"Do not think yourself so mighty, do not turn so smug a nose up at eternal life," cried the voice of Isobella-Ann. "My memory will not fade, and my life will go on far, far further than any of you… One day perhaps it will be me who is at the helm of this fine vessel."

She had since returned to her own form, that of a sylvan whose skin had obviously somewhat decayed. The curse of being a ghoul seemed to be progressing quicker and quicker with each time she used her inner magics.

"I do not wish for you to think me smug," Paechra replied to Isobella-Ann. "I cannot hide my feelings of pity, nor my personal guilt for submitting you to this voyage."

"Again, you think yourself to be far more involved in my fate, your greatness is an illusion, Paechra Lightheart," stated Isobella-Ann in swift reply. "If what you believe were to be true then all of these sisters and brothers from the sylvan lands would be suffering such transformations as I am."

"And yet, you suffer alone," stated Sarah.

"Not alone, and yet alone," contradicted Overtain.

"More can be added to our ranks from yours," suggested Isobella-Ann. "If this were to be your wish, such could easily be arranged."

"If such were to be our God-led path, I for one as leader would be first to present," said Paechra, bravely.

"Such is not the path that we began, and it is not to be our future, at least not our immediate future..." suggested Sarah.

"I am so glad to hear this," said Heidi, obviously relieved. "I do not know if I contain the bravery required to step forward and... Let go..."

"Hush, Heidi, we have much to do before we are given this same or a similar opportunity," laughed Paechra, though there was no humor in her tone or in her almond eyes.

"Enough of these games, childhood pastimes played verbally and passively," grumbled Captain Overtain. "Release to me the captured dogs, I shall do with them as the ship wishes."

"As you request, so shall it be," said Paechra with a nod.

"Fear... No... Us..." growled one of the vorsurk warriors.

"Our... Mind... Long... Too..." said another.

"Mind... Long... Like... Fang..." added the first.

"Sharp... Like... Tooth... Hungry..." promised the fourth.

"Take them, captain," commanded Paechra. "They are yours..."

With a nod of his head the ghoul placed a hand upon the broad shoulder of one of the vorsurk warriors and as a group, led all four back into the captain's cabin. Isobella-Ann followed, dutifully after.

251

The door of the cabin closed with a loud and final banging. In the silence that came next, Paechra looked around at all of the faces that were watching her. All faces that is, with the exception of the two humans. Thomas was watching Anton, while Anton was not watching much. His eyes were still firmly closed.

"Oh my, Anton," Paechra suddenly realized.

She hurried over to where the Head Truth Keeper lay frightfully still.

"He is dead, isn't he," moaned Thomas. "I'm all alone."

"Stop being foolish, butcher," commanded Paechra.

In response to this, Thomas gave a great, loud sniff.

A glowing white light appeared to surround Paechra, and she gently placed her hands upon the still and silent figure of Anton.

"What are you doing to him?" Thomas demanded to know. "Anton would not want any of your witchery to harm him."

"How would you know what I would want and not want, lad?" growled the voice of Head Truth Keeper Anton, though his voice was a touch weaker than before.

"Anton!" cried Thomas, throwing his arms around the elder human.

"Steady on!" cried Paechra, the glow fading from her. "He is still injured."

"Far from out of the fight," Anton declared. "I will have my sword back, boy."

"Of course," stated Thomas. "I shall fetch it straight away."

"And then you shall help me back up onto my feet and point

me in the direction of the battle," Anton said with a determined frown.

"The battle is over, Anton," stated Paechra.

"Witch, the battle is never over," growled the Head Truth Keeper.

"We will have a battle soon, and it shall be very short," announced Sarah Lightheart. "Especially if you keep referring to my daughter as a witch."

"Don't mistaken my wording, please," said Anton in reply to Sarah's threat.

A great shadow of a ferocious she-bear had formed around a clearly angered Sarah Lightheart.

"Oh?" she queried. "You are not thinking my daughter to be one of your spell-mixing old hags?"

"I think you are all spell-mixing hags," Anton laughed.

"You need to take that back!" shouted Thomas, shocked to hear such come from the Head Truth Keeper.

"And you don't think these Druids to be strange?" Anton demanded to know. "You understand their every thought and action do you, butcher?"

"No, I do not understand, and yes, I do fear them for their strangeness," admitted Thomas. "But there is much I do not understand and much that I do fear which I still respect... I do not call it names, especially when I wish not to cause it anger, especially not towards me."

"Fair enough then, boy," laughed Anton. "I only ask then that you handle the strange your way and let me handle it mine."

"Not when I am in range of hearing you," muttered Sarah Lightheart, that brooding shadow still threatening to lunge.

"Thomas, sword," demanded Anton.

"Of... Of... Cour... Course..." stammered Thomas, unsure of how to handle the tension. "Here, please, take it."

With that, Anton cleaned his blade and sheathed it. Turning his back to Sarah the Bear he then walked away.

Sarah then found that her anger deflated from out of her, the angry she-bear protecting her cub disappearing back into the ether.

All the while the great ship the Picturesque Picaresque with bellowing sailings continued to go where the wind chose to blow it.

Later in the day, Captain Overtain did decide to grace the deck again, two of the vorsurk flanking him, the wolf warriors somehow shrunken in stature.

"Cease your singing, sisters of Greenwood Vale," called the ghoul's voice, strong and steady. "I am the captain of this ship, and I take my rightful place at the ship's wheel."

As requested, the chorus of Druids stopped chanting, and a new song filled the silence.

Overtain sang with an unnerving, throaty warble, a sound that pushed the great ship forward, even though there were no rowers in the belly of the juggernaut, no breeze that previously filled canvas that then flapped limp and slack. It was almost as if Captain Overtain wanted to prove he was the ship and that the ship was part of him. If needed he could sail it alone, but it was his right as a captain, and his nature as a ghoul, to claim a crew.

With the arrival of the captain back on deck, the sylvan dispersed, each going their own separate way. Anton and Thomas remained, however, choosing to hover around the wheel. Anton had an obvious interest in the vorsurk, an embedded distrust of ghouls, wolves, and enemies in general. Thomas was worried about those things too, but he seemed far more concerned about the old Head Truth Keeper. Thinking that he had lost his only connection with home worried Thomas deeply. Paechra could see such thoughts clearly displayed in the changing, swirling colors of their auras. The Druid had other things on her mind though, so she left the midship, the wheel and the scene of the battle, choosing instead to engage with Mother Druid Sienna once more.

Together the pair continued to keep the darkness at bay. Paechra passing the time asking the elder Druid which ever questions that decided to drift into her mind, Sienna in turn was only happy to answer all of the questions to the best of her ability. That was until the great ship eventually, finally, came into port.

"Leave me and my ship," demanded Overtain. "And never ask of me, ever again."

"So, it shall be as you wish," replied Sarah Lightheart.

"I am not speaking with you, but instead that of your daughter," the captain rumbled.

"I understand," murmured Paechra. "It shall be as you wish."

"Thank you, Captain Overtain," stated Sienna as she confidently passed.

The voyage and her time in the cocoon had seemingly reversed a century of years from her elderly frame.

One by one, each member of Paechra's gathered disembarked down the gangplank. High Prince Ulan was one of the first, with Anton and Thomas being two of the last.

"We are still far from home, lad," suggested Anton as he looked around the port town. "But we are at least back on home, human soil."

"Where are we?" Thomas asked in wonder.

"I had forgotten you have not traveled like a Truth Keeper travels and a sage travels," Anton said thoughtfully. "We are on the kingdom's northern tip."

"And not where I had hoped we would be," said Paechra with a sigh.

As the door to the sage's tower opened out came an old man dressed in blue robes, his eyes were saved for Anton and Anton alone.

"What is the meaning of this, Head Truth Keeper?" the old human asked.

"Sage Williamsons, it is wonderful to see you still amongst the living," called Anton in reply.

"Quit the nonsense, man, what is your story?" demanded the sage. "We have had no word from Andrapaal for six whole months... And who pray tell are all these people?"

#

Paechra Lightheart stood beside her sister Druids in the human village on the most northern tip of Thuraen. She and the small army of sylvan, nicknamed Paechra's Army were still a good eleven days away from Andrapaal, the heart of the human kingdom and the place where Paechra feared the uprising of the dreaded vorsurk was already taking place. The old man dressed in the blue of Thuraen's sages had just claimed to Head

Truth Keeper Anton that there had been no word from Andrapaal for six whole months. For the sylvan race, such silence would mean very little, but the human kingdom functioned on the passing of messages and the recording of the written word. Paechra's observation had quickly led her to believe that the humankind were obsessed with writing and equally convinced of their own importance.

"Again, I ask, and I expect to be answered," stated the old sage, Sage Williamsons, in a huff. "What do you know of the happenings in Andrapaal, and who are all of these people?"

"Sage Williamsons, I sadly know as little as you do of our precious capital," replied Anton. "I have been traveling with Queen Catherine, Michael Stormsong, Thomas the Butcher, one of the Chosen Eleven, and of course, the sylvan Paechra Lightheart, daughter of Therdous Lightheart."

"Lightheart and Stormsong?" cried Sage Williamsons in surprise.

From the same tower where the sage had appeared, there came two younger figures, both dressed in robes the color red.

"Yohan, Peter, please fetch me volume eight and volume three hundred and eight of the most current series of historic tomes," requested the elder sage.

"As you so demand," stated Yohan with a bow.

"As you wish, so we obey, great sage," added Peter, his bow a little deeper and longer.

"Sycophants, the pair of them," spat Sage Williamsons in annoyance. "And yet, on occasion they prove useful."

"You had not thought to send one or both to the capital?" asked Sarah Lightheart. "If you so desperately wanted to know what was happening there, surely these two younger humans would be able to visit, take note and then report back to you."

257

"The creatures speak, and with a surprising grasp of our language," said Sage Williamsons without any effort trying to hide his disrespect.

Anton coughed and tried to hide a smile while Sarah, Paechra, and many of the other sylvan showed obvious signs of a frustration that bordered on anger.

"Might I be so bold as to remind His Wisdom that Therdous Lightheart, Paechra's and Sarah's partner was a blue robed sage just like yourself?" asked Anton.

"If it be written then so it must be true," stated Sage Williamsons. "I merely wish to consult volume eight to confirm that such is in fact, fact."

Anton nodded and gave the Druids a look that requested they hold their frustration for a moment.

"Here, Your Wisdom," stated Peter with a deep bow, upon his swift return he offered up a leather-bound tome that reminded Paechra of the spell books carried by vorsurk magicians.

"No fair!" cried Yohan, obviously disappointed. "I found that tome first, I carried it all the way down the stairs, and then YOU ambushed me in the doorway."

Paechra as well as others could clearly see blood dribbling from Yohan's split lip, an injury he had not had before rushing with Peter back towards the tower.

"Here," stated Paechra kindly, the image of the dove enveloping her form as she evoked a spell of healing. "Let me help you."

"What is this?" cried Yohan, suddenly afraid, rushing back towards the tower.

Sage Williamsons' eyes also grew wide as the younger Lightheart activated her casting. Looking at Anton for guidance and seeing that the Head Truth Keeper stood his ground, instead of running himself the elder sage called after the fleeing youth.

"Yohan, please if it be not too much trouble for you would you remember to find volume three hundred and eight and bring it to me."

"Yes, Your Wisdom," murmured Yohan.

"With your permission, Your Wisdom, I shall accompany Yohan to assist him with his search," offered Peter.

Many of the sylvan noticed the look of annoyance that crossed Yohan's face and the scheming smile that featured proudly upon Peter's. Sage Williamsons ignored both boys, instead focusing all of his attention upon Paechra and those who stood beside her.

Not hearing a response from the sage in blue robes, both boys bowed awkwardly and then took their leave, racing each other back to the tower.

"Are you always so unkind?" asked Sarah, Paechra's mother.

"Look around you, feel the sun on your face, take up the smell of the salty, fresh air," laughed the elder sage, yet not in a joyful way. "The pair that have been given to me to train and educate are already lazy, clueless, useless, thanks to the sun and the sand."

"And that has nothing to do with the teacher and your teaching?" enquired Heidi. "Nothing at all?"

"I have spent many a year here, trying to turn boys into learned men," replied Sage Williamsons. "And yet the constant sunshine and wondrous weather make it impossible for boys to concentrate, to focus such as they need to do."

"I can see your problem, Your Wisdom," suggested Thomas. "I would struggle to do anything but fish and swim if I lived here."

"There, see, the young butcher understands," said the elder sage, thankful to have someone back up his actions. "It is of no wonder to me why they did choose you for our capital's council."

"Thank you, Sage Williamsons," said Thomas with a beaming smile. It was quickly followed up with a deep bow of gratitude when he realized he had forgotten such a sign of respect.

"Hmmm... Well... Yes... Let us see here..." mumbled the elder sage as he ignored Thomas then and turned his attention to the great tome. "Therdous Lightheart arrives in Andrapaal... He befriends Chief Sage Vladamir... Joins the sages... Those last two points should be in reverse order, surely."

With unexpected nimbleness the old man flicked through the book, eyes of a light green, like fresh fonds growing from a seaside palm scanned each column searching for a particular passage.

"Ah... Yes... I do recall now to know of the man..." then announced the sage. "Therdous Lightheart, credited with the translation of lines five, eight, and ten of the fourth stanza, and lines eight, eleven, and twelve of the eleventh stanza of The Prophecy of Andrapaal."

"My father was quite the linguist," suggested Paechra. "It was the prophecy that drew him to your kingdom and its heart."

"But then your father suddenly vanishes... There is no mention of him anywhere..." continued Sage Williamsons, seemingly ignoring Paechra's comments, and yet, still, speaking directly to her.

"He was taken, I know he was... Taken by one of your...

Students..." suggested Paechra.

Williamsons raised both disheveled eyebrows. This accusation, he obviously did hear.

"Well, perhaps not one of YOUR students specifically," added Heidi. "But Paechra has told me some of what she did experience during her time in Andrapaal, and she swears that she did actually see her father."

"Ah, yes, the fate of the father..." said Williamsons.

By then Yohan had returned with yet another volume from the tower's library. A long, deep scratch marked his left cheek. Peter was nowhere to be seen.

"Thank you, boy, you are now dismissed," Sage Williamsons said, taking the tome from the bowing Yohan.

"Thanking you graciously, Your Wisdom," stated Yohan, reverently.

The sage in blue ignored the boy.

"I believe it is about halfway... Yes... Here it is..." muttered the old man. "Therdous Lightheart, slain in cold blood by the outcast, Johann Stormsong, son of Michael Stormsong, also known to some as Raven."

"No!" cried Paechra as memories flooded back to her. "That passage is false; the boy was framed."

"If it is written..." Sage Williamsons began.

Sarah looked at her daughter, eyes wide in disbelief.

"You knew of this?" she mouthed, her voice a whisper.

"But you yourself have already pronounced that passages are recorded incorrectly to the timeline," suggested Heidi. "Could it not be possible that information is also written wrong, a person's own remembrance of a situation where surely other viewpoints of the same scenario would be sought by you sages to collaborate or to shine light upon a variation of the telling?"

"What is the meaning of this, Anton?" huffed the old sage. "Are you not still the defender of the truth, of our truth and our way of life?"

"Of course, Your Wisdom," replied Head Truth Keeper Anton, gruffly, he then turned towards Paechra and raised his finger accusingly. "Be silent, witch!"

"Paechra, Sarah, Heidi, please walk with me," interjected Mother Druid Sienna Alknown.

Paechra made to reply to Anton but then thought better of it. Sienna had not raised her voice, nor had she altered her tone, and yet, Paechra could sense that it was in her best interest to not reply to the human.

Without waiting to see if she was going to be obeyed, Sienna turned away from the tower and headed back for the ocean. Standing barefooted with the waves gently lapping over her ankles, the elder Druid smiled up at the midday sun. There were a few clouds littering an otherwise blue sky, the day was far calmer than the people. Paechra and her mother joined Sienna, with Paechra's friend Heidi not far behind them.

"The humans do so frustrate me," Paechra muttered.

"Hush, daughter Paechra," soothed Sienna, taking Paechra by the hand but all the while continuing to look out to sea.

"But" protested the younger Lightheart, a squeeze of Sienna's hand in hers causing Paechra to pause.

"Look out there, daughter," urged Sienna. "What do you see?"

Sarah, Heidi, and Paechra all turned their attention towards the distant horizon.

"There is something there," suggested Heidi. "I cannot make out what it is, but it is there."

"I see it too," said Sarah. "Is it that accursed ship?"

"This is the most northern point of Thuraen," said Sienna. "In fact, we may not even by standing within the boundaries of the kingdom anymore."

"What do you mean, Mother?" asked Sarah Lightheart.

"I do not believe that what we see on the horizon is the ghoul ship," suggested Sienna. "That has left our sight long ago."

"What then?" asked Paechra. "An island, maybe?"

"Perhaps," replied Sienna. "It is most likely that your assumption is correct, daughter, although I do not recall passing an island before we arrived here."

"Nor do I," said Heidi. "We were all quite distracted though so it could have easily been missed."

"My point is, sisters, we must respect the beliefs of these humans whom we wish to save," stated the Mother Druid wisely. "Else there is truly no point in us being here."

"It would be just like in the past, we gifting humankind the written word and their so-called freedom and then vanishing to leave them to fend for themselves," added Paechra.

"Infants, left to battle with dogs, no worse, wolves in truth," mused Sarah. "Is there little wonder then that they cling to their beliefs and wish not for us to interfere?"

"It is still infuriating though to think that Thuraen refuses as a whole to consider to their north is an island, potential friendship, possible ownership, and yet because it is outside their eleven-day radius it is deemed non-existent," said Paechra to which the others agreed.

"So, we may return then, turn our backs also upon said island, whatever else is in the far distance, and focus our attention wholly and solely upon the here and the now?" suggested Sienna.

"You always know the right things to say, Mother Druid Sienna," said Heidi with a smile.

"I guess that may be due to my years of experience, daughter," replied Sienna as she released Paechra's hand.

Suddenly Paechra, Heidi, and Sarah noticed that Sienna's skin shimmered and then began to wrinkle. The effects of the time spent in the cocoon while aboard The Picturesque Picaresque were suddenly wearing off. In an instant, Sienna appeared to age another century.

"Mother!" the trio cried out as one.

"Fear not, my daughters," croaked Sienna as her frame that stood straight and strong only a moment before, was now hunched. "This is merely a sign that I must return to my cocoon if I wish to see out this journey."

"Is there nothing that we can do to help you?" asked Paechra, the blue aura of healing already shimmering over her skin.

"Nothing at all?" asked Sarah, and then Heidi, both taking one of Paechra's hands in theirs and adding their own magic to the spell.

"No, daughters, but I thank thee all for your offered support," answered the elder Druid. "All I need is rest, perhaps a few days only, Prince Ulan can be my company if he so wishes, though I doubt I will be of much."

"No," consider Paechra. "Our High Prince Ulan can do many things, but he has not the ability to join you in your cocoon."

"I hesitate to suggest that perhaps it is you, sister who accompanies the Mother Druid then," added Heidi. "I sense that your leadership will be needed while we remain here with His Wonderment and the two servant boys."

"Yes, I wonder about this Sage Williamsons, and also how it is that Anton and Thomas will change as we venture closer and closer to their home," suggested Sarah.

"We must watch the two humans who will accompany us, they will be our guides, but they will discover the world that they lead us into will have changed," suggested Sienna.

"Anton will show little of his emotion physically, but his aura will betray his true feelings as it always does," said Paechra. "Thomas on the other hand is easily read; I shall make note to keep an open eye upon both of them."

"Nay, daughter, you shall not take on this responsibility alone," suggested Paechra's mother.

"No, we will help you," agreed Heidi. "You will have much that will require your focus over the coming days here and when we travel again."

"Such is the fate of a leader," sighed Paechra. "Such is the responsibility I have undertaken gladly."

"Then we must return to the tower, to our people, and to those people that we are trying to save," said Sienna. "Come, daughters, destiny awaits."

With that said, all four turned away from the horizon and strode in time with each other, back to the tower.

#

The remainder of the day passed in reasonable peace. As

suggested, Mother Druid Sienna Alknown retired to a tent that was erected upon the beach for her. High Prince Ulan was introduced to Sage Williamsons, but he too claimed weariness from the sea voyage and joined Sienna. Paechra did ask that she be allowed access to the tower and its library of tomes, but she was quickly informed that this would not be possible.

"I only wish to discover more about my father and his time spent in your kingdom," Paechra requested.

"Good lady, why should you focus upon the past, so long ago, when you yourself have a story that has yet to be captured," Sage Williamsons gave as a reply. "As a matter of fact, it will take me many a day to meet with all of you in groups or as individuals to capture your recent times, the difficulty will be in pinpointing the when from which we must begin our recording."

Paechra considered suggesting that what Williamsons was proposing would be an obvious waste of time, but then she considered Sienna's wise words that advised the respect of the human culture. Paechra remembered arriving with Raven at the gates of Andrapaal and his surprise at discovering nobody there to greet him. That same memory reminded the younger Lightheart the emphasis that Raven had placed on the importance of reporting to the Hall of Records. Her friend's voice echoed in Paechra's mind encouraging her to tell the sages where she had been and all she had seen, all for the benefit of generations yet to come. Thinking of Raven made it suddenly so evident just how long they had been apart.

"I wonder where it is that you have been, what you have seen, and where it is that you are now," murmured Paechra.

"You are indeed a strange one, just as Anton suggested," replied Sage Williamsons.

"Oh, I am sorry Your Wisdom, my mind was elsewhere,"

admitted Paechra.

"Have we need for swords and such?" asked the old sage, suddenly alarmed.

"I see that Anton has told you much about me," observed the Druid. "Much that he has seen but certainly does not understand."

"If it is written, so must it be true," said Williamsons. "Such is the motto taught to sages of all ages and all robe colors."

"Words can have a magic all of their very own," Paechra gave cryptically as a reply.

"Would it trouble you greatly if I wrote that down?" asked Sage Williamsons.

"Do you believe it to be true?" Paechra asked in return.

"Magic is forbidden in all of Thuraen, as you well know, even here at our most northern point," the sage said, a reminder. "I merely wish to record the words as yours, should any want to look back upon them at a later date."

"Then fetch your student sages and ask them to bring many a page, and ink," said Paechra. "I've a story for you that will fill a tome all by itself and it just so happens we seem to have the time for me to tell it."

Chapter Twelve

Not All Shall Be Chosen

The winds blow like tongues of flame where the grains of sand are slick with blood.

What it is they value so highly, the fortress gone, sunken away.

From the First Stanza of the Prophecy, translated by the sages of the Kingdom of Thuraen 5th year

PAECHRA LIGHTHEART SAT upon the beach, watching the sun set upon yet another day. Beside her sat her good friend Heidi, and behind them sat Sage Williamsons, the old human, his book held unsteadily between the far younger sages, Yohan and Peter. The far elder sage that was dressed in the blue robes of his station berated his two apprentices for the silly games that they played, Peter and Yohan trying their best to cause the other to fail in one duty or another.

"Will the pair of you please just stop!" cried Williamsons in utter frustration.

Yohan had leaned slightly to his left, causing the tome to weigh heavier for Peter, in turn causing that boy to stumble back a step. As the great book of history shifted, Sage Williamsons quill splodged upon the page. A great, dark spot began to spread, ruining everything that the old man had written, the twenty lines or so on that very page anyway.

"I shall grab the blotting paper!" announced Peter, hurriedly. "So sorry, Your Wisdomness."

"You'll take too long!" cried Yohan. "Here, Oh Knowledged One…" He added as he shoved the book into Williamsons' arms.

"What..? What…? Just like bloody children…" cried the blue-robed sage, exasperated.

"They are no longer young, and not yet old," mused Paechra, pausing midway through the retelling of her tale.

"The sylvan of a similar age would be running through the forest, or if here, splashing in that sea and seeing just how far out they could swim," added Heidi.

"I would say, that there little island, just on the horizon, that would probably be my limit now," suggested Paechra, making conversation with her friend, not really directing what she was saying at the old human.

Never-the-less the old human was the first to interject.

"That there island is no longer part of our kingdom, and so I doubt greatly that any apprentices would have thought to swim there."

"No longer part? Did you lose a great battle for territory?"

asked Heidi, confused.

"It is written, so it must be true," began Sage Williamsons, as he opened the tome to a fresh page. "When the sylvan, you people, first came to our aid and drove off our mutual enemy, the vorsurk, well the lands that we were given were large and vast."

"So why not retain such lands?" asked Paechra, she was as keen as her friend to hear this tale.

"Kings and Princes make their decisions as the tomes of history are interpreted by the sages of blue, red, and yellow..." explained the sage. "It is written that one of our rulers was fascinated by the enemy, their interest in the strength of mathematical patterns and numbering..."

"It sounds like a kind of magic to me," laughed Heidi.

Paechra nodded her agreement and turned to smile at the old man.

Sage Williamsons would have none of this though.

"Preposterous! How dare you suggest such a thing!" the sage cried, suddenly going as red as the robes the younger sages wore. "Such a thing as magic is forbidden in our kingdom, and you Druid ladies had best remember that while you are here."

Mother Druid Sienna Alknown had taken refuge with High Prince Ulan and had once more encased herself within her strange cocoon. Paechra had wandered into the tent in need of asking Sienna for advice on something and had received a shrug of the shoulders from the high prince. After choosing to confide such to her friend Heidi and her mother Sarah, it had been agreed amongst the three of them that such spell casting should not be discussed further, so, their host could remain at ease. As Williamsons mentioned magic, and its forbiddeness, the two sylvan Druids had shared a look and a smirk between them but had not made a sound.

"Where are those two boys?" the elder sage demanded to know.

"Your Wisdom, we could attempt to tell you, but it would require the use of that which you cannot believe in," suggested Heidi.

"You jest, surely," the sage replied.

"Of course she does," stated Paechra. "We would not dare to break any laws while we stay thanks to your generous hospitality."

"Yes, well, of course," said Williamsons. "Any companion of Head Truth Keeper Anton is indeed, a friend of Thuraen and Andrapaal both."

"As you do so speak of the kingdom's capital, can I please ask again, Your Wisdom, just how long has it been since you have heard any news from the city of Andrapaal?" asked the younger Lightheart.

"Do you wish to know of the city, or of one of its residents?" asked Heidi with a grin.

"It is the city and the kingdom, in fact humanity that we have gathered to save," answered Paechra, a little hurt that her friend would make such a suggestion.

"Yes, of course," said Heidi, her smirk fading.

"Although, it would not hurt to discover the welfare of a friend," mused Paechra, causing Heidi to beam again.

"Alas I have no new news to give you, although what has been unwritten, floating upon the wind as idle gossip does suggest that your friend, The Raven, is less hero and more villain," muttered the blue-robed sage, Williamsons straining his eyes to see if either of the red-robed boys were returning.

Just at that moment Yohan did appear, Peter not far behind him was attempting to pull him back. Heidi and Paechra with their far superior sight witnessed the boys squabbling. It would still be a while before the pair tired of their fight and remembered the urgent need for blotting paper.

"What do you mean by such a statement, Oh Knowledged One?" asked Paechra, doing well to keep from her tone the worry that filled her heart and mind and caused her aura to grey.

"Yohan is the newest of my apprentices to arrive, much to Peter's discomfort," began the elderly human. "Yohan is a quick study, but is prone to gossip, knowing little still what is the difference between news and myth."

"Such students must surely be of a great burden to you," suggested Heidi.

"Indeed, it is almost as if I have been cursed twice," said the sage.

"How so?" asked Heidi and Paechra together.

"If only I could combine the two and have Peter's interest with Yohan's ability..." pondered Sage Williamsons, wistfully. "Yohan has a habit of sometimes just disappearing, and when he returns he refuses to allow me to record where it is that he has been,"

"What if we offered to take young Yohan into our care?" suggested Paechra. "We are headed for Andrapaal after all, I strongly sense that your apprentice is trying to find his way back home."

"What?" asked Heidi, shocked at her friend's suggested

idea. "You want another human, and

a child at that, to join the army that we are gathering?"

"Hush Heidi, I suspect that Yohan does not come from the capital city, but some other town that lies upon the North road," said Paechra, a hurried whisper.

The younger Lightheart waved at her friend to keep quiet as Sage Williamsons pondered

Paechra's rash proposal.

"No, no, no," replied the sage. "Something such as this has never been done before if it had then surely it would have been recorded."

"Then think of just how well you shall be received in the kingdom's very heart when you are written as the first to try it, especially when it is reported as having turned out to be such a great success," suggested Paechra.

"What are you doing, Paechra my friend?" murmured Heidi, but Paechra chose to ignore it, and it was difficult for the two sylvan to tell if Sage Williamsons was too elderly to hear.

"Do you truly believe that it will be a success?" asked Sage Williamsons, his milky eyes peering out at the sunset. "Do you truly believe that I would be welcomed back to Andrapaal, I could live out my final years as a citizen, not some sort of outcast... I still don't know what made Bearheart so... So... If only it were written down..."

"Yes, I suppose, if that is indeed the dream of every old man in blue robes," said Paechra. "I do not know if the Andrapaal you return to will be the city you so fondly recall."

"All that I want is for my chance to go home," said the sage.

"And leave this?" asked Heidi, indicating the beautiful scene, the soft sand, the perfect beach, the calmly lapping ocean. "Why would you leave paradise?"

"It is too hot for an old man, too hot, too humid, and far too wet," complained the sage. "I I grew up in the capital, I grew up with books, and therefore I never had a need to learn how to swim."

"What about when you wore the robes of red?" asked Heidi. "Did you not spend time by the sea then?"

"No, I was lucky," stated Sage Williamsons, his thoughts far away. "I was certain that I was being groomed, certain that I was going to be Chief Sage Williamsons... And then I ended up here..."

The old man slapped his arm as an insect landed upon his robes.

"I know that this will most probably offend you, but I would far prefer the cold stone and lifelessness of a city to all of this... This... Nature..." said the sage, the longing for change blatantly obvious. One of the evening insects buzzed around Paechra's nose, landed, and bit savagely.

"Oh!" she cried, waving the creature away. "No, Your Wisdomness, please believe me when I say that I have grown up with nature and I have witnessed Andrapaal, and as confusing as the city was to someone like me I could still see both her charm and beauty." Just then the two boys arrived, Yohan first with the blotting paper and a deep scratch across one cheek, and Peter not far behind, carrying a pair of blazing torches and a limp.

"Here you are, Oh Knowledgable One," said Yohan as he thrust the roll of paper into Sage Williamsons' elderly face and snatched the tome from the old man's arms.

"I brought torches," announced Peter, puffing slightly.

"Yes, thank you boys," muttered the sage dressed in blue. "A little late with the paper, but right on time it seems with the sources of light."

By then the sun had set and the last of the twilight was fading. Yohan's head dropped slightly as Peter shot him a smug look.

"If you are worried about writing without the aid of the sun's light, I could scribe for you

instead, if you so require," offered Paechra. "My father has taught me many languages."

"If you would not have Paechra write, then perhaps one of the boys could do it?" Heidi then suggested.

"No, I will not have anyone other than myself record the histories of this region," announced Sage Williamsons. "It has been so, since my arrival a decade ago, and I will not be changing such a tradition now."

In the flickering torchlight both Paechra and Heidi could see the disappointment in both Peter's and Yohan's eyes and their auras.

"And it so seems," the elderly sage announced as he tore his most recent page from the book with a sigh. "We have much to rewrite before we can continue your tale, Miss Lightheart."

The page was sacrifice to one of the torches that Peter still held, the action surprising both boys.

"Come, quickly then, Peter," ordered Sage Williamsons. "Place those torches near me, but not too close."

"Your Wisdom, would you at least allow Paechra and me to hold the torches aloft while the boys assist you by holding open the tome?" suggested Heidi.

"Yes, I suppose that would work," considered Williamsons. "I fear what would happen if the boys held the torches and the two of you held the book."

"My story may write itself," laughed Paechra.

"I was more worried that the boys would set each other alight, or you both, or me, or worse still the tome…" said Sage Williamsons, humorlessly. "To burn words would require us calling upon Anton, Head Truth Keeper, protector of the tomes.

"But you just tore out a page, a page of words that is now ash, vanished upon the winds," said Paechra, confused.

"That was disposing of a mistake, a blemish upon an otherwise pristine recording," explained the blue-robed sage. "Do you understand the difference?"

Heidi and Paechra did understand. That statement had not been made for them, but instead for the pair in red, the future scribes of history. The sylvan both wondered how many other so thought mistakes had been torn from the tomes, how many passages had been rewritten, changed slightly, or made to be utterly different if a new version of the past better suited the present day.

"Now, please Paechra Lightheart, can we begin again from the moment you left Andrapaal?" requested the senior sage. "And with Queen Catherine of all people…"

The night proved to be a long one. Sage Williamsons refused to rest, he was determined to capture all of Paechra's story. At one point Paechra needed to hold both torches as the old sage finally agreed to send the young boys to their rest.

"You must go and fetch us two new torches and two of your kindred, to hold the tome steady," commanded Sage Williamsons.

"Your Wisdom, I'm not one of your apprentices..." began Heidi.

The old man waved such a suggestion away.

"I understand that, but we cannot leave this recording unfinished, and the boys have no coordination at this time of day, and the torches are close to going out..." argued the blue-robe. "Now hurry along... Please?"

"As you so wish, Oh Wise One," Heidi replied.

While Heidi was gone Williamsons turned his attention to the two tired boys.

"Now Peter, I will require you to lift your efforts with your studies from tomorrow forward, am I clear?" the elder sage commanded.

"Sure... Yooooouuuuuurrrrrr Wiiiiissssssdddddoooo... Aaahhhhhh..." agreed Peter.

"No instructions for mmmeeeeeee... Thooooouuuuuggghhhh right... Oooohhhhhh aaaahhhhhhhh Wiiissseeee Oooonnnnneeee... Aaaaahhhhhh..." Yohan said with a great yawn.

"You, Yohan will act as a guide for our visitors as they travel along the North road towards Andrapaal, a great honor boy, I'd ask that you do the red colored robes proud," said Williamsons gruffly, but proudly. "You were asked for personally by Miss Lightheart here."

"What, me?" asked Yohan, suddenly awake at hearing such news. "Travelling with the sylvan army?"

"Yes, Yohan, I will be recording the news tomorrow so that it is official," promised the elder sage.

"I guess that has been decided then," said Paechra, a little taken aback. She had thought it was merely a suggestion, not yet agreed upon.

"I am leaving tomorrow? Your All-Knowingness?" asked Yohan, still surprised.

"Yes, yes, Miss Lightheart has need to speak to you tomorrow morning about a friend of hers, and when you inform her of the rumors that you are trying to sprout as facts I am sure enough that you will all be wanting to hurry southwards as swiftly as you can manage," explained Sage Williamsons.

"Why can't Yohan speak with me now?" asked Paechra, unsure of how she was suddenly responsible for a red-robed apprentice sage.

"I have borne witness to the boy's so called news from the city once already, it was not written and so it was not recorded, so it cannot be considered as fact," said Williamsons.

"And why have you not chosen to record this, making it fact?" suggested the sylvan.

"Ripples in a pond, young lady, ripples in a pond," suggested the old sage.

Paechra considered revealing to Sage Williamsons just how young she actually was, but decided against it.

"Are you referring to the principle that information from the source will alter in state the more often that it is shared, especially when it is not the owner of the information that is doing the sharing?" asked Paechra.

"Why yes, Miss Lightheart, yes that is exactly what I am referring to," said Sage Williamsons, genuinely surprised. "So, if you understand the principle so well you must know why, living upon the outskirts of the great kingdom of Thuraen, I can only record what I, myself witness, or what it is that gets

relayed to me, firsthand, by visitors such as yourself."

"Of course, Oh Knowledgeable One," said Paechra with a nod of her head. "But I do appreciate your clear and precise explanation."

Yohan stifled another great yawn and swayed upon his feet.

"No fair, you get to go back to the city," whispered Peter.

"No fair, you get to stay here by the sea," Paechra overheard Yohan whisper back.

"Come, Your Wisdom, please allow me to take the book, send the boys to their rest," suggested the younger Lightheart. "See, there, I can already see my friend Heidi has returned with two from my army, and for whatever reason, my mother is accompanying them."

Paechra's superior sight did indeed see the two male sylvan, Heidi, and the figure of Sarah Lightheart.

"If that is indeed true, and I do not doubt that it be so," replied the old sage. "Indeed boys, give responsibility of the tome to Miss Lightheart and the two of you will immediately retire."

Without another word or yawn, the pair of red-robed sages gave their senior a bow of respect, and Paechra a nod of thanks.

"I hope to see you both, tomorrow," said Paechra. "You especially," she added, her words directed towards Yohan.

Yohan nodded to show that he understood, and then both boys turned away from the shore and sped toward their beds.

#

It was Sienna who woke Paechra the following morning at dawn. The ancient Druid, who was named as Alknown had come out from her cocoon of shelter, perhaps sensing that it was time for the army of sylvan to continue their journey. The High Prince Ulan waited respectfully a few feet away, pretending not to listen as the two women spoke.

"I have been told that we will be accompanied by another on our journey southwards," the elder began, no greeting, no pomp or ceremony, straight to the point.

"Yes, Mother Druid," said Paechra as she tried to stifle a yawn, but failed.

"Enough of the dawn's hours have been wasted already," grumbled Sienna. "Arise girl, be a leader and ready us all."

"But I must first speak with the boy," said Paechra in reply. "I must know that he will be as useful as Sage Williamsons suggests."

"Do what you must, but do so quickly," Sienna ordered. "Rise, shine, eat, talk… The time to do all is now…"

"As you so command," murmured the younger of the two.

"Command, demand, creak and croak," scoffed Sienna. "I do not lead, I only speak."

"And what we the listeners choose to do with such words is entirely up to us," continued Paechra.

"I have taught you well," Sienna then said, smiling. "Your mother should be proud, just as I am."

Paechra nudged the sleeping figure of her friend Heidi, the pair sharing a tent.

"Come, it is time we were up," the daughter of Sarah suggested.

Heidi groaned in reply and rolled over.

"Hmmmph," said Sienna.

"Shall we find some sustenance?" suggested Ulan, offering Sienna his hand. "Would yo care for a piece of fruit or something else to sweeten your mood, perhaps?"

"Perhaps…" Sienna agreed as she allowed herself to be led away.

"Come, Heidi, up," urged Paechra. "I need your help to find the boys."

"If I must," groaned Heidi. "If I must…"

In truth, Paechra did not need Heidi's help at all, she just felt that she needed her friend there, or someone there whom she trusted when she took the opportunity to ask about Raven. The two boys were already up, sharing a freshly caught fish between them. The sweet smell of coconut milk could easily be detected by both Paechra and Heidi as they approached the pair, along with a mixture of spices. Paechra's stomach growled, but she chose to ignore her hunger.

"Is your master not with us, yet?" asked Heidi.

Yohan and Peter both shook their heads.

"We would be lucky to see him before midday sometimes," said Peter.

"I am truly shocked to see you risen so early," laughed Yohan, this causing Peter to pull a face.

"Now boys, please," said Paechra, at her stern tone Peter's fists uncurled and he somewhat relaxed.

"Would you care to share in our morning meal?" Yohan offered. "You can have Peter's half."

"No thank you, we shall find our own," said Paechra.

281

Heidi made to speak but then thought better of it.

"Now that we have found this pair, perhaps I may be relieved?" Paechra's friend asked.

"I guess you may," replied Paechra. "But do not return to slumber, you heard what Mother Sienna said."

"I shall find for us something to eat then," grumbled Heidi.

"And please send my mother this way, if you cross paths with her," requested Paechra. The younger Lightheart still wanted someone to witness her questioning the boys, but it had become clear to Paechra that Heidi was not right for that role.

Heidi nodded but wandered away grumbling under her breath.

Paechra's stomach growled again.

"Are you sure that you did not want to try some of our fish?" asked Peter, kindly.

"Fresh caught by this boy right here, not even an hour ago," boasted Yohan, giving Peter a mighty slap on the back.

"I could perhaps keep you all well fed, should you decide to take me with you instead," suggested Peter, hopeful as he smiled up at Paechra.

"I am so sorry, Peter," said Paechra kindly. "You are quite book smart from what I have learned of Sage Williamsons' words."

"That is true," said Yohan. "Book smart is good, no?"

"Good for a sage, especially a student sage," continued Paechra. "But book smart is not what we are looking for, not what we need right now."

Peter looked crestfallen when he heard this news.

"You are right," the boy moaned. "I never get to do

anything fun."

"You love fishing," Paechra suggested. "Don't you?"

"I love reading," admitted Peter. "I fish because the old man wants me to do it."

"We would only have fruit to eat if Peter did not drop a line every so often," Yohan agreed. "I'm a hopeless fisherman."

"In fact, I hear that the fruit trees are tended by you also," said the gruff voice of Anton as the Head Truth Keeper arrived.

Both Peter and Yohan bowed toward the older human, a sign of respect for his role.

"Yeah, that's true," said Peter. "Old Williamsons would need to part with some of his treasure trove if it were not for me."

"Treasure trove?" queried Anton, an eyebrow raised. "Sages are not supposed to charge to record the words of history."

"Well, you tell that to the miser still slumbering in his bed," laughed Yohan. "I would be talking out of turn if I told you all the things that Williamsons does so far away from the heart of the kingdom."

"Well, boy, we still have plenty of days on the road ahead of us," suggested Anton. "I would be most eager to hear of everything you can tell me, leave no detail out."

"Oh, please don't," said Paechra and Peter together.

"I can only imagine the trouble that you will land me in when Truth Keepers travel this far north to investigate," sighed Peter. "Are you sure that Yohan is the one that you want to take with you."

"Yeah," agreed Yohan. "Leave me here with the old man and take little Peter back with you, home to his family."

Anton looked from one boy to the next and then back again. He shook his head and then locked eyes with the sylvan.

"He wouldn't even make it marching a day," the Head Truth Keeper said.

Paechra nodded.

"Sorry Peter, I agree with Anton," she said.

Peter sighed and then took another mouthful of the fish. Paechra could see he did not even taste the food as he thought of home. The aura around both boys had gone from a dull orange to a washed out purple. She felt sorry for them, especially Yohan who really did not want to go. She wondered if either boy would choose to cause trouble, just for the sake of making a point. Paechra hoped to remember to regularly check in with the human boy, her short time with Raven in the city of Andrapaal had opened her almond shaped eyes to the emotional pendulum that was humanity. The sylvan's thoughts then drifted to focus upon herself, and she examined how her own psyche had altered since visiting Thuraen. There was much to unpack, and right then was not the time.

"Cheer up, lads," Anton suggested. "Yohan I am certain that there will be other opportunities for you to visit, and Peter very soon you will be wearing the robes of blue and if you are lucky you will find a station in the capital."

"If there is an Andrapaal to go home to," suggested Paechra.

"What do you know?" blurted out Yohan, almost choking on his mouthful.

"Now, lass, they are only boys," said Anton.

"We have come from the city, and return there now, by the long route I guess you could say," Paechra replied, ignoring Anton's hidden warning, much to the human's annoyance.

"How long ago were you in Andrapaal?" asked Peter. "Yohan has told me some stories and none of them are good."

"We left early on," said Anton.

"Just as the city fell and a vorsurk fortress rose up in its place," butted in Paechra.

"So, the rumors are true," moaned Peter. "I do hope that my family is all ok."

"As do I lad," said Anton as he frowned at Paechra.

"Yes, yes," said the sylvan. "But more importantly I need to ask you about another human."

"Paechra, perhaps now is not the time to interrogate the children," said Anton.

"Nonsense," said Paechra in reply. "Would you have me ask only Yohan my questions, and miss all of the additional information that Peter could possibly supply?"

"Yes," said Anton flatly. "The child Peter offers nothing of value in my opinion."

"Well, you are not the leader, you do not get to make the decisions this time," said Paechra. "And I would ask you to save your suggestions for when the children are not present."

"Boys need to learn early on just how to deal with disappointment," huffed Anton. "The sooner they learn, the better for all of us."

"These boys are sages in training," said Paechra, calmly. "They are not your Truth Keepers that need to be given a week of sleeping in thunderstorms to breed some respect into them."

"I spent a month in a cave in the snowy south, and that was all before I was ten," boasted the old man. "It never did me any harm, made me the man that I am."

Paechra looked with wide eyes of shock and surprise, from Anton to Peter and then to Yohan.

"This explains a great deal, thank you for sharing, Anton," she said.

285

"We are not sleeping in thunderstorms, are we?" Yohan asked.

"Yes," said the Head Truth Keeper.

"No," said Paechra at exactly the same time.

"Well, which one is it?" asked Peter.

Yohan stayed quiet, but Paechra saw his aura turn grey.

"You know better than any of us," said Paechra quickly, she seeing that Anton was ready to jump in with his own opinion. "Do you get many thunderstorms in this part of the kingdom?"

"Not during this time of year," replied Yohan, relieved. "Further south I heard that the weather is far wilder."

"Well then, you'll be gladdened to know that we will not be travelling further than the kingdom's heart," said Paechra. "We should have no need to sleep in wild weather or freezing cold caves."

"More is the pity," suggested Anton.

"Please," offered Yohan. "Master Anton, may we share with you our meal."

"Why yes, thanks lads," said the Head Truth Keeper as he chose to sit with the boys. "I will never understand how these strange sylvan can turn down a fine feast."

Silently Peter placed a fillet upon a stone plate and heaped upon the fish a hearty serving of greenery.

"Ah, no, thanks, boy," coughed Anton. "Just the fish will be fine."

"As you wish," Peter mumbled.

Gently he removed the mixture of herbs from Anton's plate to his own and then passed the fish over. As Paechra caught a whiff her stomach growled yet another time.

"It is delicious," said Anton, turning to the sylvan. "Are you sure we cannot tempt you?"

"No," said Paechra. "What I hunger for this early hour is information."

It was just at that moment that Heidi returned with Sarah Lightheart, Mother Druid Sienna linking arms with the pair to make a humorous trio, stumbling along the shoreline.

"Good morn to you, Mother, mother, and friend," said Paechra, bowing.

"Yes, greetings daughter," said Sienna and then Sarah.

The oldest of the group now gathered took a look at the two boys.

"Will you not find for an old woman something to fill her heart, her stomach, and her smile?" she asked.

"I forgot the fruit," sighed Heidi. "I shall be back in a minute."

As Paechra's friend rushed off, there came another growl.

"Have you not eaten yet, daughter?" asked Sarah, to which Paechra shook her head.

"No, she is hungry for something other than food," laughed Sienna. "Or at least she thinks that is what she needs."

"I know that these boys can tell me something," suggested Paechra. "What Sage Williamsons thinks is merely gossip could have meaning that will be of use."

"Use to us and our cause, daughter, or use to you and your own private quest?" enquired Sarah Lightheart.

Anton almost chocked on his morsel, and he quickly tried to swallow.

"Private quest?" asked the older human. "When was I to

discover about this."

"My mother merely hints at my interest in Raven, Anton," explained Paechra. "For those who know how to read an aura mine is obviously an open book today."

"Hmmm…" said Sienna as she interrupted the conversation she was ignoring.

The Mother Druid grabbed one of Yohan's cheeks and squeezed tightly.

"This one seems likely to be troublesome," the ancient sylvan suggested. "Are you certain Paechra that you have chosen wisely?"

"As I tried to explain to everyone, including Sage Williamsons before," said Paechra, on the edge of exasperation. "I did not ask to have yet another mouth to feed, especially not the responsibility of a child's life."

"Then please leave me here," begged Yohan. "I simply love the sun, the sand, the warmth and the sea."

"Your master wrote the words last night," lamented Paechra. "Your fate and my fate are now intertwined."

"Well then, if that is the case," huffed Sienna Alknown, Mother Druid. "I shall have him as my personal servant."

"And what pray tell does such a role require?" asked Yohan, unsure.

"I merely need my old aching feet to be rubbed each and every night, and a steaming hot bath run to keep my old limbs from stiffening up," suggested Sienna. "Ulan has been doing such tasks thus far, but these belittle the high prince."

"Surely you jest," Yohan suggested.

"Boy, you are about to discover just how much of a jester this old woman can be," laughed Sienna as she gave his cheeks a second squeeze. "Come now, gather your things and say your farewells, for it is high time we were back on the road."

"Oh no," groaned Yohan.

Peter simply smiled and gave his fellow sage in training a pat on the back.

"It seems, Yohan, you and I simply cannot escape our fates, as much as we dislike them," sighed the boy who was destined to stay.

"It seems that the words you speak are true," sighed Yohan. "But you were always far better at the truth than I was."

"Come servant," cackled Sienna as she hooked her arm in Yohan's. "Lead me to your things and then we can add to them my own."

"Why me," moaned the youth.

#

Sage Williamsons did not rise in time to see Yohan, the sylvan army or Thomas the Butcher and Anton, Head Truth Keeper of Andrapaal and Thuraen depart. Peter shrugged his shoulders and shook his head as he waved. Others of the township watched on too, but they did not seem too happy or too said to see off the visitors. Paechra and Anton were focused upon their own thoughts as the midmorning hour passed by. Paechra had taken her opportunity to ask about Johannas Stormsong, the one she knew as Raven. Peter had been about to recite many a verse from the tomes that mentioned a dark raven that was the right hand of Vladimir, Sage-King, but none of the words sounded to Paechra like they could have been her friend. Yohan's gossip was far worse than the official ones Peter knew.

289

"The dark raven is a thunderstorm," Yohan had said. "He strikes with the sword and keeps the city in his fearful gaze."

"I always suspected that the boy did not differ much from his father," Anton had added, but Paechra refused to believe.

"My experience with Michael Stormsong has been nothing but kindness and support," Paechra had argued.

"I guess we will just have to agree that I am right, and you are wrong, and to leave it at that then," suggested the Head Truth Keeper, gruffly.

Even though Paechra had not wanted to leave things be, there, Sienna's decision to take Yohan away with her had prevented Paechra from asking the boy any further questions. And, although Peter was still eager to show that he could be useful to Paechra, there was nothing else that the young sylvan wanted to learn from Williamsons' writings. She vowed to make some time while they were on the road, thinking that Sienna could not keep the boy busy the whole journey.

"Did you discover what it was that you desired to know?" asked Heidi, side by side with her friend at the head of the column of sylvan.

"No, not yet, but I will," vowed Paechra, finally accepting a plump and juicy fruit that was offered by her friend.

"I do not doubt it," replied Heidi. "Not for one moment."

And with that the pair led in silence, the munching and slurping of friends the only sound. Finally, Paechra's stomach grew still, and the long walk was a pleasant one.

Not so pleasant for Yohan though, with him sitting beside Sienna in a wagon, pulled by a stubborn steed. Every few miles the old sylvan demanding of him some menial task or another.

"Why couldn't have you just left me behind and taken Peter instead," the young boy moaned.

"You have a part to play in all of this, young Yohan," suggested High Prince Ulan who also shared the wagon.

"Do you see it?" asked Yohan.

"No, I do not," admitted Ulan. "But I see how it is that Sienna looks at you."

"Yeah, creepily," suggested Yohan causing the prince to laugh.

Chapter Thirteen

Youth Wasted on the Young

Who is the dark shadow in the blackbird's skin?

The harborer of darkness doth bar the way.

Darkness meets light.

None shall remain unscathed.

From the Sixth Stanza of the Prophecy, translated by the sages of the Kingdom of Thuraen 498th year

"HOW MUCH FARTHER?" moaned the young voice of Yohan the student sage.

"You tell us, boy," growled the distinct voice of Head Truth Keeper Anton.

The pair of humans had been traveling as a part of Paechra's army for two days, moving southward along the North road. Yohan had tried as often as he could to escape from under the wing of Mother Druid Sienna Alknown, although it was not often that the oldest sylvan rested, even though the wagon that she, Yohan, and High Prince Ulan rode upon rocked the trio like an infant's cradle. Sienna was getting far too much enjoyment from ordering the young boy about. Sleep would only rob her of her fun.

"Fetch me some red berries," Sienna demanded, and then reprimanded Yohan when he returned with poisonous fruits colored a rich, bright shade of pink.

"Trim my nails!" commanded the old one.

Again, Yohan was scolded when he broke Sienna's parchment-like skin. A dark blue oozed from the slice as the Mother Druid gasped in pain. Paechra watched on from afar, just within eyesight and earshot, trying not to laugh.

"You fool of a boy!" cried Ulan as the high prince attempted to help with the wound.

"Keep away!" Sienna cried. "I can fix it!"

"Go find some kindling to start a fire, Yohan," suggested High Prince Ulan.

Paechra almost chortled as she witnessed just how quickly Yohan made to obey.

The youngest Lightheart had hoped to speak with Yohan and discover more about the rumors he had overheard which mentioned Paechra's friend Raven, and anything that the boy had heard about Andrapaal; the vorsurk, the citizens, whether it was a peaceful or hostile occupation of the capital, but Sienna had had other plans. Thus far, two whole days in and at noon

293

on the third, there had been no time that Paechra and Yohan could have privately talked.

Paechra had begun to wonder if Sienna Alknown was living up to her name and had her reasons for keeping the two apart.

"Do you not agree that this could be possible?" Paechra had asked of her friend Heidi.

"Yes?" was Heidi's uncertain reply.

"Yes you do not agree?" asked Paechra. "Or yes, you agree that our Mother Druid does not want me to speak with the boy?"

"Yes?" suggested Heidi again, this time even less sure of her response.

"My thoughts also," Paechra had said with a nod of understanding and satisfaction. "I shall find a time to discover if what we think is true is…"

"And what is it that we think is true?" Heidi had asked, but Paechra was by then deep in thought, plotting and planning.

With Yohan finally away from Sienna and the keenly-eyed Ulan, Paechra thought it an opportune time to take the boy aside.

"Yohan!" she called, as the young sage stepped away from the column of sylvan and went searching for sticks.

Paechra made to call again, but before she could she saw Anton place an arm around Yohan's shoulders like a caring father would.

"This I need to hear…" Paechra said to herself, and she hurried to catch up with the pair.

"… and then he raised the prices at the market, but none of the merchants saw any of the additional profits…" Yohan said, causing Anton to cry out in surprise.

"I just want to turn around and march back up to that Sage Williamsons and give him a large piece of my mind," growled the head of the Truth Keepers.

"I do hope that you don't," murmured the young sage in reply.

"Nonsense," said Anton, trying to reassure. "Everything you have told me will be kept in the strictest of confidences."

"That may be the case," Yohan replied. "But Sage Williamsons will know that it is me…"

"Impossible," huffed Anton.

"Impossible for it to be anyone else other than Yohan…" suggested Paechra.

"Lightheart, when did you sneak up upon us?" asked Anton.

"Only just now, Truth Keeper," the sylvan replied.

Anton's aura changed from one of guilt to that of relief, making Paechra wonder what it was that she had missed. The aura of the young sage was a constant pinkish haze, telling Paechra that he felt very much out of place.

"My feet hurt," Yohan complained.

"You spend most of your time on the cart, with the elderly and royalty," Anton snapped. "Try walking all day and then tell me such things."

"I would happily walk all the way back to the beach," said Yohan. "I would not care how much that my legs ached after such a hike."

"You say that now," growled Anton. "But I doubt very much if you would still sing the same tune should we let you make such a journey."

"Hush, both of you," ordered the Druid. "Such speaking has done naught but cause you both angst."

"So, what is it that you would like to discuss?" asked the Head Truth Keeper, though the question sounded very much like the accusation that it was.

"Raven?" said Paechra in surprise.

For out of the forest that ran alongside the road there came a figure upon the back of a charger, he was encased in dark metal armor, a great sword was held aloft, and his free mailed hand was wrapped around a helm shaped to resemble the messenger bird.

"Who are you and for what purpose do you come with such forces into these lands?" came the booming voice of the figure astride the great warhorse.

"Raven, it is me, Paechra... Paechra Lightheart..." said the sylvan.

"Johannas, cease this ridiculous charade and get down off your high horse," shouted Anton, angrily.

"I do not know you or your kind," the figure announced, addressing Paechra directly. "All I see is a foreign force on Thuraen soil."

"Look at me boy, I am your master," ordered Anton.

Paechra looked again at the one who she thought was her friend, discovering his aura was missing, completely absent.

"Go back and warn the others..." she whispered to Yohan. "Go... Go now..."

Without needing to be asked twice, Yohan ran as quickly as he could.

"You there, boy!" called the figure upon horseback. "Stop now or I will stop you."

"No friend of mine would harm a child!" Paechra stated cooly.

"We are not friends," the warrior replied.

"He has a crossbow!" Anton suddenly cried.

Paechra saw in the same instant that this fact was true. The one whom she first thought was Raven did have a loaded crossbow. He drew it forth as he sheathed his sword. Ignoring both Anton and Paechra he aimed the weapon at the fleeing Yohan.

"One more step," boomed the mounted figure. "And you will step no more."

"Fire upon the child and you will regret it," warned Anton.

"Then perhaps I will fire upon you," the warrior replied.

Paechra watched as the crossbow swung so the bolt was inches from Anton's face. That was when the warrior pulled the trigger.

#

Paechra looked up at the human dressed in dark mail, her almond shaped ears gladdened to hear the thudding footsteps of the fleeing child, Yohan, whom she had sent off in search of aid. The knight upon horseback looked like her friend Raven, the one known throughout the human kingdom of Thuraen as Johannas Stormsong, Johannas the Betrayer, but Paechra knew Raven, knew his kindness, his tenacity, his heroics, and most importantly his aura. This figure before her was not Raven, could not possibly be her friend. The figure upon that high horse was someone, or something else. His threat to fire a crossbow bolt through the back of a retreating teen, and now the very act of shooting that bolt without hesitation, straight into the face of an old man, Anton, Head Truth Keeper of Andrapaal and the whole human kingdom, a man that each and every Truth Keeper was supposed to respect and obey. Then there was the evidence she discovered by opening her second sight, evidence that where any aura should have been, there actually was none. Those actions were not the actions and the words of a friend, not even those of a sane human being, and every true creature carried an aura with them, around them, telling those who knew how to look what a creature was feeling and vaguely thinking. No, Paechra very quickly determined that these were in fact the words and actions not of a human, but in fact of a monster.

Standing beside Paechra, Anton had none of this knowledge or forethought to guide him. He only had his past dealings with Johannas, with Michael Stormsong, Johannas' father, a decade of broken friendships, the Stormsong family's very public fall from grace, and now, in that precise instant, the arrogance of one whom Anton considered an inferior. But all of this fell away, and Anton's world became a single point in time, thanks to the figure on horseback that swung his crossbow from Yohan to him. The old man watched the gauntleted hand pull that trigger and Anton felt the shadow of the Reaper right behind him. If he had been alone, or if he had been surrounded by a whole battalion of Truth Keepers, he would most definitely have been dead. But Anton was not alone, and he was far away from any battalion of Truth Keepers. Luckily for Anton he was standing at that very moment right beside the only person who could possibly save his life.

In the moment that the crossbow fired, Paechra's mind swiftly moved from disbelief, to horror, to savior mode. The Druid quickly realized that there would be no reasoning with the weapon or the projectile, the monstrous figure upon the great warhorse was impervious to reason, but the horse, the proud beast, that was a normal, everyday, run of the mill steed, trained for battle, ready to be guided by whomever or whatever was its master; but at the very heart of the matter it was a horse, just the same as any other. Paechra's aura reached out and touched the dark-grey aura of that beast and immediately scared it, spooked it and its simple mind. As the bolt began its short journey toward Anton's eyes the horse reared up, changing the angle of the shot and sending the bolt skimming between Anton's salt and pepper head of hair. Twenty or so feet away the bolt thudded into one of the trees that lined the road and vibrated noisily with a reverberating hum.

"What insubordination is this?!" cried Anton as he fumbled to get his sword loosened from its sheath.

The knight who somehow immediately regained command of his horse, somehow settling the spooked steed in the blink of an eye, was far faster with his weapon than Anton was, and his blade was drawn and swinging downward while the Head Truth Keeper was still fussing with his. Paechra, in disbelief of the stubbornness shown by the old human bumped him out of the way and somehow managed to catch the point of the knight's sword in her off hand. Blood welled where the point cut.

"Let go, girl," ordered the dark-mailed knight. "Else my next blow will take your hand, and then your head for a trophy."

Paechra did as the knight demanded, but not because she had been ordered to do so.

"All-ash-ara... Jthu-lu-ana... Ashrak... Al... Tuu..." murmured the sylvan.

The blood from her wound poured out in a sheet that began to wrap around the knight and steed both. Before the encapsulation spell could be complete, the knight clicked his tongue and both he and the horse simply disappeared.

"I did not need your witchcraft to save me," spluttered Anton as he finally chose to get back to his feet.

"Nonsense, stubborn old man," bit back Paechra, frustrated and afraid. "It was my so called witchcraft that saved your sorry hide."

"What is the meaning of this?" called the voice of High Prince Ulan. "The boy, Yohan, came to Sienna and I crowing about trouble, and yet all I see here before me is two who have been arguing the whole of this journey."

"There was a third," cried the boy, Yohan, a few paces behind the high prince. "A hulking black knight on a horse that was bigger than I was."

"Look around you, Ulan," suggested Paechra, there was none of the respect that a sylvan was supposed to give to the high prince, but Ulan had already grown used to this.

"I am looking, young Lightheart," replied High Prince Ulan. "What is it that you hoped I would see?"

"The hoof prints, maybe," offered Paechra. "That bolt in that tree which was supposed to be in Anton's head..."

"What prints? What bolt?" asked Ulan, amused.

Paechra took her eyes from staring, defiantly into Ulan's and she looked down at her feet, and then toward the trees. Where the horse had stood, and then reared up, there was no evidence that such a beast had ever been. The bolt that Paechra and Anton had both witnessed narrowly miss claiming the Head Truth Keeper's life, had disappeared.

"I don't understand?" said Anton and Paechra, together, for

once in unison.

"Perhaps this is more of your magic, Druid," Anton suddenly accused. "You feel threatened by my presence since we are now returned to my world."

"Are you truly as stupid as you are stubborn?" asked Paechra of the old man, a genuine question, but Anton immediately took offense.

"How dare you…"

"Oh, I dare," declared Paechra. "I just saved you twice from certain death… I think that I have every right to dare…"

"The horse reared," Anton argued.

"It only reared with thanks to me," suggested the Druid.

"I guess you are claiming you cast some sort of split-second magic spell, slowed time, can talk to animals at some acute level…" grumbled the Head Truth Keeper. "Shall we call you Paechra the horse whisperer?"

"And you think that the horse reared up on its back legs all by itself, do you?" accused Paechra, a glint in her eye.

"It is possible," argued Anton, but his argument was no longer a strong one.

"And then the knight in the next second managed to get it under control again?" asked Paechra, one eyebrow was raised, daring Anton to suggest that this was true.

"Um… Yes..?" asked Anton. "I think so… Maybe..?"

"What horse, what knight?" Ulan demanded to know.

It was then that Sienna hobbled up, aided by Sarah and Heidi.

"I sense it, Ulan," the ancient sylvan stated. "There was a presence here, not long ago, a creature of dark magics."

"I know what I saw, and it was Michael Stormsong's son," suggested Anton.

"You saw what you were supposed to see," replied Paechra. "Just the same as I did, Anton, at least at first."

"It seems that we are at a disadvantage, you and I," High Prince Ulan suggested, patting Anton on the back.

"Yes, I admit, I guess that is true," grumbled Anton. "I understand that these Druids can perhaps see things we cannot, make things happen that we would only see in dreams or nightmares."

"But you do not have to like it," laughed Ulan. "To be honest, sometimes I don't."

Sienna gave Ulan a look then, one that caused the sylvan high prince to smile.

"Although we cannot see what it is that they can see, although we cannot do what it is that they can do, we can choose to respect it, and we can choose to support and protect it," Ulan said.

"Before witnessing the fall of the fine city that I call home," began Anton. "I would not have seen things in the way that you have put them."

"But now?" asked Sienna.

"I must reluctantly admit that the time I have spent with Paechra, traveling to and through the sylvan lands, and now, traveling with you all..." said Anton in reply.

"Yes?" prompted Heidi.

"I know what I want to feel and say, but the things I am seeing with my own eyes, seeing, hearing, feeling," said Anton. "These things are getting more and more difficult for me to explain."

"Then let's be happy with that," suggested Ulan.

"I guess," grumbled Anton. "So, let's all pretend that I believe that the figure who nearly killed me wasn't the boy, Johannas Stormsong, no matter how much that it looked like him, sounded like him, probably even smelled like he smells."

"Yes," said High Prince Ulan. "Let us all pretend that, just as you have suggested."

"Well then, if that is the case, what do we do now?" asked the Head Truth Keeper.

"We move on from here, and quickly," announced Sienna, interrupting.

"Do you sense something, Mother Druid?" asked Heidi, suddenly enveloped in a blue aura, shaped as a deer ready to fight or flee.

"There's nothing coming, at least not yet, daughter," Sienna reassured. "But our location is now known, and I can tell you it needs no great wisdom to determine where our enemies will send their soldiers, all one thousand three hundred and thirty one of them."

"Oh my," said Heidi. "Shall I go and order the packing of the tents then?"

"Yes, please, Heidi, my friend," said Paechra. "Please express the need for us all to hurry."

"Of course, Paechra," said Heidi, hurrying then, back toward the sylvan and human camp.

"What do you see, Mother?" asked Sarah, when Heidi had gone.

The ancient sylvan looked to Anton.

"Please, speak," urged the human.

"Very well," said Sienna. "I sense magic from one of the

vorsurk tomes of darkness, one of their sacred eleven texts, but I cannot be certain which."

"But there is something more," suggested Sarah. "There is something that is missing that is usually always there when we come across the signature of such arcana."

"Very good, young Sarah," praised Sienna, causing the older Lightheart to blush.

"It is almost as if the one who has cast the spell is unfamiliar with such power," continued Sarah as she closed her eyes again and re-opened her second sight. "The tome itself is what is in control."

"Then we must pray for the one who holds such a tome, the one who believes that they own such power, for their life will not long be their own," murmured Sienna saddened.

"May the light guide them to abandon such a foolish quest," stated the Lighthearts, mother and daughter, together.

"So, let them come," stated Anton, not understanding. "We can handle some vorsurk soldiers."

"A party of eleven, yes," agreed Paechra. "Perhaps we are ready to take on even one hundred and twenty-one."

"Yes, our numbers are sufficient, and well enough trained to survive without too great a loss should we battle a force of over one hundred," suggested Sienna. "But any more than that and we will struggle, perhaps not any of us will survive."

"Then what is the point of this?" asked Anton. "Be it one thousand, ten thousand, more? We will need to defeat all of the vorsurk to regain Andrapaal and the other cities and towns that have been overrun by those dogs."

"We have defeated the vorsurk before now, and we will defeat them again and return the lands to you and your people," vowed Sienna.

"Anton, those who have gathered to this cause have not done so lightly," suggested Paechra. "We choose to run today and not stand and fight against an enemy unknown."

"I get it girl," said Anton, sourly. "We live for the tomorrow to fight the battles of our choosing."

"Exactly," agreed Paechra.

"I have been a commander of armies for decades," Head Truth Keeper Anton declared.

Paechra tried not to smile at such a reference to time.

"As you say, Anton," she replied.

"I do say," rumbled Anton.

He unsheathed his sword and this time it came easily free.

"This very blade has felled at least a thousand of the barbaric brutes."

"But you cannot fight them all yourself," suggested Ulan. "And if we chose to remain here it may very well end up being you against the world."

"Then hurry and return to your wagon," ordered Anton. "We move out, immediately."

"As you so order," said Paechra, offering Anton a curt bow.

"I guess such an acknowledgement is the very best that I can expect," said Anton. "But know this, had you been one of my Truth Keepers I would have very early on had you peeling vegetables."

"You remove the outer skin of your vegetables?" asked Paechra, surprised. "There's no end to the bizarreness of your race."

"Enough of this nonsense," laughed Ulan. "Your complicated bickering merely delays us longer."

"You are right, Ulan," Anton said, giving Paechra a curt bow of his own and then offering the sylvan high prince a deeper, more formal one. "If we are not to fight here and now then I would prefer we make our way to where and when we choose to fight."

The old man slid his blade away and marched with stiff shoulders and straight back, away from the remaining sylvan, toward the dismantling campsite.

"Did I miss much?" Paechra heard Thomas call as he came running up to the Head Truth Keeper.

In reply, Anton huffed.

"It seems that the sighting of an old friend means we must not dally but must instead hurriedly continue southward again."

"And that means?" asked Thomas, still none-the-wiser.

"It means that I need you to pack up our things," explained Anton, obviously frustrated.

"But I just got things the way that I wanted them," Thomas the Butcher moaned.

"I know, lad," sighed Anton. "I know."

#

It took at least an hour for everything to be packed up, for Ulan, Sienna, and Yohan to climb aboard the wagon, and for Paechra's great army to get back on the road again. In that time nobody saw any sign of the stranger on horseback or the vorsurk. A day further down the road, still at least a half day of trudging away from the next township, the army halted, for there ahead was the figure Anton, Yohan, and Paechra had seen. This time he stood just beyond a corpse of trees. His horse was tethered, back off the road, but within view, like all horses, it happily munched on the grass that grew up among the tree roots.

"I told you to turn around and return homeward," called the figure.

His deadly crossbow was loaded and ready and he brought the weapon up to his eye line to sight a target.

"We could say the same of you," Paechra called back. "We know that you are not what it is that you claim to be."

In response to this the figure gave a laugh, a confident, dry sound, but not a human one.

"Perhaps this bolt is destined for you," said the figure.

It was difficult for Paechra to not see that figure as her friend, but each time she opened up her third eye she reminded herself of the truth.

"Or perhaps the old woman on the cart, or that boy beside her, so many choices..." the figure suggested, with each possible target his weapon swiveled to realign the sight.

"Kill one of us and all of us will destroy you," Heidi called out, bravely.

"Destroy me and my army will avenge my death," declared the stranger.

"What army, your horse?" scoffed Yohan.

"What army, you ask..." said the stranger. "This army..."

As if on some sort of silent cue, out from the forest filed line after line of vorsurk troops. Tens became hundreds, and the hundreds grew in number, until it seemed like there were no longer trees, but in the place of the forest a brutish band of barbarians instead. Paechra lost count at five hundred and still

307

the numbers continued to grow.

"You wanted a battle, Anton," she whispered under her breath. "And now I guess we've got one."

"I'm right here," growled the voice of the Head Truth Keeper. "If we all do as we have been trained then this will be like a dance in the moonlight."

"Sunlight is far better for us," suggested the sylvan.

"You dance where you like lass," laughed Anton. "I prefer the dark."

Paechra noticed that the old man already had his sword drawn free. She then, like her sisters, brought to mind the spells she would need, the blue aura of power cloaking her.

"What did you want me to do?" asked Thomas, surprising Paechra as he snuck up behind her and Anton.

"Stay by me," ordered Anton. "And remain out of trouble…"

"Get the wagon to safety," ordered Paechra.

In a split second Anton agreed with Paechra. Battle was about to begin, and Thomas would be a liability.

"Aye, lad, do as the witch says…" the Head Truth Keeper urged the young butcher.

It did not please him, but he knew that Paechra was right.

#

Miriam was her name, the name shared with Raven when her master bought him. She was his inspiration, his reason for living. Not in the same sense that Paechra his friend gave him a feeling of delight each time he thought of her, worried about

her, remembered their times together. Raven and Derek had been split, each going to a separate vorsurk bidder. Raven at first was unsure how he would cope without the sylvan's guidance, this world between worlds still so strange. Raven considered what Mick, his dwarf friend would have thought seeing him in his new life as a cattle herder. Raven was treated poorly by the other slaves, and vorsurk who also worked with the beasts of burden. Miriam was the only one who showed Raven any kindness.

She survived as the keeper of the secret elixir, Miriam the mistress of mead. Honey mixed with the blood of the oxen and then allowed to ferment in caves found beneath the rocky earth. Many tried to copy the mixture, but, without the knowledge Miriam had brought from her homeland, the elixir never turned out right. A human, but one from lands beyond Thuraen, Miriam's presence and memories of Paechra inspired Raven to break the bonds of slavery. The blackbird, wings clipped, had learned to fly again.

Chapter Fourteen

Fire Burning Where a Heart Should be

Ho! The black bird spreads wings of earth.

Its twin has fire burning where a heart should be.

From the Twelfth Stanza of the Prophecy, translated by the sages of the Kingdom of Thuraen 514th year

A CAST THOUSANDS barred the way of Paechra and her army. The strange creature that looked like her friend Raven stood at the enemy's front. Beside Paechra was Anton, his sword already drawn, the old man eager for battle. Paechra had tried to tell Anton that the one who looked like Raven, the one Anton thought he knew to be Johannas Stormsong, was not in fact a man at all. Paechra's special sight told her such and she believed what magic told her more than what the illusion before her said. Anton, like the other human, Thomas the Butcher, struggled to believe in magic, struggled to accept that what he could see was what was real.

"Stay back, lass," Anton ordered. "I know this boy and I have been waiting for this moment for quite some time."

"You cannot be serious?" said Paechra in reply. "This is NOT Johannas, not some battle between the old and the new."

"You tell it your way and I will tell it mine," replied the Head Truth Keeper.

"Do I stay, or do I go?" asked Thomas, meekly.

"Go!" ordered Anton and Paechra together.

"Take the wagon and lead it behind the lines," added Paechra.

It frustrated her to see that Thomas looked to Anton for confirmation before he obeyed. Precious seconds could mean the difference between life and death, and they were wasting many of them.

"Come," Thomas clicked as he stepped through the throng of Druids, Paechra's sylvan sisterhood, all shimmering faintly with a blue glow, evidence of the magic they were preparing to use.

The sea of sylvan parted allowing the butcher to lead the boy Yohan, the ancient Sienna, and High Prince Ulan to what Paechra hoped was safety.

"Where did you want me?" asked the voice of Ulan from behind Paechra.

The ruler of Greenwood Vale had jumped clear of that wagon and shirked the offered safety, that was how it so seemed to Paechra.

"Back on the wagon," Paechra ordered, giving the prince a

glance.

Ulan had a great big hunk of wood in his hands, brandishing it like a club or cudgel. Coupled with the determined look on his face, Paechra could foresee trouble.

"I have not travelled all such distance with you, Miss Lightheart, only for you to ask me to wait on a wagon with the young and the old," announced Ulan. "Tell me where you want me to go and I will be there, but do not treat me like a wilting flower."

"Please at least tell me that Yohan has stayed with Mother Sienna," said Paechra.

"Sienna Alknown has the boy and Heidi with her," replied Ulan. "All three are safer than most right at this moment."

"Not as safe as Michael Stormsong and Queen Catherine," considered the younger Lightheart.

Raven's father was back in Greenwood Vale with the human queen awaiting the birth of her child. For a moment Paechra thought it a good thing that Michael was not there but wished that she and all that had chosen to follow in her footsteps could have been anywhere else too. Paechra hoped that this was not to be the end of her story, nor the end for any of her friends.

"What would you do, Raven?" the sylvan asked, out loud, but to herself.

"Not knowing your friend, but knowing common sense, I would suggest this Raven's actions would be the opposite of Anton's," suggested Ulan.

Paechra turned her attention to where the Head Truth Keeper had previously been and discovered Anton was already three determined strides toward the figure dressed in black.

"Come step forward boy and face me like the man you claim to be," called Anton.

Immediately the sight on the loaded crossbow held by the figure that looked like Johannas Stormsong trained on the advancing Anton.

"Perhaps I will have the opportunity to shoot you after all," said the figure dressed in black mail. "Or, perhaps I should have my army tear you limb from limb until all that remains is a bleeding shell of a proud man."

"You and I can finish this," ordered Anton. "We should just send all the others home.

"I told you to turn away," laughed the dark knight. "I gave you that chance, but you all refused."

"So now we fight," said Anton. "But this battle shall be only between you and me."

"Wrong!" called back the figure that stood at the front of the army of wolf-like vorsurk. "Why would I give up such a great advantage, you call yourself a leader, and yet you act as if you are the lost little lamb."

In that moment Paechra felt something change. There was something in the nature of the man with no aura, the aura that was not there seemed to warp into something evil, or more evil, if that was possible.

Without a thought the Druid reacted. A flash of blue in the image of a sparrow flew forth from her clenched hand that opened. The bird flittered about, diving in and out between Anton, who had again stepped closer to the one dressed in black, and that strange figure who threatened them all with his loaded crossbow. As the bird passed between the pair of combatants the crossbow fired and struck it true. There was a gasp from the army of sylvan behind Paechra, but she ignored them. Instead, she closely watched Anton. She had saved his life yet again, and yet again he ignored such a favor.

313

"Foolish boy," announced the old man with a cocky smile. "Have I taught you nothing about the importance of advantage?"

"Foolish human," replied the figure who looked like Raven. "You do not realize that it is I who still hold all of the cards."

With impossible speed the figure unsheathed a long blade that burned with pitch colored flames. In an instant the weapon swung upward in a strike that aimed to open Anton from his navel to his throat. Somehow Anton managed to get his own blade in the way of the swift strike, clumsy instinct more than trained warrior skill. The magical blade that burned with dark fire sliced through Anton's un-enchanted one, but the block was enough to turn the weapon from its deadly course.

"Ha-Ma-Moosh!" called Paechra, and a great wall of wind knocked Anton to his knees while also pushing the warrior dressed in dark mail backward into the throng of vorsurk.

Behind her, Paechra heard other Druids cast similar spells, the wall of wild wind buffeting the barbaric vorsurk back into the corpse of trees from whence they had appeared.

"Attack, you useless hunks of muscle!" ordered the one without an aura.

Eagerly the wolf-like creatures howled as one and rushed toward Paechra and her army.

"My blade!" cried Anton as he picked up the fallen piece from the ground. "My sword I have had all my life as a Truth Keeper."

"Get up!" yelled Paechra as the vorsurk frontlines drew up level with the kneeling Anton. "This is the fight that you wanted, old man, so get up and fight!"

It was almost as if these were the very magic words that Anton needed to hear. Paechra witnessed Anton's aura change from grey to a burning, bright white. With what remained of his sword Anton feverishly stabbed and swiped, cutting down the barbarians that he could reach, a pile of bodies swiftly growing around him. Paechra heard strange grunts and growls, animalistic sounds emanating from Anton as he fought, sweat quickly creating a thin sheen across the old man's skin.

"Everyone hurry, to Anton's side!" Paechra ordered with a shout.

The young sylvan had quickly noticed that the vorsurk were not rushing forward en masse, instead funneling their attacks in pairs and triplets solely focused on Head Truth Keeper Anton as their target.

Druids shrouded in blue auras shaped like wolves, bears, doe, and the likes moved forward toward the skirmish, driving the vorsurk back as swiftly as they came forward. Peering into and beyond the line of trees, Paechra discovered that there was no source from whence the enemy came, they just seemed to appear.

"They have no aura," she whispered, the fact surprising her.

"You are correct," agreed Sarah Lightheart, Paechra's mother, she having made her way through the fighting to stand beside her daughter. "These creatures, this man, even the very trees and road we follow, and pass seem to be of pure imagination."

"I have blindly taken us down a road that is not real," stated the younger Lightheart in disbelief. "I have allowed myself to be guided by emotion and have placed us all in great danger."

"Cease your personal pity and join the fray," called Anton over his shoulder.

"Anton!" Paechra cried as the figure that resembled Raven took another swing at the old man.

315

The burning blade sliced with ease through Anton's guard, his armor and then his collarbone; blood the color of royalty spraying out like a pretty fan.

"Turn away and return to your forest, witch," ordered the warrior encased in black, dark, empty eyes catching Paechra's as Anton collapsed from the savage blow dealt.

"Daughter, wake from this dream," pleaded Sarah. "We do not need walk such a path."

"Do you not see, mother?" Paechra replied. "We are being shown the way, and the way is full of death and sacrifice."

#

"Daughter, come back to us," commanded the voice of Sienna Alknown.

Paechra opened her eyes and discovered that she was in her tent.

"Your aura turned black, almost like it was disappearing," gasped Heidi. "I did not know what to do, so I found your mother."

"And I in turn brought with me our Mother Druid," added Sarah Lightheart.

"And I am the one who found a way to bring you back to us," said Sienna, she gave Paechra a small smile as she squeezed the young Druid's hand. "It was a close call, but we are glad that you have returned."

"I still smell the sea," murmured Paechra weakly. "Have we not yet left?"

"You have been dreaming for two days," said Heidi. "We could not wake you."

"We have lost time, but we have gained much," said Paechra. "The road is not the path we need follow."

"You talk nonsense now, girl," grumbled the voice of Anton.

"It gladdens me to see you alive and well, Head Truth Keeper," stated Paechra, smiling, not the reaction that any in the tent expected.

"Paechra is deluded," announced Sienna. "Everyone out, allow her to rest…"

"No," said Paechra firmly as the Mother Druid began to herd the others out. "My vision showed me the dangers of walking the road, taking the child, doing the expected."

"Never once have I known you to do the expected, Paechra my friend," Heidi stated.

"And that is why I now know how we need travel to Andrapaal," said Paechra. "How I think we will be able to surprise the vorsurk, save the kingdom, and return the lands to the humans."

"How?" asked Anton.

"We travel by boat."

Anton rolled his eyes.

"We build our own boats from the great palms which guard the beachfront like sentinels," continued Paechra.

"If you truly believe that this is the way," said Sienna.

"Mother Druid Sienna, the North road leads to danger," announced Paechra. "I trust that my vision has taught me such."

"Fear dream, you mean," growled Anton.

"Such a dream showed me your death," Paechra bit back.

"A death in battle I would gladly accept," the human

317

declared.

"Then you are the fool we all thought you to be," stated Sienna. "You should instead strive to live, at the very least long enough to see out this quest."

"Is that what you wish?" replied the old man. "Mother of the Druids, are you journeying toward an ultimate gesture of sacrifice?"

"None of us know our futures," replied Sienna. "And none of us should."

"But what I have foreseen I fear shall come true," stated Paechra. "Whether we take the boy Yohan as promised or not, it will be by way of the rivers we shall travel to Andrapaal."

"I have need of the earth beneath my feet," said Anton, firmly. "I shall not be asked to row again."

There was a glass-eyed look for remembered horror etched on the Head Truth Keeper's features. Paechra nodded when she saw it.

"It shall be too long and too difficult to construct enough rafts from the trees to accommodate all of us," she said. "We will follow the river then, but travel by land, the road is watched, and it is not safe."

"As crazy as your words seem to sound," said Anton. "I sense that there is no swaying you from such a course."

"You speak the very truth that you aim to protect," Paechra replied.

"Then let me ask of the sage here for his permission," suggested Anton. "It would be better I deliver your strange plan."

All eyes turned to Paechra as she nodded her agreement.

"Thank you for your offer of support," she said.

318

"I am merely seeking a way to make the best of this," replied the human. "Do not make the mistake and believe that this is friendship."

"No, of course not," said Paechra, trying not to laugh. "Never would I believe for a second that a man such as you could befriend a forest witch like me."

"Hmmm..." said Anton.

His lips were turned downward in a frown, his arms crossed, but his eyes showed signs of thoughtfulness. Without another word he pushed his way through the small crowd that had gathered in the tent and made his way toward the sage's house.

"What is this talk of taking a child?" Sienna asked as soon as Anton had left.

"I thought that I could discover vital information about the one who is named Johannas Stormsong," said Paechra. "But the dream vision has revealed to me much that I wanted to know."

"Out, all of you get out of this tent," commanded Sienna Alknown. "Young Paechra and I have much to discuss."

"Including me, Mother Druid?" asked Heidi.

"Yes, child, including you," said Sienna.

"But this is my tent too," Heidi pleaded. "Where shall I go?"

"Perhaps I could suggest that you take a walk along the beach?" offered Paechra to her friend.

"Yes," said Heidi with a smile. "The gentle lap of waves upon the shore shall calm me, thank you, sister Paechra."

"I believe I shall join you," Paechra added. "Once you are finished with me of course, Mother Druid," she continued, respectfully.

"Perhaps wait outside, this should not take long," Sienna suggested to Heidi.

"As you wish, Mother Sienna," said Heidi with a nod.

With the tent emptied of all but the two of them, Sienna closed her eyes, and the aura of a dawning day enveloped her. Paechra felt her own eyes close, and a similar glow surrounded her as well.

"Show me everything that you can remember," requested Sienna's ancient voice.

Paechra cast her mind back to the time she led those who had chosen to follow her cause down the North road. The vision felt so real, every step she could sense the presence of Sienna, watching, listening, and learning. There came a gasp that threatened to break the bond and cause the recollection to come to a halt, Sienna reacting to the first time that Johannas appeared in the dream, but the Mother Druid was strong, especially in the ways of magic, and somehow she was able to keep the connection intact. When the battle upon the road broke out there was no way though that Paechra could relive such a vision twice. She herself chose to step away, discovering that Sienna held her hands so tightly that they had turned white. Paechra gently freed herself from Sienna's grip, the elder choosing then to open her eyes.

"A broken blade, the attacks all focused on Anton, what can it possibly all mean?" the ancient muttered while Paechra shook her hands vigorously, trying to get the blood flowing again.

"All that I know is the one who Yohan has heard all of the gossip about is not my friend," stated Paechra with certainty. "It gladdens my heart to know this but also chills it as I now fear for his safety."

"Your friend is on his own journey," said Sienna cryptically. "One that may help us, or hinder us, but not one that we can know of now."

"Forgive me, Mother Sienna," begged Paechra. "I cannot yet let go of my worry."

"Keep it with you as you would a locket," suggested Sienna. "Place it in a pocket of your mind such that you can examine it at a later time."

Paechra nodded and then did as she was asked.

"Thinking back over the vison and the discussion between the one dressed in black and the Head Truth Keeper, I did see my friend's steed acting as any steed would," said Paechra, thoughtful. "I have ridden upon that horse and swear I would know it anywhere."

"Then there must be a connection between the one with the tome, and the Truth Keepers..." considered the ancient.

Paechra's mind filled with an image of her father. Beside him stood a man dressed in the blue robes.

"Vladimir," murmured the younger Lightheart.

Then the vision changed, and the blue robed sage became a puppet on strings. A young hand pulled upon those strings making the puppet dance.

"This is all beyond even me," suggested Sienna. "We need gather together our sisterhood."

"Allow me," offered Heidi.

Sienna nodded.

"Ask them to gather at the foreshore," she ordered. "We have much to discuss."

#

The waves of the North Shore lapped gently as the Druids of Greenwood Vale stood before the shore. Mother Druid Sienna Alknown stood amongst them, flanked by Sarah Lightheart and Paechra's friend Heidi. Paechra Lightheart was the only one with her back to the waves. Again, she had been thrust into the spotlight of leadership, it was she who had suffered the dream that had brought them all together.

"…And then, from the trees there came what seemed like thousands of vorsurk, but each warrior had no aura, no presence, only a basic hunger to kill…" Paechra tried to explain.

"The trees that were not there?" asked one of Paechra's sylvan sisters.

"That ran along the road that was not real?" asked another, wanting to believe, but obviously struggling.

"A broken blade too," laughed the Head Truth Keeper of Andrapaal, Anton. "This one…"

Drawing his sword free of its sheath, Anton showed all who could see that his sword in fact was not broken.

"Anton…" said Paechra, asking for quiet from the old human, but Anton did not want to remain quiet.

"What notches and nicks that can be seen upon this blade I myself have caused, earned even…" he said, pushing his way through the crowd of sylvan, until he stood beside Paechra. "Everyone can surely see that my blade is far from broken…"

The younger Lightheart could not catch Anton's eye no matter how much she tried.

"I have fought many a vorsurk and this friend of mine has

stayed strong, straight, and true in every skirmish," the old man continued. "No blade of mine has come to pieces, the story this one is telling you is far from true."

"Such is the nature of a dream, Anton," suggested Paechra.

"I sleep quite soundly," Anton bit back. "Such things as dreams have rarely bothered me with their desire to confuse and amuse."

Paechra noticed he did not say the word witch, but when he turned his head and stared into her eyes his look basically said it for him.

"The sage did not allow us the use of his precious palms?" the Druid asked.

"No," said Anton. "I tend to agree with the thinking of one so wise as His Wisdom."

"Nobody would be asked to row," said Paechra, a whisper that she hoped only Anton would hear. "We would coast down the river, propelled by the current."

"And the boy Yohan stays," Anton stated, bluntly, seemingly ignoring Paechra's comment.

"I have seen what Paechra has shown me, what it is that the road of the dreamer has been able to reveal," Sienna's voice called out with strength.

"The ancient one speaks, and my blade falls from its hilt," roared Anton.

"Each moment you spend upon this shore makes you sound greater and greater the fool," replied Sienna. "Go find a beverage and break your fast, or if it is fueled folly, go stroll far from my seeing and prepare for orders."

"I am Head Truth Keeper Anton of Andrapaal," the old man announced. "I give orders, I don't get given them."

"We are not in Andrapaal though are we," said Sienna, lips tight, showing a rare sign of anger.

"Neither are we in Greenwood Vale," replied Anton.

"But unlike you, Anton, I need not be home to demand respect," said Sienna.

"I am home," huffed the human. "Though even this far from the heart of the kingdom it is difficult to recognize that here is where I belong."

"So, a crisis of identity is it?" asked the Mother Druid. "I knew it could not possibly be a fear of ghouls, or the water, or of Paechra's dreams."

"Dreams and crisis both be the playthings of children," mumbled Anton.

Paechra could see fear in the human's eyes when Mother Druid Sienna mentioned the monstrous ghoul, hinting at the time spent on the ship, The Picturesque Picaresque.

"Mother…" warned Paechra. "Perhaps you push too far?"

"Very well, daughter," agreed Sienna. "It may very well be as you suggest."

"I do not need you to fight my battles, Paechra," said Anton. "Be they battles in waking and in dreaming."

"No, but I do need you to help me to fight mine," the young Druid replied.

"Then know that I am ready with my blade should you require it, for the betterment of Thuraen of course," said Anton. "Just understand that I do not do boats."

"You can rest assured that I have clearly received such a message," stated Paechra.

"Good then," nodded Anton, acting as if he and Paechra were alone on the shoreline. "I think I shall go forth and break my fast."

#

By midday Yohan and Peter had heard the news that neither boy would be leaving, travelling south with Paechra's army.

Yohan showed signs of obvious relief, Peter was disappointed, but his feelings, he hid well. Paechra and the other Druids were able to detect Peter's true feelings in his aura, but they respected his privacy enough not to push.

Sage Williamsons was furious though.

"What is written MUST be true," he spluttered. "I have dried the ink, so you will be taking the boy Yohan back to Andrapaal, you cannot go against the words of truth."

'Did you not hear of the Dream Clause, Your Wisdom?" asked Anton. "I have heard on good authority that it was newly introduced to Andrapaal, just before the disruption."

"No, I cannot say that I was made aware of this new clause," muttered Sage Williamsons. "Little that which is new has come this far up the North road; it is like we are our own island, cut off from the heart... A heart that I do so truly miss..."

"Of course, Your Wisdom, a true pity if ever was spoke such a trifle," suggested Anton.

"And on what good authority do you claim to have heard of such as this new Dream Clause?" asked the sage, after a thoughtful pause.

"What greater authority is there, Your Wiseness, but the authority of truth?" replied the Head Truth Keeper, his face serious, yet plain, not giving anything away.

Paechra remained silent, she herself struggling not to smile during the exchange of words between the humans, knowing that even a small smirk would give the game away.

The old man in the blue robes nodded sagely and made the noises that Paechra associated with humans pondering and then agreeing with something, someone, or both.

"I shall have those two boys begin researching any possible solutions," decided the sage. "There simply must be some sort of solution."

"As you feel is the greatest use of their time," agreed Anton. "Especially now that you have both Yohan and Peter, and for longer than expected."

Again, Paechra's smile that threatened to appear was quickly hid. She understood that it would be rare that she and Anton ever agreed, but the Head Truth Keeper definitely had a knack for handling sages, Williamsons in particular.

"Yes, yes, but are you sure of this new clause?" the sage asked again. "The ink is dry and under normal circumstances..."

"And what of us, Your Wisdom?" asked the younger Lightheart. "Is there any way that we could be of assistance?"

"The written word is a very complex thing, young one," began the sage, addressing Paechra in the way that an elder grandfather figure might speak with an inquisitive child.

Paechra did not mention that she was hundreds of years older than Williamsons was, nor did she remind him that it was her own people, the sylvan, who five hundred or so years before had taught the humans how to write and record. No, Paechra merely nodded.

"As you so say, Your Wisdom," and with that, she could hold her smile in no longer.

"Strange beings," Sage Williamsons said to Head Truth

Keeper Anton. "I find them to be so interesting and yet so impossible to comprehend."

"Truer words have never been spoken," agreed Anton. "Truer words indeed, Your Wiseness."

#

The final days spent by Paechra and her sylvan kin in the balmy north of Thuraen was busily filled with sourcing trees from beyond the shore. The dream had revealed birch not quite a half-day away from the coast and with the assistance of the other animals and wagons located within the township that had formed around and near the tower of knowledge, it did not take long to build a fleet of twenty sturdy raft. Anton had finally realized that Paechra was not going to budge from her idea of floating into Andrapaal, and the open road was owned by nobody but the Sage-King, and as Sage Williamsons suggested, the Sage-King did not seem to care about his citizens along the North road, and trees seemed even less important that people. Paechra saw that both Thomas the Butcher, and Head Truth Keeper Anton were impressed that she and the other sylvan knew a thing or two about working with wood. Logs were cut to near identically perfect lengths, shifted by wagon, and then cut by hand into great long planks.

Before the sun rose to the midway point of the fourth day of working, the fleet was finished. Paechra had shown just how clever she could truly be, having the planks roped together just inland beyond the point where the sea and river intertwined. The craft were roped together to form a floating train, and then a great number of the sylvan clambered aboard one. There was a cheer when it refused to sink as more and more bodies clambered aboard.

"You will definitely not get me on one of those," grumbled Anton.

"What are you afraid of?" asked Thomas.

The young butcher had joined in the bark stripping and the creative part of the building process. Since his involvement Thomas had become quite protective of the fleet.

"You are a fool to think you are one of them," said Anton in reply. "And you are twice the fool if you think you are more than a butcher."

"I know what I am," said Thomas. "But it gladdens my heart to discover what I was does not have to be all."

Overhearing all of this, Paechra was proud to discover how Thomas had seemingly grown since reluctantly leaving Andrapaal.

"You were one of the select eleven, The Eleven of Andrapaal, Vladimir's chosen, and you believe that raft builder and tree chopper are greater achievements than such a role," scoffed Anton.

"Unlike you, Anton, I can admit that my time beyond the capital has given me the opportunity to grow and change," argued the young butcher.

"I should have cut those wings clean off," shouted back the older man.

"Then he would have whipped you with his fishy tail," cried one of the sylvan.

Thomas stood upon the raft beside that sylvan, and Paechra in turn stood, balanced upon the boards of the same raft, watching and listening. Yes, she was happy that Anton seemed to be warming to her and her other sylvan kin, a little bit more each day that the journey progressed, but, where Thomas had a far longer leap from beginning to then, Anton himself had altered very little.

"You have been rubbed by the forest peoples," accused the warrior.

"Such news fills my heart with happiness," Thomas cried back toward the shore.

At such bravado, the sylvan clapped the butcher upon the shoulder, a hearty, friendly blow. An unexpected blow too, one that sent Thomas off the raft and into the water.

"Where is your fishy tale now, fool's fool?" Anton begged to know.

"Here, in my hands," laughed Thomas as his head broke the surface and with a big, smug smile he presented a fish that he had caught using hands alone.

Anton shook his own head, unable to believe what he had witnessed. Turning away, the old man left the river's mouth without another word.

"Come back, Anton!" called Thomas. "I was hoping that you could fry up my find while I work on another of our raft."

"Worry not for your friend," said the sylvan, offering Thomas a hand to help him out of the water. "There are stone souls and water souls, and he is definitely a man of the earth."

Thomas relinquished his catch and accepted the offered help.

"Anton is nobody's friend," said the butcher. "In fact, I think the only thing he would miss is his precious sword if it did so happen to break."

"A man of steel, with a soul just as hardened," laughed the sylvan. "I am sure that the Druid sisters can easily see such in a man like him."

Paechra did not utter a word, although she certainly knew

such to be true. It gladdened the Druid to see how Thomas was growing in confidence, some days seemingly more rational and thoughtful than the older Anton.

"Are you sure your dream did say we should not travel by road?" asked the voice of Heidi, breaking Paechra from her thought.

Friend of the younger Lightheart, Heidi was trying to be supportive of the newly formed plan, but the ghoul ship was a frightful experience for all on board, and some were struggling to see the difference between the Picturesque Picaresque and the birch planks tied together, bobbing on the surface of the river.

"I have spoken with our Mother Druid and we both strongly agree, to walk the North road south to Andrapaal will be to announce our arrival to all, both friend and foe," murmured Paechra, though kindly, it was the third time the two were having such a conversation.

"Yes, of course," said Heidi, obviously still nervous. "But there will be a group of us following along the bank?"

"I believe that it will be faster for us all to be on the raft," said Paechra, again for the third time. "But, I have been unable to convince Anton to take to the water again."

"I do not blame him," Heidi said, but then gave her friend a sorrowed look.

"I do not blame him either," Paechra laughed. "Nor do I blame you or any others who wish to travel by foot, connected to the earth."

Heidi sighed with unhidden relief.

"Thank you, friend Paechra," she said. "I shall inform the others."

"The others?" queried Paechra. "What others do you speak

of?"

But it was already too late. Heidi was caught up in her own euphoria and, either did not hear her friend or did not wish to stop and explain. Paechra was forced to wait another day before she discovered how badly her numbers were split.

#

"What is the meaning of this?" Anton begged to know.

Paechra merely shrugged in reply.

"I was planning to follow your bundles of sticks by myself, upon horse, perhaps with Thomas acting as my squire," the Head Truth Keeper continued.

"I cannot speak for the people, just as I cannot order you," stated Paechra. "Mine is an army of individuals, each one deciding for themselves."

"Then, in my eyes, you have failed as a leader," Anton announced.

"No, Anton," said the Druid, calmly. "In your eyes I have failed as a commander... But I never claimed to be in command..."

"I see young Thomas like a duck awaiting the arrow shaft," said Anton to Paechra, but loudly enough that the butcher would hear him. "You cannot tell me that this is a decision made solely by that boy."

"You are right, Anton," Paechra said, but quietly, so only the elder human would hear.

The look of victory on Anton's face was short lived.

"I believe that you played a major part in helping the

butcher make his own decision," the younger Lightheart added.

"Come, boy, make the right choice and join me!" Anton said, beckoning for Thomas to hop off the raft and stand beside him.

"I will follow the dreamer, thank you Anton," stated Thomas with a determined smile. "I do not wish to march all the way into Andrapaal, and I see that there is only one horse."

Anton grunted and then turned said horse to face southward.

"I would ask that you care for those who follow in your wake," Paechra called to the old man's back. "But I know you are a true commander who will not needlessly sacrifice any in your care."

There was no obvious response from Anton as the horse took him slowly away, but using her special sight, Paechra could see his aura change from a deep purple to a shade of light grey.

"Farewell, friend Paechra!" called out Heidi, one of the fifty or so that remained on shore.

"We will still see each other!" Paechra called back.

And then the chanting began and the sisters that stood upon the birch raft spoke to the river and asked that the current move them along. There came a churning of the waters beneath and then the train of simple rivercraft left the bank and floated away.

The two groups, the one on the earth and the one on the waters travelled parallel for almost half a day, but then the lay of the land forced Anton and those in his care east and into the corpse of trees that existed near the river's edge. Paechra and her floating army lost sight of them all as the river continued to take the raft in a southerly direction.

"Stop chanting, we must follow after," said Paechra, thinking of her dream and the risk in splitting her forces.

"We must trust," said Sienna. "Trust that each of us will meet again."

"But what if I cannot trust?" said Paechra, unsure if she worried more for Anton, or Heidi, or all.

"You must learn," Sienna Alknown said, smiling sagely.

Chapter Fifteen

Parting Ways

Logs float. Ideas don't.

Local saying from the North Road

PAECHRA LIGHTHEART CALLED from her raft, Thomas the Butcher and Sienna Alknown standing beside her.

"Stay along the river's bank as much as you can!" she ordered Anton and those in his care.

The Head Truth Keeper ignored her cries, turning his back to the younger Lightheart, the rafts, and the river. Upon the back of the white steed, he quickly vanished beyond the tree line and the small group that he led followed after. Heidi, sister Druid, the lone figure who chose to pause long enough to give a half wave before she, the last of that group, also vanished from sight.

"I cannot trust," said Paechra as the raft drifted further along with the current. "My dream has predicted trouble, danger, death will befall us…"

"Yes," said the voice of Mother Sienna. "We have chosen the way of water because your dream did warn us of what would happen if we all followed the line in the land."

"And now some whom I call friend, some we know and love, will walk this path and they will fulfil my dream," sighed the young Druid.

"What do you mean?" asked Thomas, very concerned. "Anton is going to die?"

"Yes," said Paechra.

"No," Sienna said, disagreeing.

"We need to stop them," said the butcher. "I will swim out and guide them back."

The elderly hand of the ancient Mother Druid held Thomas' shoulder in a surprisingly strong grip.

"The dream will not come true," Sienna said.

"How can you be so certain?" asked Paechra, unconvinced.

"Your vision did show the one known as Raven who was not Raven meeting all of us upon the North Road," said Sienna. "All of us."

Thomas and Paechra thought on what it was that the Mother Druid said.

"Your argument holds some logic," said Paechra.

"But it is a great risk that we are taking in hoping it will be true," added the human, still worried.

335

"Trust," said Sienna. "Trust that what you have seen already cannot be."

"I guess that is something I can believe in," agreed Paechra. "That will need to be enough to satisfy me for now."

"We will see the others again," said Sienna.

Paechra gave a quizzical glance but said nothing.

"Oh, no dream, no vision," laughed the elder. "Just a feeling I have got, nothing more."

"And so, we just trust in a hunch?" asked Thomas. "Dreams and gut feelings, and an inkling of hope that Anton and the others don't meet Raven on the road?"

"Yes," said Paechra and Sienna together.

"Trust," Sienna said again, choosing then to sit and allow the water to take her where it willed to go.

"I guess we do not have a lot of choice," Thomas sighed.

"I guess we don't," Paechra agreed.

It was at that moment that Paechra realized just how many were still looking to her for leadership.

"We may have parted ways," she called, loud enough for all to hear her. "But I vow we shall meet again."

There was a murmured response from the other rafts, and then a silence that was briefly broken by the lapping of the river's waters upon the wooden craft.

The day upon the waters passed slowly, Paechra ordering a meal of fruits, nuts, and other nibbles to be consumed mid-travel. Conversations flowed, but Paechra, missing Heidi, remained quiet, wondering how her friend fared.

"Do not worry so," Thomas tried to tell Paechra on a few

occasions, but the Druid chose to ignore him.

As the day eventually turned to afternoon, Paechra's thoughts morphed from Heidi to that of her friend Raven, the real Johannas Stormsong, not the strange figure from her dreams.

"Where are you, Raven?" she whispered.

"You need to stop focusing on troublesome thoughts until they truly trouble you," suggested Sienna, Mother Druid.

"Are you not the one who taught your daughters to be prepared for dangers and disappointments?" suggested the younger Lightheart, quizzically. "Besides, I think of the human, not the apparition."

"I wonder though what of this dark, aura-less one that plagues your sleeping moments," mused the elder Druid. "It is not like you, Paechra, to visualize that which is not and that which cannot be."

"I does feel strange, mother," Paechra replied. "I know that this is not Raven, not the man that I have spent time with, and yet there is something about him that seems familiar."

"It frightens me to suggest this, daughter Paechra," Sienna said, her words almost whispered so quietly that the river wind stole them before they were heard. "Perhaps your friend is caught in the in between."

"You believe my friend Raven has gone where?" asked Paechra.

In all of her years, the young Druid had not come across such a term and certainly thought that she had never visited such a place.

"It worries me if our enemy does in fact know of how to banish those we love to the world beyond our own," said Alknown.

"We do not fear the in between," laughed Paechra, just as quickly she had gone from a state of fear to one of relief as she realized where it was that Sienna Alknown did suggest. "I did walk such with ease, guiding Queen Catherine, Thomas, Michael, Anton… But never did Raven accompany me…"

"Such was dangerous, just as you were reckless in traveling aboard the great ship, The Picturesque Picaresque," berated Sienna. "You were lucky in all circumstances that no soul or life was lost to the ship or the world."

"But you did teach us those ways and instructed us yourself that we should use them when and if we need," argued Paechra. "Was that wrong of you, mother?"

"I am too old to know of how the world will change, child," sighed Sienna. "I am far too tired of seeing the moon wax and wane."

Paechra nodded at this, and the pair spent some time staring into the trees, seeking signs of Anton and his party. There were none.

"I am sorry to have added to your worries," Paechra said next, choosing to break the silence.

"It gladdens me to know that you thought it time to use such skills and had enough knowledge and practice to make such happen," said Sienna in reply. "My only hope for you now daughter is that you can use such knowhow and that which else I have taught to find your true friend and bring him back."

"Thank you, Mother Druid," said Paechra, grateful. "I sense that the true Raven is close to finding his way home, that he has a guide, someone that I know, but, again, that which is remembered has morphed and evolved, and together, I feel, each will lead the other along that path they need walk."

This time Sienna Alknown was the one who nodded to

show that she understood.

"I hope though, mother, that once returned there will be a home recognizable for my Raven to see," murmured Paechra.

"As do I, daughter," Sienna replied. "As do I..."

Late in the afternoon Paechra ordered the rafts to shore.

"Why can we not continue?" Thomas demanded to know.

Paechra saw in the butcher's aura an eagerness to be home, back walking the streets of the city of Andrapaal. It saddened Paechra to see this, to discover just how quickly the young human had managed to block from his memory how his home had changed. Paechra still recalled sensing the spirit of Andrapaal cry out in pain as the city beneath, the vorsurk fortress that had been buried for centuries rose up through the earth and stone, forcing the new Andrapaal, the human Andrapaal deep down below.

"It is too dangerous to travel by dusk," Paechra said. "I will not allow it."

"The current is flowing toward the city, and the river is dragging us home, where is the danger?" questioned Thomas.

"Any travel by night is a risk," said Paechra.

"What of the travel you made us undertake?" said Thomas, his question disguising a threat.

"Forcing you, your queen, our party to travel at night was a risk, but a risk I judged to be necessary," replied Paechra. "Just as I deemed our travel by boat a risk that was worth taking."

"And who made you our leader?" the butcher asked.

"You did," said Paechra.

Thomas made to reply, the human's face flaring up with

frustration, but then he stopped.

"Thomas I know why you worry," Paechra then said, kindly.

"You are strange, Paechra," Thomas whined. "I struggle to see how any of you sylvan can think like a human."

"I see you watching the shoreline for signs of your people," Paechra said.

"I see none…" Thomas began, head hung. "Does this mean that we are too late?"

"I sense that the lives of those who live along the river have changed," said Paechra. "It gladdens my heart to know that such change has not travelled all the way to Sage Williamson and those in his care."

"But surely it is only a matter of time," said Thomas.

"And that is why we travel by raft," said Paechra.

"We are too slow… We need to keep travelling, to not stop," argued Thomas. "By horse, by road, we would have been eleven days to the heart of the kingdom, but now, will it take us all phases of the lunar cycle?"

"We are slower than a horse, yes," Paechra agreed. "Such has been our travel this day anyway."

"And how far do you think we shall travel tomorrow, Paechra?" Thomas demanded. "What if the river changes direction and sends our journey backward?"

"We have magic on our side, that and nature, and all things we need to get done what needs doing," the Druid promised. "I will forgive you for your forgetting, but you need eventually to learn to trust and have faith in me and my people if we are to succeed."

"You wish to gain my trust and faith, and thus the belief of my kith and kin?" asked Thomas. "Then prove such is warranted, just light the way and help us go further and faster this day."

"You are correct in believing we have travelled less in one day as a horse would upon the open road," Paechra replied, trying to remain calm. "But such a horse would not go far if my thinking and dreaming is to be considered and believed."

"Your kind are always taking a dream to be more than what it is," sighed Thomas, his frustrations boiling to the surface. "I fear that I and my people will never see life and everything about it the same way as your people do, but what I fear most is that there will be far less of my people left to try once we do finally arrive."

"I shall try my best as leader of this army to make certain your fear does not become reality," promised Paechra. "But I tell you with honesty, my thinking tells me that travel by night is not the answer to settling your worries."

"Then what is?" Thomas begged to know.

"Tonight, we rest," said Paechra. "And tomorrow we shall make up for such time that you believe we have lost."

With the river flowing calmly, it was with ease that the fleet of raft were drawn into shore. Paechra considered the risk of lighting small campfires, but by Thomas' estimate they were still a little way off from the next township. Low spirits were given a much needed boost when some of the sylvan warriors managed to pull fresh fish from the water. When chatting and singing started up, well Paechra let that go on also, even after her mother and the Mother Druid warned of how such could attract attention.

"What must we fear from the forest by night?" scoffed Paechra at such warnings. "Should we fear the shadows? Be afraid of spirits? Will the very trees become animated and drive us back to the waters?"

"Do not jest so," berated Sarah Lightheart. "Be more respectful of your elders."

"I show you respect, mother, and you know of my respect for your kindness and wisdom oh Mother Sienna," replied Paechra. "But what of my respect earned from leading this army? Should that not also be given and shown?"

"Come, Sarah, take me to my tent that we may talk, and leave this leader to make her mistakes," suggested Sienna.

"As you so suggest, mother," Sarah replied, offering the elder both hands so Sienna could more easily rise from sitting.

"Fine," grumbled Paechra. "Advise me, my elders, that I may not learn from my own mistakes."

"Oh no, no, no," said Sienna with a smile. "There is only so much one can be told, especially one such as you, Paechra."

"I swear she is her father's fruit," sighed Sarah. "One must certainly have been plucked from a branch of the same tree."

"Wishing you no criticism of self, Sarah Lightheart," cackled the ancient sylvan. "But such was why I did choose for Paechra to lead us."

"Oh, I know," replied Paechra's mother with her own voice hinting at laughter. "If Paechra were anything like me we would still be back in Greenwood Vale."

Annoyed, Paechra listened to the pair vanishing into the night. She longed to turn to seek the council of her friend Heidi, but such council of course had followed Anton. The younger Lightheart considered staring into the campfire flames in an attempt to contact Heidi, but that would only have worked if Anton had allowed campfires also.

"What would Anton do if he was here and believing that he was in change?" Paechra said to herself, speaking out loud.

"He certainly would not allow this," Thomas' voice came from the darkness in reply.

"You yourself suggested that a fire would be fine along the river's edge," Paechra said to the young butcher.

"Yes, one fire, for cooking," Thomas argued.

"This army is large," said Paechra. "Too large a group for just one fire, we would need at least ten for cooking and warmth."

"And who said anything about warmth?" asked Thomas. "Cook, clean up, bury the evidence... That would be what Anton has done."

"That is if he has stopped at all," considered Paechra. "He was very eager to get off the water and back onto land."

Thomas sat in silence for a moment, thinking. Paechra chose to patiently wait for him to respond, even in the dark of the evening she could sense the human's aura showed signs of a struggle.

"I should have gone with him, but I thought Anton's decision a foolish one."

"And what now?" asked the sylvan. "Has our slow progress changed your mind?"

"I don't know," Thomas replied with a shrug. "I thought that travel by water would get us where we needed to be far faster than travelling blindly through the trees."

"I still feel like this is the way," said Paechra. "But I am wondering about this vibrancy, a party when your people are enslaved once more."

"Are all the stories true?" Thomas asked. "The stories

343

recorded about vorsurk enslavement, the prophecy, the passages scribbled in the tomes by the sages of old?"

"I do not know," admitted Paechra. "That was over five hundred years ago, and although I am far older than you, even I was not born at that time."

"The one you call mother was though, right?" said Thomas. "Not your mother, but the all-knowing one."

"Yes, that is right, Thomas," said the sylvan. "Sienna Alknown, Mother Druid of Greenwood Vale was but a youngling at that time, but she certainly was alive then."

"We could ask her what to expect..." said Thomas. "We could be forewarned and such."

"Yes, we will certainly ask the Mother Druid for her council when we draw closer to Andrapaal, closer to danger," agreed Paechra.

"We?" asked Thomas. "Do you mean you and me?"

Paechra actually was hopeful Anton would be able to help her concoct some sort of plan, as she still believed that their paths would cross again before humanity needed to be saved. There was a change in Thomas, both his physical stature and his aura. The butcher grew in confidence as he listened to Paechra. The sylvan weighed up the pros and cons of revealing her thoughts and quickly decided to retain them.

"You are the sole voice of your people, Thomas," she suggested instead. "Your council was always important, but now, in this moment, it is even more so."

"I shall not let you down," said Thomas. "I must tell Athru, Bekros, and Urmunt..."

Paechra watched Thomas go off with a greater spring in his stride. It was truly amazing to her in witnessing the power of words upon the strange human race. Finally, alone, she considered still trying to contact Heidi, but the day upon the water had been a long one. Instead, she went in search of her own tent and dreamless slumber.

#

The following morning camp broke up quickly and the convoy was upon the river just as the sun was rising.

"Now we shall see what cost is fire and fun," announced Sarah, causing Sienna to nod sagely.

"You are two of little trust," stated Paechra in reply. "You need see through kinder eyes my own abilities and the nature of those we are trying to save."

It only took an hour for Sienna and Sarah to be proven correct.

As the forces of Paechra's army drifted along there came a volley of arrow shafts from the tree line.

"Vorsurk!!" cried Thomas, horrified as feathered shafts disappeared into the otherwise calm waters.

"Shields up," commanded Paechra, and she and her sisters cast their spells.

#

The convey of raft continued to float down the river, toward Andrapaal, the heart of the Thuraen kingdom. As Paechra and what part of her gathered forces she commanded floated past a particularly thick corpse of trees a volley of arrow shafts rained down, coming from the tree line.

Thomas' cry had alerted all, and immediately Paechra and her sister Druids had created a magical barrier of protection. This did not make the sole human who floated upon the waters any safer though, Thomas still struggled with his feelings about magic, still did not like it cast and created in his presence, but as was usual for the butcher he remained silent on the matter.

As the poorly aimed arrows plopped into the waters, missing each raft, Paechra considered whether this enemy was the wolf-like vorsurk as Thomas suggested, or something else.

The youngest Lightheart was pleased to note that her command for shields was respected by her sister Druids and quickly obeyed.

"Mother, do you know those who attack us this day?" Paechra asked Sarah Lightheart, the question relating to a handful of comments that her mother and the Mother Druid had both made before retiring to rest the night before.

"Know them by name?" asked Sarah, looking toward Sienna Alknown and smiling. "No, I do not know these attackers by name, daughter."

"You know what I am asking," replied Paechra, annoyed. "If this is supposed to be some foolish way you are trying to teach me a lesson then cease immediately, for you are scaring Thomas, and possibly others."

"I do not fear the vorsurk," stated Thomas the Butcher of Andrapaal, but the wavering of his voice suggested that the human did fear something.

"It is not the barbaric horde that we need be afraid of, at least not now," murmured Sienna sagely.

"Then who?" asked Paechra. "Do we strike back?"

"I shall protect you," Thomas promised as he indicated the

sword he had hanging at his hip. Over the distance between the convoy and the trees, such a weapon would be useless. Paechra considered whether to suggest this to Thomas or not but decided to let the human's bravado balance out his fear of the unknown.

"Nay, daughter," suggested Sarah Lightheart. "Please ask the human to stay his hand and order no spells from we your sisters until the enemy reveals themselves."

Another volley of arrows flew from the tree line and splashed within the otherwise calm river's surface. One arrowhead found a gap between the barrier of shimmering blue magic, woven and created from sylvan sister spell craft. It landed between Thomas' spread legs and hummed as it vibrated for a short period.

"Attack!" shrieked the butcher. "Attack with everything we have!"

Beside him, Paechra plucked the arrow from the raft's wood.

"Open your eyes, Thomas," she said. "This is not vorsurk, nor is it from my dream."

"Then who is attacking us?" Thomas demanded to know, his eyes wide with fear.

"It is you, Thomas," stated Paechra with a sigh.

The human gave the sylvan a look suggesting that she was mad, that he did not understand her at all.

"It is maybe not you, butcher," Paechra then added. "But your people, the humans."

"No, impossible," stated Thomas in utter disbelief. "My people would do no such thing."

"Humans who considered themselves to be under attack would not protect themselves against those whom they consider to be a threat?" asked Sarah Lightheart.

"If that were so," added the ancient Mother Druid Sienna. "Then everything we sylvan thought we knew of your kind would need to be scrapped and retaught."

"We would most certainly protect ourselves," said Thomas. "Of course we would."

"This arrow," said Paechra as more shafts rained down. "This arrow is human-made, definitely sourced from the trees we are looking upon now.

"Is that a duck feather?" asked Sarah as she took the shaft from her daughter and gave it an examination.

Floating close to the raft, but far enough away to not be bothered by any arrows, a family of ducks bobbed their heads into and out of the drink, seeking a morning meal.

"It certainly resembles such fowl feathering," agreed Sienna. "I would suggest a female, old enough to be a mother."

"Certainly, no vorsurk weapon this, the birds that nest in the sandy sea are not ducks, more likely sparrows, or some breed of scavenger," mused Sarah.

"I still find it hard to understand why my own people would be attacking us," stated Thomas. "We are friends, we are of one blood, one kingdom, or so it is written."

"You may be of humankind, Thomas," said Paechra. "But we sylvan certainly are not, and you alone are quite outnumbered."

"Think of your fellow citizens of Thuraen, the disruption that has affected them most recently, and then think upon the citizenry who are beyond the capital of Andrapaal and the lack of correspondence where previously your people would be constantly hearing from the sages..." suggested Sarah.

"Your whole society has suddenly been placed in a darkened world of no news, and false news, and a complete lack of guidance from those who supposedly know," added Sienna.

"And now they watch as we, wild and free as we seem, a force, and not a small force at that, float down their river toward the heart of their kingdom," Paechra said, causing Thomas to change from mystified to someone who now understood.

"Halt! Cease your attacks!" the butcher then shouted, stepping through the magical shield and madly waving at the wooden sentinels. "It is I, Thomas the Butcher, sworn member of The Eleven of Andrapaal."

More arrows flew up into the sky, more arrows struck the wooden planks that made up the rafts. But then, one by one, people, humans, began appearing upon the riverbank.

"Andrapaal?" the crowd murmured.

"You there, Thomas!" cried the loudest voice. "What news from the Great City of Knowledge?"

The figure looked strong, perhaps a blacksmith, certainly a leader within that township.

"Sadly, I know little of Andrapaal's fate, but that it has fallen to our enemies, we fear betrayal from within," called back Thomas as Paechra waved for the magical shield to be dispersed.

The translucent barrier evaporated just as quickly as it had been woven.

"I am Nathan!" called the booming voice on the riverbank. "I have family further north…"

Thomas called back with a wave.

"Greetings Nathan, we have just come from Williamson's tower. Things are well there; the people are safe."

"But why do you float upon the waters and not travel by the dust and the earth?" asked Nathan.

Thomas, Paechra, and the other sylvan upon the rafts could see and hear the group of humans that still stepped forth, out from hiding. One by one, all seemed to agree that such a question deserved an answer, travel by waters was unheard of when such a road existed.

"We are guided by dreams and by magic," suggested the butcher, and as the gathered crowd of humans gasped as one, Thomas immediately regretted his blunt choice of words.

"Thomas of the Council of Eleven, you of all people should know that magic is forbidden in our lands," called Nathan. "That is if you are who you truly state that you be."

"I am Thomas the Butcher," Thomas called back from the raft to the riverbank. "Citizen of Andrapaal and member of The Eleven."

"Then come ashore that we may make our own judgement and decide the fate of you and your trespassers," suggested Nathan.

"You rely upon this river for your livelihood..." called Paechra.

"Hush, child," whispered Sienna, but Paechra would not be hushed.

"You fish from it, you drink from it, just as you take from these trees," continued the youngest Lightheart.

"Please hush," murmured the Mother Druid.

Paechra ignored her elder.

"But you do not own it, the river, the trees, the land..."

"Is this more magic, butcher?" called Nathan, causing mutterings from the crowd of humans.

"Um… No..?" stammered Thomas.

"This is OUR land, OUR water, these are OUR trees," called out one from the crowded riverbank.

Another arrow was fired into the sky and Nathan did nothing to stop it.

"We go to save them from the evil that threatens that land, this water, those trees," said Paechra as the blue shielding magic flared up around her and blocked the well-aimed arrow.

The shaft disintegrated into dust as it struck Paechra's powerful aura of protection, a sound of dismay emanating from the crowd of humans who witnessed the spell.

"They do not know what they have yet to be told," explained Sarah. "And it seems like not much has been shared from the south as of late."

"We are under attack," exclaimed Thomas. "Again…"

"So, it does seem," said Paechra with a humorless smirk. "Sisters we need hurry this convoy along somewhat."

Thomas and the other humans drew silent as the sylvan Druids took up chanting. The singsong words held deep power, causing the current of the river to increase, propelling the raft further south. The family of ducks gave protest as they too were suddenly sped from their meal. Arrows flew into the patch of sky that existed behind both ducks and raft, and then again, each time further and further away, until Thomas and Paechra could see the tiny pins rise but not where they fell.

"Is this what you had in mind when you thought raft and river?" asked Paechra with the human mob far behind them.

"It is what I had hoped would be our everyday, without the

attacks from the forest of course," replied the butcher.

"Of course," agreed Paechra.

"Now do you see what it is that we were expecting, daughter?" asked Sienna and Sarah, a harmony of two voices sounding like one.

"Yes, you were right, we should not have had any loud noise or fires, or anything else signaling our presence," Paechra agreed. "When we next stop I will make sure to better heed your advice."

"Maybe there is something of her mother in her also," mused Sienna, Mother Druid.

"I would not have needed to learn such a lesson," suggested Sarah. "I would have already know to trust and to listen to my elders."

"It is the lesson to listen to all advice, be it elder given, a comment from the next generation, or the wise words of self-wisdom," suggested Sienna. "Experience is not just the gift of the old, some my age have very little to say that is worthy of the time that is required for listening."

"As you so suggest, Oh Wise one," said the two of the Lightheart name, this time mother and daughter harmonizing.

"What now then?" asked Thomas. "Do we slow our speed?"

"We can safely suggest we will pass more human settlements as we travel, hopefully more densely populated the closer we get to Andrapaal," said Paechra. "We cannot assume that each group will be as hostile as what we just witnessed, but our most recent experience leads me to caution."

"Thomas you must understand that magic takes a physical and mental toll on the caster," explained Sarah. "We cannot drive the raft for the rest of the journey, no matter how much you hope and pray it can be so."

"Prayer?" asked Thomas, a mixture of surprise and annoyance. "I would believe in magic, as full of faults as it is before I would even consider placing any belief in so-called deities."

"Even after all that you and Anton have witnessed?" laughed Sienna with eyebrows raised.

"What do you mean?" asked Thomas.

"The statue in the forest clearing?" asked Sarah. "Have you already forgotten?"

"I for one certainly have not," stated Paechra. "I am surprised that it is Raven and not stone statues that haunt me when I sleep."

"Be wary of your wishes, dear daughter," said Sarah Lightheart. "Else you start dreaming of statues and ravens and both come true."

"Mother, please," stated Paechra in shock. "I wish to have neither haunt me, in my thoughts and my life both."

"There is enough evil in this world and the next that we need not invent it," said Sienna.

Even Thomas could agree with that.

"Sisters, cease your song," the eldest sylvan commanded.

With those words spoken with such authority the sylvan sisterhood fell silent.

Thomas could still feel the river's current pulling along the raft that he shared with Paechra, Sarah, Sienna, and others, yet it was slowing as the effects of the sylvan song wore off, and the river's current did eventually return to the sluggish speed from earlier.

"So, Thomas, what knowledge do you have of these lands?" Paechra asked, after a few moments of silence had passed.

"More than most," Thomas admitted. "As a member of Vladimir's Eleven we were trusted to give advice on decisions for the whole of the kingdom."

"So where upon the North South road would we have so warmly been welcomed then?" the sylvan asked.

"By my memory that would have been the township of Boarder North," said the butcher after a moment's thought. "The Tower of Knowledge at the very edge of Thuraen, each major point of direction, of course is where the true boarder lies, but the townships prior to those tower settlements are named by their direction."

Paechra nodded.

"So, we should be arriving close to the next township south before nightfall, thanks to our burst of speed, and the current as it is," calculated the sylvan. "That must please you somewhat, butcher."

"I guess," replied Thomas, again uncertain.

Paechra opened her other sight and witnessed the swirling coloration of the human's feelings.

"You worry for Anton?" the younger Lightheart asked.

"Of course," said Thomas. "You do not?"

"I do," replied Paechra, not offended. "I worry for Anton, for Heidi, for all who followed the Head Truth Keeper beyond the trees."

"Will we see them again?" Thomas begged to know. "Do your dreams suggest that our paths will cross?"

"So now you are willing to trust in magic?" laughed Paechra.

"This is the humanity that we believe we know so well," added Sarah.

354

Thomas would not be denied an answer to his query.

"You can jest all you wish, but such laughter tells me nothing that can ease my pains," the butcher said solemnly.

"That is true, Thomas," agreed Sienna, and both Sarah and her daughter nodded, suggesting they thought the same.

"If I were to step now into the hallowed Hall of Knowledge and have my words recorded by one of those sages dressed in the robes of blue I would tell them that I see no visions of the future, in fact I have had no dreams since that one which has placed us all upon this watery path," admitted the young Druid.

"As disappointing as that is to hear," replied Thomas. "I thank you, Paechra, for giving me such an honest answer in words that I can understand."

"I do wish that my words were capable of giving more comfort to you and to dispel many of my own fears," Paechra added. "Alas, they are not."

"You are not the only dreamer, you alone do not solely hold such power," suggested Sarah, kindly, but with some parental force mingled within her tone.

"Perhaps this evening, when the clouds do pass and the sun has vanished for slumber, we may gather as a sisterhood and ask the moon for a sign," proposed Sienna, nothing but kindness heard within her words.

"We would like that," replied Paechra, grateful.

"We would?" asked Thomas, again unsure.

Paechra immediately made a noise like a disapproving mother bear scolding one of her cubs.

"Um… I mean… Sure, yeah, we would be… Yes please…" the butcher stammered, immediately changing his tune.

#

The remainder of the day passed by somewhat uneventfully, as the sun began to set the keen eyes of the sylvan detected signs within the trees that another town was near.

"Let's push on for a few more miles and try to create a safe distance between us and the town," suggested Paechra.

"I thought that we did not want to travel by night," said Thomas.

Sylvan on the shared raft agreed with the butcher's comment.

"Call it a risk steeped in wisdom," Paechra replied.

When Sienna nodded her agreement, those of the sylvan fell in line. Thomas though was still curious.

"What if we hit a log and your so called wisdom sinks us?" the human asked.

"Yes," agreed Paechra. "That is a possibility…"

Thomas, and others, waited to hear more.

"But a broken raft can be repaired or replaced, there are many trees that line this river," Paechra continued. "If we are attacked again, and caught unprepared, my kith and kin are more difficult to fix."

"What is more, Thomas," added Sarah, supporting her daughter. "We will only travel by dusk light, never in the pure darkness."

"As you so suggest," the human grumbled, knowing he would get no better answer from the strange forest race.

As suggested the convoy of raft drifted silently onward, until Paechra deemed her forces were a safe distance away from humanity. With a hand signal she ordered all to shore, and a makeshift camp with swiftly erected. By the time stars blanketed the inky sky accompanying a crescent moon, all were settled, feeding upon dried fruits and seeds.

"Is it time?" asked Thomas, revealing his true reasoning for questioning Paechra earlier.

"Are all of humanity as impatient?" asked Sarah.

"It is the shortened life expectancy," suggested Sienna.

"Yes, Thomas, it is time," said Paechra.

Guards were posted around the campsite and the sisterhood gathered to dream as one.

#

Raven fought hard and long to be free of the firm grasp of the vorsurk oppressors. He did not forget his friends, the ones who made his time so bearable. Low Prince Derek, minus one hand, joined Raven in his escape, as did Miriam the Mistress of Mead. As a trio they supported each other beyond the harsh lands of the dog-like barbarians, but the way back home still seemed so far for Raven to fly. Derek refused to try again to walk the way of the sisters of the grove, instead vowing to shadow his new friend, each step of the way.

Chapter Sixteen

Plucked from the Darkness

Those who fight, must always

Those who run, run far

The minds of all are now open

We now know who we are

From the Thirteenth Stanza of the Prophecy, untranslated by the sages of the Kingdom of Thuraen 514th year

"HOLD MY HAND," Paechra suggested to Thomas. "Take it and that of Sienna's."

"Me?" asked the butcher, uncertainty evident in his tone.

"It is for your purpose that we gathered to dream,"

suggested Sienna. "Did you think that you would have no part to play?"

"I thought that I would merely need bear witness to what it was you all say," suggested Thomas.

"There will be speaking," laughed Sarah. "But it will be the voice of a shared consciousness."

"The voices you will hear, Thomas, will be in your head, in all of our heads," Paechra explained. "If you do not join in the dreaming then you will see and hear silence, sleeping."

"Is this a gift from your magic or is it a connection with one of these deities you believe in," asked the human, unsure. "I do not know what it is that I fear more."

"If you must fear something, butcher," continued Sarah, Paechra's mother. "Fear that this does not work, and that we remain as blind as we currently find ourselves."

"Can magic fail?" asked Thomas, surprised, and concerned.

"Of course," admitted Paechra. "Or worse…"

"Worse than failure..?" Thomas wondered. "What can be worse than magic that fails?"

"Magic that is used against the caster," Paechra replied.

"I remember," said the butcher, his eyes widening. "In the forest, you tried to open some pathway or other…"

"Yes," Paechra admitted, shuddering as she recalled the moment.

"Were we in danger then?" Thomas asked.

Sienna and Sarah both looked openly straight at Paechra, awaiting her response. Thomas chose that moment to stare away at the thick tree line, skyward toward the first stars of the evening, anywhere but at the youngest sylvan.

"Grave danger, Thomas, just as you were correct in believing we were in danger upon the ghoul ship," Paechra admitted, dropping her head as she admitted this.

"I knew it!" cried Thomas, triumphantly.

"Daughter, why make such a flawed decision?" asked Sarah and Sienna, a chorus of condemnation.

"I did it for Queen Catherine, and I would do it again," Paechra replied. "I did it for the child, the hope of the human kingdom."

"I see," said Sienna, placing an elderly hand upon young Paechra's shoulder.

"But the queen would have been in great danger..." stammered the butcher. "How would such a risk help?"

"We needed to reach home quickly," Paechra tried to explain. "Things were... I could sense... There were difficulties..."

"I know that there were difficulties," said Thomas, his voice getting louder. "You and Anton fighting, the queen so quiet, I was scared like a pig in the slaughterhouse... All of the things that you put us through."

"I admit that I made the same decision, took the same or a greater risk, and for similar reasons," admitted Sienna.

"My daughter had her reasons," reassured Sarah Lightheart, but Thomas refused to listen.

"There is no reason that could possibly excuse so much risk," he argued. "Things for my people could be different, already, if we had not left, and left in such a strange, mysterious way."

"Thomas, we will never know if what you are saying is true," stated Paechra. "And that is my fault."

"I could have made a difference," said Thomas. "You should have let me stay, or at the very least you should have given us all a choice."

"Human, you wanted to have a choice, then, there, at that precise moment?" scoffed Sarah. "If you had chosen to stay you would have been under the firm rulership of a vorsurk sorcerer, your Queen Catherine would have been imprisoned, or worse, killed, and her child would have had no chance at life."

"You don't know that" argued Thomas. "You know nothing of the desert barbarians."

"Maybe Sarah and all of the others have had little but stories about this wolf-like race, but I still remember the great sylvan warriors who clashed with the vorsurk," said Sienna Alknown, her voice cold. "I remember witnessing the dead and hearing of the plan to break the bonds of slavery… Lifting the shackles for sylvan-kind and for humanity… I remember it all…"

Thomas made to reply, but then the anger and uncertainty drained from his face, and he hung his head.

"Fine then," he sighed, relinquished. "If this will help I will join the circle."

"Good," said Sarah with a smile.

With nothing more to be said Sienna called together the Druids who waited for her summons. As the circle formed the butcher took hold of the hands of two Druids he did not know. Both looked to Paechra for permission, the younger Lightheart giving a curt nod. Thomas wanted to show that he had at least some control in the strange situation. For Paechra it was enough of a victory that they were able to have the butcher join them. With the circle complete, the Druids began a droning chant that lulled each one into a state of slumber. Thomas found too, as much as he tried to resist the spell, he began mumbling the same words as his hands linked him and thus his mind into the shared dream.

All in all, there were twenty-one who joined in the circle, Thomas being the only member who was not a sister of Greenwood Vale's Sacred Sanctuary. High Prince Ulan spent some moments watching on, but, just as Thomas had been told, there was not a lot for those not joined by the hand to witness; some murmurings, the occasional sigh, but nothing special or revealing. The Greenwood Vale high prince turned away in search of more talkative company after only a short time. He considered returning later to ask the sisters if it would be at all possible to somehow check upon his brother using the same dreaming technique, but that was something to discuss much later.

For those such as Thomas who found themselves in the middle of the circle, the experience was quite the opposite. A great blazing bonfire erupted, growing larger and louder, until it formed into the shape of a gigantic, flaming bird.

"What is this?" gasped Thomas.

It surprised the butcher to hear his question not come from his mouth, but instead it echoed in the cosmos, separate from his self, and yet so obviously belonging to him.

"It is the phoenix," Paechra's voice replied, it joining Thomas' query, hanging in the dreamscape.

"It is our messenger bird, our dream guide, it is through this phoenix we have manifested that we will try to make contact with Anton and the others," explained Sarah's voice.

"Look, it takes flight..." murmured Paechra's voice.

Thomas watched on as the winged flames rose up with such power and elegance. With a great gasp he revealed his shock as the image then took to the inky black night's sky.

The eyes of all in the dreaming circle looked down upon themselves as they shared the view of the mythical creature.

"What is this sorcery?" stated Thomas' voice, his panic creating vibrations in the cosmos.

"You are safe, we are all safe," reassured Paechra. "Our guide is now our eyes, and our ears, it is a copy of our self."

"The dreamers become the dream," Sarah added. "There will be no harm that we can suffer, as we can wake at any time of our choosing."

"Then wake me now," begged Thomas. "This is too much, magic, faith, all things I have spent my life believing is not real, forbidden…"

"Butcher, my daughter has surely shown you that our ways are real," stated the voice of Sarah Lightheart.

"Too often," Thomas admitted. "Such evidence has been difficult to ignore."

"So, ignore it now, if it helps you to help us," suggested the ancient voice of Mother Druid Sienna Alknown. "We must focus, watch, and see what we can learn tonight."

Although not happy at being berated, Thomas grew quiet, his whining ceasing, at least for a moment.

In the tranquil quiet that followed, all watched the dream bird rise to a great height and then fall, so far and so fast, igniting trees and bushes as it crashed through the tree lining and into the forest that bordered the river's edge. Deeper and deeper, it flew, always straight, regardless of the obstacles in its way.

"Should we warn the others of the fire?" murmured the butcher's voice.

"Hush, Thomas," stated Sarah. "It is merely a dream, remember."

"Of course," the human replied, and was silenced again.

The phoenix continued its flight, ignoring those who joined it. Then abruptly it stopped.

There was a single squawk that made the dreamscape shudder.

Ten wagons, each drawn by a pair of jet black steeds slowly made their way as a convoy along the North South road. Lined either side of these, a small force of vorsurk slowly drudged, guarding the contents of what could only be assumed to be some of Paechra's army.

"Curses, they have been captured," echoed Sarah's voice.

At the head of this procession was a figure dressed in armor the same color as the night.

"Raven," cried Paechra, recognizing the figure immediately.

"Surely not," said Thomas. "I have heard the rumors, but I still cannot believe such is true."

"I feel the same, Thomas," replied Paechra. "This is not the Johannas Stormsong that I know, so it must be the stranger from my dreams."

"That is worse," suggested Sienna. "True dreams are poor company, more oft than not."

"At least we can confirm our worst fear," said Sarah Lightheart.

"You mean to tell me that Anton is dead?" cried Thomas. "Tell me, please, it isn't so."

The phoenix cried again, and this time the head figure in the dark mail turning toward the noise.

"Quiet, Thomas," hissed the voice of Sienna. "You must keep calm."

"How can I after hearing such news?" asked Thomas, frightened, his voice a mere squeak.

"Our emotions are shared by the phoenix," explained Paechra. "You upset the bird, and it may fly us away, or betray our position, our presence, open a window for this strange Raven to attack…"

"There is just so much that I do not understand," said the human.

"We are here to learn," said Sarah. "So let us learn."

The Druids directed the dream messenger toward one of the middle wagons. Peering within the canvas, all of the dreamers discovered Heidi, Anton was lying still beside her.

"Friend Heidi," whispered the voice of Paechra.

"Paechra, is that you?" Heidi called, stifling a yawn.

"We are here, child," said the voice of Sienna.

"Where are you?" Heidi asked, looking around the innards of the wagon. "Here is not safe."

"We know, Heidi, the phoenix has shown us the wagons, the wolves, the dark figure who leads you," continued the Mother Druid.

"So, I am dreaming?" asked Heidi.

"Yes, friend Heidi, you are asleep," Paechra confirmed. "Slumbering, just like us."

"I did not think that such was possible," stated Heidi. "It was almost immediate…"

"Slumber?" asked Paechra. "Such sounds impossible, friend, you seem surprised to finally be at slumber."

"No, Paechra, capture was almost immediate," sighed Heidi. "Anton led us into the forest and then the fool of a human continued to guide us through the trees."

"Hey, you are speaking of the current Head of the Truth Keeping Force of Thuraen," protested Thomas.

"I am sorry, butcher, but the man is a fool," muttered Heidi.

"Please continue," requested Sienna, everyone else, including Thomas, choosing to listen.

"We almost made it to the North South road," Heidi continued. "But then the shadows of the trees that looked like vorsurk warriors revealed themselves to actually be barbaric soldiers."

"My dream came true then," gasped Paechra. "That must have been frightening for you all."

"Fifty of us caught by surprise were no match, although the number of vorsurk was few," explained Heidi. "Anton of course refused to give in."

"Is he dead?" asked Thomas, not sure he wanted to hear the answer.

"Your Head Truth Keeper made the first mistake, drawing his sword," said Heidi. "His second mistake was confronting the one dressed in black."

"Typical Anton," murmured the voice of Sarah.

"The human who we so foolishly chose to follow was not given the opportunity to make a third and final mistake," admitted Heidi. "One blow from the one called Raven was enough to knock him out."

"And then..?" prompted Paechra.

"We thought that the end of all of us," admitted Heidi. "But it was as if they had been awaiting our arrival…"

"How so?" asked Sienna. "What do you mean, Heidi?"

"These wagons, they were there on the side of the North South road, enough for those captured to be transported, but I know not where..." Heidi explained.

"We can assume one of two things," suggested Sienna. "Yes, dark magic has been used to predict that there would be a small force of sylvan caught in the forest..."

"Or the second option..." began Paechra. "The wagons originally held the vorsurk forces and they patrol the main roads going into Andrapaal, they have known of our approach."

"Correct, daughter, that was also my thinking," agreed Sienna.

"Either way, our kindred are captured and need to be saved," suggested Sarah.

"Anton has yet to wake after the blow he suffered," said Heidi. "His aura is all over the place, his breathe shallow and slow."

"Heal him the best that you can, please friend," requested Paechra.

"Of course," Heidi reassured. "I only hope that we are allowed enough time that I can revive him."

"We will leave at the sun's rising in search of you," said Sienna. "You will not be imprisoned long."

"What if we left them?" Paechra then suggested.

"You talk nonsense, sylvan," cried Thomas. "We cannot leave them."

Again, the phoenix gave a piercing cry.

"Calm, Thomas, and please listen," begged Paechra.

"We shall listen, but we will need some convincing, daughter," said Sarah.

"The wagons travel throughout the night, in the direction of Thuraen's heart," Paechra began. "If the wagons are going to enter the city, the vorsurk fortress, should we not just let them?"

"And then what?" asked Thomas.

"If we can time our arrival with that of the convoy we can create a disruption at the gates…" the younger Lightheart suggested.

"And if our timing is wrong?" asked Thomas, his voice filled with concern. "What if all of our raft are delayed, or what if travel by water we do not arrive at all?"

"Each suggestion has merit," said Sienna.

"You will leave us here?" asked Heidi, shocked.

"What you say daughter could work, and could work well," said Sarah. "But Heidi and Thomas have concerns which we cannot discount."

"A good leader is one able to choose the best decision for all," advised Sienna.

"Then it is my decision that we will attempt to rescue our captured friends on the road," announced Paechra. "The risk is too great to hope that the wagons will help us, and that my thoughts will play out just as I predict they will."

Heidi and Thomas both sighed with relief.

Paechra sensed in the dreamscape that her mother and the Mother Druid both looked proudly down upon her.

"Be safe, friend Heidi, as safe as you can be," murmured the younger Lightheart. "And please do what you can to heal the fallen."

"And wait for us to appear in the next day or two," said Paechra's mother, Sarah Lightheart.

"Come, we must away," suggested Sienna. "The sky lightens and the time for dreaming is coming to a close."

"I will await your signal," said Heidi. "I shall also inform Anton of your visit once he awakens."

"Thank you," said Paechra.

The phoenix screamed in pain and all in the dreaming felt the burn of a sword strike.

As one the consciousness retracted from the wagon's interior and surveyed the forest. Raven was there with sword raised, ready to strike again.

"More for the master," he announced.

"We shall meet again," vowed Paechra. "But now is not the time, nor the place…"

"I and my forces shall await your signal," laughed the figure dressed in the color of the night, but there was no humor in his eyes.

As Paechra looked deeply into them she discovered nothing.

"Daughter, come, we must away," called Sienna's voice, suddenly far away.

Breaking from the contact with the stranger, Paechra discovered that the phoenix had somehow left without her. She was dragged up and away, like the tail of an erratic kite. Into the blossoming sky went the flaming bird, taking all who slumbered in the dreaming with it. Through clouds as pink as ripening strawberries they went, and then down through the brush again to wake in the circle, holding hands, tired and wounded after their journey of the mind.

"How is this possible?" asked Thomas, a shallow wound

burned across his chest, an identical wound found on each one of the dreamers. "I thought that you told me we were all safe."

"I do not know," admitted Paechra. "I thought such to be impossible."

"You also thought that we should leave Anton and the others in that monster's clutches," Thomas continued.

"Yes, I am sorry, that was a poor decision," Paechra admitted. "But now we have made the right one."

"And what decision is that?" asked High Prince Ulan.

"Your citizens have been captured, as has the human, Anton," stated Sarah, before anyone else could speak.

"Paechra originally suggested that we wait for the wagons to arrive at the city gate," scoffed Thomas.

"But now we believe it is better we rescue our comrades sooner rather than later," Paechra interjected.

"You had best inform me of the plan then," said Ulan.

"Gather everyone together..." Paechra requested.

#

Paechra stood upon the bank of the river, the sound of the waves gently lapping upon the shore gave her courage as she addressed the crowd before her. It was a crowd of her peers, it was a crowd who were keen to hear what she had to say, as their leader. Regardless of this, Paechra was nervous. The dreaming of the night had revealed that the dark one had captured those who had followed Anton off the rafts and into the forest. Such dreaming had also revealed the strange nature of the one who looked like Paechra's friend Raven Stormsong, his ability to see dreams and dreamers, something that not even

Paechra and her sister Druids could do.

Paechra, with help from Sienna, Sarah her mother, and other Druids, had tried to explain such discoveries to High Prince Ulan, but this only left him confused, concerned to the point where Paechra Lightheart now stood before so many and tried to think of what to say. The words refused to form. Silence dragged on, and on.

"Paechra, they must know," called Sienna Alknown.

"Please tell us," cried a voice from the crowd. "What do you know?"

"Yes, please!" called out another. "What have you discovered?"

"Our friends and family are in trouble," Paechra began, not knowing any other way to tell such a sorrowful tale.

"We have followed you; we have left our homes..." the crowd replied.

"I know, and I am sorry," said Paechra. "I should never have let them go."

"It was not your choice," called Sienna.

The Mother Druid's voice was indeed ancient, yet it was still strong and loud enough to be heard over the murmuring discontent that rippled through the gather sylvan.

"It was your choice to allow those who left to have their choice," continued Sarah Lightheart who stood beside Sienna.

Paechra took heart from hearing such voices.

"We are the ones who remained, you are they who placed their trust in me and my leadership," Paechra stated. "And I ask that once more you put that trust in me."

"I will follow wherever and whenever you lead, Paechra Lightheart," boomed the voice of High Prince Ulan.

"I will follow, Paechra," cried another voice.

One by one, more called out their faith in Paechra. The swell of support grew larger and louder until more than three quarters of the group that had gathered in the night admitted their belief.

"We will save our family, save those who have become lost along the way," Paechra promised.

"And how do you propose that we do such?" cried the distinctive voice of Thomas the Butcher.

"We abandon the raft," Paechra replied. "We break them apart, we turn the pieces into weapons, and we take the fight to the enemy."

The gathered sylvan, especially those who had been training with Anton and Thomas, responded with hollering and hoots, strong sounds of support.

"Our enemy is waiting for us, they know that we are coming," warned Paechra.

"But we shall overcome them with numbers," promised Sarah, giving her daughter a look of encouragement.

"Yes, we shall all be with our loved ones again soon," added Sienna.

"Come, let us bring the raft to shore," one sylvan said.

Others took up the same cry. Knives and dagger blades busily worked through tightly tied cord, fraying it, causing it to snap and give way. Then, just like that, the crude boats that had been their form of travel over the water became nothing but splinters, sharpened poles, pokers, clubs, and walking aids.

"Lead us into battle, Paechra," demanded the crowd. "The

night will not end until two becomes one again."

"Come, the phoenix shall be our guide," announced Paechra.

And looking skyward all could see the stars in the sky had taken up the pattern of the spirit guide. The moon's light beamed down and a spectral trail lead through the tall timbers.

"To victory and to saving those who need it," said Thomas, even the butcher becoming caught up in the thrill of taking the fight to the enemy.

"May the gods of the forest watch over us tonight," prayed Paechra, quietly, to herself and nobody else.

"Keep your light within your heart," ordered Paechra as she and her sisters followed the moon and the phoenix. "Wait until I give the word."

Those without the powers of the Druid followed loyally after the sisters of the forest, the vorsurk could be detected in the scent on the wind. All from the sylvan grove and their kin knew when the enemy could be detected it was high likely that you could be detected too.

"Slowly, sisters," urged Paechra.

The vorsurk numbers were small, maybe thirty compared with the two hundred that followed Paechra, yet in the dark, with friends in such peril, it was difficult to say who had the upper hand. In small groups Paechra sent her forces onward to engage with the sentries who guarded the wagons. The figure who pretended to be Raven must have thought he was so clever, thought that Paechra would use her superior numbers and rush forward as one. Pits and traps lay hidden near the trees, above them and below them, but Paechra and her sisters asked the trees, spoke with the animals of the night that hunted or fled. The forest knew what was right and what was wrong, and it was most happy to tell those who were able and willing to listen.

"I see," whispered each sylvan sister in turn. "Thank you…"

Nature speaks in image and riddle, what is a moment seems a lifetime and what is an eon takes the form of a blink. And so, the slow and steady approach resulted in none of Paechra's forces caught in the snare traps Raven had prepared for them. Thomas narrowly managed to avoid falling foul, in his rush to tackle a scarecrow soldier, he stumbled into one of the hidden pits, only for Ulan to catch him by the arm and yank him back.

"Many thanks, to you your Kingness," called the butcher as he stabbed the man of straw.

Ulan could not help but laugh.

"Hush," hissed Sarah, close by.

That was enough to cause the whole forest to erupt that night.

"Now!" called the commanding voice of Paechra, accompanied by the same boomed order from the man in black.

Vorsurk ignited sword blades that burned bright in the darkness. Sylvan sisters wrapped themselves in the color of right. Amongst such brilliance the soldiery of Paechra's force brought their bits of raft to bear and the night was filled with the sounds of the skirmish.

"Where is he?" Paechra begged to know. "Where is the one who calls himself Raven?"

In the heat of the fight none knew of where the great adversary had hidden, they had only knowledge of what was in front. With no aura, Paechra found it impossible to locate him. And then he was before her, sword raised.

"Do you seek death regularly?" the figure of evil asked, grinning.

"Your blade cannot harm me," declared Paechra. "But my magic can send you back to where you came from."

"Do not be so certain that what you so say is true, daughter of the wind playing in the leaves," said the voice.

The blade fell impossibly fast, slicing through the moonlight, and then Paechra's magical field, treating both as if they were the waters of a stream.

"Sisters, I beg for your aid," Paechra pleaded, relinquishing her shield and embracing her own form of the dark.

She allowed herself a single smirk of pleasure as Raven's face contorted into confusion. He made some uncertain stabbing motions, testing the emptiness before him, but found only tree trunks. Paechra then stepped through the space between Raven and the wagons and ended up with Heidi again.

"Paechra?" gasped Heidi.

"Silence," ordered the younger Lightheart. "We can speak as friends again once the night ends and day shines bright."

"I shall be quiet," promised Heidi. "But just tell me this… Are you here now or am I dreaming again?"

"I am here, friend," assured Paechra. "I have come to fulfil a promise."

"Then I shall not keep you," said Heidi with a sigh of relief.

"You are freed," Paechra said next. "Go if you can and join the others."

"My injuries are minor compared with Anton's, but he is now much healed," said Heidi. "I will help you here if it pleases."

375

"To work with my best would give me the greatest of joys," said Paechra. "Go spread the word that we will light up the night and then follow the north road south."

Heidi nodded.

"It shall be as you so request, friend Paechra," she said.

The two sylvan embraced, briefly, and then Heidi escaped from the wagon's covers.

"Now what shall we do with you?" Paechra said, turning her attention to the pale form of Anton.

The Head Truth Keeper looked much older, almost comparable with Sienna Alknown.

"I cannot give up all my future years," continued Paechra. "But it seems our enemy was stealing yours."

With care and precision Paechra placed one hand upon Anton's heart and then leached five years from her own future and pumped them straight into the failing human.

Anton gasped and convulsed violently.

"What did you just do to me, witch?" he groaned. "For whatever it was I am truly grateful."

"It gives me great hope to hear you speak, Anton," stated Paechra with a sigh. "For it means I do not need to carry you home."

"Carry me? Me?" spluttered the old man. "I'd much rather limp."

"Your voice encourages me, but I'd love to hear it less," suggested the sylvan.

"Then pass me my blade and I shall let such do the talking for me," commanded Anton.

"This will must do, for now," suggested Paechra handing

the Head Truth Keeper the wooden club she had with her.

Anton gingerly sat up and then took the offered weapon.

"I guess that beggars cannot be choosers," he mused.

"You are indeed correct," Paechra said in reply.

"Well, I'm off," said Anton next, and then, like Heidi, he slipped from the wagon's covers and vanished into the night.

"Stick with what you know," prayed Paechra. "We none of us are ready yet to take on alone what we cannot comprehend."

Whether Anton heard her, Paechra could not tell. Yet, she spend a moment pondering, if he had heard, would he choose to listen. Of that she was certain that she knew the answer. So, without further ado, she herself escaped the wagon's confines and ventured up the line to the next one.

Just over an hour passed by, and within that time Heidi and Paechra managed to clear each and every wagon of its captives. Paechra gave a shrill whistle, the signal for her forces to move through the forest in search of the road. They chose not to use the wagons, an easy to track and easy to find target, but they did spend some of their precious time freeing the horses from their tack and sending them galloping back the way that they had come from. Paechra noticed the steed of Raven and considered freeing it also, but the risk was too great. The sylvan did not know if the beast would still recognize her, still see her as a friend, someone who could be trusted. It had been a while since Paechra had left her friend, the actual Johannas Stormsong, in the captivity of the sage Vladimir, the city of Andrapaal under threat, the vorsurk in the very heart of Thuraen. Who truly knew whether Raven's aura had been extracted, or whether that figure was an imposter. Who could truly say what affect such strangeness had had upon that poor horse? No, Paechra made the decision to wait for now and to leave the poor beast be.

"Come, we must away," ordered Paechra, guiding her kith and kin into the cover of the forest over the way.

"We must not stop until the deed is done," demanded Anton.

But Thomas was beside the Head Truth Keeper, hurrying the older man along.

"There will be more days, more fights, and more victories, Anton," the butcher promised.

"I want no more victories, man," grumbled Anton. "I want my deserved revenge."

"Night is turning into day," announced Sienna, she being helped along by the strength of High Prince Ulan. "We must not be caught by the dawn's light."

"Did you see how the vorsurk did fall?" asked one of the sylvan males to another.

"All of that training has shown its worth," agreed another.

"Quickly, do not delay," ordered one of the sisters of the sacred grove.

She sensed what it was that the Mother Druid knew. Paechra and her mother also felt the need for haste.

Paechra's final glimpse as the sun began to rise was that of the figure dressed in black bringing back from the edge of death's abyss one of the fallen vorsurk. The spell used by Raven's twin was not that of healing but of a forced animation.

"Undead," she muttered, shivering.

The game just got that much harder.

#

"We must stop, Paechra, please," Heidi begged of her friend. "Some are still showing the worst of the skirmish, battered and bruised."

"Of course," Paechra replied with a sigh.

The force, still at least two thousand strong was not as strong as it once had been. The mission to rescue had come off as a success with no human or sylvan still imprisoned, and yet everyone seemed to be suffering some sort of melancholy, causing travel to slow.

"Halt for a half hour break," suggested Heidi.

Anton was quick to find Paechra.

"Break! You have called for us to finally cease this running away, I hope," the Head Truth Keeper demanded to know.

"Anton look where we are headed," suggested the sylvan.

"I see where we are going, witch," Anton replied. "Andrapaal is that way, but the enemy is the other way."

"I cannot allow you to go on some foolhardy solo vendetta that is just going to get you killed," stated Paechra, plainly and with as much clarity as she could muster.

"It is you who is the fool, Paechra," Anton stated. "The man in black is the threat."

"And you believe by getting rid of him you win the war," said Paechra, trying to stay calm. "At least you did not refer to him as Raven this time."

"I know what I'm seeing, lass," Anton argued. "If it looks like a horse and it sounds like a horse…"

"Knowing what it is that I know of vorsurk magic, that

379

horse could be a dragon," Paechra argued back.

"You and your kind only know of what the stories tell you," said Anton.

Paechra made to argue back, but it was true what Anton said. Her people had left the humans to battle with the vorsurk for over five hundred years. If any race knew what the vorsurk were familiar with it would be Anton, Thomas, and their people. It was foolish to ignore the past though, and Paechra had had her own recent experiences with the enemy, barbaric soldiers as well as cunning sorcerers.

"You know what you know, Anton, and I have my own experiences," said Paechra.

"And I guess you're going to suggest something along the lines of a good leader listens to all before deciding what is right," grumbled Anton.

"I would prefer it put as wisdom can only come from listening, learning, and remembering all," suggested Paechra. "There is merit in what you say also."

"True wisdom comes with age," suggested Sienna as she hobbled up to confront the pair.

"I need no more lessons taught by you, or any of your daughters," grumbled Anton.

"Then you are indeed the fool that Paechra has suggested," scoffed the ancient sylvan.

"All that I am asking is that you people leave me alone," said Anton.

"We are bringing you home," suggested Paechra. "It surprises me that you do not wish to show some gratitude for that."

"A threatened home, with the enemy in reach," Anton

argued.

"And have you found that sword of yours yet, mighty worrier?" asked Sienna.

Paechra noticed the purposeful difference between warrior and worrier, but she noted sadly Anton missed such subtle hints.

"I am certain that one of your men has hidden it," Anton grumbled.

"Or the enemy has taken it as a trophy," Paechra suggested.

"All the more reason to go back and get it," demanded Anton. "Or if not that blade, I would love to swing that blade of his against him."

"One word, Anton…" said Paechra. "Undead, and lots of them."

"That's five words," argued Anton.

"Five words that mean your certain death," stated Sienna.

"And then, you rise up and join their ranks," added Paechra.

"Nonsense," scoffed the human. "I'd cut them down before they got anywhere near me."

"With what?" asked both Paechra and Sienna, a chorus of disbelief. "Would you choose to use the air, the leaves, or perhaps a twig?"

"I cannot win…" grumbled Anton, he then storming off in search of Thomas and some human company.

"Don't wander off too far," called Sienna.

"We have our eye on you," Paechra added.

That was true. Having less than a day's grace between them and a strange enemy, Paechra had requested that all the sylvan kept a close eye on Anton, so he did not sneak away. Even

Thomas had taken it upon himself to make sure that the Head Truth Keeper continued upon the path to Thuraen's heart. Paechra was determined that all of her forces would at least arrive safe.

#

"What is this trickery?" asked Raven.

He stood with Low Prince Derek and Miriam, Mistress of the Mead beside him.

Derek motioned with the stump of his left hand.

"Here... Below... Fate awaits..." the sylvan suggested.

"But... But... Why here?" Raven asked, somewhat disappointed.

"What is the problem?" asked Miriam. "These men nestled in the valley of the mountains seem strong, yet kind."

"They are," groaned Raven. "Derek, you have lead me back to where it is I started."

"To overcome fate... Travel the path... Should you return... Know you are ready..." replied the low prince.

"Then take me back to the place where my reflection awaits me," said Raven. "I shall show everyone just how ready I am."

"I shall be with you," vowed Miriam. "For your home shall be my home too."

"You shall be welcome," stated Raven. "All shall be welcome."

Chapter Seventeen

Return to Andrapaal

The die rolls through the hall of Haven.

The thunder rolls.

The storm sings.

A city sleeps.

Nothing is eternal, but the goddess Herself.

**From the Twelfth Stanza of the Prophecy, translated by the
sages of the Kingdom of Thuraen 514th year**

PAECHRA THOUGHT THAT the old Truth Keeper Anton was
going to cause her trouble, but he proved to be nothing short of
a nightmare. Even with everybody watching for signs that the
old warrior was attempting to leave camp and head north,

Anton still tried to seek out the man in black. There was something about his experience as a prisoner, though short as it was, that had affected Anton's aura, making it obsessive, angered, embarrassed.

"Perhaps we should just let him go, face his fate, learn the lesson that must still be acknowledged," suggested Heidi.

"Yes, just let me go and I and my sword can decide whether I return," added Anton, his gruff voice on the border of pleading, but refusing to go that final step further.

Paechra scoffed at such a suggestion.

"You wish to pit your wooden toy and your tick-tack style of play against a man of mystery and promised death?" she asked.

Anton still had not been able to find his sword, lost when he who looked like Raven Stormsong along with a small force of vorsurk had caught the old man and those who had followed after him. Paechra had risked much but gained so much more in respect from her army when she decided to rescue the old man and those sylvan imprisoned. Anton still refused to thank her, and stubbornly he continued to believe that the warrior dressed in dark mail was something other than human.

"A sharpened stick slid through gaps in armor still manages to slay a foe," stated Anton with confidence.

"At least allow us to improve the sharpness or the strength of your mighty blade, or both," offered Heidi, an orange shimmer faintly outlining her fingers as she reached for the weapon that hung at Anton's hip.

"I need no such help," declared the Head Truth Keeper, stepping away so that the blade was out of Heidi's reach. "Just allow us a time and a place and the chance to fight man against man."

"Truly, Anton, you must stop this nonsense, this belief that our enemy is the boy that you trained to be a soldier," pleaded Paechra. "This skirmish you request will be elder against monster which can only end one way."

"You have little faith in me, don't you, witch," Anton stated, but Heidi was somewhat pleased to see that he was smirking, not frowning.

"Anton, please understand that I have the utmost faith in your knowledge and experience in the field of battle," replied Paechra. "But in the realm of the unknown and mysterious, your lack of understanding, and therefore your dismissive nature does cause me great concern."

"How can you still not believe in the power of the sisterhood when we are demonstrating such for you almost every day?" Heidi asked, both curious and concerned.

"Your glowing lights and so called magic tricks mean nothing to me, girl," replied Anton to Heidi. "I'm just glad that those vorsurk barbarians are foolish enough to fall for such religion."

Both Paechra and Heidi sighed together but then laughed at the impossibility of the situation.

"We travel to Andrapaal, just as I believe does this mysterious man you need to fight," stated Paechra. "Be satisfied that we will try to save what remains of your capital, your home, your identity, and we offer you a chance for your fruitless fight then and there."

"Scouts have returned with news we are no longer being pursued," announced Sarah, Paechra's mother, as she approached the trio.

"There, see," said Heidi to the human. "Now you will just have to wait."

385

"I refuse to believe that the one known as Raven has somehow galloped by us," grumbled Anton. "We should have seen evidence of his travels, even if the vorsurk that follow him have vanished through their own form of witchery."

Paechra sighed again, this time while watching Anton march off in a northerly direction.

"Do we try to stop him?" asked Heidi.

"No," said both Lightheart women.

"Let him go," suggested Paechra. "It will not take him long to figure out we are telling the truth about the mysterious man in black."

"As stubborn as humanity can prove to be, Anton is a most special case," added Sarah.

"But, for better and for worse, he is one of our forces, and an important one if we are to succeed in this quest," continued Paechra.

"May the spirits keep us all protected, from the enemy, and ourselves," murmured Paechra's mother.

Paechra and Heidi both nodded in agreement, and all three Druids made the sign requesting celestial aid.

#

Anton was gone for two whole days, returning at dawn on the third day.

"Impossible," he muttered. "There is a clear trail of footprints and then a burn mark upon the road."

The pair of sylvan men that Paechra had sent to aid Anton in his tracking remained silent.

"And what is your theory," asked Sienna.

"Could they all have grown wings and flown away?" asked Anton.

"A flying horse?" asked Paechra. "They are not common in our mysterious belief system, but they do exist."

"No, a flying horse would have been impossible to miss," said Anton, talking to himself more than anyone else.

"We could show him what a flying horse looks like," suggested Heidi.

"That would indeed be quite the sight," said Thomas, the butcher thoughtful. "I fear such would be too much for any human mind to witness."

"Yes, of course," said Paechra. "We must allow Anton to live in his bubble of denial and disbelief while the rest of us just get on with the problem at hand."

"And what do these proposed solutions look like, daughter?" asked Sienna.

"Unfortunately, of all the modes of transport we can conjure there is only one that would be deemed acceptable where Captain Doubtful is concerned," muttered Paechra. "I have used it with the small group I had but have never tried with a force of this size."

"Manipulating time and distance both can be quite challenging," agreed Mother Druid Sienna Alknown, immediately understanding what it was that the young Lightheart was suggesting.

"There are many of us now, not just the one," added Sarah, Paechra's mother. "The spell that you cast can be supported."

"Or, better yet," exclaimed Paechra's friend Heidi. "The same spell can be cast numerous times."

"Difficult and dangerous," muttered Sienna. "What you say could only be attempted by the most senior of us Druids."

"Multiple time streams, the possibility of individuals falling under the influence of multiple castings," added Sarah, giving both Heidi and Paechra a look of concern.

"Mother," said Paechra, addressing the term to both her own mother and the Mother Druid. "I am confident that if we allowed Anton to arrange our gathering into militant groups then a sister dedicated to each group would be able to focus upon just that group."

"No member of any group would then stray into the area of effect of any one particular casting and therefore the risk would be controlled regarding any one of us falling victim to the dangers associated with such a spell," added Heidi, obviously eager for her idea to be tried.

"And how will you convince the Head Truth Keeper and the butcher to take part in such obvious witchcraft?" asked Sarah.

"Leave that to me," said Paechra.

"You are not going to tell him, either of them, are you?" questioned Sienna.

"You are going to let him believe that it is his idea," Sarah added. "I know you daughter; you are perhaps more my child than initially believed."

"Thank you, mother," said Paechra. "I think it is a compliment."

"Oh, it is, child," said Sarah, with a rare smile of pride appearing across her face. "Oh, indeed it is."

"Come Heidi, my friend," Paechra then said next. "We have a human to find…"

"A human to fool, you mean," Heidi answered as she

hurried after her friend.

"I do not know whether to be proud or not," murmured Sarah as Heidi and Paechra left the clearing and conversation both.

Paechra caught her mother's final comment to Mother Druid Sienna before the two elder Druids laughed between themselves.

#

"Paechra, to what do I owe this pleasure?" asked Anton, after Paechra and Heidi found him in the tent that he shared with Thomas. "Have you located my sword?"

Paechra and her friend had spent a good portion of an hour searching the camp, following after the Head Truth Keeper's movements, seemingly as if Anton did not wish to see them.

"You know that we will not find your missing blade," replied Paechra. "I am certain that you know very well where it is that your blade has gone."

"What I know and do not know is none of your business," Anton declared in a huff. "Unless it is that you can somehow read my very thoughts."

"We can sense your aura," explained Heidi.

"Heidi, please…" said Paechra. "Anton is well aware of what it is we as sylvan Druids can do."

"Actually, you tree huggers are a complete and utter mystery to both the butcher and me," said Anton.

"Thomas probably knows far more than you do, actually," Heidi muttered, remembering that the butcher only most recently took part in the strange dream vision shared by the

Druid sisterhood.

"Heidi!" stated Paechra and Anton together.

"I know… Be quiet…" Heidi mumbled. "Don't interrupt when the two of you are fighting…"

"We were not… Fighting…" suggested Paechra. "And we are sorry that we shouted at you."

"I never shouted," grumbled Anton.

"Just like you never lost your blade," suggested Paechra.

Just then Thomas popped his head in, seemingly searching for something he had misplaced. The Butcher of Andrapaal took one look around the tent's interior, at the three figures standing in the lamp light.

"So sorry," he said quickly. "I'll come back later."

"No lad, no, please stay," urged Anton, grabbing the other human about the bicep and drawing him closer.

"Although it is nice to be wanted," Thomas stammered. "I truly must be going… Only wanted to stop for a moment…"

"Let him go," Paechra urged of Anton. "You have nothing to fear of Heidi and me."

"Yes," Heidi agreed. "In actual fact we were looking for you to ask about how we should travel since the situation is growing more dangerous the closer we get to Andrapaal."

"Oh, well, in that case…" said Anton, his gruff demeanor vanishing.

"So, I can go?" asked Thomas, his voice full of uncertainty.

"Yes, boy, run along…" Anton urged.

"I will, of course," promised the butcher. "As soon as you let go of my arm."

Released, Thomas swiped a carving knife that lay close to

his sleeping place, before hurrying back out from the tent again.

Paechra wondered what Thomas was planning to create. He had been spending some quiet moments with the sylvan males, learning the craft, and producing some wonderfully life-like statues from those branches the trees allowed to drop. Her almond eyes drifted around the tent's floor space, and she spied a half finished Anton with sword raised ready to strike.

"You were asking..?" the real Anton queried, bringing Paechra's focus back to the conversation at hand.

"Oh yes, formation," stated the young Lightheart, as if a single word could explain everything.

Luckily, enough Anton on that occasion was on the very same trail of thought.

"I could not agree more with you, Paechra," Head Truth Keeper Anton said. "The way you sylvan wander among the trees and bushes it is as if you think you own them all."

Heidi made to argue that such was certainly not the case, but Paechra placed a gentle hand upon her shoulder, causing her to pause.

"What would you suggest instead of us aimlessly wondering about with the swaying of the wind?" Paechra then said.

Heidi witnessed the subtle smirk upon her friend's face, but Anton missed it.

"A march would be recommended if the numbers were trained…" began Anton.

Paechra imagined the cloud of dust that would have formed if Anton's dream vision became a reality. Heidi caught her friend's eye, and the pair tried not to laugh.

391

"And if we do not have the time to drum such discipline into my kindred?" asked Paechra.

"I fear the best we can accomplish even in eleven days is a hope that we can keep the rabble in some sort of groups," grumbled Head Truth Keeper Anton.

"Heidi, please friend, spread the word we are to pack up camp ready to move onward, and await Anton's command," ordered Paechra, trying not to smile.

"Yes, Paechra, as you instruct," replied Heidi.

"Satisfied?" Paechra then asked, turning away from her friends and focusing solely upon the human.

"Um… Yes, very satisfied," stated Anton. "I did not think that it would be that easy."

Neither did I, Paechra thought to herself but dared not say such out loud.

"Good, I'm glad," she said instead. "Give us an hour and we will be ready to move on."

One thing Anton had learned was that the sylvan race was very efficient with setting up and packing away. When Paechra suggested an hour, he assumed that it would be quicker than that.

"I'll go tell Thomas to gather our things," he said while giving Paechra a curt nod.

"It would not hurt you to also lend a hand," the young Lightheart suggested. "I'll find the butcher, you stay here."

Anton counted out fifty heads, a mix of men and women, sending them along a forest track that vaguely headed in the direction of Andrapaal. Paechra made certain that there were at least two of her sisters among those sent.

"You should be leading the way," Thomas said to Paechra, but the sylvan shook her head.

"There is time for that later," she told him.

The Druids sang, quietly, their song as each group took up a steady-paced walk. By mid-morning, there were at least twenty groups following after each other, spaced out just enough that no group was caught in two magical fields. By the end of that day, Paechra estimated that she had taken them all seven.

"Strange, did you not think we would see signs of our kindred?" Thomas asked of Anton when they met in the evening.

"Too risky that we could warn the enemy of our arrival," suggested Anton. "It is all according to plan, boy."

"Yes, but according to whose plan?" Heidi whispered to her friend as she covered up her smile.

"Quiet Heidi," scolded Paechra, but Heidi could see her friend's eyes twinkling.

The following day as the sun rose up to the middle of the sky, Paechra ceased her singing and allowed the wagon containing High Prince Ulan, Mother Druid Sienna Alknown, and Head Truth Keeper Anton to travel at its own pace. Guiding the horse beyond the thick forest's trees she heard a great gasp from Anton.

"What have you done?" queried the old human.

He looked from Sienna to Paechra, and then to Ulan.

High Prince Ulan shrugged his regal shoulders.

"Don't look at me," he said. "I had nothing to do with it."

"But you knew though, didn't you," the Head Truth Keeper Anton accused. "Did Thomas too?"

"Know what?" asked the butcher.

"Look around you, boy," urged Anton. "Open them eyes."

"How did we...?" Thomas asked. "Everything looks so familiar, yet different."

"The vorsurk," said Anton.

"They have a way of polluting everywhere that they invade," agreed Sienna.

"And that is why we needed to hurry our journey," suggested Paechra. "We have left the human kingdom in vorsurk claws for too long already."

"If it were not for you we would still be here fighting the invaders," Anton grumbled. "It never felt right to leave."

"It is thanks to me that your queen is safe and so is Her child," Paechra argued back. "I am sure you will agree it is much better to have some hope than no hope at all."

"I know that Queen Catherine is alive and well, Thomas knows this too," agreed Anton. "But how do you propose we tell the rest of Thuraen?"

"Do you plan to magic us past the walls with your... Your... Witchery?" asked Thomas, panicking.

"Be still, Thomas, we shall enter the same way that we left," stated Paechra, calmly. "We need only seek out the city beneath."

"We know the streets," agreed Anton.

"Hopefully we know the people too," Thomas added.

Paechra could see the worry in the butcher's aura. She could also see that darkness that swirled within Anton's.

"Here," she said, taking from High Prince Ulan a blade of ironwood and offering it to Anton.

"What am I supposed to do with such a stick?" Anton asked.

As he took the blade, ignoring Ulan's protests, Anton discovered to his surprise it was perfectly balanced, slightly top-heavy, and aptly designed for cleaving.

"Use it to guide us to victory," Paechra suggested. "Or at least until you can claim your own sword back again."

"Thank you, Paechra," Anton said, quietly, his voice full of gratitude.

The younger Lightheart examined his aura and discovered sincerity, something that surprised her.

"Yes, thank you," added Thomas who was always sincere. "Now do you have a blade for me also?"

"Here," sighed Ulan.

From beneath his gown the high prince produced a much shorter blade.

"It seems I have no need for this one either," he muttered as Thomas accepted the offered weapon. "The sisterhood has me guarded by the elderly."

"Go, and go now," commanded Paechra of her monarch. "Witness this historic moment but do so please from afar."

And so, beneath the noon sun, Anton led Paechra and her army into Andrapaal.

#

Within the halls of the mighty vorsurk fortress, Sage-Prince Vladimir the Young paced, nervously. The boy he truly was,

Morthos and nothing more, tried time and time again to resurface.

Resist your weakness, listen only to me, demanded the tome, stabbing pain filling his mind each time it spoke to him.

"Master? What can we do, with the enemy upon our threshold?" asked one of the sages dressed in blue robes.

"Is there something written in the unknown book? Some sort of clue that speaks of our future?" asked another of those ancient sages.

Peering through the hazy fog that enveloped his thinking, Vladimir the Young barked orders to his underlings.

"Go to the hall of prophecy... If there be knowledge that shall save us it will be found there..."

"Of course, Your Honor," chorused the old men.

A sea of robed figures vanished, leaving only the metal-clad Truth Keepers.

They will not protect you... hissed the voice of the tome.

"Silence!" demanded Vladimir.

"We should run while we can..." said the voice of Morthos, a mere whisper.

The boy's words coming out from the ancient frame of Vladimir caused the soldiers, all ten of them to give the Sage-Prince a look of concern. Each one knew better though and chose to remain silent.

Opening the tome, Vladimir felt another piece of himself vanish into the pages.

"Reveal to me the power that I need, the power that will lead me to victory..." Vladimir demanded.

The pages fluttered, although no wind blew. About half the

tome flew by and then just as suddenly they stopped.

The ancient runes written in human blood, immediately translated in the sorcerer's mind from vorsurk into the common tongue equivalent.

The worrisome frown changed into a grin of confidence upon the old man face of Vladimir.

"Come, accompany me to the city below!" Vladimir commanded.

Unable to refuse an order from the ruler of Thuraen, the ten Truth Keepers bowed as one and then filed out of the palace library. All of them knew of the city below. All had been there before.

#

"What else do I have to do?" growled Raven, impatiently.

He was staring intently at the broken mirror, willing himself and his companions back into his home world.

"Magic words, lad?" suggested Mick McHallowhill. "Did ye learn any in yer time away?"

"No," said Raven, sourly.

"Yer certainly did not learn any less manners either," the dwarf suggested.

"Sorry," Raven stated. "I just thought this would be different..."

Miriam placed a hand upon his shoulder.

"Visualize where you wish to be," she suggested.

"Ok, I'll try..." Raven replied, uncertain.

He gasped in surprise as the mirror began changing.

"Son? Is that you?" asked the figure who appeared in the mirror's reflection.

"Father?" asked Raven. "Are you in Andrapaal?"

#

Zerrick, master vorsurk sorcerer of the Fifth and Sixth tomes, grinned evilly as more and more vorsurk soldiers flooded the streets of the fortress. Citizens of Andrapaal fell to the sword and spear, young men foolish enough to believe themselves a match for true warrior spirit. The master of magic had ordered that the women and children be captured, enslaved, herded into cages, and transported through portals back to the homeland. If all went well this day the homeland would be expanded, but for now, it was the safest choice to get the humans away. Zerrick sensed his brothers, keepers of the other tomes had finally arrived. The race for spoils had begun. No vorsurk liked to share.

#

Thurzuk watched on in disbelief as more and more magic circles appeared just outside the walls of Andrapaal. Thousands upon thousands of his kindred were swarming into the sleeping city. He imagined that the battle would be short if there was any fight in the slave race at all.

"When do we enter?" the few soldiers who still stood by Thurzuk demanded to know.

"When the eleventh tome remembers who its true master

is," Thurzuk replied, but immediately regretted his words.

"You have no plan," stated one of the barbarians. "Wait and see is the words of weakness."

"You dare?!" Thurzuk roared.

He tried to will the dark energy of magic to his fingertips, but nothing came.

"You are weak, you are afraid, you are no vorsurk," growled another of the warriors.

Four against one was not terrible odds, but Thurzuk knew it would still be the most important fight of his life.

"Come," he commanded. "I shall show you how weak I am…"

#

In the place of mirrors where Vladimir had once had his office, where dark spells had been cast before, here was where the sorcerer commanded his soldiers to stand.

"What worked once will surely work again," he mumbled to himself.

The words of power crackled as he spoke them. Each of the Truth Keepers clutched at their heart. The mirrors went dark, and then, like each reflective surface was an opened door, copies of the men sacrificed came marching into the room.

Give me more… whispered the voice of the tome.

Vladimir clutched his own heart then.

"Stupid old man," he cursed. "Don't die on me now…"

"It is still not too late…" murmured the voice of the boy, Morthos.

The mind of the sorcerer was too far gone to listen though.

#

"We are safe, Queen Catherine and I," stated Michael Stormsong, Raven's father. "Far from the evil that has invaded our home."

"I need to be there; I need to help…" stated Raven. "But I do not know how to go through."

"Son, you have returned to us, forgetting yourself," suggested the elder of the two. "Know who you are and there will not be a barrier anywhere that can stop you."

"Who am I though?" Raven pleaded to know.

"You are Johannas Stormsong, the blackbird of prophecy," replied Miriam.

"You are… Sylvan friend…" suggested Low Prince Derek.

"You are my boy, and I love you," added Michael.

Suddenly, the image of the cracked mirror changed, and Raven could see the figure of Sage-Prince Vladimir standing uncomfortably, seemingly in pain. The dark figure of Raven's reflection stood beside him. The time felt right, the moment was now. Raven stepped through the broken mirror and Derek, Miriam, Mick, and the whole dwarf clan strode through after him.

#

Paechra motioned for Anton to lead part of the army of sylvan down the left passage, the road that had once been the way to

Greggory's forge.

"We shall meet at the palace steps and make our way up from there," she whispered.

"Right, witch," Head Truth Keeper Aton said with a nod.

He brandished his wooden sword like it was made from steel.

"Please don't die along the way," the sylvan suggested.

"Don't worry about me," barked the human. "You make sure you get there."

And then he was gone.

Slowly, with caution, she led her forces, over a thousand in number, through the streets that had once felt the sun's rays. Quite quickly small groups of vorsurk were discovered. Pockets of humans hiding, seeking safety, they were waved away out from the city whose streets would run with sylvan and vorsurk blood alike. Paechra did not like this part, but gritted her teeth, knowing the price of failure would be death.

#

Zerrick followed after his forces, ignoring the screams of the dying and the smell of fear that filled the air. He was after only one thing, the eleventh, and most powerful of the tomes of magic. Deeper and deeper into the fortress he went.

"Find it!" he called out to his loyal fighters. "Find the book and bring it to me!"

#

"What is this that I see?" Thurzuk asked himself, curious.

Like rats abandoning a sinking ship, humans looked to be pouring out from tunnels located beneath the vorsurk fortress. Survivors, just as he was a survivor. He had a decision to make, should he go against the tide and wade his way into the chaos? Would he risk it all? Slinking deeper into the shadows, he made his decision, like always, to hide, to lick his wounds, and to wait to see just how weak the victor would be.

#

"You fool!" laughed the image of Raven as Johannas Stormsong entered the place of mirrors. "You think that you can defeat me?"

"I, not you, am Johannas, son of Michael, Truth Keeper, and sylvan friend," stated Johannas bravely. "You have my sword, and I vow I shall take it back."

"I have more than just your sword," laughed the figure of darkness.

The blade was taken from the sheath and swung in a deadly arc.

Johannas Stormsong was like lightning though, striding forward without fear to grasp the arm the dealt the blow, twisting it savagely.

"Kill them all!" demanded the crackling voice of Sage-Prince Vladimir.

Some of the spiritless Truth Keepers responded to his order, but most of them simply ignored the sorcerer.

You are weak, hissed the tome. *It is time I sought another master...*

"No, wait, I can be stronger," promised Morthos.

The ancient disguise of the blue-robed Vladimir fell away, and the frightened child was all that remained.

"Asss-lak mi-rath..." the child whispered, as the tome in his hands fell open.

The two figures who battled ignored the child as he simply just disappeared. The blade that they fought over clattered to the stone floor as Raven dropped it and then kicked it away.

Derek, and the dwarf clan made short work of the soulless Truth Keepers, returning them one by one back to the mirror world.

Miriam quickly scooped up the hefty blade, but when she looked upon the two who battled she could not tell which of the pair was Johannas.

"Run Miriam, go find Paechra," called one of the pair, and in that moment the mistress of mead recognized her friend.

"I shall go, but first receive this gift," she called, launching the blade with all of her might toward the combatants.

"With thanks," called the two, together, and with a single blow, those two became one.

#

Morthos sat upon the towering chair where vorsurk kings had sat before. The tome lay heavy upon his lap.

"Share with me your secrets?" he begged, but the book remained shut.

The great throne room filled with wolf-like warriors and figures dressed in arcane robes.

403

"Hand over the tome, child," growled one of those figures.

"Nay, give it to me," cried other voices.

Morthos brought his hands to his temples as the voices began to echo in his mind.

Make it stop!" the child begged.

"As you so wish," replied Zerrick.

A bolt of acid flew from the sorcerer's outstretched hand. It struck the boy in the middle of the chest and then hissed as it burned him.

Morthos screamed until his lungs were gone.

Zerrick ignored the noise, marching up to the throne he took up the tome and lofted it skyward in triumph.

"It is mine!" he announced, just as three bolts of crackling lightning struck him, one after the other.

\#

Anton thrust his wooden blade into every vorsurk warrior who barred his path. Some fell instantly as he scored a lucky blow, others took two or three more strikes, before they toppled to the ground and remained still. Each time a weapon of steel clattered to his feet he ignored it, refusing to fight with the steel of his enemies.

"What do you think of that, lad?" he asked, almost laughing as another of the barbarians met a grizzly end.

It was in such a moment that Anton remembered he had ordered Thomas away. The sylvan beside him gave a nod and fought on. Anton still wished though that the butcher was beside him.

#

The battle for Andrapaal and the human lands of Thuraen came to a final moment in the throne room. Paechra, Johannas, and Anton, all arrived at the same time to discover the skirmish between the vorsurk sorcerers that was unfolding. Realizing what an opportunity they had then, Paechra pointed at the first of the books of magic.

"Destroy the tomes," the Druid ordered.

The sylvan and human forces did what they could, but when the third and fifth books were torn to pieces and their wielders slain, the other sorcerers vanished from sight.

The remaining vorsurk soldiers put up what fight that they could, but without the power of their masters, the odds were against them.

Paechra cried out in gleeful victory as the last of the brutes met its end.

"Now to end this," the youngest Lightheart stated as she reached for the eleventh tome, still waiting for a new master.

"No!" cried Thomas the butcher, one of the chosen eleven of Andrapaal.

"Thomas?" yelled out Johannas Stormsong his voice so loud that it bounced off the great stone walls of the hall.

"I vowed to you, Raven, that I would protect the sylvan," stated Thomas. "And such a promise I shall keep."

Paechra cloaked herself in an aura of flame and made to devour the book and throne with her mighty magic.

Thomas secured the tome before she could touch it, the protective magics of darkness striking him down dead, just as they would have the sylvan.

#

The eleventh tome was wrapped in the robes of Zerrick and the other fallen sorcerers, then buried deep below the city of Andrapaal with Thomas, now known as Tomas the Guardian. The city below rose again, to stand atop the vorsurk fortress, neither sinking back into the earth. Queen Catherine gave birth to a heathy son whom she named Fredrick in honor of the princeling's father. Catherine ruled over Thuraen until her son came of age. Johannas and Paechra discovered the power of their friendship, just as Derek learned his true feelings were for Miriam. Ulan welcomed all to return to Greenwood Vale. Johannas decided with his new love to stay in Andrapaal though, and the Stormsong name was again renowned as champion of the kingdom. Most importantly of all, the prophecy of Andrapaal was taught to all, not just the sages, and reading and writing became a joy for every human throughout the land.

And Thurzuk, what became of him? Of that, nobody knows... He has remained in the shadows, biding his time, licking his wounded pride, and waiting for the day that the slave races will become ripe again for the picking.

Epilogue

Celebrations begin at sun fall

The blackbird and the lioness are finally one

Torches shine bright in the darkness of night

As few recall, even in the day there be places forever left in shadow

Those who win, those who lose, the die is cast again

The goddess watches, the balance of fate, never remains in one place

THE PROPHECY OF Andrapaal, thirteenth stanza, untranslated by the sages of the Kingdom of Thuraen 514th year

Palidine, representative of all things good, watched in triumph as the city of Andrapaal rose up from slumber, but then frowned as the Fortress of Evil remained. Sinestri, twin brother of Palidine hissed his displeasure, but such a sound became a tittering laugh.

"It seems neither of us as fully won the day, brother," the shadow declared.

"It does so seem our battle must continue," agreed the figure who sat within the square of white.

#

The spirit of light, Aiera scrawled the newest verse of the prophecy upon the walls of the vorsurk fortress, still standing proudly erect in the evening rays of the sun's light. The runes of so many different languages blended and blurred together, creating mystery. The people of Thuraen were now opening their minds though. No prophecy would stay untranslated long.

Ithulii once more appears

From the safety of the land of light it comes

Just as the hounds again do turn and run

Uncarne drifts back to shadow

Bidding its time, impatiently waiting

Celebrations begin at sun fall

The blackbird and the lioness are finally one

Torches shine bright in the darkness of night

As few recall, even in the day there be places forever left in

shadow

Those who win, those who lose, the die is cast again

The goddess watches, the balance of fate, never remains in one place

Those who fight, must always

Those who run, run far

The minds of all are now open

We now know who we are

About the Author

Author Tim Law has been a dreamer for years. He grew up in libraries, his head firmly stuck in the pages of a book. Fantasy, the realm of dreams was always his favorite of all the genres, so naturally when it came to writing, his mind traveled there. A comment made by his wife one day about a feisty friend created Paechra, and a city inflamed, part of a roleplaying campaign became the city of Andrapaal. Everything else about this story seemed to flow on from there.

Tim is a loving husband, with a beautiful wife, and a proud father of three amazing teens. He resides somewhere in Southern Australia but spends many an hour in a world of his own.

Many more of Tim's stories and poetry can be found online,

especially at *www.theworldofmyth.com* as well as other sites. This is his fourth book published by *Dark Myth Publications,* and far from his last...

www.ingramcontent.com/pod-product-compliance
Lightning Source LLC
Chambersburg PA
CBHW071640260626
47170CB00001B/173